A Simple Hope

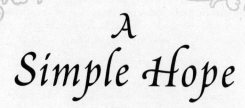

A
Simple Hope

A LANCASTER
CROSSROADS NOVEL

Rosalind Lauer

BALLANTINE BOOKS TRADE PAPERBACKS
NEW YORK

A Ballantine Books Trade Paperback Original

Published in the United States by Ballantine Books, an imprint of Random House, a division of Random House LLC, a Penguin Random House Company, New York.

This book contains an excerpt from the forthcoming book *A Simple Charity* by Rosalind Lauer. This excerpt has been set for this edition only and may not reflect the final content of the forthcoming edition.

ISBN 978-0-345-54328-8
eBook ISBN: 978-0-345-54329-5

Printed in the United States of America on acid-free paper

www.ballantinebooks.com

2 4 6 8 9 7 5 3 1

First Edition

Book design by Karin Batten

For Violet Dutcher,
My bridge to the other side

PART ONE

Greener Pastures

Blessed is the man that trusteth in the Lord,
and whose hope the Lord is.
For he shall be as a tree planted by the waters, and
that spreadeth out her roots by the river . . .

—JEREMIAH 17: 7–8

1

The gentle spring breeze sent cherry blossoms floating through the air, pink petals settling over Rachel and James as they walked hand in hand through the orchard.

Rachel King stepped away from him and held her arms out, wanting to breathe in the beauty of the petal shower. "It's like falling snow!"

James Lapp planted his legs apart and tipped back his hat. A slight smile appeared as he watched her reach out to catch falling petals. "That's the difference between us, Rachel. You see a shower of flower petals. I see early blooms that'll wither if we get a late frost."

"So practical."

"That's the good in living off the land. It keeps a man down-to-earth."

"I know you're used to this wonderful sight, working in the orchard every day, but there's something about blossoming trees that makes the heart burst with joy."

"Ya, if you don't have to prune them." The warmth in his dark eyes told her he was teasing.

"Is it a chore when you love what you do? You've told me yourself that your dat used to call you a tree monkey. When it was time to pick peaches, he couldn't get you to stay on the ladder."

James chuckled. "That was me." He leaped up, grabbed on to an overhead branch, and hung there a moment before doing an easy chin-up.

"You're still a tree monkey!" she said, glorying in the cascade of petals loosened by the jolt to the tree limb.

"Ya, but I've learned that a ladder is the easiest way up a tree." With dark hair that framed his handsome face and smoky eyes that warmed for Rachel, James was solid and grounded. His steady calm was one of the things that had won Rachel over a year ago when he'd started driving her home from singings and youth gatherings. At a time when other Amish fellas were putting boom boxes in their buggies and tossing back beers, James followed a simple path, choosing baptism and the management of the Lapp family orchards. Rachel liked to picture him as the root system that anchored her to the earth.

James dropped to the ground and leaned down to pick up a fallen bud. "Here's one for you."

Rachel held her breath as he came close, brushing back the edge of her prayer *Kapp* to tuck the pale pink bud over her left ear. His touch sent shimmers rippling down her spine even as the gesture warmed her from head to toe. Ya, he kept her feet on the ground, but he let her heart soar.

"There." His dark eyes held her as his broad hands dropped to her shoulders. "You are the finest blossom in the Lapp orchard." His arms encircled her, and she melted in his embrace. Rachel loved the way he made her feel small and delicate against his strong, solid body. His lips touched hers gently, quick as a butterfly's glance, but she felt the spark of love in that kiss.

"We should go to the sugar shack," she murmured. "Out here in the orchard . . . people can see. Your parents might be watching."

"With these trees so thick with blossoms? I think we're well hidden." He caught her in his dark gaze. The flicker in his eyes let her know that he was feeling the same love that stirred her heart. Could he feel the quiet tremble of her limbs? Or the wooziness that overtook her when his lips nuzzled her jaw, leaving a trail of tingling sensation that became heated by his warm breath?

"Besides," he whispered, "I don't care if they see us. I don't care if they know that I love you, Rachel."

I love you, Rachel.

His words swelled and blossomed inside her, filling her heart with goodness and light. But just when they were about to kiss, the sweet moment faded, slipping away like sugar sifting between her fingers.

A dream . . . it was all a dream.

In the pink light of early morning, Rachel opened her eyes to blots of color that made up the large bedroom shared by the King girls.

All a dream.

Rachel closed her eyes and clung to the sweetness, holding tight to the scent of cherry blossoms and the sureness of love. James loved her! And James was strong, standing and walking and swinging from a tree, healthy and hearty as ever!

She tried to hold in the goodness of the dream, but reality tapped on her mind like fat raindrops. James would not be grabbing on to a tree in the orchard today, or anytime soon.

Before she could ease herself away, she was back in that terrible moment, hearing the sickening screech of tires on the road, the grind of metal. The accident. Although Rachel had been able to walk away from the wrecked van, James had not. He was still recovering from spinal injuries, confined to a wheelchair for now. Maybe forever.

Sighing, she rolled over to see her younger sisters asleep in the double bed. Twelve-year-old Bethany's bare foot hung out from under the quilt, and nine-year-old Molly's sweet lips were pursed like a rosebud. Sleep was the only time Molly's lips were still, but Rachel didn't mind her chatterbox little sister. In fact, her sister's gabbing was just the sort of reassuring company Rachel had sought when she gave up her room in the attic to move down here with the younger girls. Rachel had hoped to spend more time with sister Rose, too, but Rose, now sixteen, had other notions. Eager to leap into *Rumspringa,* Rose had missed the point of companionship and moved up to Rachel's room, sure that a young man would soon come courting at her window. Oh, Rose, so full of dreams!

Still, Rachel was grateful for the chance to talk more with her other sisters, whose steady breathing in the bed across from her was reassuring. Let Rose have the room upstairs; no young man would be calling for Rachel anytime soon, not with James still unable to walk.

Rachel closed her eyes in the hopes of recapturing the sweet dream—reliving the time when James had moved freely and managed the family orchard without fail. With a deep breath, she tried to bring back the scent of blossoms and the warm strength of James's arms around her.

But the dream was gone, and so was the James she had fallen in love with. The accident had pulled him away from her . . . so far away. Many things changed when a vehicle had hit the van Rachel and James had been riding in back in January. The other driver, a young Englisher girl, had been killed, and James's uncle Tom Lapp had died later in the hospital. So much heartbreak for two families, Englisher and Amish alike. The accident had sent old Jacob Fisher into a terrible fit of breathing, but he seemed to be recovering, thank the good Lord. And James, her James had hurt his back, really bad.

The golden wash of light told Rachel that it would be time to start the day soon, a fine Monday morning. Time to wake her sisters and roust them from bed. There were chores to be done, a breakfast to prepare. Cows to milk, and a house and barns to redd up. All tasks that went against Rachel's grain. But now, she would do the stinkiest chores gladly if it meant that James could get better.

She slid out of bed, pulled the quilt over her shoulders, and padded barefoot to the window seat Dat had built. Outside, sunshine shot over the green and purple hills in the distance. The morning air was cold, but the sun promised warmth to the day—Gott's promise of springtime and light and hope. Rachel thought of the colors in the paint kit her Englisher friend Haley had given her and wished she had time to paint right now. How she would enjoy mixing colors to come up with spring-field green, daffodil yellow, crocus purple, and the rich blots of pink and purple and orange and red that made up a sunrise. Upstairs in her old room, among the many unfinished canvases, was a new painting she had just finished for James. It was different from her usual style, but she thought it might spark some joy in his heart.

And James was so very much in need of joy.

She kneeled beside the window seat and clasped her hands together for a silent prayer. *Dear Gott, please heal James. Teach him to walk again. Please, don't let my selfish dreams get in his way.*

Long before the terrible accident, Rachel had thought of marrying James, and their relationship had been moving in that direction. But Rachel had secretly dreamed of a life away from the work of a farm or orchard. Her paintings sold well at the Country Store in Halfway, so well that she had been invited to sell them in a gallery in Philadelphia. In the back of her mind, she had always wanted to leave farm life behind and live in a small house in town. With her love of peace and quiet and her yearning to paint all day and all night, Rachel longed to break free of the bonds of milking cows twice a day, tending the chickens, and weeding the family vegetable garden.

Plenty of Amish had moved away from tending the land. Her cousin Market Joe traveled to Philadelphia six days a week to run the family cheese shop in the city's market. James's cousin Elsie Lapp ran their family's store in Halfway. Why couldn't she be among those who left the farm behind for a job or craft? She knew the bishop would allow it. The only fly in the ointment had been James. He loved working the orchard, a life of sunshine, he said. Before the accident, he would not have considered living in town.

And now? She wasn't sure what James was planning for the future. The James she loved, the man in her dream, was so hard to reach these days. And how she missed him! Without his sure, steady footing, she felt unsure and scared, like a seed blowing in the wind with no say in its direction, no idea where she might land.

Dear Gott, please bring James back to me.

"Rachel?" Molly's voice chirped from the bed. "Are you praying for James?"

"Ya, always."

"Me, too. Every morning and every night, and sometimes in between, I pray for Gott to heal his legs so that he can walk again. Bethany says I shouldn't tell Gott what to do, but Bishop Sam says we can pray for anything. Bishop says that Gott always listens, but He doesn't always give us the answer we want."

"I've heard Bishop Samuel say that, too." Rachel turned back toward the bed, where her little sister was sitting up, twisting one of her long braids around one hand. Sprigs of Molly's golden hair had worked loose along her hairline, and the fluffy hair and shiny eyes made her resemble a baby chick.

"Thank you for praying, Molly," Rachel said. "Right now, I think James needs every prayer he can get."

"Do his legs hurt him really bad?" the younger girl asked.

"I don't think it's pain that's the problem." Although James had not offered to discuss his medical condition with Rachel, from what she'd overheard during her visits, it was the lack of sensation in James's legs that left him unable to walk. A few times a week, therapists visited the Lapp house to help James through exercises so that his muscles wouldn't weaken and atrophy. The doctors were still not sure about his future—whether or not he would walk again. No, pain wasn't what was bothering James. It was fear that he wouldn't recover.

Pulling the blanket up on her shoulders, Rachel went over to the double bed and sat down facing Molly. "You have a big heart, *Liebe.*" Too big to take on worries about James.

"I pray for everyone who was in that van," Molly said. "It must have been a terrible thing, being in a crash. Ben says two cars can crack each other in half, just like eggshells."

"Don't let Ben scare you. He's full of stories these days, and he wasn't there." At eighteen, their brother Ben was feeling his oats, as Dat said. Although rumspringa was meant to be a time for parents to look the other way while their teenaged son or daughter found a mate in the Amish community, some young people pushed the walls out way too far. Rachel had heard talk of Ben learning to drive a car and racing motorbikes. But mostly, he seemed to collect tidbits of Englisher culture, gobbling up stories about the Englisher world as if they were candy.

"Are you still scared to ride in a car?" Molly asked.

"A little," Rachel admitted. "But I don't get that tight feeling inside anymore. The meetings with Dylan have helped me a lot."

Dylan Monroe was an Englisher counselor who had offered free sessions to help the passengers deal with the aftermath of their accident. Post-traumatic stress, he called it.

"You're so brave."

"Not really." As Rachel smoothed back her sister's hair, she thought of the story shared by Ruben Zook, one of the other passengers. The notion of angels had come up when the group members were questioning why they were spared while Tom Lapp was taken by Gott, and James was seriously injured. "Ruben says that we had angels with us that afternoon. Gott's angels, watching over us."

Molly flung her arms around Rachel and hugged her close. "I love that story. Sometimes when I can't sleep at night, I pretend that an angel just slipped into bed beside me. And that helps me sleep."

"That's a wonderful good way to doze off." Looking down at Molly's honey-blond head, Rachel thanked Gott for her sisters. She closed her eyes, surrendering to a yawn.

"Tired?" Molly asked.

"Ya, but now it's time to get up."

"Time to greet the day!" Molly pushed back the covers and popped out of bed with her usual enthusiasm, bright as a daisy. "Bethany?" She leaned over her sleeping sister. "Don't you want to check the stand before school? I wonder if anyone bought any flowers."

"Mmm." Bethany rolled over onto her belly.

"Most likely, you didn't get a lot of customers overnight," Rachel said, amused by her younger sister's interest in the roadside stand the girls managed. "But you can check."

"I'm so glad you moved back down with us." Molly's eyes shone brightly as she looked up at Rachel. "I missed you."

Rachel smiled. "I'm glad, too."

Molly prodded Bethany, whose face was pressed into her pillow. "Now it's really time to get up, sleepyhead."

"I'm up," Bethany groaned. "How could I sleep with you two yakking?"

"Rise and shine," Rachel said as she began to pin her long blond hair back. "It's the early bird that gets the worm."

"I want to sleep." Bethany rolled over and groaned again. "I don't need any worms."

Chuckling softly, Rachel was glad to be back down here sharing a room with her sisters. Gott did work in wondrous ways.

2

*M*orning was a good time for James Lapp. Actually, it was the last hour of darkness that he enjoyed, when sleep held the rest of the house, still and silent but for the creaking of floorboards under his chair. Waking fresh from sleep, moving quietly from bed to chair, he thanked Gott for the promise of another day and wheeled himself into the bathroom. There was a certain satisfaction in ticking off the grooming chores he'd been taught to manage in occupational therapy. This was something he could do completely on his own.

Because he could no longer reach the bathroom shelves, the Englisher medical folk had given him a vinyl bag that attached to his wheelchair to hold his razor, shaving cream, toothbrush, and toothpaste. With the bars that Dat and brother Peter had installed in the washroom, James could use the toilet and maneuver himself onto the shower seat in the tub. These things took longer now that his legs would not bear the weight of his body, but still, James could manage, and without help from anyone.

That was what mattered to James—getting washed and dressed on his own. Although he lived in a supportive community, James was not one to wait around for a helping hand or lap up pity. In the orchard and in life, his father had taught him to do his part and do it well. Ya, there were many chores that he couldn't do while he was healing from the back injury. But James wasn't going to let his rehabilitation become an extra chore for family members like his mamm and his sister Verena.

Having spent his youth climbing trees, James had good power in his arms. He was grateful for that. Since the accident his upper body had grown even stronger with the necessity of having to lift and lever his body from one chair to another. By the light of a single kerosene lamp, he washed up and brushed his teeth. He shaved off the stubble on his chin and jaw, checking his face in the small mirror. Not long ago, he had looked forward to the day when he would let his beard grow. Growing a beard was but one small joy of marriage, a rite of passage in the Amish community. He had planned to marry Rachel King next wedding season, in the fall. Their friends and family had expected it.

Now he couldn't count on marriage or even Rachel's love. Now, when he tried to see ahead down the path to the future, his sights were set on walking—nothing else. When doctors had told him that his spinal cord had not been completely severed, that he had a chance of walking again, James had snatched at that hope as if it were the first ripe pear on a tree.

At the hospital and rehab center, there had been many tests and continuing physical therapy. Dat had taken James to a local chiropractor who many believed had healing power, and Mamm had purchased a few healing elixirs advertised in *The Budget,* the Amish newspaper. A couple of pills or one spoonful a day promised to temper all ills, and Mamm was convinced that the bottle of thick brown liquid James had consumed was responsible for the sensations in his legs. There were two surgeries and medications and talk of medical trials. James did everything the doctors asked, holding so tightly to hope that the notion of walking was beginning to seem as sure and rock-solid as the ground beneath him. As long as they kept saying that it was possible, that he might regain the use of his legs, James would keep digging deep inside himself for more strength, pushing and dragging and pulling himself up until that glimmer of chance burst into a roaring fire.

Back in his room, James glanced at the Bible on the edge of the bed. He almost stopped to read it over again, but he knew the section that was marked almost by heart. Mark 2:11 told about how Jesus met a man who couldn't walk. And he told the man, "Arise, and take up thy bed, and go thy way into thine house." And the man got up and picked up his mat, and all those who doubted Gott believed in the Almighty's power.

Ya, James knew that Bible story by heart. He had mentioned it to his dat, wanting to remind Jimmy that miracles could happen, but his father had told him not to brag about his Bible knowledge. *Hochmut,* or pride, was a sin. Most Amish didn't spend a lot of time reading from the Bible, but every man wanted to have a few Bible stories in his toolbox.

James carefully strapped each foot into black shoes with Velcro straps—shoes designed for wheelchair patients. He frowned, thinking of his dat's crisp remarks when the shoes had arrived a few weeks ago.

"I don't know why you're bothering with shoes at all." Dat had made his disapproval plain when one of the nurses, Haley Donovan, had held up the shoes that she'd ordered for James.

"These are lightweight, and easy to get on and off," Haley had said. "And besides that, they'll keep your feet warm and dry when you're out on the farm, taking care of the trees."

"But James isn't going to go out in the orchard in a wheelchair,"

Jimmy had told the therapist. "His brothers and I will tend to those chores." Dat had become a naysayer lately. Whenever James talked about the future, of getting better and walking again, his father grew agitated, as if James were breaking the Ordnung, going against the ways of the Amish.

"They go on a lot faster than my boots," James had said, pressing the Velcro tab into place.

"Seems like a waste," Dat had said, shaking his head. "For the amount of time you're going to be outside, a pair of thick socks would do just fine."

Despite Dat's displeasure, when Haley had looked to James for a decision, he had told her the shoes would serve him well outside, and they had. With the spring showers they'd had in the last two weeks, the shoes had proven their worth—especially when James had no choice but to direct his all-terrain wheelchair through mud and puddles of water. A few times his pants had gotten splattered and soaked, but his feet had stayed dry.

James pulled his jacket on, then wheeled down the hall. The kitchen sat cold but expectant. In a few minutes, the gas flame would be lit for coffee and the house would begin to stir. James would have liked a cup of coffee to ease into the day, but this was his time in the orchard—his chance before everyone else began their day.

From the simple porch at the front of the house, James breathed in the chill morning air, and then efficiently transferred himself to the all-terrain wheelchair. Between this chair and the ramp his father had built with his brothers, James was now able to come and go through the orchard on his own. He rolled down the ramp and steered toward the uneven path. As golden light sifted through the green crowns, shadow and light brought a sense of movement to the patterned rows of trees, punctuated by the rising chatter of birdsong.

Morning had broken.

In the past few weeks, this had been James's spot every morning at sunrise. There was something warm and good about the sunrise, the sharp light glowing through the leaves as the sky was washed pale with morning. Ya, there was hope in the first light of day. Even if the day held rain and a soupy sky, Gott brought enough light to find your way. The sureness that Gott brought a sunrise each and every day, that was a foundation a man could build on; the hope that this would be the day when Gott breathed life back into James's legs and blessed him with the strength to begin walking again, that was his morning prayer.

In his mind, he made a list of the things to be done this month. His grandfather had taught him that managing an orchard was a year-round task.

If you want to make cider in October, best to start checking your apple trees for leaf rollers in May.

He moved past apricot trees, already in bud. They would be the first to bloom, toward the beginning of May. Down on the ground, James was glad to see the specks of fertilizer his brother had scattered in a wide circle around each trunk. April was the month to fertilize everything except the peach trees. He had told Peter and Luke that over and again, but those two were caught up in girls and buggies—spring fever, Luke called it. "It must be a strong fever," James had teased his younger brother, "because it hits you in summer, fall, and winter, too."

For now, Luke and Peter were stepping up to get the work done. As long as James gave them specific chores to do each day, they had been able to tend to the fruit trees. But James didn't want to think of what would happen to the acres of trees—their whole family business—if he wasn't there to oversee things. Who would maintain the trees if James stepped away?

James had learned the orchard from his grandfather Elmo Lapp, who had shared his way of nurturing trees to bear healthy fruit. Doddy had taught James all the basics. When to prune, and how to clip so that the remaining branches would grow in the sun and within reach for picking season. James had learned about fertilizing and watering and mulching. How to fend off fruit moths and borers, and what to do about diseases.

You spray to ward off apple scab, Doddy told him, *but if you find a canker on a tree? Don't waste your time with sprays. Cut off the diseased limb and burn it. That's the only way to take care of that.*

Doddy had tips and solutions and rules for every season of the year, and James had soaked them all up, trailing the older man through the orchard from the time he was a small boy through his teen years.

Steering off the path, James moved close to an apple tree and ran one hand over the bark. Now was the time to apply a dormant oil spray, an organic way to prevent infestations of apple scab, the most common disease to damage apple trees.

An ounce of prevention is worth a pound of cure, Doddy used to say when he told James about measures to ward off damaging insects, fungi, or diseases.

Rolling his chair back to the path, James looked up at the bare branches of apple trees reaching to the sky.

"I still hear your voice, Doddy. Gone two years, and you're still telling me what to do." He laughed at himself, talking to the heavens, and then looked around to be sure he was alone. Anyone else in the orchard would think he was *verhuddelt,* talking to the sky. Maybe he was a little crazy in the head. Dylan had talked to James many times about shock and post-traumatic stress. Talking with the counselor had gotten James out of the mud pit, where his heart and mind had been stuck for the first few months after the accident. Now the only thing holding James back was these legs, still and dormant, like the orchard in the winter.

James slapped his thighs, checking the sensations that hovered there, the dull thunk and slight buzz. Sometimes it was as if his legs were wrapped in thick quilts. They were not blind to sensation, but all feeling was dull and muddled.

"There's still something there, Doddy. And I'm not giving up. I'm going to walk again. Walk and run and climb these trees."

This time, he didn't hear Doddy's voice.

Well, that was no surprise. Doddy knew his trees, but he had not spent much time telling James how to run the rest of his life. For Doddy, the trees were the source of all lessons and advice.

Unlike Dat. Ever since the accident, Jimmy had been scowling down at his son for one reason or another. First it was the cost of medical treatment and rehabilitation. Tens of thousands of dollars. It used to make James sick to think about it, but the Amish community had come together to raise money to pay those bills. An auction had raised two thirds of the expenses. Some doctors had made big donations, while others had cut their fees. Their church district had an emergency medical fund that had paid for James's first surgery. Dr. Dylan's services were paid for by the county, and Haley provided free physical therapy to get credit for her nursing degree.

As James picked up speed along the main path, heading toward the sugar shack at the very back of the orchard, he wished his father would take a step away right now. He knew Dat didn't trust Englishers—many Amish felt that way—but Amish folk didn't have their own doctors, and English were the only source of reliable medical assistance. If James wanted help getting back on his feet, he would have to rely on Dr. Trueherz and the other medical workers. Besides, Dat seemed to be ignoring the generosity of folks like Haley and Dr. Monroe, Englishers who were being Good Samaritans. It was one thing to live separate from the world, as Gott told His people. James would always live simple and keep the ways of the Amish. But he didn't understand Dat's insistence that they push away Englisher folk who wanted to help.

In the distance, the sugar shack seemed to be tucked into the hill. The land on the north end gave way to a low gully, where a stone-lined creek zigzagged along one side of the small structure. The maple woods were a natural border behind the shack, stretching all the way to the Lapp property line, which was marked somewhere behind those woods by a fence meant to keep cows on the dairy farm. Although the wide stovepipe chimney jabbed into the sky and the stack of wood under the lean-to was plentiful, the shack hadn't been used this year. Since Doddy died, James had been the one to get his brothers going when it was time to tap the trees. Doddy had taught him that the sap began to flow when daytime temperatures rose above freezing, and since he was a child, James had dutifully watched the outdoor thermometer in the late winter. But this year, with the accident, there would be no maple sugaring.

The last time he had been inside the shack, snow had covered the land. Every detail of that afternoon was etched into his mind, like a very good story told over and again. The blustery cold outside had made the fire inside seem warm and welcoming. The back of Rachel's black coat had been soaked from when she'd flopped down on the ground to make snow angels, and he had hung it to dry near the potbellied stove while she had sketched a quiet scene of a single tree leaning into a fence dusted in snow.

He used to like watching her sketch. The whisper of pencil on paper. The shapes that grew into flowers and trees and buildings. The smooth contentment on Rachel's face as a picture flowed from the lead of her pencil. She always hummed as she drew, often the same song, "I Need Thee Every Hour." James had begun to think of it as their song.

This had been their hideaway, their quiet place to be alone together. That was one of the drawbacks and blessings about living Plain: You were almost never alone. But here he and Rachel had found a place with privacy. In cold weather they huddled inside by the fire. The rest of the year, they sat in the grass that had overgrown the lane. Sometimes they stretched out and found shapes in the passing clouds. Sometimes they kissed. And he had spent hours holding her, her softness pressed against him as he breathed in her scent and dreamed of the life they would have together. A big Amish family with a dozen boys to man the orchard.

He wanted to think they would huddle inside there again, Rachel in his arms. That van accident on a cold winter's evening was not going to change him for the rest of his life. James would not give up. He was counting on walking again, because without these legs under him, he would be useless to this orchard.

Useless to Rachel.

His jaw clenched at the thought of her, blue eyes calm as a river, smile as bright as a candle in the night. He'd been in a foul mood since the accident, but Rachel had stayed by him, encouraging and cheerful.

Somehow, someday when he was walking again, he would make it all up to her.

3

*A*s she turned a slice of scrapple on the griddle, Rachel hummed a song about the hourly need for Gott. Since the accident, she'd found comfort in calling on Gott in silent prayer throughout the day. As a child, she had thought worship was reserved for every other Sunday, when the community gathered at a barn or house for church. But turning to Gott was one of the things suggested by Dylan. The notion was seconded by Bishop Samuel, who agreed that it was good to remember that the Almighty was behind every part of nature and life.

Emerging from the pantry, Mamm placed two jars of peaches on the counter and began to sing the words to the tune Rachel had been humming.

"I need Thee, oh, I need Thee; Every hour I need Thee . . ."

Smiling, Rachel sang with her. "Oh, bless me now, my Savior, I come to Thee."

"That's got to be your favorite song," Mamm said, "since I hear you singing it nearly every day."

"Singing makes work into play." Rachel moved a brown piece of meat toward the edge of the cast-iron griddle.

"If that's so, why don't I hear you singing when you're mucking the stalls?" Betsy King asked.

"No amount of singing will turn that into a game." Rachel grinned, knowing her mother was only half teasing. Her parents were well aware of the way she tried to wake before her siblings so that she could dig into household chores and breakfast preparation, leaving them the barn chores.

"Thank Gott in heaven, most everyone favors something different. Jacob and Amos don't mind tending to the cows. Abe is the farmer of the family. And whenever I need to run an errand, Rose is quick to head out and harness a horse for me."

"Rose understands the horses," Rachel said. "If one of 'em is limping, she'll figure out what's wrong. She's good in the stables. Just keep her out of the kitchen when you're baking cookies." Last week, when Rose had been helping with a batch of peanut butter cookies, she had accidentally added a cup of salt instead of sugar.

Betsy chuckled softly as she spooned raisins into a serving dish. "When will you children let Rose off the hook? It was an honest mistake. Sugar and salt look alike."

"But they sure don't taste alike," Rachel said.

There was a simple peace on Betsy's face as she stirred the large pot of oatmeal. Mamm had always seemed so content at home with her family of eleven. Rachel wanted that peace in her own heart. Sometimes she wondered if her desire to sketch and paint was the thing that made her discontented with doing the work of an Amish woman.

"Here's the last of the peaches from James," Mamm said, twisting the lid of one jar. "How are the Lapps faring without him to manage the orchard?"

Rachel shrugged. "His brothers are picking up the slack. But James goes out in the orchard every day. Sometimes for hours. He's still managing. Not climbing ladders or pruning. But James is the one who really knows the trees."

"Well, I'm sure the family will let us know if they need help."

"I'm hoping to go over and visit with James on Saturday," Rachel said. Saturday night was the traditional courtship night. Usually an Amish young man came calling for his girl, but since it was so difficult for James to travel, Rachel had taken to visiting him.

"You give him my best." Betsy removed the lid and stirred the oatmeal. "Breakfast is ready. I'll send Molly out to fetch the others." She turned toward the arch, then paused. "Let's not forget Ben. He's going to need a lunch pail for the market in the city."

"Is it his turn again already?"

Mamm nodded. "The van will pick him up shortly after breakfast. They're a little shorthanded at the cheese stand, with Lizzy keeping close to home now."

Usually, the King family cheese stand at the Reading Terminal was run by Market Joe King and his wife, Lizzy, but with cousin Lizzy expecting her first baby, the family was considering who might replace her at the market.

"I'll make a lunch for Ben." Rachel shut off the burner under the last batch of scrapple and turned to the cutting board to slice bread. "A cheese sandwich?"

"Put a hard-boiled egg on there," Mamm said. "The children dyed three dozen or so for Easter. We'd best get using them."

As she prepared an egg sandwich for her brother, Rachel realized that it was not really Ben's turn to go to the city. As they usually rotated the chore of going to Philly among the teens in their family, it had to be Rachel's time to go. She was grateful that her parents were letting her off the hook on account of the way her nerves iced over at the prospect of riding in a car or van.

"That's not a problem at all," the bishop had said when she'd told him about her fear. "Stick to a horse and buggy and your life will be right as rain." Samuel had a way of making it seem so simple, but in her heart, many things were still jumbled and twisted as a knot of yarn. Trusting her faith, Rachel looked to Gott to let her emotions settle, smooth as a pond. Three months after the accident, she was still praying for that simple peace.

The silver lining in the cloud was the way the young folks from the van had come together after the accident. In the past few months, Rachel had grown closer to Elsie Lapp, Ruben Zook, and Zed Miller, the other young passengers in the van. Well, Zed was a good bit older than the rest, but having spent years away on his rumspringa, he had been lumped in with the young folks now that he was back in the community. With Dylan Monroe guiding their discussions, just talking about the accident and their fears had helped everyone in the group. Unfortunately, James's injuries had kept him away from the meetings. Rachel was sorry he hadn't enjoyed the benefit of support from the others. These days, James seemed so alone. Ya, he was surrounded by family, but he reminded her of a lone eagle, hovering and circling on its own.

Sometimes she wondered if her secret plan might cheer him up. She had never mentioned it before, but now, with James confined to a wheelchair, she wondered if it might give him hope just thinking about a small one-story home in town. James would take the buggy to the orchard each day, and they would live Plain, but, oh, how nice it would be to buy milk at the market instead of having to milk a few head morning and night.

And her paintings were a part of that plan. If she could sell her work, she could help pay their home expenses. The day of the crash, she had met with an Englisher woman who had thought she could sell Rachel's art in her Philadelphia gallery. Claudia Stein had told Rachel to get busy, because she would need a dozen paintings to stage a show.

A dozen paintings!

On that January day, Rachel's spirit had jumped for joy at the prospect of so many sweet hours spent dabbing paint into pictures. She had wondered if that much money would convince her mamm and dat to let her skip some of her regular chores on the dairy farm so she would have more time for her side business. After the crash, she had backed away from Claudia's offer, but now she considered the practical side. She and James might need a good source of income. Especially if James wouldn't be working for a while.

Now she considered telling James about her secret plan. Maybe it would give him hope. He might begin to see a good life ahead, a future with Rachel that would be workable whether or not Gott healed his legs.

The kitchen grew warm and noisy as the family assembled. Dat talked about the spring weather and Mamm ladled out bowls of oatmeal from the head of the table. As her siblings began to take their places at the kitchen table, Rachel carried the large platter of scrapple to the table.

"That's enough for me," twenty-year-old Abe said, eyeing the platter of meat. "What are the rest of you going to eat?"

With quick hands, Jacob served himself. "I could eat a bear."

"Why are you guys always so hungry?" Molly asked as she passed a bowl of oatmeal down the line.

"Hard work gives a man a good appetite," Davey said, stabbing a slice of meat with his fork. The boy was six years old, but he copied his older brothers to a T.

When everyone was seated, Nate King called for the prayer. Rachel bowed her head and silently gave thanks for the meal and for the love of her family. Before the accident, she had taken the love and comforts of home for granted. Now, each day she reminded herself to keep her eyes wide open to the blessings of her family.

The conversation turned to the new calves, born last month, who were still being bottle-fed by Molly and Davey.

Twelve-year-old Bethany said she wished she could care for the calves instead of milking. "Or maybe the cows could be milked later in the morning. That way, I wouldn't have to get out of bed so early."

"But then you'd be late for school," Rachel pointed out.

"I wouldn't mind that," Bethany said as she reached for her glass of milk.

"But the milking is easier with the machines," Rachel reminded her sister. Three years ago, Dat had brought in milking machines powered by a gas generator. Once the machines were hooked up, milking was done quick as could be. They cut milking time down to almost nothing.

"When *was* the last time you milked a cow?" Rose asked her pointedly.

Rachel shrugged. "I didn't mark it on the calendar."

"It's been that long?" Rose shook her head. "I knew it. If Rachel doesn't have to help with the milking, how come I do? I'd rather work in the stables."

"Cows need milking," Dat said without looking up from his oatmeal. "That's what we do."

"Not Rachel," Ben said. "She paints."

Rachel pursed her lips together to keep from snapping back. Leave it to Ben to say something like that. He'd caused their parents so much worry, going off on motorbikes and trying to dodge chores. He was eighteen now; he'd never taken much to dairy farming, and he had no trade in sight.

"No one's painting pictures when there's chores to be done," Mamm said. "Rachel's a big help to me, here in the house."

"But Mamm, the cows need her, too," Jacob teased. "They miss her."

"Brownie says she's forgotten what you look like, Rachel," said ten-year-old Amos, who knew every cow by name. "When I asked her about you, she said, 'Rachel moo-who?'"

Laughter filled the room. Molly and Davey joined in with Amos's mooing, and everyone laughed some more.

"I always knew that Brownie was a funny cow," Dat said wryly.

Taking in the happy faces, Rachel let the gentle ribbing slide off her back like rain on a duck. Besides, she couldn't stop chuckling at the thought of Amos talking with the cows, and the cows talking back.

Davey's brows knitted together. "Did Brownie really say that?"

"We all know that milking cows don't talk," said Dat, ever the voice of reason. "But if they did, I'm sure Amos would speak their language."

"Ya." Amos wiped his milk mustache with one sleeve. "I speak English, Dutch, and cow."

4

After breakfast, James was about to head back out to the orchards when his father called to him.

"James, will you wait a little bit?"

Stopping the chair, James waited until Peter and Luke grabbed their hats from the wall peg and squeezed past. How he wished he could follow them out the door on his own two feet. Then he turned back to his father.

"I was just going to check on our supply of Bordeaux spray. We need to start spraying. Don't want fire blight on the apples or pears."

"You can do that later." Dat motioned him toward the living area. "*Kumm*. I want to talk with you before the bishop gets here."

"Bishop Samuel?" Unease prickled the back of James's neck. The leader of their church was kind but intimidating. It wasn't easy to pass under the stern gaze of a man who decided what was right by Gott. "Why is he coming here?"

"I asked for his help." Jimmy sat down and rested his large hands on his thighs. From the way Jimmy kept his gaze on the floor, James could tell that his father was uncomfortable, too. "At a time like this, we need to look to our bishop for answers."

Answers about what? James wondered as he rolled his chair to a stop beside the sofa. "What do you want to ask the bishop?"

Jimmy lifted his dark eyes to his oldest son. "James, there's no denying you've been through the wringer since that accident. It was a terrible thing, and we've all done our best to move ahead and do the right thing for you."

"And I'm grateful for all that you and Mamm have done. All the support from the community. The auction and fund-raisers. I know the chiropractor and doctors and hospital cost a lot, Dat, but with everyone's help, the bills are nearly paid off, aren't they?"

"Close to it." Dat pointed toward the old carriage house, which had been turned into an office for the orchard. "I got a special file for the medical bills. You can take a look next time you come into the office."

Which might be never, as far as James was concerned. He couldn't abide the stale air and mountains of papers that made up the office. Ledgers and files. As if this wheelchair wasn't enough of a hindrance; a desk seemed to be invented to strap a man down to the earth without an inch of movement.

It was James's turn to stare at the floor. "I know my injury used a lot of the family's money, but the orchard is a profitable business. And I'm going to keep it running for my grandchildren and their grandchildren, too."

"Grandchildren? You don't even have children yet. You're counting your chickens before they've hatched."

More disapproval. James could not say anything without his father cutting it down. He rubbed the knuckles of one hand over his smooth-shaven face. How could he explain his connection to the orchard? How winter, spring, and summer had become synonymous with dormant, bloom, and harvest? How few joys could rival the sheen of healthy bark and the scent of peach blossoms? And all of Doddy's lists of things to do, categorized by type of fruit and season—they were all in James's mind, a fruit gardener's encyclopedia.

You'd think that Jimmy would understand all this, having grown up on the orchard, too. But Dat had left the growing to his father, while he had focused on the business side of the orchard. It was an arrangement that had worked fine, until the accident. Now, as James dared to take in the older man's square face, framed by dark hair and a beard below his chin, he wished that his father understood that the injury hadn't changed James—not really. He was still Jimmy's oldest son, still capable of overseeing the acres of fruit trees, even if he did it from a wheelchair.

In the awkward silence, James heard the clipped patter of horses' hooves in the distance. The bishop was approaching.

James pushed up on the armrests and shifted in his chair, wishing he could roll down the ramp and escape to the orchard. "Lots of work to do outside," he said, hoping that this meeting would be short.

"You've always been a good worker," Jimmy said with a flicker of approval in his dark eyes. "But now that you're off your feet, it's time you learned the other end of the business. Get acquainted with the bookkeeping and sales."

"But I've always managed the orchards. Right now I can't do everything, but that'll change when I get walking again."

"Mmm." It was the growl of a discontented bear. "We'll have to see about that. I'm not sure of Gott's plan for you, but I know you're not meant to be tangled up with these Englishers. Isn't it enough that they come in their buses and vans, swarming like ants in the town? I see them in Halfway and then I come home to find my house full of doctors and nurses, drivers and therapists. There's an outsider here every day. It's getting so you'd never know this is an Amish home."

Jimmy kept his distance from Englishers, which was not so unusual. Most Amish kept to other Amish; that was how their community worked. But living side by side with the English, there were times when they couldn't be avoided, and this was one of them. There were no Plain folk in the medical profession. Amish children finished school after eighth grade, and then worked the farm or learned a skill. Preacher Dave had told James that no Amish settlement had ever allowed a person to go to medical school. Dave thought it was a matter of pride—hochmut. He pointed out that the higher knowledge gained in worldly society might override a person's good Amish values. If James wanted to work with doctors to get rehabilitated, he had no choice but to deal with Englishers.

"Dat, they taught me how to get myself in and out of bed. How to wash myself and . . . all the physical therapy, moving my legs so they don't wither and die. Folks like Haley and Dylan, like Doc Trueherz, they've helped me come a long way."

"I'm grateful to them, but they're not our friends or family. It's time to back away." It was not the first time Dat had spoken of keeping distance from Englishers. His dislike of fancy folk had been forged years ago, when he was a boy, and an Englisher had injured his best friend. An incident so upsetting that Jimmy refused to talk about it.

"Dat, all Englishers are not bad people."

"Ya, this is true, but the Bible tells us to stay separate from that world. I know the bishop will agree with me on this. A man must keep a good Amish home. So . . . next time the Englishers visit will be the last time. It's wrong to have so many dealings with outsiders."

"But the orchard has dealings with outsiders. We work with the Englisher stores. We sell our fruit to thousands of Englishers."

"That's different. Englishers can enjoy Gott's bounty as well as

Plain folk. But here's the difference: Selling fruit doesn't bring the outsiders into our homes. Into our lives." Jimmy's brow was stern as he rose and moved toward the door. "Samuel's here."

Stewing in misery, James watched his father greet the head of their congregation and make small talk about the weather. James didn't know what his dat had told the bishop, but he sensed that they were coming at him with a shared purpose. This was not going to be a good talk.

Magnified by his glasses, Samuel's eyes were round as an owl's. He listened as James answered his questions about the orchard, telling about the spraying and fertilizing that had to be done in April.

When the bishop got down to business, it soon became clear that he was here to convince James to give up all hope.

"It's been a few months since the accident, and from what Jimmy tells me, you seem to be in a rut." Samuel's tone was gentle, but his words cut like a hunting knife. "It's time to accept the truth. You will probably not walk again."

James felt his nostrils flare in defiance, but he held his tongue. No one argued with the bishop, and a young baptized member like himself did not dare say that their community leader was wrong . . . that Englishers had predicted otherwise.

"It's a tough thing to say." Dat frowned. "But Gott tells us how it's going to be, and we must accept His ways. Contentment is not getting what we want, but being satisfied with what we have."

"Gott's will is hard to understand and accept, but we must. 'Thy will be done.' That's the Lord's Prayer, ya?"

James felt his heart harden as the bishop's words crackled in the room.

"Now, how does that apply to you?" Samuel went on. "For whatever reason—we can never understand why—Gott's plan for you has put you in that wheelchair. It's time to stop mooning over what used to be and accept what is. It's not the end of the world to be in a wheelchair. Many of Gott's blessings can still be enjoyed. A sunny spring day. A funny joke. A good meal."

Dat sat there beside the bishop, nodding in agreement. "And there's another blessing to be thankful for. The doctors keep saying James is lucky to be alive," Jimmy added.

Alive, but trapped in a chair. But James could not give voice to his feelings; he had to remain respectful. The bishop had the final word on all things in their community.

"'Thy will be done,'" Samuel repeated, his gray eyes magnified by the lenses of this glasses as he studied James. "This part of the Lord's Prayer, *this* must have a new meaning for you. You must take it to heart."

"If I knew that it was Gott's will for me to be paralyzed, I would accept it," James said, struggling to keep his voice even. He patted his thighs. "But Gott left me some feeling in these legs, and I'm going to do my best to see if I can make them work again."

Samuel's eyes were steely as he stroked his graying beard. "Determination can be a very good thing, but sometimes Gott puts us on a bumpy road to shake our hand loose."

For a brief moment, James could appreciate what the bishop was saying. He was trying to save James the grief of disappointment. He was trying to help James settle in and accept that his was a lifetime injury.

But James would not, could not settle for that.

"James is determined, all right," Dat said. "And a hard worker, too. I told him he wasn't needed in the orchards, but he wouldn't sit back. He won't linger in the house when there's work to be done outside."

"Maybe some wouldn't mind the rest, but I'm itching to get back to work, back to climbing trees." James forced a smile, trying to lighten up the conversation. He didn't want to be handed any orders from his father or the bishop today. He didn't want to be bound by their decisions. "And Doc Trueherz thinks it's possible—that I might walk again—because I didn't lose the feeling in my legs. There's a new therapy. Something that wakes up the spinal cord. I'm supposed to meet with a man named Dr. Finley."

"And how much will that cost?" Dat asked.

"If I get into the study, I won't have to pay anything. I just need to get to the clinic in Paradise."

Jimmy folded his arms across his chest, a gesture that told James he was closing his mind. "And if it's not free, I reckon there will be more bills."

Crinkly lines grew deep around the edge of Samuel's eyes. "Ach! Medical bills can be sky-high."

"They tell me that Dr. Finley's program has no charge." James did not expect his father to bring up the money issue in front of the bishop. "But even if it costs money, I want to do the treatment. You just said that we're caught up on the hospital bills."

"We've paid for a lot more than the hospital and doctors," Dat went on. "Don't forget the money for the two wheelchairs. The one with the fat wheels cost nearly a thousand dollars. And the ramp we built for you. And so many car rides to the hospital and rehab center. Even if this Doc Finley is free, there's the matter of getting there. It's a busy time in the orchard and no one can be spared to drive you."

"Gott has given you a heavy burden. Sometimes, all we can do is accept the load, and accept the familiar road." The bishop faced James. "Listen to your father. He is wise when it comes to falling in with the Englishers. And you know your parents can't keep pouring out money. Who could? And the Englishers, I've seen them advise medical tests and exams that amount to nothing but a lot of debt."

"But they have therapies that can help me walk again," James said, keeping his voice respectful. "By the grace of Gott, they might have a cure for me."

Disappointment burned in Bishop Samuel's eyes. "Did you not hear anything we've said? Doctors might help, but it's Gott who heals. It's time to accept His will."

"But there's still hope . . ." James insisted.

"Hope is a good thing, ya?" Samuel said coolly. "The Bible says 'Blessed is the man that trusteth in the Lord, and whose hope the Lord is.' But the main thing is to trust in the Lord. You do that, and the other things will fall into place. For now, you'd best listen to your dat. Find ways to pitch in with other things while your brothers work the orchard."

"There's a lot for you to learn in the office," Dat said. "Get to know the business end of the orchard. I'll be happy to have you working side by side with me."

And I'll shrivel up and rot, like a fire-blighted apple.

As the bishop put on his hat and headed out to his buggy, James felt sick inside. He reminded himself to stay strong, keep pushing himself toward recovery, but when the bishop's words replayed in his mind, he felt frozen in place.

Dat and Samuel wanted him to give up, and they wouldn't be satisfied until the last flame of hope inside him was snuffed out to a charred, sizzling wick.

5

"Isn't today Friday?" Shandell Darby asked as the car whipped past green fields of corn.

"I guess. Where'd I put my sunglasses?" Gary pulled the visor down against the sun as he steered with one hand. There was a harsh quality in his normally handsome face when he squinted that way. "What's it matter? When you're on a road trip, you don't have to worry about what day it is. We got the wind in our hair and the open road in front of us."

"Yeah, but I thought you said we'd be home by the weekend."

"What's your rush?" Agitation prickled in his voice.

Shandell squirmed in the passenger seat, not sure how to answer. It seemed the more she pushed Gary toward going back to Baltimore, the more obstinate he became. It was a side of him she'd never seen back home, but when their road trip had begun to unravel, so had their friendship. She opened the console, fished out his sunglasses, and handed them over.

He took them without a thank-you. "I wish you could talk about something besides going home," he said as the car swung on a curve. She wished he didn't drive so fast. "It's getting a little played out."

"But you're the one who said—"

"I don't know what you think you're going to find when you get back to Baltimore," he said pointedly. "It's not like a fairy's going to wave a magic wand and get old Phil off the couch."

That hurt, maybe because she knew it was true. Since her stepfather had lost his job as a plumber, he seemed to be sinking deeper and deeper into the couch, a can or two of beer always on the end table beside him.

She scraped back her blue-tinted black hair as she stared out the window at her own reflection in the side mirror. The round-eyed, button-nosed face in the reflection was pathetically childish for an eighteen-year-old. It didn't help that she was petite, with the small body of a pixie. When would she begin to look her age?

When will you begin to act your age?

Maybe that was a better question. She had made a lot of mistakes in the past few days, and now she was beginning to see the consequences.

Shandell stared at the cornfield beyond the window. She had never seen corn so young—short green stalks reaching up to the sun. So hopeful. Shandell wished she had that kind of hope in her heart. She wished someone would hire her stepfather and give him a reason to stop drinking. She wished that she was anywhere else but driving in Gary's big boat of a car.

Three days ago, when her mother had freaked out over a notice from the school that Shandell was failing math, Shandell had taken Gary up on his offer of a road trip. Maybe it wasn't the best decision Shandell had ever made, but the prospect of escaping her sorry life for a visit to Gary's sister had seemed like a great idea at the time.

"Road trip!" Gary had shouted, pumping a fist in the air. In need of relief, Shandell had found his enthusiasm contagious.

In the past six months, life at the Darby house had become unbearable for Shandell, who was expected to keep house and cook for Phil while Mom worked two jobs to make enough to keep up with the rent.

Chelsea Darby's plan for a stable, happy life had not worked out the way anyone had envisioned it. No one had anticipated that Phil would lose his job, and as if the loss of income weren't enough, Phil had dwindled into a bitter, critical man when he turned to drinking to ease the pain. The shriveled core of a person who now sat on the couch in their living room barely resembled the kind, athletic man who had once told Shandell that he considered it an honor and a privilege to be her stepfather. Lately, Shandell had focused most of her energy on coming up with ways to stay away from home. That had led her to hang out in Ryan's garage with her more low-key friends, like Lucia, Kylie, Ryan, and Gary. She'd passed many a lazy hour there talking and listening to music. "It's your therapy," her friends always told her when she felt nips of guilt over missing school to hang out. Ryan had some great music on his iPod, and his mother understood that the teens had nowhere else to go. With music and a Ping-Pong table, a deck of cards, and snacks that everyone picked up from the convenience store on the corner, hours passed easily in Ryan's garage.

School . . . that was another sore spot she didn't want to think about. She was supposed to be graduating in June, but now there was probably no chance of that. *And it's not my fault,* Shandell thought, frowning. Although Shandell loved history and writing, she was terrible at math and science, and with Mom working the evening shift at the hospital laundry, Shandell lost her tutor. From the first day that she failed a quiz in Algebra 2, Shandell felt herself sinking fast without Mom to teach her the lessons. By the time midterm grades came out, she was drowning with no lifeboat in sight. They couldn't afford a tutor, and her teacher could not spare the time to work with individual students. At this point, her high school diploma was in jeopardy.

And if that wasn't bad enough, there was her stepdad. She raked her silky black hair away from her forehead and tried to let the neat rows of corn beyond the window chase the dark thoughts of her stepfather from her mind. Thinking about Phil made her want to cry, despite the Amish farmland, bursting with the colors of springtime. She had enjoyed her time out in the bright countryside, a nice break from the shadowed living room where Phil carped at her from the blue light of the television screen.

What's wrong with you? You can't even pass dummy math.

With grades like that, you'll never amount to anything.

"Aw, come on." Gary slung his arm around her in a conciliatory gesture. "Don't forget why you wanted to leave home in the first place."

"I haven't forgotten." The images of her stepfather passed out on the couch and her mother raging through tears were branded in her memory. After the terrible fight with Mom, she'd wanted nothing more than to be far away from home. But now they were out of money and running out of gas. Twice she had washed her hair in public restroom sinks, and sponge baths left her feeling grungy. She just wanted to go home. "It was fun in the beginning, Gar, but you said it yourself. Our plan didn't work out. Your sister couldn't put us up, and you can't really live in a car. We need to go home."

"You can't go back there." His voice was soft, but there was an insidious edge that was beginning to wear on her. "Your mother told you to go, didn't she?"

Chelsea Darby had told her daughter to leave, but Shandell didn't think she meant it, not really.

"I already missed three days of school," she told Gary. "If I miss too much, I won't graduate."

"Too bad, so sad. You're old enough to drop out of school, and what would you do with a high school diploma, anyway? There are no jobs for people like us anymore. We have to blaze our own trails. Do something different."

Gary considered himself to be industrious, but at twenty-one he was three years older than Shandell and still didn't have much to show for it. He had dropped out of school when he was seventeen and taken a job with a moving company in Baltimore. But there were slow periods when they didn't need him. Like now.

When they'd left Baltimore, she'd thought that Gary might be her savior; now she recognized that he was an ordinary thief. Twice they had bolted from gas stations without paying for the gas, and she realized that the hot food from the convenience store was probably stolen, too. The excitement of the road trip had soured into a bad dream, one of those feverish dreams where Shandell kept climbing a mountain but every time she looked up, she was miles from the top. And when she looked down, the steep drop paralyzed her with fear.

She wanted out of the road trip.

"Maybe I want to do something different," she said, "but just back in Baltimore. It would be nice to sleep in a bed again. I'll be better at blazing a new trail with a good night's sleep."

"You can be such a dweeb. But okay. We'll head back after dark. I just want to hit a few more of these Amish towns. Lancaster County is full of them."

"They are really quaint," she said, though she was surprised that Gary was into patchwork quilts and buggies.

When they passed over the rise, the road descended steadily into a green valley flanked by farms on either side. The dark road seemed to reach into the future. *My road,* she thought, not sure where it would lead. Still, it was a lovely road, smooth and steady. And the green, growing life surrounding it gave her hope. She would work things out with Mom when she got home. And Phil? Well, that wouldn't be so easy if he didn't want to help himself. But maybe Mom would help her convince Phil to get help.

Up ahead on the right was a little farm stand—a small white shack with a sign that read FLOWERS & PIE FILLING. NO SUNDAY SALES. It was tidy, with flowers and jars set out on the counter. Shandell was wondering about the Amish people who ran it when Gary pulled off to the side of the road and rolled to a stop in the gravel near the white hut.

"It's closed," Shandell said. That was too bad, because she wouldn't have minded seeing some Amish people again. They were kind of brusque and blunt, but they didn't gush or waste words. She had gotten used to their uniform clothing—the way all the women parted their hair in the middle and pinned it back under a kapp. All the women wore brightly colored, loose dresses and the men could be seen in black pants, colored shirts, and black felt or straw hats. Although they kept to themselves, there was something intriguing about them, as if they knew a secret path to peace that they couldn't share with outsiders like her.

"Let's see what they got," Gary said, cutting the engine.

She shot him a suspicious look, but he ignored her, leaving the car door open as he strode ahead. She followed him over to the counter, which was nearly covered in neat rows of potted yellow daffodils and fragrant hyacinths. The crowded blossoms of the pink, purple, and white hyacinths reminded her of fireworks exploding in the sky. Only these had a deliciously sweet scent.

Gary moved out from behind the counter and circled round to the back of the stand.

"What are you doing?" she asked.

"Just checking. There's nobody here."

"I told you, they're closed. They're probably in one of these farmhouses, eating dinner." With their family. Longing blossomed in her chest, but she tamped it down. She would be home soon enough. Right now, she just needed to keep Gary on track.

"We should go," she said, "unless you suddenly have a yearning for hyacinths." She turned to the jars on the side of the counter. "And cherry pie filling."

He rubbed his ear, considering. "You know, I think I do need some flowers."

He lifted up the entire carton of hyacinths.

"You're kidding, right?"

"Nope. These are a deal at a dollar apiece. We'll take them home to butter up your mother."

"Wow. That's kind of sweet, Gar." It had probably been years since anyone gave her mom flowers, and once these were planted in the yard, they would come back year after year. She softened as he carried the flowers to the car and placed them in the trunk.

Shandell calculated what they owed. Basic math came easily to her; it was the multistep procedures that lost her. She lifted the lid of the little gray cash box. "That's twelve dollars," she told him. "You just leave the money in this box."

He grabbed two jars of cherry pie filling. "Since we're here, might as well take these, too."

"Then that'll be twenty, even."

She imagined the pleasure of the Amish people when they noticed the big sale tomorrow. The thought of it made her smile, too.

But that faded when she heard Gary cackling behind her, on his way to the car.

"Get in the car, girl. You don't pay for stuff when you can get it for free."

"But it's the honor system," she insisted, wheeling around to face him. "You can't steal that stuff."

His laugh was giddy. "Oh, yeah? Watch and learn."

"Come on, don't do this. It's wrong and . . . and you don't even need it. Come on, Gary, just leave the money."

"I'm not leaving these people a nickel. Honor system, my ass. They don't need my money. They got plenty of money and cows and horses. Look at all the land they got. Now get in the car, before I throw you in the trunk, along with the flowers."

This time, Gary was not laughing.

Her jaw dropped as she stared at him. Did he mean that? He wouldn't hurt her, would he? She didn't think so, but then again, she hadn't thought he was a thief when they'd left Baltimore three days ago.

"Get in the car."

Biting back tears, Shandell got into the car and began to plot her escape.

6

The lavender light of sunrise filtered through the curtains in the attic room as Rachel put the finishing touches on her painting. Wanting to bring James a little gift today, she had risen early and crept upstairs to her old bedroom to finish this small canvas, a close view of a ripe peach still hanging in a tree.

As this was the only space in the house suitable for painting, she had to work quietly while Rose slept in the single bed against the wall. The steady whisper of her sister's breath reassured Rachel as she sat at her homemade easel, a pyramid of wood sticks her dat had built for her last year as a birthday gift. She hoped that the soapy paint smell and stirring noises didn't disturb Rose, but so far there'd been no complaints from the lump curled under the patchwork quilt.

Rachel swished her brush in water and added a dab of cerulean blue to the palette of bright colors. She had finished painting the peach in a combination of magenta, cadmium orange, burnt umber, and sienna, and she had to admit, the sight of the fat fruit made her mouth water. Usually her work wasn't so realistic. Most of her paintings focused on the colors of Amish life: a patchwork quilt, gem-toned dresses swaying from a clothesline, flowers blooming beside a bright blue watering can, a dark horse and buggy silhouetted against an orange sky and autumn gold fields. But today, for James, she had tried something different—a close still-life. She had worked hard to make the peach look real and delicious, with sun-dappled rose streaks and dewdrops on the skin. Even a bit of peach fuzz.

Now as she layered on a cloudless, bright blue sky, she hoped that James would like the reminder of the orchard he so loved. These days he was able to move through the wide aisles between trees, but he wasn't able to help much with the mulching and spraying. When it came time to prune or harvest . . . Well, no one could say if James would be able to run the orchard in the coming seasons. Only Gott in heaven knew if he would ever be able to rise from his chair and climb the fruit trees like the monkey he once was.

A tender smile softened her lips as she painted, circling the brush to create round texture in the sky. How easy it was to lose herself in her art! James sometimes teased her about it, telling her to return to the farm, but she found such contentment in re-creating the stillness of Amish life. And the bright colors of life brought her such joy! The temptation to paint the day away was strong, but Amish life was not a life to be spent alone. Although her parents enjoyed her artwork as a gift from Gott, they often reminded her not to spend too much time on her hobby. And many Amish thought that things like art and music were an indulgence—a way to show that you were special and superior, which was never a good thing for a person.

"It's good to have a little something on the side," Mamm always said, "but the center of life is your family and your community.

Family is among Gott's greatest blessings—the unbroken chain of life."

Before the accident, Rachel hadn't really seen their noisy, boisterous family as such a blessing. Her tall, muscular brothers who swiped the last of the bacon or spiked the ball right at her in a volleyball match? And her sisters, who seemed glued to their beds nearly every morning? One look at the kitchen after a meal, and any person in his right mind would run in the opposite direction. Her siblings teased one another mercilessly at times, and they could raise some thunder, but when one person was hurting, the way she had been after the accident, they all pulled together to help. She loved them dearly.

After the accident, folks had come through for her in small and large ways. Mamm and Dat had rushed to the hospital to see her, even though she was unharmed. The main concern had been to take care of the injured folk, and after the first few days that had included all the young people in the van who had been spared physical injury but hurt inside—traumatized. Dr. Monroe offered to do group counseling, and it was a blessing that the bishop allowed it because talking about the worst parts of the crash had eased the terror in Rachel's heart. It was still a sad thing, especially losing Tom Lapp and seeing James and old Jacob injured. But now Rachel could talk about the accident without quivering inside.

Stepping back from the painting, her blue brush tipped in the air, she thought about James. How she wished he'd been able to join in the group therapy. Dr. Dylan had been going to see him, but that wasn't the same as hearing that Elsie, Ruben, Zed, and Rachel were battling the same feelings, suffering the same dreams. Was James getting the support he needed from his Amish family—the folks in the church district, the Plain folk of Halfway?

She hoped so. Now, more than ever, James needed his Amish family.

๖๏ะ

Later that morning, James was still on Rachel's mind as she drove the buggy toward town. Mamm had given her a list of items to buy at the bulk store, but first she was going to drop sisters Molly and Bethany off at the farm stand on the road by the other family dairy farm, run by cousin Adam King.

"I can't wait to see what's come out of Mammi Nell's greenhouse," Molly said, clapping her hands together in delight.

This was the first year that the younger girls had been put in charge of running the family farm stand, which was used to sell off extra vegetables from the garden as well as items their grandmother grew in the greenhouse. Last year at this time, Rachel had managed the stand with her cousin Sadie. Dear Sadie! She had gone off to the city during her rumspringa, and Rachel missed her so.

"Look at that! Ruthie's already there." Bethany pointed ahead at the white roadside hut down the hill. Today the chalkboard sign said FLOWERS & PIE FILLING. Underneath was the painted sign that read NO SUNDAY SALES.

"Do you think we'll get many customers today?" Molly asked, holding a hand up to shield her eyes from the sun.

"I reckon so," Rachel said. "A lot of Englishers come out this way on weekends, especially in the good spring weather."

As Rachel drew back the reins to slow the horse, cousin Ruthie emerged from the cover of the hut with her hands on her hips, her face set in a scowl.

"Ruthie King, I've never seen such a look from you," Rachel said as her sisters hopped down from the buggy. "You need to turn that frown upside down."

"But I'm not happy." Ruthie pointed to the stand. "Somebody came by and stole our hyacinths. Every last one."

"Don't tell me that!" Bethany rushed into the little booth to see for herself. "We've been growing those hyacinths for weeks, checking them every day. And now they're stolen?"

"I don't believe it. Who would steal flowers?" Molly picked up two pots of daffodils, as if the money might be hiding under them. "Maybe they're coming back to pay us later."

"I thought of that," Ruthie said, "but the cash box is empty. Whoever came by took the money we left here to make change."

"Oh, dear girls, I'm afraid Ruthie is right." Rachel understood their disappointment. "Someone didn't obey the honor system."

"The sign is very clear," Bethany said, reading: *"Honor system. Place money in box. Thank you."* She squinted up at the sign, shaking her head. "Why didn't they follow directions?"

Molly blinked. "Maybe they couldn't read. That would be a shame."

"But it's still wrong to take something that doesn't belong to you," Ruthie said firmly. "And there are two jars of pie filling gone. They might have been sold, but I can't be sure. No one made a note in the book."

"What a terrible day," Bethany said crossly.

"Don't be that way." Rachel slipped an arm around her sister's shoulder. "Nothing good will come of this if you let it ruin your day."

Bethany shook her head. "How could there be anything good in this?"

"Maybe Gott means it as a lesson to us. We need to learn to forgive and forget."

"Especially if the thief doesn't know how to read," said Molly.

"Either way, we must forgive." Rachel was watching Bethany, whose steely eyes seemed set in anger. "Take your anger and roll it up." She pretended to be working cookie dough. "Pack it into a ball, and toss it down the road. It's too heavy to be carrying around."

Molly and Ruthie exchanged a smile, then did the same, scooping up the air and cupping it between their hands.

"And then throw it away!" Ruthie called, pitching it toward the road.

"Good throw, Ruthie. Next softball game, I want you on my team," Rachel teased.

"Kumm, Bethany," Molly urged her sister. "Toss your anger away."

With a snort, Bethany went through the motions quickly. "I forgive, but I'm still upset."

Rachel nodded. "Gott heals the heart. Sometimes it takes time."

"Mmm." Bethany crossed her arms.

"Maybe they needed the money more than we do," Molly said.

"Then why did they take our flowers, too?"

"Wasn't Mammi Nell the one who gave you the bulbs in the first place?" Rachel pointed out. "So, really, they're her stolen flowers."

Ruthie wiped a few dirt crumbles from the counter. "If you want to go back that far, you could say the flowers were stolen from Gott, since He is the creator of all things, large and small."

Bethany scowled. "So they stole the flowers from Gott?"

"Nay . . ." Rachel said slowly. "Because the flowers still belong to Gott. So in a way, they weren't stolen at all."

"Oh, this is such roundabout talk," Molly said. "Were the flowers stolen or not?"

The girls looked at one another and began to laugh.

"I don't think it matters anymore." Ruthie hitched up the skirt of her dress and bent down to reach under the counter. "And look here. Mammi gave us a whole lot of parsnips to sell, along with some potted tulips."

"There you go. Parsnips are good in stews." Rachel helped load the vegetables onto the counter. She had always thought of parsnips as a cross between carrots and sweet potatoes.

"I hope we can sell them," Ruthie said as she added another bunch to the stack, "because I'm getting kind of sick of eating them."

"Make room for the tulips, too." Bethany pushed the parsnips to the side so that all the flowers could be together.

No sooner had the girls reorganized the display than a car pulled up, and an older couple purchased some parsnips. The woman was still chatting with the girls when a little red sports car roared to a stop, and two women got out to look over the flowers.

For a few minutes Rachel hung back near the horse and watched the younger girls handle the customers. Then she went on her way to the bulk store, thinking that she must remember to tell Dat about the theft, though there was nothing to be done about it. Plain folk didn't report crimes to the police; Gott in heaven was the only judge of a man.

As Banjo's hooves clip-clopped on the road, she felt a twinge of sadness for the girls, so disappointed that someone would steal from them. Still, it was a lesson to learn, one that she had faced with the accident. Sometimes bad things happened, but Gott healed the heart and renewed the spirit. As Mamm liked to say, "Gott could save us from trauma, but instead he sends us a comforter."

7

Saturday afternoon, bright Englisher voices and scattered laughter filled the Lapp home. The Englisher medical folk were here for the weekly visit that had been the norm since James had checked out of the rehabilitation facility. After Dat's order to distance himself from the Englishers, James felt an uncomfortable resistance from his father when he greeted the visitors. When you ran your palm over an unfinished piece of wood, splinters would get in the hand.

Luckily, Jimmy stepped out the door when everyone settled into the kitchen. What did that mean? Would Dat back down on his decision to tell these medical folks to stay away? While Mamm and Verena served coffee and shoofly pie, James soaked up the familiar faces and friendly conversation.

He was glad to have Doc Trueherz here. In his denim shirt and jeans, Henry Trueherz had a friendly manner and a streak of common sense that made him different from other doctors. Although

Doc had an office in Paradise, for many years he had made house calls far and wide. Most Amish folk in Halfway liked and trusted Doc Trueherz. James wished his father felt that same solid trust.

As Haley Donovan poured a cloud of cream into her coffee, Doc asked her when she would finish nursing school.

"Graduation is the last week in May," Haley said, pushing her gold hair back behind her ears, "if I make it that long. There's a killer meds test coming up, and everyone is freaking out about it." A nursing student at Lancaster County General Hospital—LanCo General—Haley had witnessed the van accident that had injured James. He didn't remember much from that night, but Rachel told him many times how Haley had helped in countless ways, probably saving old Jacob Fisher's life. Folks were grateful that Gott had brought her onto the road at that moment. Even after that night, Haley had helped. When she learned that the Lapps couldn't afford a physical therapist, Haley had volunteered to make his therapy part of her studies. Since then, she'd been out here every week to supervise James's exercises.

"Ah, I remember those med school exams." Doc sighed. "My advice? Try to study a little each week instead of leaving it to the last night."

"What did I tell you?" Dylan Monroe pointed to Haley.

She laughed. "Dylan warned me about procrastination. He's been quizzing me, twice a week."

"And it's working. You've got most of the vocabulary down."

"I do, thanks to you," Haley said, her eyes on Dylan.

James had noticed the looks that passed between these two. Like two blue jays, chasing each other over fences and brambles, Haley and Dylan favored each other. Sometimes it reminded him of the way he and Rachel had talked and joked around and walked hand in hand.

Dylan lifted his mug of coffee over his plate. "Edna? Do you mind?"

Mamm looked over from the sink and grinned. "Go ahead. It's what we do when Englishers aren't around."

With the wink of an eye, Dylan poured his coffee over his shoofly pie, causing Haley to let out a little squeal. "Dylan! Have you gone bonkers?"

"It's delicious." With a flourish, Dylan scooped up a bite of moist pie.

"Some people like it that way," Doc Trueherz agreed.

"Without coffee or cream, shoofly pie can be like a mouthful of dry sand," James said, holding back a grin. He'd been the one to tell Dr. Dylan about the custom of pouring coffee on pie.

Mamm chuckled. "Soon we'll have ripe plums and peaches. You don't need to tip coffee or cream on fruit pies."

Everyone agreed. As the conversation went on, it dawned on James that these people had become good friends. After the bishop's dismal advice the other day, James felt like these Englishers had brought water to a man in the desert. He looked forward to their visits, clinging to their advice and jokes. Still, Dat was wrong to worry. Nothing would turn James's head from living Plain.

While Edna talked with Doc Trueherz, James and Haley went out to the living room to review his physical therapy exercises. Dylan tagged along as usual. He had taken to talking with James during the sessions, and now after weeks of prodding, James answered.

James had told Dylan what it had been like to grow up on a family orchard, following his grandfather around through the trees, climbing ladders even as a child to pick peaches and pears and apples. Dylan's childhood had been very different, centered on riding his bicycle, playing basketball, and swimming in a friend's pool.

"The only time I ever climbed a tree, I got stuck up there," Dylan had admitted, spurring laughter from James.

"You've made a lot of progress," Haley said as they completed the thirty-minute workout. "How's the all-terrain chair working out for you in the orchard?"

"Good. Though I'd like it better if it could climb the trees," James answered.

"I bet you would," Haley agreed, tucking a lock of blond hair behind one ear. "We'll have to get someone to design that feature."

"Nay. I want to climb on my own again. My arms are strong enough. Now it's only my legs that need to follow."

"What's the latest update on your prognosis?" Dylan asked.

"The doctors say it's possible I might walk again. I went through some testing a few weeks ago to qualify for a study. They want to use electricity to wake up the spinal cord."

"And it's okay to do that?" Dylan's arms swept through the living room. "I mean, considering that electricity isn't allowed in your house?"

"It would be all right to use electricity outside the home. Amish do it all the time—in Englisher shops, under streetlights, sending faxes." James checked the kitchen to make sure Dat had not returned before he continued. Mamm was in the kitchen alone. Doc Trueherz had stepped outside to take a call on his cell phone. "The problem is my father, and now the bishop. They're worried that I've become swept up with the Englishers. They don't want me to lose sight of the things that matter. My family and community. And Gott."

"Ouch." Dylan leaned forward in his chair. "Are you questioning your faith? Have we been a bad influence?"

James lowered the small barbells to the floor and straightened in the chair. "There's no muddy water for me. When I look inside, there's only a clear spring. I know I'm Amish through and through, and I won't be swayed by Englisher friends or doctors. But my dat, he doesn't see it that way."

"And there lies the problem," Dylan said. "Does that mean Haley and I are getting you in trouble? I mean, our visits here . . ."

"Your visits have eased my mind and helped me keep my eye on the target. I've learned that healing is more than lying back in bed. But Dat and the bishop don't agree."

"Are they going to make you stop therapy?" Haley asked, a glimmer of concern in her blue eyes.

"It looks that way. After today, Dat wants no more Englishers in the house. I'm sorry, but today will have to be your last visit."

"Oh, no, that can't be!" Haley frowned, hands on her hips. "How will you continue therapy?"

"That I don't know." James tucked the weights under the chair. "But when the bishop comes out to the house because he thinks a person is drifting away . . ." He shrugged. "They're going to watch me like a hawk now."

Dylan rubbed his jaw with the knuckles of one hand, taking it all in. "Sounds like you're in a pickle. What can I do to help?"

"There's nothing to be done. I'll respect my father's wishes, and Dat and Bishop Samuel will come to see that I'm not falling away from Plain living."

"Okay, my friend." Dylan sat back in the rocking chair, gripping the armrests. "So I guess this would *not* be the time to persuade you to try our group counseling session? Because the other members of the group keep asking when you're going to join, and Samuel has given us the nod of approval."

James shook his head. Rachel had been asking him to go to those meetings, and he'd given it some thought until Dat had come down on him. "I can't do that now."

"Understood." Dylan held up his hands. "You just keep me in the loop. Tell me to back off or step it up, whatever you need."

The door opened and Doc returned, along with Jimmy.

"James!" Doc held up his cell phone, a twinkle in his eyes. "I just checked in with Alec Finley, the doctor doing the experimental spinal cord treatment—epidural stimulation, it's called. He's gone over your X-rays and scans, and he says it's a go. He wants to see you in his office Monday morning."

"That's great news," Haley said brightly.

Dylan grinned, and even Mamm seemed happy, her hands pressed to her lips in a gesture of prayer, as if she were silently thanking Gott.

"It's good." Warmed by hope, James nodded, trying to keep the excitement buried inside him. This study had helped previous patients learn to walk after similar injuries, and it didn't require any medication or surgery. But he kept his hope hidden. He didn't want to give Dat a reason to buck against yet another Englisher treatment.

"Let me give you Finley's number right now." Doc Trueherz tapped his cell phone. "Edna, can I trouble you for a pencil and paper?"

"Mmm." Jimmy grumbled as the doctor wrote the information on a notepad Mamm produced. "We'll take the number, but we must give this some thought before we rush into anything. James has already had two expensive surgeries. We can't keep going back to the hospital, hoping for something that the Almighty has not willed."

"I can't speak for God," Dr. Trueherz said, "but I can tell you that Dr. Finley's study will not cost you any money. You just need to get James to the rehab center in Paradise."

"That's not too far," Edna said, but her lips clamped tight when Dat turned stern eyes on her.

Jimmy's broad, friendly face was tight with disapproval. "We'll see. It's a busy time in the orchard. It would be hard to spare James and someone to drive him."

"How about if we hooked James up with some transportation?" Dylan suggested.

A flame of hope sparked in James's chest, but Dat's scowl snuffed it out. "No. Don't need any more help. From now on, the Amish community will give James the support he needs." And quick as a lightning bug's flash, Dat had dismissed the Englishers.

James wanted to point out the good things about the study. The potential. The fact that they had accepted him. The fact that it was free. The hope of standing and walking on his own again. But he knew better than to argue with his father, especially in front of the Englishers.

Silence swallowed the group that only minutes ago had been joking and laughing. Clearly, the visit was over.

"I've got a few more house calls to make." Doc Trueherz checked his watch. "Thank you for the pie, Edna. And I hope you folks give Alec Finley a shot. I've read up on this procedure. In one of the early trials back in 2011, the patient was able to stand on his own within three days of the treatment. It's not often you see results that quickly." He clapped James on the shoulder. "Think about the study, son. I think it's worth giving it a try."

James was a drowning man reaching for a lifeline. He looked to his parents, but they were miles away, no doubt concerned about what the bishop and others would think about their son trying yet another Englisher medical procedure.

Dylan rose from his chair, but then dropped down on one knee so that he was eye level with James. "I'd like to keep checking up on you, if that's okay," he said directly to James. "Haley and I want to keep the strong ties we've made here in your community."

James nodded, aware of his father's eyes burning a hole into his back. "You'd best not come around here anymore. Don't take offense, but my father, he's had bad experiences with the English. It's not about anything you've done." The words were sour on James's tongue, a bitter pill. James knew his father had been crushed by a bad experience, but why couldn't he let bygones be bygones? "But I'm grateful to you, and to Haley."

"Just doing our jobs," Dylan said casually, though James knew it wasn't true. They had given help and coaching and consolation in their personal time, and now . . . now Dat wanted to send them both away.

Haley and Dylan said their good-byes and headed out.

Without looking back at his parents, James followed them, rolling himself out the door and onto the porch. Once outside, he breathed deeply, trying to find calm in the cool spring air. Steering the right path through Dat's obstacles was exhausting.

"You okay, buddy?" Dylan asked, his brows lifted in concern.

James glanced back at the house. At least Jimmy and Edna had not followed them outside. "There's an expression folks around here say: 'If you get to the end of the rope, tie a knot and hang on.'"

Dylan pursed his lips, thoughtful for a moment. "So you're tying a knot."

James nodded. "Every day."

"That's the way, one day at a time."

❧❧

After the visitors left, James returned to the house to find his parents sitting in the living room—a rare event for any afternoon.

"James." Dat's voice summoned him, and from the grim slash of Mamm's mouth, James knew the weather was not improving.

"I'm glad that's the end of the visits." Jimmy stroked his beard. "No more Englishers in our home."

"I wanted to ask you about that. What if just Haley and Dylan kept coming out?" James asked, his voice thin as a dying wind. "Just for physical therapy and counseling."

"Counseling." Dat winced over the word. "Why not get counseling from Samuel or Preacher Dave? When you were baptized two years ago, you agreed to live in this world, but not of it. You should be looking to the church leaders for answers. Not to fancy folk, who are putting dreams and notions of walking in your head."

"Dat, please," James begged. "Don't blame them because I want to heal. It's my dream, my plan. And you know how I am. When I set my sights on something, I don't back down."

"We can't have the Englishers here anymore," Dat said.

"But that means I'll have to stop physical therapy." *The therapy that got me out of bed . . . out of the stew of dark thoughts.*

"You can go see a doctor if need be, but I won't have the Englishers in this home anymore."

"So then . . ." James pushed back. "I'll be doing the experimental therapy with Dr. Finley."

"Just as long as you don't go riding in a car."

James sank back into the chair, feeling like a hollowed-out tree, a mere shell of life, solitary and decaying. "You know I can't climb into a buggy just yet."

"Maybe that's Gott's way of telling you to stay home," Dat said.

James set his teeth, staring at his father. He had always known that Jimmy Lapp had backbone, but he'd never bumped up against this solid wall of resistance. He looked to his mother for help, but Edna was staring down at the floor. Did she agree with Dat?

He didn't want to think about the days and weeks ahead without visits from Dylan and Haley. Physical therapy had gotten him out to the orchards again. And sometimes, talking with Dylan was the one thing that kept fear from flapping in James's chest. Dylan had a way of helping James break the knot of tension in his chest so that he could line his ducks up in a row. It was a wonder, the things that Dylan could do, just by talking.

"So, that much is settled, then." Dat's eyes were dark as shiny lumps of coal. "No more Englishers in the house, and you'll begin to see that this is where you belong. Walking or not, this is where the Almighty wants you to be, living Plain with your family."

James gripped the arms of his chair, longing to push himself up and stand before his father.

Look at me, Dat, he wanted to say. *I am here, living Plain, and I'm not going anywhere, trapped in this chair.*

Anger tasted sour on his tongue, and James worked hard to swallow it as he relaxed his arms and sank back. If he was going to be stuck in this chair, half a man forever, he would shrivel and dry like a fallen leaf.

But he could not say this to Dat, who already thought that James was acting fancy. For now, James had to swallow the bitterness, and hope that, in time, Dat would see his oldest son in a new light.

8

*T*hey had been driving in circles.

Gary was still trying to make it sound like they would be turning toward home any minute, but Shandell had figured out his game.

He wanted to stay in Lancaster County because it was so easy to steal from the Amish. Both Gary and Shandell knew that Amish people wouldn't fight him or get violent. The Amish were pacifists; fighting back went against their beliefs. That made them an easy target.

So far they had spent the day driving from one Amish town to another so that Gary could snag things while vendors were looking the other way. He had stolen a brick of cheese and popcorn and a leather belt. He had made off with a quilt that had to be worth a lot, and a wooden cradle that he had absolutely no use for. When she'd asked him about it, he'd told her that he would sell it off, just like the flowers. While they'd been parked at a rest stop, he had traded some lady the entire carton of hyacinths for five dollars.

"This is found money," he'd told Shandell.

More like stolen money.

The cherry pie filling stolen from the roadside stand had been his dessert last night. Watching him pluck out a fat cherry with a long white plastic spoon, Shandell had felt sick about how low he had fallen and worried about how she would extract herself from his crime spree.

"We could be just like Bonnie and Clyde," he had said last night. "Except that instead of robbing banks, we rob the Amish." He'd laughed at his own joke. "I just wish we could come up with a way to get free food from that Amish diner in Halfway. They've got good eats. I would dine and dash, but it might attract too much attention. You never know if there's a cop nearby."

A cop . . . that would be a relief. Shandell could turn herself in and ask for help getting home. Right now, she was beginning to doubt that Gary would make good on his promise. Even worse, when she had asked him to drop her at a bus stop, he had squinted at her as if she was the crazy one.

She had almost called him on it. *Oh, I'm not allowed to go home? I can't go off on my own? What, am I a prisoner? Is this a kidnapping now?*

She thought that Gary might back down if she confronted him, but she wasn't sure. And what if he didn't? Would he stick her in the trunk, along with the stolen quilt and cradle? Fear shivered down her spine, despite the warm sunshine streaming into the car. She didn't know how low Gary would stoop, but she wasn't going to stick around to find out.

He turned off Halfway's Main Street and pulled in to a parking lot shared by the library and the ice-cream shop.

"I'm gonna hit the restroom in the library," he said. "You coming along?"

He was giving her a choice. This was her chance. "Nah. I'll wait here. All those books remind me of school."

Gary snickered as he slung the car door open. "I told you, you don't have to go back to school at all. You're eighteen now."

But she wanted to go back to school. Even with all those floating, angry equations in algebra, even if she had to go back over the summer to get her degree, school was better than the guilt and shame of tearing through these peaceful hills and valleys to rob the Amish. She would spend hours sprawled on her bed, studying. And then hug her pillow and slip under the comforter covered with puffy white clouds on a background of blue . . .

Oh, she missed the comforts of home!

"I'll be right back," Gary said, slamming the car door.

She nodded, pretending to be distracted by searching for a radio station as he went through the parking lot to the front of the library building.

Watching him from the corner of her eye, Shandell calculated. The sheriff's office was just down Main Street, over to the right, but she would have to cross in front of the library to get that way. No, she couldn't take the chance that Gary would see her through the library's floor-to-ceiling windows that looked out on Main Street.

She would have to run in the other direction. The back of the parking lot stretched out to the other side of the ice-cream parlor, allowing plenty of extra room for Amish buggies and horses. In fact, there were two buggies parked there now, their horses nickering as they waited in the mild afternoon sun. She would cut over that way, around the far side of the ice-cream place, and then run like crazy.

As soon as Gary disappeared from sight, Shandell popped out of the car. Her hands shook as she opened the rear door and reached in for her backpack, but she warned herself to stay calm. Keep breathing . . . and run!

Her pack thumped against her back as she bolted across the parking lot, cutting a wide arc around the ice-cream place. Once she flew out onto the sidewalks of Halfway's Main Street, she had to watch for pedestrians. She darted past two chatty teenaged Amish girls and cut around a woman helping an elderly man out of the car parked at the curb. With tourists and local people dipping in and out of shops and chatting casually, Halfway's Main Street was no place to be in a hurry.

Her heart raced, more from fear than exertion, as she passed a cute little tea shop and Kraybill's Fish and Game, where some handsome wooden ducks were on display in the window.

At the next corner she paused and peered behind her. No sign of Gary yet, but there was no telling how long he would be. She couldn't outrun him. She would have to hide.

Bracing herself, she bounded ahead, feeling a sense of relief with each step she put between herself and Gary. She had to get away—now.

She raced past the bakery, its window teasing with iced pastries and buttery pretzels. The scent of baking rolls made her stomach growl, but right now hunger was the least of her worries. She had to get away and time was running out. But where could she hide?

Her heart thumping, she slowed to a jog and paused at the door to the Country Store. It was as good a place as any. Bells jingled as she stepped inside to the mixed scents of lavender and sweet chocolate fudge. Old, white-scrubbed wood shelves and display cases held crafts like crocheted potholders, wooden birdhouses, handmade quilts, and Amish rag dolls. The quaint shop beckoned to her, a refuge.

"What should I do with these, Elsie?" a big Amish guy asked the young woman sitting behind the counter.

"Put them in the storeroom for now," she answered.

A quick glance told Shandell that Elsie had an unusual smile. Shiny dark hair was pulled back under her white kapp, and her eyes seemed kind as she focused on Shandell. "Can I help you find something?"

Swallowing back her pride and fear, Shandell pressed her palms to the counter.

"Please . . . Elsie, that's your name, right? I need your help."

The young Amish shopkeeper's eyes grew wide. "Tell me what I can do for you."

"Hide me." Shandell's heart was thumping fast now. She checked the door, sure that at any moment it would burst open and Gary would barge in, flashing the handsome smile that didn't connect to his heart. "My friend is . . . well, he's gone a little crazy and I need to get away from him. I ran from his car just now, but he'll be coming after me. Please, will you help me?"

Elsie's dark brows lowered as she shot a look at the door. "Come with me."

As the Amish woman slid down from the stool, Shandell saw that she was barely three feet tall. A little person. Still, she moved with authority as she led Shandell past an aisle of wooden plaques and quaint paintings of green fields and Amish quilts.

"You can stay in here," Elsie said, pulling the curtain back on a doorway.

Shandell quickly scanned the dim, windowless storeroom, its walls lined with shelves of neatly arranged boxes, jars, and fabric. "Thanks, but there's no door. Gary could just walk right in here, and he probably will. Maybe I should go out the back way . . ."

Elsie stepped behind Shandell, her compact body blocking her from backing away. "What's your name?"

"Shandell Darby. I live in Baltimore, and I don't know how I ended up here with Gary, but I just want to get away from him and go home." Shandell didn't mean to blurt out her life story, but there it was, bald and true.

"Then get away, you will." Elsie nodded at the storeroom. "But for now, you're better off in here. We'll cover you up right good. Put your pack in there and sit on the floor by this wall."

Shandell followed Elsie's instructions. First she stashed her backpack inside a wooden love chest with a seat that opened. Then she huddled up against the wall by the shelves holding bolts of fabric.

"Now, this is thin muslin cloth, so I reckon you'll be able to breathe through it," Elsie said as she unwound a bolt of tan cloth. She opened the material and doubled it up so that it would cover Shandell. Then she slid the bolt onto the shelf just above Shandell's head. "There. How's that?" Elsie asked.

"I feel like a mummy. Can you see me?"

"No." Elsie patted Shandell's head gently, then adjusted the cloth again. "Are you good under there?"

"Fine."

"Okay, then. I'll be out front, but you just sit tight."

She was about to thank Elsie, but the Amish shopkeeper's footsteps were already receding. Shandell pressed against the wall. If she closed her eyes and melted into the floor and wall, maybe she would be invisible to Gary.

Shandell took comfort in the voices from the main shop. Elsie seemed to know how to please customers, and the Amish guy had a deep, low voice that complemented Elsie's high-pitched tone.

The place had a peaceful atmosphere, like one of the scenes in the paintings by the storeroom door, with patchwork fields lined by purple hills, black hats on hooks, a horse and buggy silhouetted by a brilliant orange sunset. For a few minutes, Shandell let herself float in the good memories of the past few days.

Then, with a jingle of the door bells, she felt him enter the shop.

"I'm looking for my girlfriend." Gary's voice chilled the air. "We were just on our way home, and we stopped in town."

Liar. She wasn't his girlfriend. And he wasn't going to take her home. It was all an act.

Tears of frustration and anger sprang from her eyes. How did she get into this mess?

"Did you see a girl with black hair?" Gary asked.

"Lots of girls like that around here," Elsie answered.

"Yeah, but hers is sort of tinted blue."

"You can take a look."

"I figure she went off to browse in a shop and lost track of time," Gary said. "You know how women are."

His voice was growing louder, a sign that he was creeping closer. Shandell clenched her jaw, fighting to remain very still. She held her breath as she sensed him closing in on her.

Was he in the storeroom?

Go away! Leave me alone.

To keep from quivering, she imagined herself floating away from him on a thick white cloud.

"All right. Whatever." His voice, coming from the shop once again, let her breathe again. He talked with Elsie a minute more, turning on the charm. Then, at last, he said good-bye.

Shandell's heartbeat began to steady as the bells jingled. A minute later, she heard Elsie's voice.

"He's gone, but you best stay put for a few minutes, in case he pops back in."

Shandell spoke through the muslin. "Thank you. I . . . I really need a break from him."

"I'll say. He talks sweet, but I wouldn't trust him. He made off with two bars of lavender soap. Tucked them right up under his shirt."

"He did? I'm so sorry." Shandell thought of the few dollar bills she had hidden in a pocket of her backpack. "I'll pay you for them."

"No need," Elsie said. "From the looks of him, I reckon he could put the soap to good use."

A few minutes later, Shandell still felt shaky as she emerged from her fabric cocoon. Elsie peered into the storeroom while she was smoothing out the muslin and wrapping it neatly.

"I can't thank you enough." Shandell replaced the bolt of fabric and stepped back into the shop, where the Amish man was tending to customers. She kept her voice low, not wanting to make a scene. "Really. I . . . I had to get away from him."

Elsie nodded, her brown eyes wide with concern. "How will you get back home? Baltimore is too far to walk."

"I'm hoping my mom will come pick me up." Shandell swallowed against the knot in her throat. That was going to be a difficult phone call to make, but she was ready to apologize. "I want to go home," she said, her voice raspy with emotion.

"I'm sure you'll find a way." Elsie patted her shoulder, her brown eyes aglow with concern. "Do you have a cell phone to make your call?"

The Amish woman was kind, even motherly, though she seemed young to have children herself. "I do, but the battery ran out." She hadn't thought about bringing the charger, and she couldn't afford to buy a new one.

"Then use our phone. We just got it. The bishop allows shop phones if the wiring is already there." Elsie pointed to a white phone hanging on the wall over a tidy little desk in the storeroom.

Swallowing back her nerves, Shandell picked up the handset and punched in the number. It was late afternoon, almost suppertime, and she imagined her mom in the kitchen, the scent of roasted chicken in the air and a wispy cloud of steam rising from a pot on the stove.

As it rang, she rehearsed her apology. *Mom, I'm sorry for the bad choices I made. I should never have argued with you. I'm sorry about failing math. Give me a chance to fix things. I'll make it better . . .*

The line clicked, but the low snarl wasn't her mother. "Hello?"

"Phil . . ." Disappointment tugged at her. "It's Shandell."

"Shandell who?" He slurred her name, but the malice in his voice was sharp and clear.

"I know that's a joke, but right now I don't feel much like laughing. I was hoping to talk to Mom."

"She's not here. She's working the laundry. Trying to pay the bills. *Your* bills."

"I'm sorry, Phil. About everything." It hurt her to think of him sitting there in the folds of the couch, tossing back a beer, while their family was crumbling like a cookie. "But I need to talk to Mom. I . . . I'll call her on her cell." She should have done that in the first place.

"Good luck with that," Phil Darby said. "There's no cell phone reception in that laundry. Besides, she couldn't talk with you, even if she wanted to. She's got a job to do. A job. That's what you need, instead of whining over school. When are you going to wise up?"

A wave of remorse swept through her when she thought of the mistakes she'd made. Granted, she had been trying hard in school, and the math grade wasn't her fault. But instead of shutting down and letting herself fail, she should have stood up and gotten help. She should have appreciated the support her parents gave her—good food and a roof over her head. And then it had been wrong to cut off Mom, the only person who was really on her side. Instead, she had jumped in Gary's car, dazzled by the thought of adventure. She'd actually thought that a few days at his sister's house would be like a vacation.

What an idiot she was! And she had no one to blame but herself.

Shandell told Phil: "Tell her I called, okay?"

"I'm not your secretary," he grumbled.

"Please, Phil." She ran her hand over a little scar in the surface of the desk, bracing against the sting of his retorts. Although she knew it was the alcohol talking, it still hurt. "Listen, I gotta go—"

"So busy doing nothing," he snapped.

"Bye, Phil." Wincing, she broke the connection and quickly dialed her mother's cell phone. Phil had been right; there was no answer. She left a message saying she was all right, that she was in a town in Lancaster County, and that she would try again later.

When she hung up, the Amish guy was standing behind her with a plate of food.

"Ruben got some fresh rolls at the bakery, and we have cheese and apple butter." As Ruben put the plate on the little desk, Elsie scooted the chair out for Shandell. "Sit. Have a little bit to eat."

"Thank you." Shandell smiled at the tall young man, who nodded. Next to Elsie, he seemed like a giant, but she liked the way he looked at the Amish teen. There was fondness in his eyes, as if Elsie were a bright bouquet of flowers. They were a cute couple.

Shandell's mouth watered at the sight of the soft rolls with a wedge of buttery cheese. "I haven't eaten for a while."

"I thought so." Elsie opened up a folding chair as the door bells jingled. "We'll be right with you!" she called toward the door.

"I'll go," Ruben offered, heading out to tend to the customer.

"Did you talk to your mamm?"

"I left a message for her," Shandell said, breaking off a piece of roll.

"A message? But how will she find you?" Elsie sat down in the folding chair, and frowned over the cloth bag in her lap. "Is she coming for you?"

"She'll be coming later." Shandell didn't want to pile more worry on Elsie; the young woman had done enough, hiding her from Gary. And she certainly didn't want to try to explain about Phil. She had kept her stepfather's bad behavior a secret from her friends; Gary had been the only one to figure it out, and that had been only because he'd been pushy. "What's in the bag?"

"Scraps of cloth to make quilt squares. If you have to wait, it's good to have something to pass the time."

"But I've never made a quilt," Shandell said.

"I'll teach you." Elsie pulled out a square of maroon cloth and smoothed it down on the desk. "You'll get the hang of it."

Watching her go through the scrap bag, Shandell had a feeling there was nothing Elsie couldn't smooth over. Maybe there was hope for Shandell, too. Maybe, with Elsie's caring touch, her ragbag of a life could be pieced together.

9

Nervous excitement fluttered in Rachel's chest as she washed pots while her sisters Rose and Bethany dried and put away the last of the dinner dishes. It was Saturday night—courting night—and Rachel had been thinking about James all day.

"Here's a stubborn patch," Rachel said, putting some muscle into the scrubbing of a fat kettle that had been used for bean soup. She lifted the kettle for a look. "Still there."

Rose wound her dish towel around the pitcher she was drying. "At this rate, you could be scouring all night."

"And I've got somewhere to go."

"Are you going to see James?" Bethany asked. "Did Dat say you could use a buggy?"

"Mamm and Dat trust Rachel with a horse and buggy," Rose said, rising on tiptoe to put the pitcher on its shelf. "And we'd best help her get going, so she can start before dark. Why don't you finish that last pot, Bethy, while I hitch up Pansy for Rachel."

Bethany shrugged. "Sure."

Rachel squeezed the sponge, surprised by her sisters' generosity. "Gott truly blessed me with loving sisters."

Rose smiled. "Ya. Sisters who hope you'll be helping us out when it's our time to be courting."

"I would help you in a heartbeat." How she loved her sisters! She dried her hands as Bethany stepped to the sink. Rachel patted Bethany's shoulder, placed a kiss on Rose's cheek, then bounded up the steps. She wanted to wash the grime from her face and fetch the painting.

Out in the barn, she helped Rose harness Pansy. The girls brought the horse to the side of the barn, where they worked alongside brother Ben, who was hitching up his own buggy, obviously going off to see a girl—probably Hannah Stoltzfus. Rachel felt a little awkward, calling on her beau. By tradition, an Amish boy came to visit his girl on Saturday nights. But James hadn't been able to drive a buggy since his accident.

"So you're off to see James." Ben held up the heavier part of the rig while Rachel fastened the lines. "I heard the Lapps might be looking to hire a few men, come the summer. Did James say anything about that?"

"He didn't mention it," Rachel said.

"I might want a job like that. It would sure beat working in the factory."

"I thought you were going to take the job at the family stand in the city?" Rachel said.

"Maybe. Right now, nothing really grabs me."

That was Ben . . . already eighteen but still waiting for the right star to twinkle in the sky for him. Meanwhile, the family was counting on him to work the cheese stand at Reading Terminal Market. The Philadelphia hub was one of the oldest markets in the country, and sales in the city were a major source of income for the King family's two dairy farms.

Rachel carefully tucked the painting into the buggy, then came up behind her brother and clamped her hands on his shoulders.

"That tickles." Ben winced, chuckling. "What are you doing?"

"Just showing you that something's grabbing you," she teased. "And what is it? I think it's the job at the market. A good job for a young man who needs work." She squeezed his shoulders, causing him to squirm and laugh.

"Cut it out," Ben exclaimed.

From the other side of the rig, Rose joined in their laughter. "Rachel? Did you hitch the wrong horse?"

"Looks that way. This one's wild and untamed." Rachel dropped her hands, and her brother scrambled away, still chuckling.

"You're going to make me late."

"We can't let that happen," Rachel said.

"Tell Hannah we didn't mean to keep you," Rose called. She was only guessing that Hannah was the girl their brother was courting; like most Amish young men, Ben kept his love life close to the cuff.

Ben just swatted her comment away, and then climbed into his buggy. He called to the horse, and was off riding into the pink and orange sunset on the horizon.

જ્જ

Pansy's black tail swished back and forth contentedly, no doubt in anticipation of some attention from Lovina and Mark, James's two younger siblings who enjoyed tending animals. As they passed the neat rows of trees leading to the Lapp house, Rachel searched the foliage for the lovely blossoms that had burst from the branches in her dream. So far nothing was in bloom, but many of the trees were thick with buds.

She turned toward the farmhouse, where the porch had been rebuilt to include a wide ramp for James's wheelchair. It was one of the ways the orchard house had changed in the months since the accident. These days, Englishers came twice a week—doctors and medical folk, checking on James's health and updating his exercise program and such. James's parents had also given him their bedroom on the ground floor and moved to the second story so that he didn't have to be carried up the stairs. There were the wheelchairs, the bars suspended from the ceiling beams so that James could lift himself and make the transfers. The widened doorways. So many changes.

But the renovated house was just the outward shell. The changes that frightened her were the dark moods that James slipped into from time to time. Dylan had said that depression and post-traumatic stress were normal for a person with an injury like James's. Rachel understood that. She had lapsed into her own bad moments of guilt and sorrow, a dark and sour time. Thanks be to Gott, those clouds had lifted from Rachel's heart. But James still had his bad times.

His path will be different from yours, Dylan had told her. Ya, James had gone through lots of physical therapy, lots of work learning how to do basic things from a wheelchair.

And then there was the fear . . . the terrible possibility that James would never walk again. Rachel had made her peace with this, trusting James's future to the Almighty. She couldn't change the past, and Mamm had hammered the reality of Gott's will to Rachel and her siblings. *Gott doesn't make mistakes,* Mamm told them every time tragedy struck. One day, Rachel and James would accept that the accident was not a mistake. But for now, they both had to trust Gott and keep moving on.

Eleven-year-old Lovina emerged from the barn and offered to tie Pansy up in a good spot. Rachel dropped down from the buggy and passed James's father, who was splitting logs by the woodshed. Jimmy gave a curt nod, then kept going with his work. On the grass by the picnic table, Verena was tossing a Frisbee back and forth with sister Hannah and brother Mark, who were racing the dog for the plastic disk. Rachel wished that James was out here, teasing his siblings or giving the Frisbee a toss from his wheelchair. She always felt a twinge of sorrow when she saw life going on around him. Sometimes, when James was in despair, he let his injury hold him back.

Edna met her at the kitchen door and went about making tea for her, while Rachel pulled a wooden rocker up beside James, who was staring at an open book. The Bible.

He nodded in greeting, but there was no flare of warmth in his smoky, dark eyes, and he didn't hold his hand out to touch her or pull her close. It didn't bode well for her visit. Already she could tell that today he was a million miles away.

"I brought you a gift," she said, holding the canvas board out for him to view. Bracing herself, Rachel watched as James took in the painting she had done for him.

He squinted. "A peach?"

"A peach hanging on a tree. It's a bit different for me, so close up you can see the drops of dew on the peach fuzz. What do you think? Is it good enough to eat?" she asked, repeating something he once said about one of her paintings of a wedge of watermelon.

"I reckon. But no matter how tasty it looks, it's just a painting. It's not real life. Sometimes I think you hole up and paint a different world to get away from the one Gott gave you."

She blinked, off-guard. "I'm not trying to get away."

"Mmm." His lips were tightly pressed together as he propped the small canvas board on the table. She could tell he didn't care much for it. Of course he didn't. Men didn't appreciate decorative things like crocheted potholders or the photos on calendars. It had been a mistake, thinking that she could cheer him up with a little picture. "I figured that if you couldn't work the orchard, I'd bring the orchard inside to you."

"But I don't need a painting to see the orchards." His words were drained of hope, as if someone had pulled the plug and all his enthusiasm had run out of the sink. "You know I work out there every day. Someone has to tell Peter and Luke and Matt what's to be done."

"And you're the one who followed your doddy around since you were a little boy." Rachel knew James was fond of his memories from when he was a toddler, traipsing through the orchard behind his grandfather, soaking up tidbits on which insects were helpful and which harmed trees, when to prune and when to let a tree be. "He taught you everything about the orchard, the gardener's alphabet from A to Z."

"Ya. All that so I could work in the office."

"Is that what you're going to do? I thought your dat managed the sales end of things."

"He wants me to learn that side of the business." He closed the Bible and put it on the table beside the painting. "He thinks I'm stuck in this chair for good."

Sensing the venom in his words, Rachel changed the subject as Edna delivered her tea. "*Denke.* Hot tea is good on a night like this. Once the sun goes down, you forget it's spring."

James's mother agreed, and they chatted a bit about how a late frost might hurt the trees. When Edna returned to the kitchen, Rachel went to the shelves to pick out a board game. She knew James wouldn't open up for a serious talk when his family was still apt to wander through the living room. They played a round of Trouble, though Rachel felt sorry for James; his tokens were trapped inside the starting spot because he just couldn't roll a six for the longest time. It was too close to reality, with him being trapped in the wheelchair, unable to walk and climb wherever he wanted. After one round of the game, she put it away and dealt the cards for Go Fish.

They played on in a shadow of tension until James's parents and young siblings headed up to bed.

Alone, sitting in the glow of the fire that James had just fed with logs, Rachel pulled her chair closer to him. "There's a group counseling session on Monday," she said. "Can you come to this one? Everyone would like to see you, and I think it would do you good to get out for a while."

"I can't."

"James, talk to me, please. Tell me one of your good stories."

"There's none to tell. I had a visit from the bishop this week. It seems he and Dat have decided I should give up on walking and stay a cripple for the rest of my life."

"What? James, that can't be."

"But it's true." He told her about the bishop's advice to accept God's will and how Dat was worried that James's association with the world beyond their community was pulling him away from Amish life. "Dat won't allow Englishers in the house anymore."

"What about Dylan and Haley? Your counseling . . . your physical therapy."

"No more, unless I can get myself into town to see them."

Rachel gripped the worn armrests of the rocking chair. This was going to be a new challenge for James, who already had a full plate. "What about that study? Will they let you do it if you qualify?"

"Doc Trueherz told me I made it into the study. The treatment is free."

"And you're allowed to do it?"

"I don't want to give Dat a choice on that. Better to ask forgiveness than permission, don't you think?"

"Bishop Samuel has never stopped you from getting treatment," she said. "When it comes to health, he knows that medicine can save people's lives."

"If it's Gott's will," James reminded her.

"Ya. Gott is the only one who can really heal you." The crackling fire was the only sound in the room as James fell back into his brooding. He got caught in that glum mood a lot these days, stuck in the muck of worry. Thinking back on how James had been so miserable, she realized the bishop's idea was a good one. Samuel was trying to help James deal with the reality of today, here and now. If James could accept the way things were, he would be happier right now.

"Maybe it's not such a bad thing, to accept what Gott has given us to work with today," Rachel said. "My mamm always says that Gott makes no mistakes. You know it's true. We have to accept the changes He sends us."

"I'm sick of hearing that. Does it mean I have to accept this? That I can't learn to walk again?"

"It's not about learning, James. You can learn how to crack an egg. But you can't learn how to walk again if it's not Gott's will. It's about accepting Gott's plan for you."

"That's enough." He turned to her, but his expression was frosty. "If I wanted more advice, I'd be sitting here listening to my dat make plans for me. I thought you, at least, would be on my side."

"But I am on your side." Rachel took his hand, holding it tight when he tried to pull away. "I've been by your side through this whole thing, and I'm not going away, James. So you can turn the table over or tell me to leave, but I'll always be nearby. I'll never stop loving you."

He snorted. "Not much of me left to love."

"You know that's not true." She pressed his hand to her cheek, then placed a kiss on his knuckles.

"Oh, James. The light's gone from your eyes." She couldn't bear it. Pushing out of the rocking chair, she paused beside him, then kneeled down. Leaning against him, she clasped his hand in hers and pressed it to her heart. "Don't turn away."

That brought his dark eyes to meet hers. She used to be able to see so much in his eyes, but tonight they were smoky and mysterious. She snuggled close, the way she used to, and she was relieved to feel James's fingers grip hers. "Tell me you still love me, James. I need to hear it from you."

"I do love you," he breathed. "But it's all so . . . it's wrong now. You can't be expected to marry half a man."

"Hush. I'm going to marry the man I love," she said with her ear pressed to the broad wall of his chest. "Hmm. Heart still beating. And still breathing. Well." She lifted her head to peer into his smoky eyes. "Still alive, though I'd never guess that, considering your part in this conversation."

James ran his fingertips over the line of her jaw, down her neck, and across her shoulder. His touch still sent tiny stars of sensation tingling along her skin. Did he feel the same thing? His eyes seemed vacant, his thoughts a million miles away.

He shook his head, his face gone white as a cloud. "It's all over for me if I can't get out of this chair. I know the orchard well— I've got a map of every tree in my mind—but I can't really work it without the legs Gott gave me. And I can never get married."

His words cut through her like fat thorns, but she tried to reason away the pain. "No one says a man has to be able to walk to get married," she pointed out. "There are plenty of things you can do from your chair. You've proven that to everyone, tending to yourself, making coffee, and doing so many chores from a wheelchair."

"I'll go crazy if I have to be stuck this way the rest of my life. Verhuddelt. And if that happens, I'm not going to make you suffer, too."

"I wouldn't give up on you," she argued. "If it's not Gott's will for you to walk again, we can make do, make some changes. We can get a place in town. I could paint and send my paintings in to that gallery, and you could do the bookkeeping for the orchard, like your dat said. It wouldn't be so bad. You know, I never felt that I was well suited for farm life. To me, a house in town would be a dream come true."

The strong, sturdy arms that had embraced her slipped away. "Are you saying that it's okay for me to be crippled because you can get the easy city life you've always wanted?"

"What?" Rachel straightened away from the warmth of his chest, shocked to hear her words twisted. "No, that's not what I meant."

"It's what you said. Your dream come true—a house in town. And you would have me leave the orchard? Just like Dat. You don't think I can handle the trees anymore."

"I didn't say that. James, listen a minute. I—"

"You'd better go." His arms went stiff, nudging her away.

Bewildered, she stood up. "James, don't push me away. I was just trying to—"

"It's late, and a girl like you shouldn't be out alone on the road late at night. There's a reason why the fella does the courting."

Rachel hated leaving like this. This was supposed to be a wonderful good night for them, like her dream in the orchard. She had imagined them joking and laughing. Talking about matters, small and large. Sitting together and holding each other close. How she longed to feel his strong arms around her, his warmth warding off the chill of night, dissolving the dread of worry. Tonight, she had hoped to snuggle close with James and remember all the reasons she loved him.

Instead, his muscular arms had pushed her farther away.

Disappointment lay heavy on her shoulders as she plodded off toward her horse and buggy. "Pansy, kumm." As she gave her horse the instruction to go, she was grateful to be by herself under the dark, velvety sky. At least this was one time when she could be alone with her tears.

10

*S*handell had never known such darkness. She had walked miles from the lights of town, far from streetlights and brightly lit rows of houses with the blue light of televisions flickering in the windows. Out in these parts, most of the farms were owned by Amish people who did not have electricity in their homes, and the few lights she saw in windows burned with the softer glow of kerosene lamps.

It seemed like she'd been walking forever, but it had probably only been a few hours since she had headed out of Halfway with her pack on her back and tears rolling down her cheeks. At least she had managed to hold it together in the sheriff's office, where they'd let her use the phone to call home. It would have been mortifying to cry in front of the dispatcher and the deputy. As it was, she felt like a fool. A stupid runaway. Only at age eighteen, she wasn't even considered to be a runaway anymore.

She was an adult, free to leave home anytime she wanted. The problem was, no one told you that you might not be free to return home.

When Elsie and Ruben had closed up shop around six, Shandell had thanked them and moved on to the library. No one seemed to mind when she sat at a table, reading quietly until closing time. She knew her mother worked at the laundry until nine, and next time she called, she had to catch her.

She timed things right, walking through the dark town for a few minutes before she found her way to the sheriff's office. The female dispatcher had narrowed her eyes suspiciously when she saw Shandell's large backpack. But once Shandell sat down and spilled her story, Melanie Bamburger clucked her tongue in sympathy.

"Poor thing. I have a nineteen-year-old daughter at home, and I would be up all night worrying if she took off. Your mother must be freaking out."

Shandell shrugged. It hadn't sounded that way when she'd called home, but then Phil was not a great communicator. "I really miss my mom. We had a fight before I left."

"Aw. Are you hungry?" With a cloud of brown hair that curled softly above her shoulders and rectangular-framed glasses with rhinestones on the edges, Mel had the soft but authoritative manner of a mother hen. "We've got some gnarly snacks in the machine here, but the pizza place across the street is still open, and I'll send you for a slice."

Shandell thanked her for the offer, but told her she had been given some food by the young woman at the country store.

"Elsie Lapp? She's a sweetheart," Mel said knowingly.

"She really saved me," Shandell said, realizing that she'd been fortunate to duck into the Country Store when she'd been running from Gary. "My friend was getting really weird. He kept promising to take me home, but we were just driving around in circles."

"Sounds like you were right to give him the slip. But now you're in a bit of a pickle, hon. Social services would intervene and get you home if you were under eighteen. Since you're legally an adult, there's not a lot I can do for you."

Shandell told Mel that she just wanted to go home. "Can I use your phone to call my mom? I'm sure she'll come and get me."

"Sure thing." Mel had set her up at an empty desk, with a bottle of water and a box of tissues. "In case you get emotional, like me," the older woman said.

This time, Shandell's mother answered, but her response wasn't half as kind as Mel's. "Do you have any idea how many sleepless nights I've spent worrying about you? And you couldn't call? Not even a text to let me know you're okay?"

"I'm sorry. At first I was mad. You were mad, too. And then I wanted to call, but the battery ran out on my cell phone and—"

"So many excuses, Shandell. I'm fed up with your excuses, blaming other people for everything that goes wrong."

"I know. I'm sorry. I've had time to do some thinking, and I know I need to step up. Right now, I just want to come home."

"Fine. Come home, then. We didn't change the locks."

"Thanks, Mom." Shandell sat back in the chair, relieved to be heading home soon. "Can you come get me? I'm in a little town called Halfway. It's in Lancaster County."

"That is hours away!" Chelsea Darby let out a sigh of frustration. "I just got home, and I have to work a double shift tomorrow at the laundry. Do you realize what you're asking? I can't blow off work or stay up all night driving just because you decided to go on a wild spree with your boyfriend."

Shandell swallowed hard over the knot in her throat. She had thought her mother would come, but of course, she hadn't considered the reality of Mom needing to work. With Phil out of a job, Mom was the only one making money now. She understood that Mom's jobs were a priority. But still, her heart ached. How could Mom abandon her like this?

"Gary got you out there," Chelsea was saying. "Tell him to bring you home."

"We're just friends, Mom. And I'm not with Gary anymore." Shandell winced. "He was . . . acting weird." She didn't want to announce right in the police station that her friend had been stealing from locals. "I had to get away from him."

"Oh, Shandell." Her name came out in a long sigh of disappointment. "What are we going to do with you?"

For a second Shandell was going to suggest that her stepfather come for her in the morning, before he'd had a chance to start with the heavy drinking, but she knew that wouldn't work. Phil didn't have the desire or focus to make the trip to Lancaster County.

Shandell eyed the tissue box on the desk as her eyes began to sting. No. She wouldn't cry here. She had to hold herself together. She didn't want Mel and the deputy, who was watching from across the room, to know just how much trouble she'd gotten herself into.

"How are you going to get home?" her mother asked.

"I don't know. There's a bus out of Lancaster and one out of Philly. But Halfway is pretty far from both of those cities, and there's no bus service here."

"Fine. Get yourself to the city and take the bus, then."

"But, Mom?" Shandell turned away and lowered her voice, mindful that Mel was watching. "I need you to send me some money. Like through a wire service or something."

"You don't have money with you? What about your savings?"

"I brought some cash, but we used it. It wasn't supposed to be like this. We were planning to stay with Gary's sister."

"And how did that work out for you?" Mom asked.

"You know it didn't."

"I don't know what to do." Chelsea Darby sounded exhausted, her voice cracking with stress. "I don't have the spare cash to wire money to you, and I don't even know if I trust you anymore. How can I be sure Gary didn't put you up to this? You know I never trusted him or any of those kids who hang out in Ryan's garage."

"This isn't a trick." Her mother's suspicion stung, but Shandell knew she deserved it. "I just want to come home."

"And honestly, I don't know how to make that happen. My next day off is Friday. Thursday night is the soonest I can come for you. But what would you do until then?"

"I don't know. Maybe I'll just hitchhike home."

Across the room, Mel was shaking her head vigorously. "Bad plan. Hitchhiking is too dangerous for a young woman."

"The police here don't think hitchhiking is safe," Shandell said.

"They're right, and I want you to stay safe. But, Shandell, I can't drop everything to come and get you. And you shouldn't expect that."

Shandell bit her lower lip, swallowing back the knot of emotion in her throat.

"You are eighteen. It's time to grow up. I feel terrible about this, and you know I'm worried about you but . . . you need to find somewhere safe to stay until I can drive up on Thursday. Maybe a campground or something."

"Okay. I'll figure out something." Shandell could not miss the raw emotion in her mother's voice as they said good-bye.

"How'd it go?" Mel asked, cocking her head to one side. "Is she coming to get you?"

"She's on her way," Shandell said brightly, keeping the happy mask on her face.

"That's good." The police dispatcher looked out the precinct window toward Main Street. "You want to get some pizza while you're waiting? My treat."

"No, thanks. I'm not really hungry." That part was true.

"Did you tell Mom to pick you up here? You can hang out there in the waiting area. We're about the only thing in Halfway that's open all night, except for the 7-Eleven on the other side of town."

Shandell hesitated. Where was she going to go? Halfway was too small for a bus station or a public place where she could spend the night, and she knew these people wouldn't like the idea of a homeless girl roaming their streets for the next few days. "You know, maybe I will wait for her here." Shandell didn't mean it, but it would be a warm place to stay until she could come up with another plan.

She settled into a comfortable chair and checked her backpack to make sure her cherished book was there. She would have liked to take it out and skim over the familiar Bible stories with their colorful illustrations, but it would be too embarrassing for anyone to see her reading a children's book. Mel came to the rescue with a stack of magazines, a warm blanket, and a hot cup of tea. "If your mom's coming from Baltimore, you got a few hours. Try to get some sleep."

She did. The comfort and safety of the waiting room allowed Shandell to doze off, stretched out on the vinyl-cushioned couch.

When she woke up, the clock on the wall was swinging toward four o'clock. It was still dark out, but Shandell felt a little better. Mom always said that things would feel better in the morning. Well, it would be morning in a few hours.

Mel was gone, and the deputy was talking on the phone with the dispatcher's headset on. She figured that Mel was probably on break. It was a good time to leave. She appreciated the woman's kindness, but Shandell knew that Halfway's police department wouldn't let her camp here for the week. She had to leave—*before* Mel realized that Shandell had been lying to her.

She left the folded blanket and the stack of magazines on the counter. The deputy glanced up and she gave him a friendly wave, then headed out the door.

Her backpack didn't seem so heavy anymore, but now loneliness was a dull ache that made her feel hollow inside. So cold and empty. Her life was in ruins, like the bag of scraps in Elsie's shop. But while Elsie could finish patches and sew them into a beautiful quilt, Shandell was clueless when it came to piecing her life together.

Feeling like the last person awake in the world, she plodded down the road in search of open land.

ᔕᓂ

The old one-room shack was rustic, and super isolated. Shandell had turned down a farm lane and walked for at least a mile, following as it passed a dark farmhouse and narrowed into more of a footpath. Her plan had been to zip into her sleeping bag under the cover of some trees or bushes, but when she came upon the old deserted outbuilding, she began to think that maybe God hadn't forgotten her, after all.

There was no electricity that she could find, but there were plenty of matches and a big black woodstove with a stack of dry wood beside it. The small fire she'd built chased away the damp cold inside the hut, and the kerosene lantern gave her enough light to do a quick cleanup of cobwebs and dust with the broom she'd found leaning against one wall. Once she brushed off the two stackable plastic chairs and the wooden bench, the place actually took on a warm personality.

Now that the cabin was relatively clean and warming up, she unzipped the sleeping bag from her backpack and spread it out on the wooden bench across from the fireplace. Good thing she'd brought that! She had thought she might need it to sleep on the floor at Gary's sister's house. She rooted around inside her pack until she found the plastic bag that had remained stashed away during most of the trip. Her fingers framed the book inside. Many times she had longed to take the book out and lose herself in the familiar pages, but she didn't dare let Gary see. She knew he'd mock her, either with laughter or with a speech about how she was eighteen years old and should be done with children's books.

Shandell couldn't count the nights when she'd been soothed by this little blue book. Sometimes just the colorful illustrations and encouraging captions gave her comfort. Nestled inside the sleeping bag, she opened the book, inhaling the sweet scent of the pages.

The book fell open to a chapter about the parting of the Red Sea. A wicked king was being mean to God's people, so God told Moses to lead the people away. But the king and his soldiers chased them. She thought of her escape from Gary that day. It seemed like long ago, but the snap of fear was still vivid in her mind. She understood the fear the Israelites must have felt at being chased from their homeland. Turning the page, she saw the happy little cricket holding a banner with the word of the lesson: *Safe.* "God's love keeps us safe," she read aloud.

With a deep breath, she let the open book fall on her chest as she took in the raw wood beams of the shack and the uneven wooden boards that made up the ceiling. Even in a deserted shack in the middle of nowhere, God knew where she was, and He had the power to keep her safe.

She snuggled into the puffy ridge of her sleeping bag and closed her eyes. Maybe she wasn't ready for the real world. If growing up meant giving away the book that soothed her troubled mind, well, then she would never grow up.

ᵒᵍ 11 ᵍᵒ

*E*aster Sunday brought sunshine that warmed the earth and thawed the chill in James's heart. This morning, as he had wheeled through the orchard, memories of Doddy's Easter traditions had sparked a smile. His grandfather had loved hiding eggs in the orchard. When Mammi had worried that it might be a waste of good eggs, he had said it was a good exercise for the children to hunt down Easter eggs. Practice for sorting out rotten apples.

Now, looking over at the pear trees, he imagined a blue egg in a crook of the branches, and a green one nestled by the roots of a tree. The thick grass would be dotted with purple and orange and pink.

"And all these years," Doddy used to tell the Amish women, "my children and grandchildren never missed an egg yet. I hide two dozen, they find twenty-four. Children can be good finders when you make it a game."

How James missed his grandfather! Elmo Lapp would have

known how to handle the doctors and balance the Englisher visits with the ways of living Plain. Doddy wouldn't have given up on the hope of James walking again. That twinkle in Doddy's eyes had always been full of hope, brimming over with Gott's love.

But Doddy was gone, and there would be no eggs to find this morning. The younger ones had dyed eggs, but with Hannah, the baby of the family, ten now, the egg hunt tradition was dwindling. Doddy wouldn't have liked that. James decided to ask Peter and Luke to hide some eggs when they got home from church in the afternoon.

With a sigh, James turned his chair back toward the house. There was no time to roll out to the sugar shack today. When he'd left the house, Mamm had warned him not to go far. After a quick breakfast of cold cereal or toast, they'd be loading up the buggies and heading over to the Beilers'.

In the lane beside the barn, James came upon his brothers Peter and Luke, who were already harnessing horses for the family's ride to church. The sight of the old apple cart, ready to be hitched to a horse, hit him like a blow to the chest.

"What's that doing out?" James asked, pointing to the cart.

Peter and Luke both glanced up from either side of Patches.

"That's for you to ride in," Luke said. "Dat told us to harness a horse to the cart for you. He says it's easier to push you up the ramp in your chair than lifting you into the buggy."

James felt his nostrils flare as he drew in a breath. It was another example of Dat's downright stubbornness. Many times James had told him how he hated riding in the back of the cart.

"I don't want to be any bother," James said, fighting to keep the annoyance out of his voice, "but there's something about riding in the back of that cart that makes me feel like a hog on its way to auction."

Peter straightened and tipped his hat back. "You don't like it, and that's no surprise. With your wheelchair lashed down in the cart, you're on display like a pyramid of apples in the market."

"We can leave the cart, and you can ride in the buggy with us," Luke said as he leaned into Patches to rub the horse's neck. "Between Peter and me, we can lift you to the buggy, easy as pie. We'll tie your wheelchair to the back of the buggy with a bungee cord."

"That's a better way to go," James said, relieved that his brothers didn't mind moving him in and out of the buggy. Peter and Luke had been a big help since the accident. Everyone in the family had pitched in to take on James's workload and care for him.

But through it all, Dat had stopped listening to James. This idea of making him ride in the cart was just one more example of the way that Dat had started pushing James to his father's way of doing things. It was as if Jimmy believed his son had lost the ability to think, as well as walk.

∽◯≺

During church, Dave Zook preached about the risen Jesus:

"Early in the morning, the women brought some spices and things to the tomb. But when they got there, the stone had been rolled away and they did not see the body of the Lord Jesus. No one was quite sure what had happened until later, when Jesus himself stood among them." Dave pressed his black glasses up on his nose as he looked over the congregation. "Imagine their shock to see him. They thought they were looking at a ghost!"

James smiled. He knew this story well. Every spring, Amish children were reminded of the true meaning of Easter: The celebration of how the Heavenly Father made His son rise up, body and soul, to the heavens. Gott's promise of a heavenly kingdom for those who loved Him.

There was no limit on the miracles Gott could do. Was it wrong of James to pray for Gott to bless him with a miracle in the next medical procedure? Was it wrong to hope that he would walk again? Dat wanted James to give up this hope, but who could know the Almighty's plan for tomorrow and the day after that?

At the thought of the future, James's gaze latched on to Rachel, who was sitting with the young women and girls who had not been baptized. Regret was sour on his tongue when he thought of how he had pushed her away last night. Throughout the past year, her sparkling eyes, clear as a blue summer sky, had held steadfast love for him. Even when his lameness disgusted James himself, Rachel seemed blind to his injury. She still saw the man he used to be. James turned away quickly, not wanting to catch her gaze now. His love for her burned strong, but he hated the way his burden was heaped on her shoulders.

And on his family.

He was grateful to the twins, lugging him around when he needed a hand. When he'd first left the hospital, it had been easier to maneuver, with Dylan driving him where he needed to go. In the beginning, Dylan had come by and driven James to church every other week. Dylan's van had a lift on it so that getting in and out took less than a minute. Not that James minded the time—he was in no rush to get anywhere—as long as he wasn't sitting on display in the back of a cart. He hated having so much attention lathered on him, like an expensive horse. He was still bristling at Dat's insistence on cutting the Englishers off, but there was no getting around it. A father's rule was law.

When the last song had been sung and the Ausbunds had been closed, James watched as the ministers left the barn, followed by the elders. Old Jacob Fisher nodded as he rolled past, his wheelchair pushed by his son Kevin. Jacob had also been injured in the van crash. A few of his ribs had been cracked, causing a punctured lung.

Gott had blessed him with good health once again, though he was now eighty-eight.

When it was their turn, Dat pushed James out of the barn.

"It was a right good service," Dat said. "Easter always brings renewal and new life. Look at Eve Beiler's flowers there." A garden thick with yellow daffodils and red and purple tulips bordered the front of the Beilers' house. "Those daffodils, reaching toward the sun, show us how we must reach for the light of the Savior."

"Ya, spring is a time of hope," James agreed. "Makes a man think he can do anything with Gott's blessing." Of course, he was hoping Gott would help him rise from his wheelchair, but he knew his father didn't see that as a possibility anymore.

As the rest of the folks filed out of the barn, Peter emerged and headed toward them. "There you are. I got James now, Dat."

As if James were a little one to be corralled, his family took extra care so that there was always someone by his side to wheel him around at church and social events. James hated it. And this was the time after church that was most awkward, as most of James's friends, like Jonah King, Ruben Zook, or Rachel's brother Abe, were off helping to reset the church benches for seating for the church meal.

"Good, because I just spotted Abe Zook, and I haven't seen him for two weeks at least," Dat said. "Let me ask him when he's planning to step up the hours at Zook's barn for the spring season."

"There's something we forgot today," James said as Peter pushed him over toward a group of young men gathering by a fence. "When we get home, you and Luke need to hide those colored eggs out in the orchard. Just at the edge of the yard."

"The Easter egg hunt. I can't believe Mamm and Dat forgot."

"They've had their hands full this year," James said. "But I think Hannah, Lovina, and Mark will enjoy searching for eggs. Maybe even Verena. Thirteen isn't too old to have a little fun."

"You're never too old to have fun," Peter said.

Looking ahead at Peter's friends, Amish youth still in their rum-springa, James knew his brother truly hoped to enjoy everlasting fun. Peter was still feeling his oats, enjoying the singings and youth events, driving different girls home on different nights. He had fitted his buggy with a boom box, and he'd even taken a job busing tables at a diner in Halfway to make more money for Englisher things, like movies and a cell phone.

By contrast, Peter's twin, Luke, said he was aiming to be baptized in the fall. Luke had been keeping company with Deb Fisher since he'd started rumspringa, and though he enjoyed taking his buggy out, his heart was at home, caring for the team of horses, the chickens, and the milk cows.

By the time Peter and James were halfway down the lane, Peter's group was hopping the fence, heading down to the pond, probably to skip rocks and maybe even dip their feet into the cold water before it was their turn to sit and eat church supper.

"Looks like your friends are off to the pond for a swim," James teased.

"They'll freeze if they do. We were just ice-skating on that pond last month."

"Hold on there." James stopped the wheelchair, knowing there was no way he'd be venturing down to the pond right now. He glanced over to the greenhouse, where Rachel stood talking with a few other young women.

"Go on and follow your friends and you'll be off the hook for babysitting me."

"I don't mind," Peter said earnestly as he came around the chair. He pointed to the far fence. "I can wheel you through the gate. Trust me, I'll get you down to the water."

"Nay. Go on. I'll go talk to Rachel, and I can get there on my own steam. These arms know how to turn a wheel."

Tipping his hat back, Peter smiled. "If you say so."

The young women were chatting and giggling together, but when James approached, they went silent. Hannah Stoltzfus had to press her lips together to hold in the little peeps of laughter, and Becky Yoder stared down at the ground. That was normal—the self-conscious feeling that came over a group of girls or fellas around the opposite gender.

But as soon as Emma Lapp asked how he was feeling, the doleful looks and words of sympathy gushed out. The girls' sad faces were enough to send James wheeling in the opposite direction. He didn't need their pity; he was crippled, not dead. Besides that, he was determined not to stay this way.

The Amish community had given him financial and moral support. James was thankful for everything, but he had no use for their pity.

"Rachel," James said, cutting right to the point, "will you walk with me up to the house?"

"Sure."

She pushed his wheelchair over to the simple white farmhouse with black trim. James put the brakes on his chair, and Rachel sat on the edge of the wooden porch, a height that was better for conversation.

"I barely slept a wink last night, thinking about things," Rachel admitted. "What I told you about living away from a farm or orchard . . . it's true, James. I can think of nothing more wonderful good than painting all through the morning, afternoon, and night. But I didn't mean that I'm happy you're in that chair right now. You know I pray every day for Gott to heal you."

"I don't blame you," he said. "When I lose patience, it's with myself, not you."

"I wish there was some way I could help you," she said, her voice hoarse with tears. "But you keep closing the door on me, James. You've got to stop doing that. Please, let me in."

Looking over at the flush of heat on her cheeks and the sparkle of tears in her sky-blue eyes, James felt his throat grow tight. He hated to see her cry over him. He had wanted to be with Rachel since the summer of long ago when she had been one of the Amish youths hired on to help harvest the fruit at the Lapp orchard. He remembered the way she had climbed the ladders, the graceful sweep of her slender arm as she reached for a ripe peach. The way sunshine bathed her golden hair and white kapp, her rose-colored dress and sun-bronzed skin.

She had stolen his heart back then. And now that he knew her well, he couldn't picture his life without her. He would never love any other woman the way he loved Rachel King.

And it was because he loved her that he needed to do this.

For the first time, he could see what he would have to do. And the terrible truth took the breath from his body, like a stab in the chest.

He had to stop pressing his burden upon her shoulders. He would not saddle Rachel with the chores of tending to him. He would not be the leper who made her friends look uncomfortable when he came over. If Rachel got stuck with him, she might as well be crippled, too, and he would not—he *could not*—do that to her.

"Since the accident, I've had a lot of time to think." Days and nights, endless hours. "I've been praying, too. And I think Gott is showing me what must be done."

"That's good," she said encouragingly.

He turned away. He couldn't bear to see the openness in her smile, the spark of interest in her eyes.

"Here's the truth. You and me, we don't belong together."

"What?" Her head snapped toward him so fast, one of her kapp strings went flying. "What are you saying?"

"I'm saying you're free to go court other fellas."

"Are you verhuddelt?" She squinted at him. "Why would I do

that, when I want to be with you? See, this is what I mean. Every time I get close to you, you slam a door in my face."

He hadn't expected her to argue. He closed his eyes and took a breath as he remembered the many things they had in common. Their enjoyment of ice-skating and Wiffle ball, Jenga and ice cream. How they had worked side by side in the orchard, talking and humming as the baskets filled with peaches and pears. The way they could finish each other's sentences and make each other laugh.

"You can't say we don't belong together, because you know it's not true," she finished.

"We've had some good times," he admitted, keeping his voice low so that all of the congregation wouldn't hear them. "But the past is long gone. Things have changed, and you need to accept that. I've changed. I'm not the man I used to be." The words stuck in his mouth like peanut butter, but he had to say it. "I can't be your beau, Rachel. You deserve a man who can stand on his own two feet, a man who can make a life with you. That's not me. Not anymore."

She swiped tears from her cheeks, then leaned forward from the edge of the porch. "I can accept a lot of things, but I'm not going to let you push me away. I'm just going to make like you never said those things."

"Rachel, I'm doing this for your own good."

"Who are you to say what's good for me?" She lifted her chin toward the spring sky. "For that, I count on Gott in heaven." She rose, smoothing down the skirt of her dress. "I'm going back to my friends. And I'm going to give you a chance to think about everything you said. You've got one strike, like in baseball." She put her hands on her hips and leaned forward, her brows knit together in a stern expression. "But no more strikes. You don't want to get an out."

Dazed, James watched her walk away. Who would have thought Rachel had that spunk? He had expected the tears, but not the

struggle of a defiant horse. Confusion roiled inside him as he maneuvered his chair away from the house, away from Rachel and her
friends, away from the prying eyes of Amish folk who had gathered
to chat before the meal.

Suddenly, the chair listed to the side and sank down.

James braced himself as the wheelchair fell back and settled into
a furrow. Ach! Just what he didn't need! He pushed with all his
might, but the wheel on the right side was clearly caught in a rut.

"James, are you stuck?" Dat emerged from a group of men, along
with his friend Alvin Yoder. Together, the two men lifted that side
of the chair and pushed until it had traction on the packed dirt
again. James kept quiet the whole time, but it didn't matter, as Dat
and Alvin kept up their conversation about the high price of land
in Lancaster County.

Without giving James a choice, they wheeled him over to sit
beside Jacob Fisher's wheelchair.

"Those are some fat tires you got on that chair," Jacob said,
squinting as he stared down at the wheels.

"It's an all-terrain chair," James explained. "It's supposed to go
anywhere. But it doesn't. I still get stuck."

"Ya. There's always some sticky patches in life that pull us in
from time to time," Jacob said. "Wheelchair or not."

In the past, James had steered clear of old Jacob, who was stern
and brisk, nothing like Elmo Lapp, who prided himself on making
folks smile. Yet despite Jacob's prickly mood, many men came over
to visit with him. Listening to the others talk, James felt abandoned,
like a man lost in the woods.

As the men conversed and chuckled, he dreamed of escape. If he
had his legs, he would jump in his buggy and leave. He snorted. Ya,
but if he had his legs, he wouldn't be wanting to leave. He would
be helping the men move benches, or tossing stones into the pond,

or teasing Rachel about the gmay cookies she'd made for the children to have during church.

Instead, he was stuck here, waiting on others to wait on him. He sank into himself and prayed that Gott would not leave him to be half a man forever.

ஒ 12 ஒ

*E*motion was a knot in Rachel's throat from the time James had words with her, through the noon lunch at the Beilers' place, a nice social affair with homemade bread, ham, two kinds of cheese, peanut butter spread, pickles, red beets, hot peppers, and large gmay and chocolate chip cookies for dessert. All that time, Rachel put on a good, social face, smiling at the little ones and helping to clear away plates. When friends talked about the singing that night, she smiled along, though she knew she wouldn't be going. She had no desire to be there without James, and he had no desire to be with her.

As the King family left the gathering, she pushed back her own ache to talk with her sisters, who shared the backseat of the buggy driven by Jacob. Rose was concerned because she didn't know how to tell if a boy liked her from the way he acted.

"He clams up when his friends are around," Rose explained. "But when we were pouring lemonade, he was a chatterbox. He said he could come to our house for dinner sometime."

"If he wants to come by for dinner, then I'd say Eli Esh fancies you," Rachel said.

"That's what I thought." Rose folded her arms as she sat back in the buggy seat. "But Ben said he's probably just coming around for Mamm's pie."

"Ben is pulling your leg. Such a joker."

"Hmph." Rose's eyes narrowed. "I have half a mind to tell him that Hannah Stoltzfus is only spending time with him because of the music system in his buggy."

"Now, don't go tit for tat. Be happy that Eli wants to come to dinner. Maybe Mamm will make her fried chicken when he comes 'round."

"Maybe."

"Does Eli like fried chicken?" Molly piped in.

"Everybody likes Mamm's fried chicken," Rose assured her.

The smiles of Rachel's sisters and the clip-clop patter of Pansy's hooves helped to soothe that cold knot as they headed down the road to cousin Adam King's farm, where they would be visiting this afternoon. This was a part of the family they were very close to, on account of working together in the cheese business and being just a few miles down the road from each other. A terrible sadness had swept through their family a couple years back when Rachel's aunt and uncle, Esther and Levi King, had been killed so suddenly in the dead of winter. Those were long days of heartache, but Gott was there to give the family strength for every hill they had to climb.

Cousin Adam and his wife, Remy, were now the heads of the house, though they had plenty of help with the farm and the little ones from older cousins like twenty-three-year-old Jonah; Gabe, who was eighteen; and fifteen-year-old twins Leah and Susie.

As Pansy turned down the lane to the Kings' farm, Rachel felt her worries ease a bit more at the prospect of seeing her cousin Sadie, her good friend who was back from Philadelphia for a visit.

Nineteen-year-old Sadie had left home last summer, and Rachel feared that Sadie might never come back from that different fork in the road.

Mamm and Dat's buggy was ahead of theirs, and already cousin Simon was patting their horse, getting ready to unhitch and give Banjo a break. Off to the right, Mammi Nell, cousin Mary, and Remy sat at a picnic table, watching as a vigorous game of kickball was being played on the gently sloping green lawn. Rachel searched her cousins for the dear girl who was like a sister to her.

"Sadie!" There she was, running in from third base, her Plain dress flapping to reveal black jeans cuffed to just below her knees.

Sadie glanced up as she stepped on the piece of wood that was home plate. Her face lit up as she spotted her female cousins waving. "Halloo!" Sadie's call was half a yodel as her arms shot up in a broad wave.

The sight of Rachel's cousin, running to the barn to meet their buggy, chiseled away at the ache of tension caused by James. Oh, dear James! She didn't know what she was going to do about him and she feared she had handled things badly today. She couldn't wait to tell Sadie everything.

There were lots of big smiles and much hugging as Rachel's family greeted Sadie. Although the rest of Adam's family had attended church, Sadie didn't dare, knowing that she was walking a thin line with the ministers. On the one hand, since Sadie wasn't baptized, there would be no ban—no shunning. But the church leaders were still putting pressure on Adam and Jonah to bring their younger sister back into the fold. Mamm always said that Plain folk were like good shepherds; they never gave up on one of their own.

There was a good amount of commotion and noise as the buggies were unloaded. This was one of the parts of having a big family that Rachel so enjoyed. There were always enough players to make a team, plenty of helping hands in the kitchen, and somehow there was always someone nearby to pick you up when you stumbled.

Taking advantage of the sunshine, everyone stayed outside for a few rounds of kickball, badminton, and Wiffle ball, Rachel's favorite. As she lined up at the plate, facing her brother Jacob, the pitcher, she recalled how James had taught her to bat. From him, she learned batting stance and follow-through. And she had come to love the satisfying crack of the ball against the bat, even if they were both plastic.

In between games everyone munched on popcorn and hard-boiled Easter eggs and homemade grape juice. Ruthie and Rose prodded Sadie to teach them one of the new church songs she had learned in the Englisher choir, and within minutes, Sadie had the family singing along to a hymn about how Jesus had died on Calvary "just for me."

When Rachel noticed that Mammi Nell wasn't singing, she turned to her grandmother. "Don't you like the new song?"

"I like it just fine," Nell said, the lenses of her glasses magnifying the creases at the outer edges of her eyes. "But it's the family singing together—all to the glory of Gott—now, that's something I want to hear. And I can't hear you if I'm singing myself."

Rachel smiled, and Mammi patted her hand. "Go on. Keep singing. It's a good Easter song."

Sadie had been blessed with a magnificent voice. With her leading the group, voices rang from hill to dale.

After a few songs, some of the kids decided to hide Easter eggs, and Rachel caught Sadie's eye across the picnic table. This was their chance to get away for a little talk.

They linked arms and headed off around the house.

"Where you going, Sadie?" asked Sam, Sadie's youngest brother.

"Down to the pond for a little bit," Sadie said.

Sam smiled, revealing two missing teeth. "Can we go fishing? Davey and me?"

"I don't know about fishing," Sadie said, "but you two can come along."

Fed by a spring that ran through the corner of the King farm, the pond was actually a wide creek that flowed on to the neighboring property. Rachel sat on a patch of grass and shielded her eyes from the diamonds of light bouncing from the water's surface. She could see clear through the water to the amber, gold, and gray stones on the bottom, and now and again a dark fish darted away from the shadowed banks. The air smelled of lilac and manure and frozen soil that was softening in the warmth of spring. The sun-drenched landscape seemed to breathe a sigh of relief that winter was truly over.

"Fish!" Davey pointed at the water. "The fish are out." He clapped his hands over his ears. "And we forgot to bring fishing rods!"

Sam put his hands on his knees and leaned closer to the water, curious. "I see them. We need something to catch them. A net."

Davey removed his black hat. "How about we use this?"

"A fish in a hat?" Sam chuckled.

"We can make a fishing rod out of a stick."

While the boys remained busy by the water, Rachel told Sadie about her terrible talk with James at the Beilers'. "I've been sick about it ever since. I don't think he really means it, but it's not my place to talk him out of it."

"Sounds like you stood up to him, though. Did you really tell him you wouldn't let him break it off?" Sadie asked.

"Ya, I did. And in front of most of the church members, too." Rachel groaned. "I was definitely feeling my oats."

"You were trying to protect something important," Sadie said. "James may not see it now, but he'll have a fine wife in you."

"Right now, marriage is not on his mind."

"Well, sure. He's suffered a lot." Sadie picked at a blade of grass, then snorted. "Did you really tell him three strikes and he was out?"

"Something like that." Rachel smiled, and then chuckled at the whole situation. Before she knew it, Sadie was laughing along.

"And I thought I was the one that gave the folks around here plenty to talk about."

Rachel slung an arm around her cousin. "Now, you know gossip is forbidden."

"Ya, but everyone talks."

"I missed you so!" Rachel rested her head on Sadie's shoulder, and her cousin gave her a squeeze. "It would be wonderful good to have you visit more often."

"It's hard to get away with school and church and my job, taking care of Katherine." Living among the English, Sadie had a full life, too. When she wasn't going to school or studying music, she took care of her boyfriend's grandmother. "And if I visit too much, the bishop will surely come calling on Adam."

"I know, but I wish you could live closer."

"Me, too. It's hard not having family around. And it's strange, living like an Englisher. With cars and cabs and buses and frozen pasta that cooks in minutes at the touch of a button. Everyone's in such a hurry, and so many folks won't even look you in the eye. There's not a lot of comfort there."

Rachel turned toward her cousin. Despite the slash of Sadie's mouth, there was a glimmer of peace in her amber eyes. "But you're staying in Philly," Rachel said, guessing. "Because of Mike."

"Mike is a big part of the reason." Sadie let out her breath in a sigh. "I feel so very alive when I'm with him. Gott has blessed us with His love, and who could turn their back on that? Ya, I miss the comforts of home, but I am quilting and baking. I taught Katherine, Mike's grandma, how to knit, and she has quick hands. Mike and I will make a comfortable home. He asked me to marry him as soon as I finish school, and I said yes."

"Oh, Sadie." Rachel hugged her. "I'm so happy for you, but sad, too. Joy and tears, all at the same time."

"I know what that's about. Some days I wake up and wonder what I've gotten myself into. Sometimes I look around and all the students in my class have their heads down, lost in their cell phones. I think they're missing life! But there are many things that are easier when you don't live Plain. Laundry and dishes are a snap. And there's no milking the cows or building fires."

"I don't think I would miss *those* things," Rachel said. "You know me. I always try to help in the house so I can miss the milking."

"Some things never change," Sadie said.

But as Sadie talked about living in a fancy house with heat and electricity, Rachel realized she could never live that way. Ya, she would like fewer chores and more time to paint. A house closer to town would take away the farming chores, but she had no desire to leave her community or her family. That much, she knew. Even if she sold dozens of paintings and her art blossomed into a profitable business, she would live Plain, under the laws of the Ordnung.

"It's hard to believe that it was just a year ago when we colored eggs and talked by the woodshed," Sadie said. "So many things have changed. There'll be babies born soon, God willing. Our family will be growing."

"Last Easter, I thought I'd be the one planning to wed this year," Rachel said. "But the accident changed all that. Sometimes James isn't himself. A different person."

"He's still healing from the accident." Sadie's eyes shone with sympathy. "Something like that leaves scars inside and out. But Gott will carry us through our troubles."

Rachel tucked her dress over her knees and hugged herself as a breeze stirred the strings of her kapp. "One thing I'm sure of: I'm not giving up on him. And I'm done with rumspringa." She would talk to the bishop about getting ready for baptism. All the doubts that had gnawed at her last year were gone now. "I can see a clear path. There's no other fella I want to be courting. My heart belongs to James."

"Well, it's good to have that much settled." Sadie patted her arm. "Sooner or later, he'll come around."

Rachel hoped and prayed that Sadie was right.

"Look here!" cried a cheery voice from the pond.

Little Sam was holding a fishing pole with both hands, tugging it up and down as if he were wrangling a fat fish at the end of the line. "I caught a whopper!"

Behind Sam, Davey laughed so hard, he hugged his sides.

"Where did he get the fishing pole?" Sadie asked as the girls jumped to their feet.

"Looks like he made it." As she got a closer look, Rachel realized the makeshift pole was just a long stick with a string of stripped ivy attached. The little ones were so creative.

"That's quite a catch," Sadie said, eyeing the bundle of fat leaves that flopped around on the ground whenever Sam gave the stick a tug. "I'm looking forward to frying that one up for dinner."

Davey giggled again. "You don't want to eat leaves!"

"He's right," Rachel teased. "The stems stick in your teeth."

❧ 13 ❧

The sky beyond the barn was ablaze with orange and red, a sunset that made James stop and thank Gott for this beautiful orchard. Inside the barn, his brothers were selecting horses to hitch up to three individual buggies. It was a rite of passage for a young man to bring his own buggy to a singing. If the night worked out good, a fella used his buggy to drive a young woman home. With that tradition in mind, James had turned down his brothers' offer to drive him to the singing, strapping his wheelchair to the back of the buggy.

"It's about time you came to a singing," Matt had said. "Everybody asks about you, and you've been out of the rehab center for a while now."

"Come with us, James." Luke's youthful face had been earnest. "You can ride in my buggy."

"Alongside you and Deb? That would really cramp your style," James had insisted. "I'm happy here, where I can move around on my own without relying on anybody."

"We don't mind lifting you in and out of the buggy," Peter said. "That's what brothers are for."

"You go on. I'm better off here." And before they could argue further, James had wheeled himself out of the barn to the path.

Since he hadn't the time to make his daily trip that morning, James decided to head to the sugar shack now. It would be dark by the time he returned, but he enjoyed the stillness amid the neat rows of trees in the orchard at night.

It took a good twenty minutes for him to reach the back acres of the orchard, but the doctors and therapists agreed that a trip like this was a good thing to build upper body strength and stamina. As he approached the small shack, he thought of the many hours he had spent there over the years. During the maple-sugaring season, there were always buckets to clean, sap to filter. And then there was the most time-consuming process of cooking the maple sap down to sweet syrup.

James was sorry Dat had decided not to collect the sap this year. Surely, Luke or Peter could have figured out which of the trees in the woods were silver maples. And drilling into the trees to insert the taps was a simple process. If his brothers had gotten the spiles in back in February, the family would be having fresh maple syrup on their pancakes, with enough spare syrup to sell it by the bottle.

But there was no use longing for something that was not to be. James, of all people, should know that by now.

As James rolled close to the shack, its dried wood silvery in the low light of dusk, he realized that he had miscalculated. Night was falling fast. He was about to turn back when he saw that the door to the shack was open and light glowed inside. Were some of the younger kids playing in here?

"Who's there?" he called, moving toward the rectangle of light.

Although there was no answer, the figure of a person sitting on the wooden bench was clear as he rolled up to the door. The glow of the lantern illuminated the girl's face and cast a silvery glow around her dark head. A halo.

For a moment he thought of the angels mentioned in the Bible. Today was Easter Sunday, and the picture of Jesus rising from the tomb was fresh in his mind.

But unless angels now wore blue jeans and jackets, this was just an Englisher girl. Ya, it was just a girl . . . a young woman. The halo was actually the circle of light from the lamp, along with gems sparkling from her ears. Her arms were wrapped tight around her knees, and her eyes were round with fear.

"Hi," she said. "How's it going?"

What kind of question was that? She had a young face: the round, innocent eyes of a baby deer, a button nose, thick lips that puckered in worry.

He paused in the doorway and squinted into the shadows, looking for others. He didn't want trouble. Sometimes kids and wanderers came through these parts. His parents usually offered them some food and sent them on their way. This one seemed to be alone.

"What are you doing here?" he asked.

"To be honest, I stayed here last night." Her voice held a calm that didn't come through in her eyes. "It was late, and I needed to sleep." She shrugged. "Sorry if I'm trespassing. I was planning to sleep outside, like camping, but when I saw this place, I couldn't resist. Is this your house?"

He shook his head. "This is my family's orchard. Most years, we use this building for sugaring maple syrup."

"I thought it was something like that, seeing all the buckets and all the burners on the stove." She spoke lightly, as if they were two old friends who'd met in town.

He took in the room as she talked. The floor and walls had been swept. Red coals glowed in the stove. She sat on a dark red sleeping bag that had been spread out on the wide bench. From the bucket of water heating on the stove, it was clear that she'd found the pump. There was no harm done here. In fact, she had made the shack good and tidy. But she had to go. Dat would not abide any more Englishers at the orchard.

"Why aren't you making maple syrup this year?" she asked, interrupting his thoughts. "Is there something wrong with the trees?"

"The trees are fine," he said. "How did you find the sugar shack?" It was at the back of the property, well secluded.

"That, I think, was luck, or else God took mercy on me and led me here. I needed a place to hole up, a place to hide, really, and for some reason, I turned off the main road in the dark last night, and I landed here." She brushed her dark hair back off her face and cocked her head to one side. When she looked him in the eye, he could see that she wasn't quite a woman. A teen, older than his sister Verena, but not old enough to be wandering the countryside alone. "I'm Shandell, by the way. Shandell Darby."

He nodded. "James. How old are you?"

"Eighteen. Too old to be a runaway. That's what the police told me."

And you can't stay here. You need to go. It's time to move on.

There were a million ways to send this Englisher on her way, but somehow James couldn't bring himself to say the words.

What was wrong with him? Paralyzed legs, and now a frozen tongue, too?

"Is it James Lapp? I mean, the sign said the Lapp orchards, and I met a girl named Elsie Lapp at the Country Store in Halfway. Do you know her?"

"Elsie is my cousin."

"Really? She's awesome. She saved my life yesterday."

"Is that so?" He hadn't heard any recent stories of Elsie's good deeds, but then Elsie would never be so proud as to talk about herself that way.

"She helped get me out of a very scary situation. I was trying to get away from this guy . . . Gary? I thought he was my friend, but I was so wrong about that. I was wrong about a lot of things. And by the time I figured it all out, we were here in Lancaster County, miles from home. He sort of turned on me. I was really scared, but Elsie helped me hide. She is one brave girl. And after Gary left, she and Ruben gave me some food. And Elsie showed me how to finish a patch for a quilt." She shifted to the side to reach down into her backpack. "She even gave me my own little rag bag to keep working on." She smoothed out a lavender patch with finished edges.

"That sounds like Elsie." His cousin had a heart of gold. "So. This bad friend is gone. Why don't you go home?"

"I've got no way to get there. No money for the bus, and Baltimore is too far to walk."

"Baltimore, Maryland?"

She nodded. "My mom is going to come get me, but she can't do it until Thursday night. She works two jobs, and that's the soonest she can get away. Do you think I could stay here until then? I won't cause any problems for you, James. I'll stay out of the orchards, and I've got enough granola bars and stuff to last me until then."

He knew the answer to that had to be no. Dat would not want an Englisher staying on their land, especially after his decision to restrict outsiders from their home. He drew in a breath to tell her, but something about this girl brought him to a place he hadn't known for many months. A place of compassion.

"For you to stay here . . . it's not allowed," he said, thinking of his father's rules.

"I know, I'm not Amish. I don't belong here, but please don't kick me out. I won't mess anything up. And I promise you, I'll leave on Thursday. It's just a few days. Please. I'll be quiet as a mouse."

James frowned. A mouse would not make a good guest. A mouse scratched around in the wall and made a mess of things. No, this girl could not stay.

Open on the bench was a child's book of Bible stories. That did not seem to match the teen sitting in front of him. A stranger and an outsider. An Englisher.

But underneath all that, she was just a frightened girl. She could be one of his sisters, gone astray during rumspringa. This one needed help.

"You can stay the night," he said. Not even Dat would send a young woman packing after nightfall.

"Thank you." Her eyes swam with relief. "It's weird, being out here in the middle of nowhere, but last night I really slept. I feel safe here."

The middle of nowhere? He squinted. Didn't she know she was sleeping in the back acres of a family orchard? Shandell seemed sweet, but not very wise of the world. "That's good. But till Thursday is a long time, and we're not in the business of putting up strangers here. It would be good if you could find some other place to go tomorrow."

Before Dat or anyone else sees you back here.

She nodded. "I'll work on that. First thing in the morning."

"All right." As he switched off the brakes and turned the wheelchair, he realized that Shandell was one of those rare people who spoke to him without even seeming to notice that he was in a wheelchair.

"Good night," she called, as he headed out the door into the darkness.

He wouldn't have minded staying and talking some more, but he didn't want to arouse concern back at the house. He didn't want Dat coming out this way to search for him.

"Good night," he answered without looking back. There was a curious ripple in his chest as he rolled into the velvety dark of the April night. An odd feeling of responsibility.

The memory of Shandell's face in a pool of light, the way her legs swung from the bench, too short to reach the ground. Shandell needed to be taken care of. And right now, James was the person Gott had chosen to do that.

PART TWO

The Long Road to Paradise

For now we see through a glass, darkly; but then face-to-face:
Now I know in part; but then shall I know even as also I am known.
And now abideth faith, hope, charity, these three;
But the greatest of these is charity.

—1 CORINTHIANS 13:12–13

14

*R*achel sat in the patch of moonlight spilling into the attic room and added dots of silver to the starry sky of her painting. Behind her, Rose's breath whispered in a steady rhythm, a reminder that it really was time to sleep. Anyone who saw Rachel now would think she was verhuddelt! Crazy to be awake so late at night.

But after such a day of hurt feelings and raw emotion, this was just the thing to soothe her. There was something calming about Gott's magnificent sky, and as she added dots of purple, blue, white, and silver to her painting, she felt her sorrows begin to fade ever so slightly.

Moving close to the canvas, she painted tiny lines radiating out from the stars.

She didn't quite understand why painting eased her burdens. Sometimes she wondered why Gott made her to think that way, in bits of color and light. It was not the Amish way. True art was viewed as self-expression, and the Amish believed that garnered feelings of pride and superiority—hochmut. That seemed funny to her, since she didn't feel proud about her art. It was just something that flowed from her, and that was that.

All done with the silver, she plunged her brush into a jar of water and stood up to get a closer look out the window. Under the starry sky, the lawn stretched away from the house, the dark grass crossed by pale paths and lanes.

It wasn't hard to remember how James had stood down there in the yard, courting her on Saturday nights last year. He used to shine the beam of a flashlight on her window to let her know he was here, and she would rush downstairs, padding quietly in bare feet, and let him in. He would add some wood to the embers in the stove, and she would ease into his arms, secure in his embrace, secure in his love.

A few times in the winter they had met at the sugar shack for innocent but delicious kisses by the fire. Now, as she hugged herself to ward off the chill, she tried to remember the wonderful warmth of being in James's arms. His strength had made her feel secure and safe. She had believed that there was no problem they could not solve if they worked together. And his unquenchable sense of humor had promised a lifetime of laughter.

Once, when he was visiting while she was working on a scrapbook page for a sick cousin, James had penciled in a little joke while she wasn't watching.

What starts with T, ends with T, and is full of T? Answer: Teapot.

"What a rascal he could be," she said aloud, and then looked behind her, glad to find that Rose was still sleeping. Sadie was the only person she'd told about what had happened that day. The ache in her heart was still too raw as she wondered if she was really losing James. Had his love for her drained away like his sense of humor?

She pulled a quilt over her shoulders and tiptoed across the cold wood floor to the dresser. There was the clock James had given her, a pretty round face with fancy arrows, set behind clear plastic with silver trim. It had been an engagement gift, a private thing between a fella and his girl. When she moved downstairs, she'd left it up here, thinking it would be safe until she and James were married and moving into a home together. But now that their engagement was in question, should she give the clock back?

No, that would be like saying she didn't love James anymore. She wasn't going to give in so easily.

Pressing the clock to her heart, she remembered how she had refused his words.

You and me, we don't belong together.

Ha! He had a lot of nerve saying that. Didn't he know how those words would break her heart?

She had fended him off, but now she wasn't sure where she stood with him. It was a terrible mess, and she didn't know how to fix it.

With a sigh, she turned away from her paintings and headed downstairs to bed. The house was silent now, but come four A.M., Mamm and Dat and the men would rise to tend to the cows and other chores. Along with the scuffle of her feet, she heard the small beat of the clock's second hand.

Downstairs, she huddled under the quilts and placed the clock at the edge of her pillow. She couldn't make it out in the darkness, but she heard it ticking softly. She yawned, listening as time moved on. This was the thing James didn't understand. True love would beat on, like the flapping wings of a bird, like the beating of a heart.

15

*W*heels turning, spinning endlessly. Arms pumping, pushing . . . the images had filled James's mind the whole night through. In his dream, he had made the trip into Paradise on his own, simply by propelling his wheelchair along the side of the paved road, one ferocious push at a time. All to get himself to Dr. Finley's clinical treatment on time.

The dream still held him when he awoke at three A.M., drenched in sweat, his biceps aching. As he washed and dressed, thoughts of escape clung to him. Much as he wanted to take control of the situation, he knew that it would take all day and half the night to wheel himself the many miles into Paradise. He needed another plan . . . a way to get to town without relying on anyone in his family. After Dat's order about staying Plain, the only solution would be to turn to someone else in the Amish community. There were plenty of folks willing to help, but many of them would be put off by the opinions of Dat and Bishop Samuel. Once they heard of their concern over this new test as well as their disapproval of James's associations with the Englishers, well, most folks wouldn't walk into that tangle of thorns.

He rolled his wheelchair out of his bedroom and was surprised by the smell of coffee, savory and warm. Who was up before him?

"James." Mamm's voice, low and quiet, caught him before he spied her bending over to poke at the fire in the woodstove. "Come. Have coffee."

"It smells good, Mamm." He maneuvered over to the hutch, where he lifted two mugs from their hooks. He stowed them in the chair's side pocket, wheeled over to the table, and set the cups on the vinyl tablecloth. "Nothing quite like coffee first thing in the morning."

"Ya." The door of the stove closed with a squeak, and Mamm straightened, wiping her hands on her apron. "I knew I'd have to get up before the birds to catch you."

"Ya. It's early to bed, early to rise for me."

"I reckon it's easy to get up before dawn when you don't stay out late at singings and such."

Was this going to be about him refusing to go to social functions? Another push for him to settle into a life in this chair? James's chest grew tight as she poured a cup of black liquid into his mug. He used to add milk, but since the accident he'd started drinking it black, savoring the bold bitterness, so like his new life. He took a sip now, silent as Mamm placed her mug beside the cutting board and began to chop baked potatoes left over from Saturday's supper. Nothing went to waste in an Amish kitchen.

"Hash browns for breakfast?" James asked.

Edna nodded. "And scrambled eggs. You'll want a good breakfast in your belly for the trip to Paradise."

James gripped the mug. "Paradise?" Had he heard right? "Are you talking about going to the clinic? The treatment with Dr. Finley?"

"Ya. I've been thinking on it, and this is a time when we must call on our friends and family, find someone in the community who'd be willing to drive a buggy for us. We'll supply the horse and all."

"It's a big task, a lot to ask." Despite his doubts, James felt a weight lifting. "The treatment has to be every day, seven days a week. For who knows how long."

Mamm nodded, and as she faced him, James noticed the new creases at the outer edges of her eyes, and that there was more silver in the hair scraped back beneath her prayer kapp. His injuries had taken a toll on her, too. "But if it's a task worth doing, it's worth doing right. I would have put the word out yesterday after church, but I didn't want to cross your father."

James frowned, his lips taut against his teeth. "He doesn't want me to get the treatment."

"That's not true." Mamm held an onion to the cutting board and cropped off the papery skin at the end. "We talked about it last night, and he's right fine with it as long as you take support from our community, not from the Englishers."

"Mmm." James took another sip of coffee to mask his concern. This would all be so easy if Dat would allow Dylan or a hired driver to transport him. But this treatment was so important to James, and he was glad for a way to get to Paradise without crossing his father and the bishop. "I'll do anything I can to get there, Mamm. Even if I have to wheel myself down the road." He told her about his dream, about the hours of strained muscles and dust.

Edna clucked her tongue. "I think we can do better than you wheeling yourself. I'm going to ask Gabe King or Lois Mast if they can take you in each morning."

James nearly choked on his coffee. "The bishop's wife?" Lois had a stern way about her. "I'm not sure I'm ready to spend so much time with the bishop's eyes and ears."

"Beggars can't be choosers." Mamm didn't look up as she diced the onion. "She's been a great help with fund-raising and all."

"I'm thankful for that. But would you try Gabe first? I'd rather ride with a man."

Mamm nodded. "I'll try, but Gabe will need to be back in the afternoon for milking. For today, I'll take you in this morning. I can stop at the bulk store on my way home. And Mark will go in and pick you up when he gets home from school."

"Little Mark?" Twelve-year-old Mark was right good with horses, but he didn't have much experience driving a buggy yet. "He's never ridden alone into Halfway, and Paradise is twice as far."

"It's time he learned. Right now, he's the only one who can be spared around here, and he's eager to do it. He's a good boy, James, and he wants to help you."

Were the tears in her eyes from the onion, or the high emotion of the situation? Suddenly, James wanted to kick himself. All these months, he had been so wrapped up in his own pain, he hadn't thought of how the accident had affected his mother. Mamm wanted the best for her firstborn son. She wanted James to walk again, and she was doing everything in her power to make it so.

"Mark will learn by doing," James said. "It's a right good plan, Mamm." Grateful, he nodded at his mother, wishing that he could undo the creases and gray hairs and worries of the past months.

"We do what we can." Her thin lips curved slightly, and James caught a glimmer of that whimsical light in her eyes, an enjoyment he'd seen there when she served up a slice of pie or savored a good joke. Edna Lapp hadn't always been a stern woman; it was the difficulties of the past few months that had dulled her smile like a worn blade.

As his mother turned away and scraped potatoes and onions into the sizzling fry pan, James breathed in the mouthwatering smells and savored the new hope in his heart. No one but Gott in heaven knew for sure whether or not he'd be able to walk again. But now at least he had a chance.

⊙ 16 ⊙

*D*own in the kitchen, Rachel and Mamm were well into frying bacon and grating cheese when Rose came down the stairs, barefoot and bleary-eyed.

"What's for breakfast?" she asked.

"We're making the bacon and egg casserole," Rachel said with a smile. The dish, a baked combination of hard-boiled eggs, Colby cheese, and cream of mushroom soup, was a favorite of the King children. They especially liked it served over Mamm's flaky biscuits.

"We're just finishing the bacon, so you've got plenty of time to help with the milking first," Mamm told Rose, who was breaking off a corner from a slice of crispy bacon.

"Off with you now," Betsy told her daughter. "It's the early bird who should be getting the bacon."

"I was tired this morning," Rose said as the door to the mud room closed behind her.

"Out late with a fella." Mamm turned to Rachel. "Did she tell you?"

"I heard bits and pieces when she came in," Rachel said, "but I'm sure I'll hear more about it later." This was big news. Rose had just started her rumspringa, and she so longed to catch a fella's eye.

"And why didn't you go to the singing last night? Last I checked, you're still a single youth."

"James has trouble getting out to singings," Rachel said. She didn't want to mention that James might not be her beau anymore. The uncertainty of it all made her feel prickly inside.

"You've a good heart, Rachel, but no one expects you to marry James anytime soon. The accident changed all that, and you can't argue with the hand of Gott."

"I know, Gott doesn't make mistakes." Rachel pressed her lips together as she scooped diced onion into the pan of hot bacon grease. There was no arguing with Gott . . . or Mamm. Still, no one would stop her from loving James. "But that doesn't change things for me and James."

"We'll see." Betsy sighed. "Put it in Gott's hands."

෨෬

After breakfast Rachel helped Mamm get some laundry going, and then she caught a ride into town with her brother Abe. Today was the group session, a time for counseling for the Amish travelers involved in the January crash.

The old folks did not attend; Rachel suspected that they talked through the crash with the ministers. For the young people in the van like Elsie, Ruben, Rachel, and Zed, and Haley Donovan, the Englisher girl who had helped them at the scene, the trauma had been eased by conversation and advice, and they had become good friends, too.

In the months since the accident in January, Dylan had helped Rachel let go of the guilt that had overwhelmed her. When James had been injured, she had blamed herself. Now Rachel knew that none of it was her fault. Not the crash. Not the fact that James's seat belt had been broken. Gott didn't make mistakes. It was sad when bad things happened, but Gott was with her. He would see her through.

Dylan opened the session by asking about friends and family. "The four of you were in the van, and I think you've benefited from these sessions," he said. "But I wonder about other people in the community. We know a tragedy like this has a ripple effect. It's my job to reach out and help other survivors work through their grief. I'm wondering if you guys can help me?"

"I think it would be a good thing for folks to talk with you," said Elsie Lapp, who had lost her father, Thomas, in the crash. "Sometimes I see Fanny, so busy at home with the baby and the house chores." Fanny Lapp had been married to Thomas, and tragically, he had died before their third child had been born. "She never complains, but I think her heart is broken. Her first husband was taken to heaven, too." She shook her head. "I have asked her to come along to these meetings, but she wants to stay close to home."

"Would it be okay if I stop by to talk with her?" Dylan asked.

"You could call during the day." Elsie's mouth puckered as she thought it through. "Maybe you should bring Haley? Folks might get to thinking the wrong thing if an Englisher man comes by to visit a widow."

"We could do that," Haley said.

"And I've been trying to get James to come join the group," Rachel said, "but I don't think it's going to happen. His dat and the bishop don't want James spending so much time with Englishers. They think he's drifting away from living Plain."

"That's a tough issue." Dylan explained that he had been visiting

James last weekend when Jimmy Lapp announced that he didn't want Englishers in his house anymore. "I'm going to try to meet with James whenever he goes into Paradise for treatment. I'm sorry I can't do more, but I respect Jimmy's decision." Dylan asked about others in Elsie's family. Thomas had left behind three little children, as well as Elsie, brother Caleb, and sister Emma, who taught the Amish children of Halfway.

While Elsie talked about her family, Rachel's mind wandered to her own concerns. James was in her thoughts all the time, but she could hardly tell the group about her courtship blues. It wouldn't do to bring such matters up, especially in front of fellas like Ruben and Zed.

After the meeting, the group walked down the street to the pizza place—Dylan's treat. They divided into smaller conversations, and Rachel told Haley how she dreamed of living in a house in town like Haley, or an apartment like Dylan.

"Not everyone belongs on a farm," Rachel said. "Mucking the stalls and milking cows doesn't suit me. And without all the farm chores, I could spend more time painting. Gott willing, I could make enough money to support James and me."

Although Amish couples traditionally kept their engagements a secret, except from family, until just a month or so before the planned wedding, everyone here knew that Rachel and James had long planned to marry in the fall.

"Elsie told me your paintings sell well in the Country Store," Haley said.

Rachel nodded. "And I've started painting again. I'm thinking I might sell them through that gallery in the city."

Dylan joined their conversation, asking where Rachel would like to live. She said that she had been thinking that her family and James's might build a house on the outskirts of Halfway. "We could build it special for James," Rachel confided in Dylan. "One of those houses with no stairs, and ramps, and extra-wide doorways for a wheelchair."

"Have you talked to James about this?" Dylan asked.

"A little bit," Rachel said. Of course, she hadn't mentioned the details about building a house for the wheelchair because she knew it would upset James, who longed to get back on his feet.

"I have mixed feelings about this," Dylan said. "As your therapist, I support your plan because it seems to fit your needs." But when it came to the long-term plan that involved James, Dylan had his doubts. Life-changing injuries like the one James had sustained often ended romantic relationships. He encouraged Rachel to look toward her long-term future with a "wait-and-see" attitude.

She imagined a life in which she and James lived in an apartment where she could spend most of the day painting. Why could no one else see that? Everyone around her would have her leave James behind. It would not be a bad life at all. She and James could be very happy together, if everyone would stop being so gloomy.

17

"Are you nervous?" asked the young doctor with the shiny shaved head and polka-dotted bow tie. Dr. Alec Finley stood in front of James, his hands clasped together expectantly.

"I reckon," James admitted. Now that it was time for the actual treatment, he was struck by how odd it was that he was pinning his hopes on electricity—the thing forbidden in Amish homes. "You won't be giving me a shock?"

"Not at all. Some patients tell us that it's actually soothing. This is a treatment that's been used for many years to help relieve chronic pain. In your case, we're trying to use the mild electrical stimulation to prime your nervous system so that it relays signals from the brain to your lower extremities."

"Mmm. So the brain can tell the legs to walk."

"Something like that. I must repeat the reminder that there's no guarantee. This is a test we're running. That said, we've had some success with a handful of patients—enough to continue the trials.

And your profile fits well in our study. I would like to start today, but you have to be ready to make the commitment."

James leaned back in the chair, hesitant. He could hear his father's voice, telling him that he was too comfortable with Englishers. "What kind of commitment?"

"We need to administer the electrical treatment every day for at least two weeks, along with two hours of physical therapy. We would like that to be daily, too, although you can take Sundays off if it conflicts with your religious beliefs."

James knew all this. "I will get here, somehow."

"I appreciate your determination, James." Dr. Finley gave a sage nod. "I know . . . you don't live so close, especially by horse and buggy. I would like to tell you that we can come to you, but these machines and monitors are expensive, and they're not portable. You would need to come here."

The travel was a hardship, but James couldn't let this chance go. Maybe Dat would let him hire a young Amish man to bring him to Paradise by horse and buggy. He thought of the old saying when a person came to a crossroads: *Gott won't lead you where His grace can't keep you.*

"I'll get here," James said. "I want to do everything I can to walk again."

"That's the motivation I like to hear." Dr. Finley clapped him on the shoulder. "We'll start today. Let me get the techs, and we'll implant the electrodes."

OC

"Did it hurt?" Mark asked, once they were on their way home with Rowdy pulling the buggy.

"Not really," James answered. "The setup took a long time."

It was something to get used to, seeing twelve-year-old Mark driving the buggy with his black hat cocked back and his chipmunk face masked by a pair of sunglasses. Twelve was a bit young to be driving such a long distance, and Mark preferred to do chores in and around the barn. "What did they do to you?" Mark asked.

"They had to put sixteen electrodes under the skin of my back, along the spine." James reached back and touched the sensitive spot under his coat. "I think maybe they left some tape on. But it wasn't painful."

"That's good."

"And after that, there were two hours of PT. That's what they call physical therapy. But the therapist, JJ, he said PT stands for personal torture, 'cause they work you so hard."

Mark frowned. "That doesn't sound good."

"It's a joke," James explained. An Englisher joke. Today had been quite a workout, even for James, who had done his exercises every day at home. He was tired now, and eager to get home. The doctors wanted him to rest. After the rigor of the treatment, he might just take a rare nap.

With the black Morgan moving along at such a quick pace, they would be home fast. Rowdy was quick-footed, but James wished his brother hadn't decided to use the new horse. Morgans were a high-spirited breed, and Rowdy had been recently purchased from a non-Amish dealer, who had warned them that the horse had been subjected to some harsh conditions.

In the English world, harsh conditions usually boiled down to animal abuse. Neglect. Malnutrition. Sometimes a trainer went too far with a whip.

The Lapps couldn't abide that. Dat had nearly walked away from the deal, not wanting an unpredictable horse in his stables. But once Mark had set his heart on the horse, Dat had given in.

"Does Mamm know you took Rowdy out on the highway?" James asked.

"She told me Ranger would be the best horse, but when Rowdy started nuzzling me, I couldn't say no."

"Rowdy has never done a trip this long before, has he?"

"This will be the first time," Mark admitted, "but he's ready for it. I've been working with him every day, strapping him on to the smallest buggy. Horses take a lot of patience. You have to do the same thing over and over again, and sometimes you think it's not working at all. At first he was too scared to move. Then he started balking at the smallest movement. He's a jittery horse."

The black horse had a full mane and good lines. "How did you get him to stop balking?" James asked.

"I taught him to put his head down when I give him a cue. It's a trick I learned from a trainer at a horse auction. When the horse puts his head down, he can't see what scares him anymore."

"That's a smart thing. What's the command?"

Mark covered his mouth, to be sure the horse wouldn't hear. "I tell him: frankincense."

"Like the gift the wise man brought to Jesus."

Mark nodded. "I reckoned it's not something folks say every day."

"That's for sure." James asked his brother about working with the horses, and Mark explained that they were like mirrors. "Horses reflect the person who owns them." Mark believed that Rowdy's first owner had been cruel to the horse. "I can tell that he's been whipped before. There are scars. That's a very sad thing for a horse."

"But if the owner's nature comes out through the horse, then Rowdy should be a good, patient horse, now that you are training him."

Grinning, Mark nudged his brother. "Are you kidding me?"

"I don't joke about things that matter."

As they talked, a milk truck came chugging up the road, heading toward them. For a moment, James worried that it might spook the horse. The heft of the huge vehicle made the earth rumble as it approached. But Rowdy kept his head, trotting forward steadily.

The truck was upon them now, the rumble of the tires blocking out Mark's voice. James put a hand on the edge of the buggy to hold himself steady.

Rowdy didn't seem bothered by the truck—until the driver hit the horn, letting out a low blast that seemed to blow right through James.

That was the horse's undoing.

The Morgan skittered to the right, reared up, and whinnied. Staging a defense against the truck, the Morgan turned off the road onto the shoulder. Dust flew as he kicked up sand and stones.

The buggy rocked crazily as it left the highway. It swayed, ready to tip, and James looked to make sure his brother was still on the bench as it bounced on the shoulder. Ahead of them, Rowdy pushed down a chicken-wire fence, posts popping from the earth.

"Stop!" Mark shouted, pulling back on the lines. "Rowdy. *Rowdy!* Stop! Halt!"

Head down and holding on for dear life, James could hear the terror in his brother's voice. In his panic, Mark had forgotten the cue to calm the horse.

Bracing himself as the buggy hit something with a thud, then bounced, James lifted his head.

"Frankincense!" he shouted, his voice booming ahead. "Frankincense!"

At that, the horse stopped and the buggy rolled to a halt. For a moment, there was a strange stillness. Then came the sound from passing cars on the highway. And the creak of the buggy as James shifted back and eyed the tangled wire fencing that was wrapped around one wheel. A sea of dark green now surrounded the buggy.

The wild horse had pulled them into a field of early spinach.

He turned to Mark. "Are you all right?"

"Ya." Mark's face was red, his eyes shiny with tears. "You remembered the cue. When Rowdy got spooked, it happened so fast that I forgot."

"It was the horn that frightened him."

"I didn't train him to ignore horns yet." Mark swiped at his eyes with the sleeve of his jacket. "We could've been killed, all three of us."

"But Gott spared us today. We're still in one piece." James clapped his brother on the shoulder, then turned to look out at the damaged field. "But I can't say the same for the Yoders' spinach."

"And look at Rowdy." Mark leaned forward to peer at his horse. "Are you okay, boy?"

"Go to him," James said, taking the lines.

A moment later, Mark hopped down among the short spinach plants to get to the horse.

A squat man wearing a plaid shirt and a bright orange vest came over to the buggy. He was the driver of the milk truck, come to apologize. James explained that they had a skittish horse on their hands. No one had been hurt, but they could use some help getting free from the fencing and back on the road. The man noticed the wheelchair strapped to the back of the buggy, and nodded.

With the driver's help, the buggy was untangled and Rowdy was led out of the field, back onto the roadside. Mark was a bit sheepish the rest of the way home. James didn't blame him, but there was a lesson to be learned. A boy needed to mind his mamm.

"After all those afternoons in the round pen, all those times I gave Rowdy the cue, over and over again, I can't believe I'm the one that forgot it."

"It happens," James said, reassuring the boy. Mark wasn't the only one with a lesson to take from this. James had felt a moment of power, a reminder that he was not a worthless man. The things he had learned in his life still came in handy. Praise Gott, he was not as helpless as he'd thought.

᠄᠄ 18 ᠄᠄

*S*handell felt bad that she had lied to James about finding another place to go. Now that she had cleaned up the shack and figured out where to get water and how to keep the stove burning, well, she wasn't going to move down the road and sleep outside with insects and moles and deer and whatever else. Not that she had anything against creatures and critters. She just didn't want them creeping up on her or crawling into her sleeping bag at night.

Maybe it was a terrible sin to lie to an Amish person, but she figured that if she could talk him into letting her stay until Thursday, it wouldn't be a lie after all.

And maybe he wouldn't even be around for the next few days. Poking her head out the cabin door, she blinked against the bright sunshine. Tall trees swayed to the right and left, their green leaves thick and abundant. She knew the little path between them led over the little hill and back through the orchard, but from here all she could see was the knoll of tall grass and wildflowers. To the left, a small creek ran alongside the hut, and she had gotten some water from it yesterday and set it to heat on the woodstove. Warm water was better for washing up, and she had decided it was safer to boil it before she drank it.

Wow, that sun was warm. She said a little prayer of thanks for the beautiful day. Bad weather would have made it hard to stay out here in a bare-bones shack.

A slight breeze tousled her black hair as she strode past the trees and up the slight rise. Not a person in sight. But the dirt path under her feet was rutted and overgrown with brambles here and there. It had to be hard, maneuvering around the orchard in a wheelchair. What had happened to James? Had he been born without the use of his legs, or had he been in an accident? In the local newspaper that she'd read at the police station, *The Budget,* there'd been two accounts of men injured in farming accidents. One of them had lost a finger; the other had died. Had James been hurt by a plow? It was sad for a young, attractive man like that to be stuck in a wheelchair.

Accidents were terrible. Her real dad had been killed in a construction accident. She'd been a little kid back then, so it really didn't hit her at the time. She told her friends that she missed him, but the truth was, she barely remembered him at all. There were vague memories of riding on his shoulders and him sitting at the foot of her bed, reading to her at night.

Reading from the book of children's Bible stories. He used to lean on one side, a pillow tucked under his arm. Sometimes when she closed her eyes she remembered the gravelly sound of his voice. He'd had a way of reading each chapter with a curious tone, as if it was the first time he had ever come across such an amazing story. And then he would finish a story and cup her face with his big hands and plant a kiss on her forehead. And Shandell had known it was time to close her eyes and sleep, safe and secure in her bed.

That was the dad she missed, but she couldn't tell her friends that she longed to go back to a five-year-old's existence.

With a sigh, she headed down toward the little creek. It was nice of James to let her stay here—she was grateful for that—but it was lonely. She crossed her arms over her chest, embracing the book that she had tucked under her zipped hoodie. After Dad died, the book of Bible stories had stayed in the back of a drawer for a long time, tucked away like so many memories. It wasn't until Shandell was fifteen and helping Mom pack up the apartment to move in with Phil that she had discovered the book she had loved as a little kid.

The heel of her boot slipped on loose stones, and she hopped down closer to the creek and walked along until she found a sunny patch with a brown stone, perfect for sitting. Was this a fishing creek? Did James ever come here with his brothers and sisters? She figured there would be lots of them, because she'd read that Amish people usually had lots of kids.

Unzipping her jacket, she opened her book and leafed through the pages of colorful illustrations surrounded by decorative borders.

The book fell open to the story of the wise builder, Shandell's favorite.

In Matthew chapter seven, Jesus told the story of a wise man who built his house on rock. When the rains came and the streams rose and the winds blew, the house was fine because its foundation was solid rock. But another man who built his house on sand? The rain and wind made it collapse.

Shandell liked the picture of builders carrying rocks, and another of a cute little stone house with two windows that resembled eyes.

The story that Jesus had told was such a good lesson in life: to lay your foundation on your solid faith, not on false promises and people who will shift away like sand under your feet.

Wow, she'd really fallen for that one, hadn't she? She'd only read this story a hundred times, and yet she had been foolish enough to trust Gary. Any house he built would be like a sand castle on the beach.

What had happened to her? She used to be such a good kid. She used to get along with her mom. But things had begun to fall apart last year when Phil lost his job. In the beginning, Phil had made Mom happy, and he'd been an easygoing guy, back when he was working.

But now? Phil was miserable, and he took it out on everyone around him. Usually, that was Shandell, who had the responsibility of keeping the house clean and putting together some kind of dinner each night while Mom was working.

In a couple of days, she'd be back home, serving miserable Phil again. She smoothed her fingertips over the orange border of the picture. She wanted to go home to Mom, but she wished that she never had to face Phil again.

Oh, grow up, Shanny.

He's your mom's husband now, and he's not a bad person.

It was Phil's drinking that made their lives so unstable. Somehow, it felt better to blame the alcohol. When Phil started drinking, the rock foundation had crumbled. Their house had shifted on its foundation of sand.

And now it was all tumbling down.

Well, not really. Shandell knew she occasionally exaggerated things. And she would be missing the point of the story about the wise builder if she blamed her unhappiness on Phil's drinking. Shandell was the one who had run off with Gary. That had been her house of sand. And as soon as she got home, she was going to have a heart-to-heart with Mom. She wasn't sure what to say about Phil, but it would be good to be honest with Mom again.

The sound of a man's voice made her heart leap. "Hallo?" his voice thundered.

Adrenaline popped in her veins. She closed the book and clasped it under one arm as she jumped up and turned toward the creek.

Someone was coming . . .

19

*S*uch a glorious day!

Rachel knew that April showers were needed for spring flowers, but she enjoyed the bright splash of colors that emerged with the first flowers of the season, along with the sunshine that made her feel calm and smooth as melted butter.

The good weather made for a perfect laundry day, and already Rachel and her mamm had taken in two loads of laundry, fresh and dry from the sun. With more clothes and sheets to pin to the line once this batch was dry, Betsy had told Rachel she could set up her easel out in the yard and paint while the laundry was drying.

"There's not much time for too many other chores on a big laundry day," Mamm said. As long as she stayed mindful of the time and took care not to get any paint on the clean washing, Rachel could paint outside beside the hanging clothes.

Now she swirled her brush in a blob of pink that was so bright, she had to smile. She had decided to cover her sorrow and brighten the shadows in her heart with wild, loud colors. These paintings were different from the quaint, pastoral scenes of cows and barns and quilts on a clothesline. One canvas showed a close-up of clothes hanging on the line, but these dresses were the deepest blues, brightest reds, and sunniest yellows she had ever seen. On another canvas, she had painted purple pears. There were also blue hens and the silhouette of a simple house with a pink and orange April sunset heating the sky behind it.

All in all, it had been a good day of painting and laundry. Rachel was happy to balance the fun of painting with a chore that kept the house in order.

The sun was dipping low in the sky when a gray buggy came up the lane. It was one of the Lapps' horses, with Edna Lapp driving. She expected James's mother to continue on to the barn and visit with Betsy, but the buggy paused right beside the daffodils that bordered the lane near Rachel. Quickly, she placed her palette on the grass and walked over to greet Edna.

"I'm on my way to talk with Gideon Yoder, but I wanted to stop in and visit you." Edna wrapped the reins around the stub and stepped to the ground. Her face looked drawn and tired.

"Do you want some tea?" Rachel offered.

"No time for that, and I haven't much of a stomach for it after this afternoon. Such a scare there was! Mark was driving James home from Paradise, and the new horse went wild. Pulled their buggy off the road."

Oh, no! Rachel's stomach dropped. As the memory of the van accident began to stir anxiety, Rachel's fingers found the pins in her apron. "Is everyone okay?"

"Mark and James are fine. James was able to stop the horse, but not before it tore through some of the Yoders' spinach. We'll need to patch up the field."

"I'm glad everyone's okay. I'm sure the Yoders will understand."

"We're grateful it wasn't worse. Jimmy was reluctant to buy this horse, and I suppose we should have thought better than to take on a Morgan named Rowdy. It's hard to train a horse that's been subjected to harsh conditions. But Mark had his heart set, and he's been working with the horse."

Rachel knew that James's younger brother had a way with horses. Loving and patient, Mark enjoyed training and grooming them—a necessary chore in every Amish home. "Some horses are more stubborn than others," Rachel said. "I'm sure Mark will have Rowdy in line soon."

"Gott willing. But it made me see that Mark is too young and inexperienced to be driving into Paradise. He was bringing James home from his new procedure. Electric wires to heal his legs! Isn't that a strange thing?"

"James told me about it. I pray that it helps him."

"He still has hope. His dat, not so much."

Rachel noticed lines of weariness around Edna's eyes, and she thought of the hospital vigil and steadfast care Edna had provided for her son. So many long hours.

"And what do you make of it, Edna?" Rachel asked. "Do you think this could help James?"

"I know my son. Right now, he needs to return to the orchard he loves. If this will help him get back on his feet, then I'm grateful to Gott and the Englisher doctors.

"I know you two are planning to marry, and I know you've tried to support James. He just doesn't appreciate Gott's blessings right now, but he could use your help. He's going to need a daily ride into Paradise for this new therapy. His dat doesn't approve, and I can't be doing it every day."

A ride to Paradise . . . Rachel wished it was that simple. She would cherish the chance to help James, but if he rejected her in front of his mamm and his family, that she couldn't bear.

"I want to help," she told Edna, "but James doesn't want me around anymore. He said so."

"Did he, now? He's been a mite grumpy lately. Can't say I blame him on that. But a mother can see past cross words, and I know he's not grumpy about you. For James, seeing you ride up the lane would be a better sight than rhubarb pie. And we both know he favors rhubarb."

Rachel blinked back tears as she smiled. "Do you really think so?"

"I know my son. Sometimes he needs a push," Edna said. "Come around. And if your parents can spare you, it'd be wonderful good to have someone to drive James. Right now, it's one more hardship that'll be difficult for our family to bear." She climbed back into the buggy, and headed down the lane.

Rachel felt lighter, a burden lifted from her heart. She left her easel and the laundry and raced after the buggy.

"Edna!" she called. In a few loping strides, she had caught up with the buggy and waiting horse. "If it's okay with Mamm and Dat, what time do you need me?"

"Eight would be right fine." Edna's smile softened the creases in her face. "See you tomorrow, Gott willing."

Rachel ran inside to find Mamm. Driving James to Paradise would be a good way to help, and it would give them time together, every day. Oh, please, dear Gott, let Mamm and Dat say yes!

There was hope for James and her. A simple hope.

20

As soon as his mother had left for the Yoders', James had rolled out to the sugar shack, not sure what he would find there. He knew Gott's will would be done, but he hoped that he was in time to stop her from leaving.

It had been quite a day. With the first electric treatment and the buggy incident, James thought he would be exhausted when they reached home. Instead, something had come alive inside him when Mark turned the buggy onto the lane leading through the orchard. As if he could feel the hand of Gott upon his shoulder, James now knew what he had to do.

"Hallo?" he called out, watching for movement as crisp green leaves crackled in the breeze overhead. When he had knocked on the door to the sugar shack, there'd been no answer. Inside, ashes glowed in the woodstove, the wood supply dwindling. He'd been relieved to see her things there, her backpack on the ground. The sleeping bag was neatly spread on the bench.

What would his parents do if one of the girls decided to leave home and travel about like this? Surely Mamm would be riddled with worry over Verena . . . or Lovina or Hannah when their time for rumspringa came around. It was one thing to let a youth in rumspringa test the boundaries. But if a young person like Shandell asked for help, the Savior himself would not turn her away.

He rolled down the path that ran along the creek, minding to avoid the deepest ruts. Although the rest of the orchard was well-tended, no one groomed the land this far back, which was used just once a year for maple sugaring.

A movement in the scrub to the right caught his eye. He turned to find nothing . . . and then Shandell's head popped up from the bushes along the ravine.

"I'm so glad it's you!" She clasped a hand to her chest dramatically. "I thought I was in big trouble."

"Because you're not supposed to be here?"

"Exactly. I was just sitting by the water, trying to think of another place to go." The sun touched her hair, and it glowed, blue as the pond on a summer day. He hadn't noticed in the dim light of the sugaring shack last night.

Blue hair? This girl was full of surprises. "That's something for us to talk about."

"I know I told you I would leave," she went on, "but honestly? The last two nights were sort of cozy here, and I'm afraid the next place I try down the road won't be so kind to me."

"The sugar shack might serve you well until your mother comes. Let's talk about this a little bit." He turned his chair and wheeled around toward the woodpile. Time for her to earn her keep. "I see you're running low on wood. I'll show you how to split some more."

"Really? Okay." She walked alongside him, then skipped ahead, reminding him of an eager child. "I know where you keep the wood, but I couldn't find an ax."

"It's tucked away, so the blade doesn't rust." For the next few minutes, he became the teacher and Shandell was an interested student. From his chair, he was able to sink the ax into the first piece of wood. He showed her how to go for the center, to split along the lines. "Then after you hear it crack, you tap it hard against the stump to separate the remaining chunks and free your ax."

Resolve shone on her face as she pounded a few times and cracked the fat log into two manageable pieces of wood.

"There you go."

"Wow." She grinned, flexing her arms in the air. "I have mad lumberjack skills."

James couldn't help but grin. "I reckon." He showed her how to bundle the wood to make it easier to carry inside. And then Shandell set to splitting another log.

As she worked, she asked him what he did all day.

"Today I went into Paradise to see a doctor."

"Are you sick?"

Her questions came without embarrassment. She didn't realize she was crossing a line.

"I'm getting a new treatment. But it was a day full of excitement. On the way home, our horse got spooked and ran off the road."

"You're kidding me." She rested the ax blade on the ground with a thunk. "That must have been scary. Is everyone okay?"

"Lucky for us, Rowdy got slowed down when we tore through a field of spinach. But the field wasn't so lucky, I reckon." He took off his hat and rubbed the back of his neck. "We're going to have to do some more planting in the Yoders' field."

When she asked who had been driving, he told her about Mark, who couldn't be blamed for his inexperience at the age of twelve. "Though he should have listened to Mamm. Rowdy isn't ready to pull a buggy just yet."

"Awww. But that's sweet that your brother is trying to rehabilitate a horse."

"Ya. Mark is good with horses."

"Have you been in a buggy accident before?" she asked. "I mean, is that why you're in a wheelchair?"

He scratched the back of his neck. This girl had nerve, but he was beginning to mind it less and less. Since the accident, too many folks had been tiptoeing around him, as if they thought talking about his injury was going to make it worse. "Not a buggy accident. I was riding in a van, coming home from Philadelphia, and a car hit us on the highway."

Her eyes grew wide as she set aside an armful of split wood. "That's terrible. You'd never think of an Amish person being hurt in a car accident. Especially since you're not supposed to ride in cars, right?"

He explained that his district allowed members to be passengers in automobiles, but they could not own them or drive them.

"When was the accident?" she asked.

"January. I got knocked unconscious, so I don't remember much." He explained that the shoulder harness of his seatbelt had malfunctioned, so his spine was jolted when he doubled over. "I hit my head, too. I had a concussion, but that was easy to get over. The paralysis, not so much."

"I'm sorry to hear that." She frowned. "Were your legs broken?"

"My legs are fine; it's the spine that was damaged. The spinal cord. I've been through rehabilitation and some surgeries. It's a new treatment I started today. The doctors think I might be able to walk again. It's possible." He nudged his thighs with his fists. "Isn't it strange that legs in perfectly good condition can't work without the message from the brain?" *Like the empty shell of a man without Gott's light inside,* he thought.

"I never was good at science," she said. "I just think the whole human body is one of God's great miracles. Of course, my biology teacher didn't really want to hear that answer on a test." She fingered the gems in her ear. "I guess I'll never be a doctor."

"Me, neither. Plain folk don't go to school past eighth grade. We pick up a trade, work the family farm. We work close to home."

"I wish I had a job close to home," she said wistfully.

"There's always the cooking and cleaning."

She rolled her eyes. "That's not a job."

"But it needs to get done. Amish or English, everyone needs food and a roof over their head to live."

"That's true. I've learned that the hard way over the past few days." Bracing herself, she lowered the ax into the center of a fat log. A good strike.

"But you're also learning a skill," he teased. "Now you can split wood."

"Like I said, I have mad lumberjack skills. At least I'm learning something positive out of my bad choices." She drove the ax deeper into the wood.

"How did you wind up out here, anyway? Why did you come here, to Lancaster County?"

"At the time, the destination wasn't important. I just wanted to run, fast and far from home. Gary called it a road trip. He said we had a place to stay at his sister's house. We were going to ride through the countryside with no deadlines or commitments. That sounds like fun, right?"

"Mmm. I've never left Lancaster County, but some Amish folk travel once in a while. My mamm went to Florida with her family when she was a girl. She got to swim in the ocean." James and his siblings had always enjoyed her stories of the miles of blue water that met the sky on the horizon. Holding hands with her sisters and brothers, she had hopped over the incoming waves—like jumping rope. The salty spray. The way her feet sank into the sand as the tide pulled the floor out from beneath her.

"The ocean is great," Shandell said, pulling her hair to one shoulder, "but I've never been a beach bunny. I'm so pale. An hour in the sun, and I'm burnt to a crisp."

"You need a hat." James pinched the brim of his black hat as he turned it in his hands. "A hat and sunscreen."

"I'm just not a hat girl. Hats always squash my hair."

James nodded. "And you don't want to crush your blue hair."

When Shandell laughed aloud, it was a happy sound, like the breeze jangling the new leaves. "Are you saying you don't like my blue hair?"

"I didn't say that." He grinned. "But I might have thought it."

With another chuckle, she sat on the splitting stump and raked her hair back with both hands. "I really am a mess, James. I admit that. I guess it was easy to leave because I didn't have a lot of good things going on. I'm supposed to be graduating from high school, but I got a notice that I was failing algebra." She shook her head. "I didn't have much going on. I figured there was no reason to stay."

"But now . . . now you want to go home?"

"I do. I miss my mom. I miss the comforts of home. I'm a lousy camper, and I'm not a very good fugitive." She sighed. "Isn't this crazy? Me, sitting here telling you my life story like we're old friends."

"Ya." She was right on that. Many boundaries had been crossed between them—maybe too quickly—but there was no going back. "And with all your questions, you've gotten more out of me than most."

"You're the sanest person I've met in a long time." When he squinted at her, she added, "That's a good thing."

James frowned. He knew he should not get involved with this Englisher girl. She was not Plain and he suspected that she had been in more trouble than she admitted. It was not appropriate for a young Amish man to spend time with a young Englisher girl. And his father had become strict about separating from all Englishers. Every bit of common sense told him no.

But it was too late. He was already getting to know her. He was already involved. And his conscience kept reminding him of the Bible story of the Good Samaritan. He had to help her.

"I'd better get back to the house. I don't want to stir anything up, me being gone for too long." James knew his family would worry if he was gone for too long without anyone seeing him around the orchard.

That was how family was—something Shandell didn't seem to know about.

He put his hands on the rims of the wheels, then remembered the food in his satchel. "I brought you something." He reached into the side pocket and removed a thermos of milk, some biscuits, and hard-boiled eggs. "I know you brought granola bars, but no one can resist Mamm's biscuits."

"They look delish. Thanks." Her eyes grew wide as she picked out an orange egg. "Easter eggs! Mom and I used to make these."

"I'll pick up the thermos tomorrow. Probably in the afternoon." With the treatments in Paradise scheduled for each morning, James would have to switch his morning trip out to the sugar shack to later in the day.

"I'll be here. Not like I've got anywhere else to go." She shrugged. "I'm usually a night owl, but when you live in the woods without electricity, there's no reason to stay up. I figured that part out the past few nights. So, you're telling me it's okay to stay until my mom comes?"

What was he to do? James had always followed the rules of his father, but never before had he seen his father's rules cross the path of Gott. He knew there would be trouble if his dat found out, but his father never came out this way. No one but James bothered with this wooded end of the orchard.

He nodded. "Stay close to the shack and away from the orchards so no one's the wiser. There'll be a stir if my father or brothers see you. Stick close and you'll be safe here."

She called a good-bye as he rolled back under the canopy of green leaves, surrounded by birdsong. This was the first time in his life he had faced such a crossroads—one path leading to the approval of his father, the other showing him the way the Savior would have walked.

Maybe he was moving toward trouble, but his heart was light with surprising relief that he had followed the Golden Rule. Heading into the gentle breeze, James knew he would sleep well tonight.

21

"Rain, rain, rain," Rachel said with a sigh. The highway before them glistened, as fat drops tapped the umbrella she held over Ben and herself on the gray Tuesday morning. Stubborn Ben had insisted on taking his open buggy when he was asked to drop her by the Lapps' on his way to the feed store, and now the sky was opening up on them.

"I don't mind it," Ben said. "It's part of the growing season."

"Ya, but you're already full grown," she teased. She knew that the crops needed rain, but this morning she could have used a bright, sunny sky to boost her confidence. She wasn't sure how James would take to her driving him into town.

"There you go." Ben stopped the buggy at the top of the orchard lane. "Take that umbrella with you. I can't be bothered with it."

Holding the umbrella aloft, she climbed out of the buggy. "Don't get too wet," she told her brother.

Ben adjusted the brim of his black hat. "I'm like a duck. If I can't fly between the raindrops, I'll swim." With that, he called to the horse, and the buggy took off at a good pace.

Ben seemed to have two speeds on the road: fast and faster. Sometimes Rachel wondered if he would ever settle down. On the other hand, she could take a lesson from the way he plunged into things headfirst. Sometimes, Rachel let doubt hold her back.

She faced the narrow road that curved down to the white, two-story house trimmed in black where James and his family were no doubt in the midst of morning chores. *Ready or not, here I come.*

She considered going to the barn first. She might catch Luke and Peter on their way out to the orchard. Mark would be there, tending the horses before school, or maybe even hitching a gray carriage for them. Talking with his siblings would be a way for her to test the waters and gauge James's mood. But as she approached the house, she felt a presence, like the big eyes of an owl upon her.

And there he was, watching from his wheelchair on the covered porch.

Emotion was a fist inside her, tight and trembling, as she met his gaze and headed straight toward him.

"Rachel?" He tipped his hat back, his chin lifted in defiance as she reached the steps. "This isn't a good time for a visit. I'm leaving for Paradise soon."

Oh, why couldn't this be easier? "That's why I'm here." She paused under the overhang, letting her umbrella sway back on her shoulder. "I'm your driver."

The confusion in his smoky eyes tugged at her. "Why would you do that?"

Because I want to be with you. Because I would do anything in the world to help you. Because I love you . . .

There were so many answers, but she couldn't make her lips form the words.

"I asked her." Edna stood at the door, two fingers poised over the pink scar on her chin in a thoughtful expression. "We told Dr. Finley we'd get you there six days a week, and that's a big commitment. Rachel here is willing to help us out, and her parents can spare her, though I'm sure it's a hardship for them." She nodded to Rachel. "Tell Nate and Betsy we're ever so grateful."

Lowering her umbrella, Rachel gave a slight smile. It hadn't been easy, convincing her parents to reassign her usual chores. Rachel had promised to work harder when she was home to pick up some of the slack. Mamm had been reluctant, but Dat had pointed out that a person in need could not be denied goodwill.

"It's not as simple as that," James said. "Rachel doesn't know how to help me in and out of the carriage."

"But she can learn, like anyone else," Edna said. "Besides, your brothers will help you in on this end and the staff at the clinic will come out and get you into the wheelchair."

"I'm stronger than I look," Rachel said, shaking water from the umbrella. It would be best to steer clear of James's exchange with his mamm. Somehow, she wanted him to know this was Edna's idea, and not hers. She didn't want James to think she was sniffing after him like a hungry dog.

"So that's that," Edna said, smoothing down her apron. "I've got Mark hitching up a carriage for you. You'd best head down to the barn and get going so you won't be late. I'll bring out a lunch pail for you." She opened the door and disappeared inside.

Her hands wrapped around the hook of the umbrella handle, Rachel was afraid to look up at James, afraid to see resentment and rejection on his face. Staring at the window box of red and white pansies, she asked, "Want me to push you out to the barn?"

"I can do it." From the crisp tone of his voice, she knew it would be a long trip to Paradise. "And, Rachel?"

She had no choice but to look up and take in his handsome face: strong cheekbones and angles, and those smoky eyes that could take her breath away. Bracing, she pressed her lips together, fearful of what he might say.

And then his brown eyes warmed as he smiled. "*Denki.* Your good help is much appreciated."

Awash with relief, she nodded. Then, all too soon, the moment was over and she was following him down the ramp.

ⓖⓔ

The journey to Paradise went quickly, with James telling her about how the doctors had set up all the electrodes on his back to bathe his spine in electricity.

"And how does electricity feel?" she asked. Everyone knew that a bolt of lightning could kill a person in an instant, so it seemed odd to be using electricity as a cure for paralysis.

"It felt fine. Relaxing. A bit like a warm bath, but also like pins and needles when your foot falls asleep. The treatment is a piece of cake compared to the physical therapy. That's always like a hard day's work."

As he talked of the new doctors and technicians, Rachel's chest swelled with appreciation for the effort James put into his treatment. He tried so hard! He really gave it every ounce of strength that he had. She prayed that Gott would bless him with a cure someday. James would never give up.

At the clinic, the technician told her she would have at least a four-hour wait. Watching them wheel James down the hall, Rachel knew she would need to find something to fill the time. Why hadn't she thought to bring her paints or some mending? A sketchbook and some watercolors? It had been a while since she'd worked with the muted tones of watercolors, but she always enjoyed experimenting, blending and swirling simple lines of paint.

To pass the time, she decided to ride back to Halfway and visit with Elsie, whose Country Store was always a hub of activity. It would give Rachel a chance to check on her paintings and see if any had been purchased. Elsie had sold many of Rachel's canvases in the shop, and she'd always been encouraging about the prospect of placing them in the gallery in the city.

As she was tying Ranger to a hitching post, she could see that the shop was hopping with tourists. A small busload of women, all of them wearing red hats, were scattered through the shop like ants claiming the delicacies at a picnic. From her stool at the counter, Elsie juggled purchases and questions with her usual charm and grace. Ruben waited on customers in the aisles, measuring boxes of Amish-made fudge for them or carrying larger purchases out to the bus.

Seeing Rachel at the door, Elsie gave her a nod. "There's the artist herself—Rachel King. You can ask her your questions in person."

Rachel was joined at the counter by a woman with jet-black hair that swept gracefully over one eye. She wore a short brown leather jacket and a lovely patchwork skirt in blues, reds, and yellows that trailed the top of brown boots. Noticeably younger than the other ladies, this one wasn't wearing a red hat.

"Rachel?" The woman's brows lifted. "I'm Kiki Grant, a designer for Bailey and Flood."

Although Rachel had never heard of this Bailey person, she gladly shook the woman's hand.

"I was just asking Elsie if you do commissions because I have two customers who would be *thrilled* to have some of your pieces in their collections." Kiki pointed out a large painting, two by five feet, which showed a quilt blowing in the breeze from a clothesline. "I'm wondering if you might want to do two more quilt paintings on the same size canvas. One of my customers loves this piece, but she has a large space to fill, and three is such a perfect number in design."

"Two more paintings of quilts in a yard?" It was a scene that brought peace to Rachel's heart. Rendering the quilts was a challenge, as she needed to get the designs just right, but it was satisfying to see it come together. Almost like completing a quilt. Rachel had given most of her savings to the fund for James's medical bills, but she probably had enough left to purchase the large canvases. She could buy them today at the art supply store in Paradise.

"Wunderbar!" Kiki spoke the German word with a clap of her hands. "Your work will be the centerpiece of their great room, which they want to be cozy and Americana. And I'm sorely tempted by the Amish doll piece, too." Kiki wagged a finger at a small painting of a faceless boy doll with a little straw hat and pants with suspenders. "You really are a talent, Miss Rachel. I predict great success. Once people discover you, you're going to be a star."

"Oh, I'm not looking for that." Rachel's face grew warm with embarrassment at the idea of being compared to a beautiful sparkling star in the heavenly sky. "Don't get me wrong. I enjoy painting, and I do it because I know Gott gave me this talent. But I don't want to be singled out as someone special. Just because I paint pictures, it doesn't mean I'm better than anyone else."

"Talented and modest, too," Kiki said. "I respect that. I can keep your reputation as low-key or high-profile as you want."

Rachel shrugged. She had been hoping to support herself and James on the money she made by selling her paintings; she hadn't given a thought to reputation. "I don't want to attract too much attention." The bishop didn't mind her painting scenes of Amish life—things like farms and quilts, milk jugs and buggies—as long as she didn't show Amish folks in them. Rachel was content with that. But if her canvases got popular—if she became a star—that wouldn't be good. Folks would think she was full of pride, and she would be attracting a lot of attention for being special instead of blending in with the other Plain folk in Halfway. "I'll do the two paintings, but I don't want any fuss."

"That we can do," Kiki said with a wink.

The designer wanted to give Rachel a down payment to "lock in a commitment," as she said, but Rachel didn't think it was right to take money in advance. Kiki put a "sold" sign on the painting in the shop, and Rachel wrote down the size of the canvases Kiki wanted, the basic color scheme, and the date that they would be due. Maybe she could get some painting done while James was getting his treatment in Paradise. If she could work out something with Pepper, the owner of the art store there, it would be a very useful way to spend her waiting time.

By the time Rachel finished with Kiki, the red hat ladies were filing out of the store, heading into the bus parked out front. The quiet that fell over the shop was welcome. Now Rachel could enjoy the many treasures found here—the scented lavender soaps, the magnificent quilts, so full of love and artistry, the handmade birdhouses that resembled tiny homes with tiled rooftops and miniature porthole doors.

"Sometimes, I think I would like to be a little mouse," she told Elsie and Ruben. "So I could stay in your shop after dark and make a little home here. I could take a little nap on a handmade hot pad or make a cozy home in a birdhouse."

"Ya." Ruben grinned. "And you could grow fat on the cheese and fudge that we sell. You would never have to leave the shop."

"Oh, that's very cute." Elsie's face glowed with glee. "But dear Rachel, you don't have to be a little mouse to hide away in our shop. You are always welcome. Oh, and it seems we're already a hiding place. Didn't you hear we had an Englisher girl hiding in here, just a few days ago?"

"I didn't hear. What happened?"

As Elsie told her the story of the teenaged girl hiding from a very bad fella, Rachel picked up a small Amish doll in her hands and touched the miniature black kapp. There was something special about these faceless dolls, on account of each of them being different. Each one was special. They were handmade, usually with a little girl in mind. Rachel still had one that Mamm had made for her when she was little, and there were others in the house that had been sewn by Mammi Nell, dolls that Molly still played with when they weren't sitting on the shelf by her bed.

"How is it that this girl can be wandering on her own with no one caring about her?" Rachel asked when Elsie finished her story. "Does she have a mamm or dat?"

"In the end her mother came to get her," Ruben said. "But plenty of young people go wandering. What about the Amish youth who leave home during rumspringa?"

"That's true, but they seem different. I know their parents are wanting them back." Rachel looked to Elsie, who smiled. Neither of them had pushed the limits much during their own "running around" time. As her thumb moved over the stitching of the doll, Rachel wondered how long it would take to sew such a sweet little toy. One day, she would be making a doll like that for her own daughter. She bit back a smile. Oh, if only it was true! The ride in to Paradise had been marked by easy conversation with James, but he hadn't apologized or taken back his words. As far as he was concerned, they were no longer a couple.

But she had to put her faith in Gott. The Almighty had a plan for them, and Rachel felt sure they were supposed to be together.

She squeezed the doll as longing surged through her. Someday, Gott willing, Rachel would be James's wife, and her hands would work a needle through a tiny kapp to sew a doll for their little girl.

"So Kiki Grant wants to buy some paintings," Elsie said. "She's already reserved that one over there."

"That's a good sale," Ruben added as he carried a box off to the storeroom.

"Ya." Rachel smiled at his retreating figure, then leaned over the counter to confide in Elsie. "And the sale would be in the nick of time. I'm starting to save for a house for me and James. It might have to be specially built with a ramp and such, depending on how his recovery goes."

Elsie squeezed her hand, her mouth open in an O of surprise. "So you're moving toward marriage? Ruben and me, too. I guess we'll be in the same group for baptism."

"Oh, Elsie!" Rachel came around the counter and hugged her friend.

"It's going to be a busy wedding season," Elsie said as she patted Rachel's back.

I hope so. Now that she had let her hopes out of the bag, Rachel worried that it would never happen. What if James kept pushing her further and further away?

Although she knew her friend would understand, she couldn't share her doubts with Elsie. To say the words . . . that would give them too much power. She had to stay positive and prayerful.

She covered Elsie's hand with hers and held tight. "Looks like you and I are heading down the same road."

22

It was late Tuesday afternoon when Shandell stacked the last of the wood under the lean-to and grinned. Anyone who knew her in Baltimore would be shocked at how well she'd adjusted to this country life, chopping wood, building fires, and heating water on a stove. Why, she was a real nature girl, just like the reality show about those city slicker girls sent to a farm.

She could imagine a TV crew following her as she drew water from the creek and carried it up the bank of the ravine. The camera would catch the smile on her face as she swung the ax over her shoulder and hacked into a log.

She wiped her hands on her jeans and winced. Each hand had a raw red spot where a blister was forming. That was the downside of working with your hands. She would admit that she missed her coffee from Starbucks, but she would hold up her dead cell phone and attest to the fact that you really get a chance to think about things when you're not busy with texts and calls, tweets and Instagram messages all day.

"And don't forget to stow the ax under cover," she said aloud to the imaginary film crew, parroting the information the Amish guy had told her. She slid the ax into a leather sleeve and tucked it in the corner of the woodpile. "You don't want the blade to get wet and rusty. That will make your job even harder." Her friends would hate to be photographed in dirty clothes without any makeup, but none of that stuff mattered to Shandell right now. She was Nature Girl, surviving in the woods, all on her own!

Oh, there were a few things missing from her Nature Girl existence. The trek to the outhouse was a little creepy after dark, and the night wind whistled through the tiny shack. She missed the convenience of grabbing an apple or a yogurt from the fridge at home, and she kicked herself for not bringing ramen noodles or mac and cheese to make on the stove. Food would be an issue if she was planning to stay here for more than a few days. But in a couple of days she would be headed home. And now that she had shaken Gary off her trail, well, this was sort of like a little woodsy retreat, a time to think about all the stuff she kept tamped down in the back of her mind.

Sinking onto the tree stump, she stared at the dense clouds over the hills, lumpy as mashed potatoes. They caught the light of the setting sun in a purple and orange glow, pretty as a postcard.

When was the last time she had noticed a sunset? All this Nature Girl stuff was not part of her life in Baltimore. Nope. Most days when the sun set, she was holed up in Ryan's garage, playing pinochle or hearts or Ping-Pong. Wow . . . she'd been hanging there every single day in the past few months. What had begun as a way to avoid going home to Phil and the cloud of negativity that lingered over him had turned into a daily habit. In the beginning, she had sort of been keeping Kylie company, because Kylie liked Ryan but didn't think it was cool to be the only girl hanging in the garage with Ryan and Gary. And their friend Lucia had come along, so it was the five of them most days. Lucia had always lied to her parents, saying she was over at Kylie's house, because her father was a cop and he was really strict about where she could go and whom she could see. Shandell used to think Lucia's father was ridiculous, controlling his daughter's life. Now she could see that he was just concerned about his daughter; Mr. Bianco didn't want Lucia to make a mistake that would hurt her future.

The way I did?

She soothed the tender spot on one hand with her fingertips and pressed her lips together in resolve. She wasn't going to beat herself up about her mistakes anymore. The new Shandell, Nature Girl, was all about moving on. Surviving. Enjoying a sunset and a warm fire and the homemade biscuits James had brought her. She still had one left—a reserve that she was saving for dinner.

With one last glance at the replenished woodpile, she headed back around to the shack entrance. It would be dark soon, and she wanted to take advantage of the natural light to do a little reading in her book. She had learned that the light of the fire was too weak for reading, and she thought it best to save the kerosene lantern for an emergency. Although James had generously allowed her to stay here, she didn't want to take more than she needed. It would be good to get home, where she didn't have to worry about taking anything. As she carried a plastic chair outside to the light, she looked forward to the time when she could just turn on the light beside her bed and read day or night.

In a chair propped on the level ground beside the shack, she flipped through the colorful children's book, landing on a page with an illustration of Jesus sleeping on a pallet that resembled her red sleeping bag. That brought a smile to her face. It was always good to remember that Jesus had walked on this earth, just like everyone else.

The Bible story told about Jesus falling asleep on a boat under a peaceful, starry sky. Suddenly, the winds shifted and a terrible storm blew in. Rain dashed against the boat, which was tossed in the sea. When the frightened men on the boat woke him, Jesus ordered the wind and waves to stop. And just like that, the storm subsided.

Shandell hugged the open book to her chest, and turned to the heavy clouds over the purple hills. Was a storm on its way? When she was a kid, thunder and lightning had scared her. Many a night she'd fled her room for the safety of her parents' bed, where Mom would hold the covers down for Shandell to dive in between her parents.

"It's just a storm, Shanny," Dad would say, rubbing her shoulder.

And in the safety of that big bed, sandwiched between her parents, Shandell always found comfort and sleep.

"Hallo?"

She turned toward the friendly voice and saw James rolling down the path. "Hey there. I was just wondering if it was going to rain."

"Looks like it. From the way the wind shifted, I'd say we're due for a thunderstorm."

"Aren't you worried about being out in the open?" she asked. "You could get struck by lightning."

"Mmm." His dark eyes narrowed as he stared at the clouds over the foothills. "It's still a ways off." He nodded toward her. "What's that book you're reading?"

Her face warm with embarrassment, Shandell closed the book. "It's sort of babyish. A silly book, really. Just some Bible stories for kids."

"Doesn't sound silly to me." He held out one hand. "Let's have a look."

She held tight to the book, staring at its cover illustration of Jesus surrounded by a field of happy white sheep. Gary would have shredded her to ribbons if he'd seen her reading it, but she suspected that James would be more respectful. She handed it over.

"*Bedtime Bible Stories?* We have books like this at home." His brows rose, his interest obvious as he leafed through it. "A very good book. I know someone who would like the pictures, so full of color."

Relief eased her worries as he focused on the table of contents.

"Noah and the Ark. God's Promise. Make Me a Fisher of Men. The Lost Sheep." He nodded. "These are good stories. So why are you embarrassed? Just because the stories are written for children, it doesn't take the truth away from Gott's word."

He pronounced "God" with a hard accent—a sign of his Amish culture, she supposed. "You're right," she admitted. "It's just that I've had the book since I was really little. My dad used to read the stories to me, and now that he's gone . . . I don't know. It's my only real keepsake of him."

He nodded, handing the book back to her. "A good keepsake. But the best memories are in your heart, ya?" He pressed two fingers to his chest, and she wondered about the memories held tight inside him, like a vault of short, poignant films that no one but James could understand or savor.

"Memories of the heart, huh? That's a pretty deep concept."

"Nay." He brushed the notion away with a swipe of one hand. "It's just the way Gott made us." There was neither judgment nor praise in his voice, just the simple peace of a man who knew he was on solid ground. "Before I forget, I brought you something to eat."

From the side pocket of his wheelchair he produced a parcel of food covered in silver foil. It was heavy and still warm as she took it from him, and the scent made her mouth water. "Fried chicken?"

"Mamm made it for dinner. I had to get help from my brother Mark to snitch some away." He also handed her a jar of peaches and honey, a napkin with fat slabs of fresh-baked bread, a thermos of milk, and a warm plastic container of baked beans.

"This is a lot of food, and it smells delish. Thank you so much!" Her arms felt heavy and her stomach suddenly ached with hunger. Carefully, she set the food on the plastic chair. "Do you want some chicken now?"

Already James was maneuvering his chair around, pointing to the house. "I have to get back. I don't want to be late for supper, and it's best to be ahead of that storm."

"Well, I really appreciate you letting me stay." As she walked alongside him down the path, she pressed her fingertips to her blisters. It hurt, but it was a good pain, a sign of accomplishment. "I'll be out of your hair soon enough, but this is turning out to be a really special time for me. I mean, people would pay big money for this kind of peace and quiet."

"Why would they want to do that? If they stop the noise, the silence is free."

"That's true." But it wasn't about silence; there was a certain serenity out here, an inner peace that involved more than lack of noise. Was James aware of that, or was it something so second nature to him that he didn't see it? "Thanks again for bringing the food out. It's nice to have contact with another human being, but don't you worry that your family will get suspicious with you coming all the way out here?"

"This is what I do." He shook his head. "I come out here almost every day. It's part of my exercise routine. Besides, these rows of trees are my home. This is where I belong."

Shandell wished she knew where she belonged. She had a million other questions for him. She wondered why he didn't have a beard like other Amish men. She was curious about the clothes the Amish wore, especially those crisp linen bonnets worn by the girls. But she knew James had to get back to beat the storm, and she needed to peel off before she was in plain sight. Beyond the scrub and the thin line of trees, she could see where the path widened into a dirt road that ran alongside the prim, neat rows of trees. Time to let James go on his own.

"I'd better turn back. We don't want anyone to spot me. See you tomorrow?"

"I reckon." He wheeled himself ahead without looking back at her, but she didn't take offense. The Amish didn't dwell on formal manners or good-byes, but when it came to good deeds? From what Shandell had seen, they were first in line.

🖎 23 🖎

$\mathcal{A}$s James rolled toward home, he imagined himself riding a wave that carried him along to a safe shore, pushed by the hand of Gott, the same mighty hand that once parted the Red Sea for Moses and Gott's followers.

The wave had begun gathering this morning when Rachel had appeared on the front porch, telling him that she would be the one to drive him into town. Her blue eyes had seemed cool, even stern, but he could see her hesitance in the way her hands worried the pins of her white apron. And then, in that moment, he knew, and his heart sang.

He hadn't lost her, after all. Despite his attempts to push her away, to cut her loose and let her swim off like a glittering fish, she simply swam right back to him.

Within minutes of her arrival on the porch, they were talking and sharing stories like always. There seemed to be no wall between them as they traveled the road to Paradise. More than once, James had felt the urge to let his hand drift toward her, to touch her arm or brush against her leg. How he longed to pull her into his arms once again!

But he had resisted, reminding himself that he was still not the complete man she deserved to have as a husband. There was hope—that strong white dove, beating its wings steadily—but it had not landed. It had barely taken flight.

And then, the treatment. Gott be praised! The bath of electricity was bringing nerves and muscles in his legs to life again. None of the docs or technicians at the clinic had asked about results, and he had kept this news to himself. "We'll monitor our progress after seven days," Doc Finley had told him. But James wasn't sure he could wait that long to put his legs to the test. Tomorrow, if these pins and needles and muscle contractions kept happening, he was going to speak up.

Even the bristly concern over the Englisher girl in the sugar shack had not whittled down his enthusiasm. Shandell's attachment to the book of Bible stories had sweetened his view of her, and the more he talked with her, the more he knew in his heart that Gott had meant him to help her.

The Almighty didn't make mistakes. Gott had put Shandell in James's path for a reason, and James was sticking by his decision to help her.

He was still a good five minutes from the porch when the rain began to fall—fat, hard drops that pelted his hat and shoulders.

Let it rain, he thought, savoring the smell of damp earth and wet leaves. *Let Gott's love rain down on me.*

☙❧

At the supper table, James bowed his head for the silent prayer of thanks. There was a tension around the table, thick as Mamm's beef stew. Sixteen-year-old Matt kept his gaze down on his plate, and Peter was hunched over as if that might make him harder to see. Luke, Hannah, Lovina, Mark, and Verena were uncharacteristically silent as they helped Mamm serve and took their places at the table. After her bit of matchmaking, James would have thought Mamm would be pleased that he and Rachel had returned home today talking and laughing.

James wondered if Dat was still sore about him going into Paradise for the treatments. It seemed to James that his father thought he would simply give up, once Dat had handed down the rules that made the journey so difficult.

He waited for Dat to start the conversation, an unspoken supper tradition among Amish families. Biting through the crisp skin of a drumstick, James watched as Dat tucked into his mashed potatoes, then shot a hard look toward Peter and Matt. Those two were the wild ones of the family, but Peter usually got the brunt of disapproval on account of him being older.

"Tomorrow is another day," Dat said. "But there aren't enough hours in the day to make up for neglected chores." His dark brows drew together. "Playing baseball while there's much work to be done?"

James blinked. This was news to him.

"But Dat, when you told us to help hoe and reseed the Yoders' spinach, you said it would take all morning and most of the afternoon," Matt said, his eyes lowered respectfully.

"Ya. But did I tell you to spend the rest of the day playing baseball with the Yoder boys?"

So that was the reason for the discomfort that hung over the supper table. James chewed slowly, relieved that he wasn't involved.

"That was only because we finished the field work early," Peter explained.

"Peter." Dat held a piece of chicken aloft. "You're nineteen. You know better than that."

"Did you fix the field first?" Mark asked. The boy obviously felt responsible for his horse's damage to the Yoders' spinach. "Is it hoed and planted?"

"It's all done." Matt nodded reassuringly. "Emanuel Yoder said we did a right good job. And before we knew it, Leah was setting out a dinner for us."

"And then when Manny and Steven needed two more for a game . . ." Peter shrugged.

"We'll talk no more about it," Dat said. "The more pressing matter is when are we going to get to the fertilizing? We're more than halfway through April and Luke tells me it's barely been started."

"What's that?" With a stab of alarm, James turned to Luke. "I've told you for weeks that April is the month for fertilizing . . . everything but—"

"The peach trees," Luke finished for him. "I know, you've said it enough times. But without you leading the way, it's just not getting done."

James knew that it was hard to corral Peter and Matt. He knew that work in the orchard could be tedious. But his brothers didn't seem to understand what was at stake: the health of the trees, the quality of the fruit, the future of this land that had been in their family for generations.

James's sisters, who had watched the scolding of their brothers in silence, now piped in.

"I can help in the orchard," Hannah said, her lips shiny with oil from the chicken.

"Me, too," eleven-year-old Lovina agreed. "I'm not that tall, but I can climb a ladder."

"And you can count me in, if Mamm can spare me in the house," Verena said.

"Of course I can."

"That's all good, but it may be too little too late," Dat said. "I have half a mind to hire someone on through the harvest. Old Jacob knows a man who used to run a fruit farm up in Lebanon Valley. He's living with his children now in Paradise. A man like that would prove mighty helpful to all."

"No!" The objection was out before James could temper his reaction, but he couldn't sit here and follow along like a trusting sheep while his father hired a man to replace him. All eyes were upon him as he tried to explain. "We don't need to bring in an outsider. We can get it done, I know we can. Besides, it would cost us money to do a job that's always been done by this family."

"I don't want it any more than you, James, but there's a lot at stake here." Dat tossed a bone onto his plate and scanned the table with stern eyes. "Something's got to change, even if it means me stepping away from the business end to be a foreman."

Dread was evident on the faces of James's siblings at the thought of that. Dat did not have his father's skill for managing the orchard.

"Then who would keep up the business end?" Mamm asked, concern in her eyes. "A plentiful harvest can be wasted if you don't get it out to market in time."

"Hmm." Jimmy grunted. "It's a matter that needs some thought. In the meantime, we'll put every ready hand to work." He turned to James. "I know you've got the treatments and all, but can you make the time to supervise for the time being?"

"In the morning, every morning," James said, determined to get the orchard back on track. "They don't need me at the clinic until ten or eleven. We can do what it takes, Dat. If we work together, the fertilizing will get done."

"I hope so," Jimmy said. "I'm counting on all of you. Any more neglect, and we'll have to hire someone."

That will not happen, James vowed. *Not while I am able to roll myself out into the orchard.*

24

*T*hat night, Rachel could not fall asleep. Her feet were cold, her pillow was flat, and her heart ached with worry and hope for James. Finally giving up, she pushed back the covers and slid out of bed. The floor felt like ice beneath her bare feet, so she slipped on a pair of socks and wrapped a blanket over her shoulders. Treading lightly up the stairs to her old bedroom, she considered getting her paint tubes and brushes out. It would be nice to get started on the paintings for Kiki, but she didn't have the canvases yet, and she had decided that her time would be better spent painting at the Paradise art store while she was waiting for James.

The door was ajar, and she yawned as she pushed it open. She was far too tired to paint, but the little window seat was a good spot to think and pray. When she tucked her feet under her and pressed her palms to the cold glass, she could see a field of stars shining between the thin clouds.

"Oh, dear Gott," she whispered, sending her prayer up to the heavens, "I'm so grateful that James has opened his heart again."

The sight of the starry sky brought her comfort. The twinkling pinpoints of light reminded her of a little song called "Tell Me Why," which she sang with Mamm and her sisters while doing chores. The song had so many questions: Tell me why the stars shine, why ivy twines, and why the sky is blue. And the answer to all the questions? Because Gott made things that way.

Her breath was clouding the window, and she rubbed the glass clear with the edge of the blanket. It was silly to think that she was going to solve her future with James in one night. You couldn't sew an entire quilt in a day. Right now she needed to quiet her racing mind.

"Rachel?" Rose murmured from the bed. She rolled over and opened one sleepy eye. "What are you doing?"

"I couldn't sleep, and looking at the stars always calms the heart."

"Mmm." With a deep breath, Rose propped herself up on one elbow. "How come you can't sleep?"

Rachel shrugged. "Different things. Mostly thinking about James."

"You'll catch a chill by that window." Rose scooted over and patted the mattress beside her. "Kumm."

The sheets were still warm from Rose's body, and Rachel sank into the cozy cocoon of blankets. Snuggled beside her sister, Rachel felt her mind easing. Here, she could be a girl again; a sister, a daughter.

"What's happening with James?" Rose asked groggily. "Mamm said you're driving him into Paradise every day."

"It's a treatment the doctors are testing, and I need to drive him to the clinic every day."

"That's a lot of travel by buggy. Can't he hire a car?"

Taking the shortcut of sisters, she quickly explained the concerns of James's father and the bishop. She told Rose how James had tried to cut her off, how she had refused to end their courtship, and how, out of the blue, James's mother had come over to ask her to drive him to his new treatment. "That was a big surprise, seeing Edna come down the lane looking for me. But in the end, it's all an answered prayer. Gott's smiling down on me."

"But I don't understand." Rose stifled a yawn. "If it's all good news, why can't you sleep?"

"It's just that I'm not sure what James is thinking of me now, after he tried to break it off. He seems like the same old James, but I don't want him to feel like he's stuck with me just because I'm the person driving him to Paradise nearly every day."

"Seems to me it would be the other way around. What with James not being able to walk and all. Don't take this the wrong way, but do you worry about being stuck with him? Especially if he has to spend the rest of his life in a wheelchair."

"I love him, Rose. For better or worse. I know we haven't taken vows, but he's the one for me. We're two peas in a pod."

"What a wonderful thing, to be so in love. I hope it happens for me someday. There's no boy that even looks at me twice."

"What about Eli Esh?"

"He's nice and all, but I think he'd rather be off fishing with his friends. My feelings for him are not strong and sweeping as a fierce wind. I want a love like that. Such sureness in your heart that he's the one you'll spend the rest of your life with."

"It will happen for you, Rose. You're just sixteen."

"And no fella has ever even given me a ride home. I'm miles away from a love like that."

"But it will happen. Gott wants you to have a husband and a big, loving Amish family. He wants our children to play together, to help each other in the fields, and to work side by side at quiltings."

"I hope so. Back before the accident, when I would see you with

James, the way he smiled for you and the way you looked at him . . ." Rose tucked her hands under her chin and sighed. "It made me all wobbly inside. I knew it was true love."

"And you could see that? Really?" Rachel smiled. "You must have very good eyes, indeed."

"Everybody could see it. Not so much, anymore. Since the accident, James is like a closed book. So quiet, and the only time he comes around is for church. How do you get him to talk?"

"Sometimes he doesn't talk at all. But today? Once we got going, he was the James I fell in love with." Rachel burrowed her cheek into the pillow as sleep nipped at her. "I still love him so. I just hope he feels the same way toward me."

"Hope is a very good thing," Rose said in a woozy voice. "One of the three things that last, ya? That's what the Bible says."

"Faith, hope, and love." Rachel closed her eyes, content now as she remembered the words of Gott: *And the greatest of these is love.*

ҩҩ 25 ҩҩ

*A*s the technician hooked up the last of the electrodes for his treatment, James took a deep breath and tried to still his racing thoughts of the orchard and Rachel and the charley horse in his left leg that had ached during the night.

Like the first rays of dawn, the feeling in his legs was beginning to return, pale and quiet, but undeniably bright and promising. Although James had told no one, the tingling stream of electricity was awakening sensation in his legs. So far, his new strength hadn't been put to the test, but Doc Finley said they would give it a try today.

"I know it's only the third day of your treatment," the specialist had told James, "but some patients respond more quickly than others." The doctor had cautioned that it was only Wednesday, and whether or not James showed a response, they would stick with the protocol for three to six months, as long as James was willing.

James had simply nodded. The aches and tweaking muscles in his legs had awakened him last night, but he didn't want to say anything, for fear that the ripples of sensation were all in his head. He knew that phantom pain and sensation seemed very real. Every Amish boy had heard the stories of men who had lost a leg or finger in a farm accident and still suffered aches and burning from their missing limbs. He hoped and prayed that this was not the story with his legs right now.

With his hopes locked on to that moment of truth, James gave his worries up to Gott in a prayer and tried to relax as the technician checked the monitor and electrodes. James had exchanged his black pants for soft black shorts that gave easy access to his legs, which were now covered with suction cups the size of large mosquito bites. He had been fitted with a harness full of equipment, though it did not look like any harness he'd ever put on a horse. The truth? It looked like a big diaper, swaddling his crotch and hips. Thank the good Lord it was black instead of white.

"Okay, we're ready to turn on your electromassage," the technician said with a grin.

James gave a thumbs-up. "I'm good to go."

Chet was a joker. When he'd been introduced to James, the tech had pointed to his own bald head and said that it was shaped like a lightbulb—proof that he was born to be an electrical engineer. Every day he had a new joke for James, who was glad to have some chuckles to add to his toolbox.

As Chet turned the switch, James leaned back and closed his eyes. He had best take advantage of this soothing treatment while he had a chance. The electrical current wasn't painful; the soft tickle was like the bristle of a callused hand against a new wool coat. When the doctors had described the treatment as a "warm bath of electricity," they weren't joking. When the machine was hooked up, he felt like a cat napping in the sun.

He closed his eyes, ever grateful for the hope this treatment brought him. *Thank you, heavenly Father.*

The minute he'd rolled out of his room this morning, he had found most of his brothers and sisters waiting to get to work in the orchards.

"Verena and I went around and woke everyone at four-thirty," Mamm had admitted as she handed James a thermos of hot coffee. "You were right about sharing the workload. If we're going to keep the orchard running the way your doddy did, everyone in the family needs to pitch in."

James thanked his mother for the coffee and tucked it into the side pouch of his wide-wheeled chair. The ground was damp from drizzling rain and the night had not yet lifted, but many of his siblings wore LED lights strapped to their heads so that they could see in the dark. James had each of the twins hitch a horse to a cart, which they brought around to the manure pile.

"We'll load each cart with manure, and then divide up into two teams," James said, explaining how they would use wheelbarrows to deliver fertilizer to the mound beneath each tree. "We'll go down each lane, beginning to end, and when we finish a row, we mark it with orange tape around the trunk of the tree at the end." The older boys had spread fertilizer before, under Doddy Elmo's watchful eye, but no one but James seemed to recall the different steps and procedures.

Mark dug his shovel into the edge of the compost heap, then turned back, his face pinched in revulsion. "Why is it still so stinky?"

"It's chicken manure," Luke said with a broad grin. "It's not supposed to smell good."

Lovina flicked the strings of her prayer kapp back over her shoulders and lifted her shovel. "I hope we don't smell like manure all day at school."

"Teacher Emma will understand," Mark said.

"Ya," Lovina muttered, lifting her shovel to the back of the cart. "But I don't want to smell bad, no matter how nice the teacher is."

Everyone had chuckled over that. Mark and ten-year-old Hannah, who usually took more to working outside than helping Mamm with chores in the house, merrily dug right in, though Verena and Lovina tried to keep away from the fertilizer as much as they could.

Once the carts were loaded and taken to the orchard, James pointed out where to spread the manure so that all the feeder roots were covered. "Spread it a little bit more," James instructed. "To the drip line. See how Luke is doing it? The fertilizer should go from the tree trunk to under the outermost branches."

His siblings could be good workers when they put their minds to it. James was grateful that they were all pitching in. By the time Mamm called them in for breakfast, they had filled and spread four carts of manure, covering about an eighth of the orchard. James hoped they could get enough work done to keep Dat from bringing in a stranger to run the orchard.

Soon after breakfast, Rachel had come walking up the lane with an umbrella overhead, bright and crisp as a school bell in autumn. The sight of her reminded him of the huge stone inside him; the immovable boulder that would not let him be her fella again until he was healed. Oh, the temptation was there to fall back into their regular patterns, and there was no denying that he enjoyed every minute of Rachel's company. But he could not tether her for the rest of her life. The thought of a future without her made him ache inside, and yet that was how it had to be unless Gott granted him a miracle and gave him the power to rise onto his own two feet.

"Am I interrupting a nap?" The familiar voice brought James out of his reverie. He opened his eyes to find Dylan standing inside the doorway, his arms crossed over a denim jacket with a fleece collar.

James waved him in. "Not much else I can do while I'm hooked up here."

"This is great, getting all juiced up." Dylan nodded, taking in the many electrodes with wires running from James back to the machine. "How's it feel?"

"Like a warm bath, with a few pine needles on the bottom of the tub."

"Honest as ever." Dylan chuckled. "I'm glad you're here, James. I wanted to check in before I head out. I'm off to Chicago for a wedding. An old college buddy. But before I left, I wanted to make sure you'd worked out the transportation issue."

James explained that Rachel was driving him.

"So your father is on board, then? He approves of the treatment now that you're coming by horse and buggy?"

"Dat doesn't have much hope for the treatment, but he'll allow it."

"Glad to hear it. And Rachel is your ride?" Dylan touched his chin, his eyes thoughtful. "That's an interesting development."

James didn't answer. He had told Dylan of his doubt about the future of his relationship with Rachel.

"How's that working out, buddy?"

"It's wonderful and terrible, all at the same time." James explained that he'd broken away from Rachel, but she refused to give up.

"I admire her spunk," Dylan said. "Perhaps she thinks your relationship is strong enough to withstand the obstacles of your injury."

James grunted. Sometimes Dylan used words that didn't have a whole lot to do with real people.

Dylan stepped toward the wall to examine a picture of a covered bridge. "So would you say things are going more smoothly with your father?"

Another grunt. "Not to complain, because I'm grateful for the good roof and food my parents provide. But every time I turn around, my father makes another decision that pushes me down. Yesterday, he said he's thinking of hiring a foreman—a stranger—to come manage the orchard. He wants to replace me."

"Whoa. First of all, no man can replace his oldest son. That's a role you've got for life. And I'm not sure it's such a bad idea to bring in someone to manage the place while you finish your treatment. You've been to hell and back, James. You deserve time to recuperate, and your family needs someone to run the orchard while you're gone."

"Gone? I'm not going anywhere. Just a trip into town for treatment a few hours a day. I can run the orchard."

Wincing, Dylan held his palms up. "I'm just sayin', it sounds to me like Jimmy is trying to give everyone a break. I would try to keep an open mind on that front."

James bit back a response. He didn't want to argue with Dylan, who had reached out to James when no one else made any sense. But Dylan didn't understand that it was up to Amish sons to keep the family business going. He didn't see that bringing in a stranger would be another loss to James, a failure in so many ways.

Just then Chet returned, and James was grateful for the distraction. Talking with Dylan usually made James feel better, but today . . . today everything was winding him up tighter.

Chet turned off the machine and parked a wheelchair beside James. As James began to tear at the Velcro attachments of the harness, Chet stopped him. "You're gonna leave that on. Doc Finley wants to check your progress before the two to three hours of hard labor. We're going to use the PT room because it's got the platform and support rails we need." He moved the machine away from the wall and pulled out two hefty plugs. "I've got to wheel this equipment down there since you'll be harnessed up for the test."

"Wait." This was news to James. "Are you saying that I'll need to be hooked up to an electric machine whenever I want to walk?"

"Uh . . ." Chet rubbed his chin. "At least in the beginning. That's the way I understand it. You'd better ask Dr. Finley to explain that."

Dylan tagged along as James rolled down the hall to the PT room, a wide-open space with stairs and platforms used by patients learning to increase mobility and strength. Dylan went off to take a phone call while Chet went to find Dr. Finley.

On the far side of the room, an elderly woman moved slowly, pushing a walker. The therapist walking in front of her smiled.

"That's right, Mrs. Freeman. Just remember not to pivot when you turn. That knee isn't ready to be twisted yet."

The elderly woman paused, her gaze sweeping over to James. "I got a brand-new knee, just two days ago," she told him.

"And you're walking already?" James nodded. "Good for you."

Mrs. Freeman smiled. "Give me another week and I'll be dancing," she said with a wink. "What are you in for, son?"

"I'm getting a treatment to help me walk again," James said. "Automobile accident."

"Well, you're in the right place." When the woman came closer, James could see the soft, wrinkled skin of her face, and the quick, dark eyes that reminded him of his grandmother. Mammi Miriam lived with his aunt in Bird-in-Hand, too far to visit often, and James missed her quick responses and humorous stories.

"This is my second bionic knee," Mrs. Freeman went on, "and I'm pleased as punch with the first one. My husband says he'll never be able to catch up with me now. He's a year older than I am."

"Maybe you will slow down for him," James said. "If you want to be caught."

The Englisher lady swatted at him dismissively. "Oh, Arty caught me fifty-two years ago and I've been a blushing bride ever since."

James grinned. He liked Mrs. Freeman's sense of humor, and talking with her was a good way to occupy his mind during this tense time. They chatted for a few more minutes while Chet rolled in the machine and set it up. Mrs. Freeman kept up her walking, gently guided by the therapist.

Like a gathering flock of birds, they came. JJ, the physical therapist with the black cross inked on his neck, came in. Dylan returned and Dr. Finley sauntered in with two assistants trailing him like ducklings.

"Let's see how you're doing. Are you ready to try and stand up?" Dr. Finley asked. Dressed in a bow tie and baggy pants, Alec Finley had a round, pink face with a large nose. The man always reminded James more of a circus clown than a medical doctor.

"I want to stand," James said, "but I thought I'd be doing it on my own, without the electricity." He pointed to the machine. "I can't be taking that thing around with me everywhere."

"No, you can't," Finley said. "But right now, you need it to get started. Let me explain how this works. We used to think that the spinal cord was just a conductor for the brain—sort of like a telephone line carrying messages, if you will. I know you're Amish, but you understand how electric service works."

James nodded. "If wires aren't attached to your home, you won't have a working telephone."

"Right. So we thought that the message to move your legs had to come from the brain, down the spinal cord and to the legs. And that's how things usually work. But we've learned that sometimes, when the spinal cord has been damaged, we can restore the connection between the muscles in the legs and the nervous system with a little electricity flowing into the lower spinal cord. We have been able to make the leg muscles function without any input from the brain." Doc Finley pressed his palms together in prayer position and touched his fingertips to his chin. "That's the treatment in a nutshell; what we're trying to do for you."

"And I hear you've had success with the treatment," Dylan said.

"There was one remarkable case, an athletic young man around the same age as James. He has worked very hard in rehab—hours a day—but he has managed to stand on his own and walk with some assistance."

"The exercises and PT are not a problem for me," James said. "I'll do what it takes."

"And so will we," Dr. Finley said earnestly. "Let's give it a try."

Chet and JJ, the physical therapist, helped him onto a high bench that faced U-shaped support bars. After the electrodes were checked, JJ instructed him on how to plant his feet solidly on the floor and slide forward.

"You can use your arms to lift you at first," JJ said, "but try to use your legs and abs. Contract the muscles, the way we do in PT."

Everyone seemed to be holding their breath, their eyes on James. Over in the corner, Mrs. Freeman sat watching, her dark eyes shining.

With a hearty breath, James leaned forward and braced his legs.

The room was silent as he pulled the muscles in his legs tight, tighter, tighter, and leaned forward. Pushing at the earth with all his strength and might, he straightened at the waist and rose, standing tall.

The silence stretched out for a moment, and then there were happy murmurs, smiles, and even applause. Mrs. Freeman clapped rapidly, bobbing in her seat. Doc Finley's face lit with a wide smile, and Dylan gave a hoot and whistle of excitement.

A strange mix of emotions churned in James's belly as he stood there, wobbling only slightly. Ya, there was joy at this success, but there was also disappointment that he needed the electric harness to make his legs work and fear that this was as far as he might ever progress. Although James was no stranger to strong emotions, this complexity of being soaked by so many contrary feelings all at the same time was new to him.

He wanted to laugh and cry, all in the same breath.

He was still far from climbing a ladder in the orchard, but he was making progress. Inch by inch, step by step, he was on his way to being a man again.

❧ 26 ❧

*T*hursday morning Shandell awoke as the pallid sunlight filtered in through the cracks of the shack. From the small porthole of a window she could see that the sky was gray, but rain did not dampen her hopes.

Today was the day. She would be so relieved to give Mom a hug and sit back in the car, heading home. She wondered if Mom felt the same excitement that bubbled inside her. Not that Shandell thought she was returning home to a perfect life. Her time here, all the quiet time, had got her thinking about that, and she'd realized that many of the bad parts of her life couldn't be changed right now.

She couldn't see more of Mom, because Chelsea Darby needed to work two jobs right now.

She couldn't cure Phil's drinking problem. No one had the power to get Phil off the couch and back to work until Phil wanted to change his life.

And she probably couldn't fix her math grade before the end of the school year.

Shandell wasn't expecting a fairy-tale ending to this trip, but she was looking forward to the two-hour drive to talk with Mom, just the two of them. They were two smart cookies, and if they put their heads together, Shandell was sure they could come up with a plan to make things better.

A plan for happiness.

Sliding out of the sleeping bag, she hopped across the cold wood floor and quickly added some wood to the embers. Before long it blazed into a flame, chasing the chill from the air. That was better.

The smell of burning wood had become a familiar, cozy part of her day. By the warmth of the fire she changed from her pajamas to her jeans and hoodie. This outfit was in need of a wash, but it would have to do until she got home.

On the way to the outhouse, she pulled her hood up to keep away the drizzling rain. The dirt path was soft with mud, the grasses glimmering with raindrops. It must have rained through the night. How lucky she was to have had a roof over her head these past few nights. She was really grateful to the Lapp family. Even though James couldn't tell his parents that he was letting her stay in the sugaring shack, she prayed that God would bless the family for their son's generosity.

Back in the house, she took the foil-wrapped packet that James had brought her last night and placed it near the fire to warm. The casserole, which James called Yummasetti, had been delicious, with noodles, ground beef, cheese, peas, and a creamy sauce. Lucky for her, he'd brought enough for her to make two meals out of it. He didn't have time to talk yesterday, and she suspected that he'd wheeled himself out here to the back of the orchard just to bring her some food. It was really, really nice of him. James was the opposite of Gary, sort of the big brother she'd never had. While the casserole warmed, she grabbed two clean buckets and headed down to the stream to collect water for heating.

This is my last morning here, she thought as she walked down the path. Tomorrow, she would just go into the bathroom, turn on the faucet, and there would be instant hot water.

She was grinning about the thrill of such basic comforts when her shoe slipped on a bald patch of mud. As her arms went up to catch her balance, the buckets went flying, and both shoes slid out from under her.

"Oof!" With a cry, she fell, landed on her bottom, and slipped down the incline until she could dig in her hands and heels to stop the momentum. When she managed to stand, her hands, shoes, and pants were a muddy mess. She wasn't hurt, but smelly brown muck streaked the back of her jeans and hoodie.

"Oh, not now, please!" Shandell could hear Mom's voice telling her: "You're not getting in my car with those jeans!" She would have to wash them and hope that they would dry by the fire before she had to head into town this afternoon.

Bending down at the edge of the stream, she rinsed her hands for as long as she could stand the icy water, and then filled the two buckets. The powdered soap she'd found in the cabin would come in handy. She would be doing a load of laundry as soon as she could get the water heated.

She turned toward the riverbank, then paused. These jeans needed some serious work. It seemed wrong to walk around half-naked out here, but there was too much mud on her jeans to clean them in the bucket. Shandell found a stone to stand on as she slipped off her boots and jeans. Her bare legs were more embarrassing than cold. With gritted teeth, she squatted beside the stream and submerged her blue jeans. They floated for a moment like a disembodied soul, then sank down, heavy and dark in the water. She scrubbed vigorously, her teeth chattering as the frigid water chilled her to the bone.

With most of the mud rinsed off, she did her best to wring them out, though her fingers were nearly numb from the cold. She rose, draped the dripping jeans over one bucket, and headed back to the cabin, laughing at her final act as Nature Girl. Yeah, she was going out with dramatic flair.

27

Oh, the lengths Rachel King would go to so that James would be surprised!

She chuckled aloud as she approached the back acres of the Lapp orchard, her arms loaded down with baskets of food and a thermos of milk. Her brother Abe had offered to give her a ride past the Lapp house, all the way to the path leading to the sugar shack. "It's raining. You'll be soaked by the time you reach the barn."

"It's just drizzling," she had insisted, pointing to the side of the road where he should pull over. "And a little bit of rain never hurt anyone." She had hopped out at the beginning of the lane, removed her goodies from the buggy, and set off down the path behind the Doddy house, away from the orchards, where she figured James and his brothers and sisters would be working. She didn't want to be spotted as she trekked to the sugar shack. James didn't expect to see her for another two hours or so, and she wanted to use that time to sweep the cobwebs and critters out of the sugar shack so that later they could simply enjoy their indoor picnic.

The picnic had been Rose's idea. "You and James need some quiet time together to talk," Rose had told her. "I know you chat during the ride into Paradise, but it's different with you having to mind the horse and the traffic and all. A picnic would be just the thing. You'll have a chance to put words to the way you feel, and he'll have a chance to answer without feeling put out because his girlfriend is the driver."

"Why, Rose King, I think you've got that right. How do you know so much about the way a fella thinks?"

Rose squinted, her nose wrinkling. "I listen when the older girls talk at singings. And I read the magazines while I'm waiting for Mamm at the pharmacy in town. You wouldn't believe some of the things that men are thinking."

"I'm sure I can't. But a picnic is a good idea. I can bake something. James's favorite cookies, the cocoa drops."

"And a good, hearty meal. Some chili or a wiggler casserole." Rose wrapped the end of one of her kapp strings around a finger. "They say that the way to a fella's heart is through his stomach."

"Such good advice," Rachel said with a smile. "Watch out, little sister. Once those fellas at the singings figure out how smart you are, they'll be lining up to take you home."

"You're just saying that because you're my sister." But despite her denial, there was a glimmer of pleasure in Rose's eyes.

"Ya. I'm your sister and I love you and it's all true," Rachel said firmly.

Now, as Rachel made her way past the second barn, she thought of the new friend she had found in her sister. That night in Rose's room had bonded the sisters in a special way. It had helped Rachel to share her worries, and it seemed that Rose had been waiting for a hand to help her navigate into the teen world of rumspringa. At a time when boys could be very judgmental and some girls could be even worse, Rachel wanted her sister to know that her family loved her just the way she was.

Rose had helped Rachel bake fudge cookies for the picnic, and this time Rose got all the measurements right—not too much salt, and just the right amount of butter. By necessity, lunch would be leftovers, although no one had ever turned away Mamm's cheesy casserole. And just this morning, as Rose had helped Rachel pack a hamper, she had asked about the business end of the Lapp orchard.

"How is everything going out there?" Rose had asked. "Folks are saying that the orchard may be in trouble. The Lapps can't stay on top of it all, what with James away at his treatments and still not able to do the work he used to."

"It's true," Rachel said sadly. "James is worried that his dat will hire a foreman, someone to see them through the harvest."

"That might save the orchard, but it will cost a lot of money," Rose pointed out.

"But most of all, it will be a setback for James. He feels like his father is pushing him out of the orchard, pushing him away."

Rose clucked her tongue. "Such a sad time for James. But a meal like this is sure to boost his spirits!"

Now, as Rachel passed through the border of green shrubs and trees thick with bud at the back of the orchard, she spotted the sugar shack in the distance. Oh, how she missed those sweet days with James in the shack. Back then she didn't have to argue her way into James's arms. He had been more than happy to pull her close and take her breath away with a kiss!

The sugar shack had been the first place she had thought of when it became clear that the weather was not cooperating with her plan for a picnic. And since it was right here on the Lapp farm, it would be easy to bring James out to this cozy little hut once they returned from his treatment in the late afternoon.

As she drew closer to the shack, she noticed that the woodpile was stacked high against this side of the building, and a puff of smoke rose from the chimney.

That slowed Rachel's pace. Someone was out here. Who? Who had built a fire? It was too late in the season for maple sugaring, and besides, James had told her that his family hadn't collected sap this year. Who was in there?

Perhaps it was a drifter, taking cover in the shack. More likely it was one of James's brothers, sneaking out here to avoid chores or find a bit of quiet. She couldn't blame them for that, but she hoped whomever it was would let her use the sugar shack this afternoon for her little surprise.

Rachel approached the shack with caution, slowing as she reached the door. She knocked and called out a hello, but there was no answer. Not a very friendly response. Concern rippled through her, and goose bumps rose on her arms. Was she intruding in a place where she didn't belong?

Checking nervously over her shoulder, she noticed a movement by the ravine and spun around. Someone was there.

"Hallo?" she called out.

Two buckets now stood on the edge of the muddy path, and Rachel headed over toward them. "Who's there?" she called.

A head poked up from the embankment—an Englisher girl with a hood covering most of her head.

Rachel's jaw dropped in surprise. The girl seemed too young to be a drifter. A moment later her surprise shifted to shock as the young woman climbed the rest of the embankment revealing a flash of bare legs. Rachel blinked, her mouth a round O of surprise.

The Englisher girl's eyes were round and full of fear, like a deer ready to spring. She shifted a piece of dark fabric in front of her bare lower body, but it did little to cover the expanse of pale flesh from her hips to her boots.

"Hey," the girl said, forcing a smile. "Are you James's sister?"

This girl knew James? "No. I'm . . . his friend. Who are you?"

"My name is Shandell. I . . . um . . ." She shifted uncomfortably, shivering and apparently trying to hide behind the dark, wet fabric. "This is so embarrassing and awkward. I slipped in the mud and gunked up my jeans, so I rinsed them in the river and . . . and now I just want to get inside to warm up a little."

Well, that explained why the girl was half naked, though Rachel couldn't imagine what she was doing here. "Better get inside," Rachel said.

Shandell bolted toward the door, leaving it open behind her, and Rachel followed her in, feeling like a stranger in this very familiar place.

Inside, a fire burned heartily in the stove. Rachel turned away as the girl began to step into some pants, but not before noticing that the plastic chairs were arranged across from the bench, like a little living room, and the floors, walls, and ceiling had been swept clean. She placed her hamper and bags on the old wooden table beside neatly arranged toiletries and a little blue book of children's Bible stories.

"That's better," said Shandell. "Sorry about that. I don't usually run around outside in my underwear."

Rachel turned back to find Shandell wearing flannel pajama pants under her hoodie. "I'm glad for that. But I'm wondering what you're doing here."

"I'm staying here until I can get a ride home, back to Baltimore. That's where I'm from. I traveled up here with a friend and sort of got stuck on my own with no money and nowhere to stay."

"And you know James?"

Shandell nodded. "He said I could stay here, only . . . well, I don't want to get him in any trouble. He said his parents wouldn't approve, so please don't tell them."

"It's not my place to tell." Though she could not lie if someone asked about this girl. "And how long have you been here?"

"James found me on Sunday, but I won't be here much longer. My mom is driving out from Baltimore to pick me up after work tonight. In fact, I was planning to walk into town today to leave her a message about where to meet me, but that was before I messed up my jeans." Shandell pushed her hood down, revealing black hair with an unusual blue glow, the color of the twilight sky.

From up close, Rachel could see that Shandell was more a young woman than a girl. What was her story? "Did you run away from home, then?"

"At the time, I didn't think so." Shandell looked over the wet jeans, frowning. "But, yeah, I guess I was running away. But I'm looking forward to going back now. Do you have any experience with hand-washing? Look at this mud. I was going to heat up some water and add detergent."

"Hot water can lock in a stain. Better try cold." Rachel took off her coat and pushed back her sleeves. "Let me have a try."

"Oh, thanks!" With a wobbly smile, Shandell handed Rachel the jeans and powdered soap. "I'll be right back! I left the buckets of fresh water behind."

"Mind you don't slip," Rachel called after her.

"I won't." As Shandell blew out the door, Rachel noticed that her pajama pants had little drawings of Minnie Mouse on them. She was familiar with Disney characters; Rose used to collect Disney books and stickers, until she decided she was too old for cartoons.

This Shandell was an interesting girl, very contrary. Blue hair and Minnie Mouse pajamas. A woman and a girl at the same time. As she spread the pants on the floor and sprinkled soap flakes over the mud stains, she saw that this day was going to hold far more surprises than she'd planned.

An hour or so later, Rachel held her breath and the reins as Mark and Edna helped James into the buggy.

"Easy does it," Mark said as he crouched on the running board and helped lift his brother into the seat. Rachel tried not to stare, but it seemed to her that James was pushing up with his legs. Was that her imagination?

She turned away, not wanting James's family to see the cloud of worry in her eyes. When she had met Shandell this morning, it was clear that the girl needed help. But now she was beginning to wonder how it had become so tricky to follow the Golden Rule and the rules of the Ordnung.

Thank goodness James was soon in his seat and ready to go. Rachel called to Patches, the horse, and soon they were trotting down the lane, approaching the highway that bordered the north side of the Lapp orchard. Last night's heavy rains coated all the grasses and bushes, and the water drained into the ditch alongside the road. The world was damp and sodden. *Just like my heavy heart,* Rachel thought.

"You're awfully quiet today," James said as Rachel paused at the end of the road to check for traffic. "What's the matter?"

"I got up extra early," she said, trying to tamp down her hurt and annoyance. What sort of fella kept a girl hidden from his family . . . and from his best girl? "I had a surprise planned for you."

"For me?" He tipped his head down so that the brim of his black hat blocked his eyes. "You do enough for me, Rachel."

"Well, I wanted to do something special. And I walked back to the sugar shack to set it up."

He lifted his chin, his dark eyes meeting hers. "The sugar shack?"

"Ya. And it turned out, the surprise was on me."

"Because she found me there, in a very embarrassing situation," came a low voice from the back of the buggy.

James's head whipped around, his face suddenly gone white as a sheet.

Shandell popped up from the backseat and leaned forward, propping her head between Rachel and James.

"Ach!" James slapped his chest. "You two have more power to shock than a bolt of lightning."

"Sorry, James. I didn't want to get you in trouble."

"I'm not in trouble. Why are you riding in the back of the buggy?"

"I was going to walk into town to call my mom, but Rachel said she would take me to a phone that I could use. I'll walk back to the sugar shack from there and pack my things up."

"This isn't wise," James said. "You shouldn't be in the back of the buggy. Folks will be talking if they see you."

"Now you're worried about what folks might think?" Rachel demanded. "Have you gone crazy? Verhuddelt?" Unable to contain herself any longer, Rachel launched into Pennsylvania Dutch. *"Taking in an Englisher girl when your father has warned you to keep to Plain folk? Sneaking around behind your parents' back? And hiding it from me, too? Me, James."*

"So . . . I'm not hiding it from you anymore," James returned in Deutsch.

"Only because you got caught!" Rachel exclaimed.

James folded his arms, a gesture that said he was closed off to her once again. This was not what Rachel wanted. She wanted to be his partner. She wanted him to count on her and trust her.

"Umm, guys?" Shandell spoke up from the back. "I don't speak that language, but I get the drift. I'm really sorry."

James turned to Rachel and asked in Deutsch: *"Do you know the story of the Good Samaritan from the Bible?"*

Rachel let out a breath. "Ya, I know the Good Samaritan," she said in English. "But this is different."

"I know that story, too," Shandell said. "It's a classic."

"She knows the Bible," James said in Deutsch. *"She is a good girl, Rachel, a person who has fallen on hard times like the Jewish man in the story. I gave her food and a place to stay. Very small acts of kindness compared to the sacrifice of our Savior. And have you forgotten Jesus's commandment to love your neighbor as yourself?"*

"I am thinking about the Ordnung," Rachel said in English. "About respect for parents. About following the rules set by the bishop."

"This is true," James continued in Deutsch, *"but when I was caught between the two sides, I chose to help a person in need, and I didn't tell you because I didn't want to draw you into it for this very reason. It's not so simple, is it? Shandell reminds me of my sister Verena, and if she were to be stuck somewhere during her rumspringa, I would pray that a stranger would give her food and shelter."*

Rachel pictured Verena . . . then she thought of her own sisters, Rose, Bethany, and little Molly. It would be a terrible thing if anyone in her family got stranded without a friendly face in sight. A few nights ago, James had come face-to-face with Shandell and he had needed to make a quick decision. Who was Rachel to question his choice—especially when he had risked angering his parents to help a girl in need?

"I hope you two aren't arguing over me," Shandell said. " 'Cause I'll be out of your hair tonight."

"We don't argue," James said flatly.

"Really? You could have fooled me."

Rachel turned to take in the man she loved, his dark eyes smoky and distant, and the young woman with a baby face and strange blue hair. It was all so peculiar, like a feverish dream. But it was real, and there was no denying that this was the way Gott intended her day to go. The Almighty did not make mistakes.

It was verhuddelt, all right.

ᘒᘗ 28 ᘒᘗ

"That's a phone shanty?" Shandell stared at the little shingled shack painted white, which seemed to spring from the corner of a farmer's field. "It's so cute! Like a country phone booth."

"My family shares that phone with a few other neighbors," James explained. "No one will mind if you use it."

Shandell hopped out of the buggy and waited as Rachel came around to open the shanty door. "I thought that Amish people weren't allowed to use phones."

"We can use them, but we cannot have the phone lines running to our house."

"Well, I appreciate you letting me use this. I'll pay you back someday. Really, I'm going to come back and make up for all the nice things you've done for me."

"You don't need to do that," James said. "But you do need to make your call so we can continue on. There's folks expecting me at the clinic, and it won't do to keep them waiting."

"I am on it," Shandell said, stepping inside. It was an old-fashioned phone with big numbers to press. Quickly, she tapped in her home number and waited for an answer, hoping against hope for Mom, though Shandell knew her mother probably had to work this morning.

"Hello?" Phil's voice made something curl inside her. She wasn't looking forward to seeing him again, but she had promised herself that she and Mom were going to work out a plan so that Shandell was no longer responsible for cooking for him and cleaning up after him.

"Phil, it's me, Shandell. Is my mom there?"

"No. You know she's working," he said, launching into a mini lecture about how her mother didn't have the time or means to live a life of leisure.

"Right. Sorry. I promised Mom I'd call her today. We need to coordinate the store where she's going to pick me up." Shandell had picked a place in town, knowing that it would cause way too much suspicion to have Mom meet her on the country road that passed by the Lapp orchard.

"Picking you up?" he asked. "Hold on a second. Let me get something to write with." She thought she heard him talking to someone else, but then maybe it was the TV. "Okay, where are you again? I'm supposed to write down exactly where you are."

"I'm in a little town called Halfway. There's a convenience store on Main Street that's open all night. It's a 7-Eleven, I think."

"The Halfway 7-Eleven," Phil said, and there was a low sound in the background. Was someone else there?

"I have to go. Just tell Mom I'll wait for her at that store."

"Actually, your mother's not the one coming to get you," Phil said.

"What?" Shandell held the handset of the phone closer as disappointment seeped in, cold and chilling. "What are you talking about?"

"You know your mother's busy. Her work schedule's crazy. And we had another volunteer. You've had a visitor here. He came by twice this week. He's sitting here now." Phil chuckled. "It's your boyfriend, Gary."

Gary! "He's not my boyfriend," she protested.

But Phil went on. Either he didn't hear her or he didn't care. "He'll be coming to get you tonight, right there at that 7-Eleven. He thinks he knows just where it is."

"No," Shandell breathed, closing her eyes. This couldn't be happening.

"Phil . . . Dad . . . You *can't* send him out here. He's the reason I never got home in the first place."

"He's been worried about you ever since you ditched him. That's not a nice thing to do, now, is it?"

"I ditched him because he wouldn't take me home," she said, trying to keep the panic out of her voice.

"Don't be a drama queen." Phil's tone was surly now.

"Tell her I'll see her tonight," Gary said in the background. "At the Halfway 7-Eleven."

"Phil, listen to me." Shandell's heart was beating fast as she gripped the phone. "Don't send Gary. That's just a waste of everyone's time. I want Mom to come. I *need* Mom to come get me. Please."

"Listen to you, making demands. Still haven't learned that it's not all about you."

"This isn't about being selfish, it's . . . it's about self-preservation."

"Easy, drama queen. You know what I always say: You'll get what you get and you won't get upset."

She had heard that one a hundred times, but it wasn't going to keep her from trying to straighten this out. "Don't send Gary. I'm not getting in a car with him."

"Oh, and now you're a snob? Too good for him?"

"That's not what I mean at all. Please, tell Mom that—"

"You can tell her yourself, when you get home tonight," he said. "When Gary drops you off."

Before Shandell could respond, there was a click on the line. Disconnected.

Quickly, she punched in the number again. She would keep her emotions in check and reason with Phil. But the phone rang on and on, and outside the door of the shanty, the sight of James and Rachel talking in the buggy reminded her that they were waiting, and James had to get to therapy. She would have to leave a message and call back later.

After the tone, she told her mother not to send Gary, because she would not go with him. She promised to call later, adding that she really wanted to come home and missed her mom.

After she hung up, she realized that Phil would probably be the one to retrieve the voice mail. He would be annoyed that she hadn't said that she missed him, too. He might even delete the message without telling Mom about it. He could be that petty sometimes.

As she left the shanty, she pressed a hand to her mouth. Would she be able to talk sense into Phil? She knew Gary could be very persuasive.

Oh, if she could just reach Mom. She tried Mom's cell, but the call didn't go through. That was no surprise; Chelsea worked in a building with zero cell reception.

"Shandell?" Concern flashed in Rachel's blue eyes. "You're shaking like a leaf. Are you sick?"

"Sick at heart, I guess."

"Did you speak with your mother?" asked James.

"No." She climbed into the back of the buggy and collapsed on the seat. "She was at work. But it turns out she's not coming for me tonight. They decided to send Gary, the lunatic that I had to escape from."

Rachel started the buggy moving, turning it around on the road. "What's a lunatic?"

"Verhuddelt," James said. "But in a mean way." Then he launched into that language Shandell didn't understand again, only this time his tone was more concerned than argumentative.

"I see," Rachel said. "This man, Gary, he was trouble for you?"

"Big trouble." Shandell didn't know how to begin describing Gary, but she tried to give Rachel and James a condensed version. "He told me we were going home, but he kept stalling and driving through all the towns around here, telling me he'd take me home when he really had no intention of doing that. I felt like one of those kidnap victims who have to break free. And he's a thief. At first he stole gas and snacks from a few gas stations. Then, when he realized that Amish people don't give a lot of push-back, he started stealing from Amish shops and stands. So, yeah, he's trouble."

She thought about her plan to call back and talk Gary out of coming. That was lame. He wasn't going to back off, especially now that he knew where she was. It would be like some sort of conquest for him, a sick victory. He would enjoy having her back in his car and under his power.

Would he actually drive her home?

She wasn't going to take the chance that he might do her that favor.

"What will you do if he is the one who comes tonight?"

"I can't go with him. If he's coming to Halfway, I'm going to get myself as far from here as I can, even if I have to hitchhike. As soon as I get back to the sugar shack, I'll get my stuff together and leave. What's the next town over?"

"Paradise," James said, "but it's a good ten miles. It will take you most of the morning to walk there. And what will you do once you get there? It's much like Halfway, but bigger. You talked to the police and they can't help you. I don't think the answer is in Paradise."

That sounded funny; Shandell would have laughed if she didn't feel nauseated.

"And don't forget, your pants are still drying," Rachel reminded her.

"Right." The ultimate humiliation; Shandell was now running around in her Minnie Mouse pajama pants. That wouldn't have been such a big deal on some college campuses, but here in Lancaster County, the attire wasn't quite so loose. "Well, I guess I'll be walking in wet jeans." She would get over it and get through it. She didn't know where she would go next.

She knew only one thing for sure: She could not go near Gary.

🍂 29 🍂

James watched the two of them move about the sugar shack, chatting like two old friends. It was hard to believe that Rachel and Shandell had met just this morning, and in a very uncomfortable moment, too.

Warm from the fire and relaxed from a good helping of cheesy casserole, James eyed the cocoa drop cookie in his hand. It was his favorite treat, from his favorite girl. Indeed, the young woman he had always planned to marry. But in the years before, James had not seen Rachel tested on big matters. He had not known that she had the strength to travel a bumpy road, full of obstacles, until she had stayed by his side throughout his rehabilitation. He had not seen her endure his harsh words until Easter Sunday. He had not seen anger flare in her cornflower-blue eyes until today. And he had not seen her take a fallen angel under her wing, until this evening when she realized that Shandell was truly in need.

What a day it had been! James had risen at four as usual and had spent nearly four hours working in the orchard with his brothers and sisters. They were making some progress with the fertilization, but he feared it was not enough to keep Dat from hiring on strangers to take over the orchard.

And a new can of worms was opened as Shandell considered her future. James and Rachel weren't sure what to do, but Rachel had been firm on getting Shandell to stay at the sugar shack until they returned from treatment so that they could talk about a plan.

And then, at the clinic, when his treatment was done, Dr. Finley gave him another chance to stand up—and he did. This time, he stayed on his feet for nearly three minutes, holding on to the bars only for balance. A true blessing! It reassured James that the progress of the day before hadn't been a fluke. After that, he had pushed himself during the physical therapy, scraping all of his might to lift each leg, just a little bit. JJ was a good inspiration, calling at him to squeeze hard here or press hard there.

"Even if you move just a hair," JJ had said. "A fraction of an inch today can be a few inches in a few months, and before you know it you're taking a few steps."

That was exactly the encouragement James needed to hear. He vowed to do everything asked of him in physical therapy. With Gott's blessing and lots of hard work, James would be a whole man once again.

And now they were back at the sugar shack with Shandell, the stranded Englisher girl. He took a bite of the cookie, letting the bittersweet chocolate melt in his mouth. So much had been packed into one day.

Watching the two of them now as they gathered trash and tidied up the sugar shack after the good supper Rachel had brought, James realized that he loved Rachel more than ever before.

No longer lost in her art, no longer distant and dreamy, Rachel had stepped out of her girlhood to become a woman who cared deeply for him and for other people. When had this change happened? He suspected the accident had something to do with it. Those first few weeks, he'd been surly and distant, sunk too deep into the muck to notice anyone else. From a terrible tragedy, Gott had blessed Rachel with new strength. She now had backbone and a kind heart. When she calmed Shandell's worries, he could imagine her soothing the children they would have. When she handed them plates of casserole warmed from the woodstove, he saw her serving up a big family supper. It was a pretty picture, imagining Rachel as his wife. It pushed him that much more to recover, so that he could be the healthy husband she deserved.

His thoughts were interrupted when Shandell jumped up and pointed to a spider in the rafters. Calm and efficient, Rachel got the broom and managed to brush the critter and his web down. A minute later, the spider was scuttling out the door.

"What's the difference between a spider and a duck?" James asked.

"Plenty of things." Shandell sat back in the plastic chair and curled her legs up to her chin. "But you don't want either of them bunking in with you."

"It's a riddle," Rachel said, her blue eyes glimmering as she smiled at him. "James used to be full of jokes. So tell us, what's the difference?"

"The spider has two feet of web, while the duck has two webbed feet."

Shandell rolled her eyes, but Rachel's chuckle was music to his ears.

"Tell us another," Rachel said, taking a seat beside Shandell.

"How do you fix a broken pizza?"

"That I don't know," Rachel egged him on.

"With tomato paste."

Now Shandell was giggling, too. "That's so corny."

"No, it's tomato-ee," James corrected. "And what gets bigger when you take more away from it?" When both women shook their heads, he answered, "A hole."

With a peaceful smile, Rachel leaned back in the chair. "Oh, James! I've missed your jokes and riddles. A good laugh eases every worry."

That had been his intention. "But there are some matters that can't be laughed away," he said, turning his gaze to Shandell. "Like the matter of getting you home safely. Rachel and I, we've been talking about this as we rode in and out of town today. It sounds like a wise choice to avoid that man, Gary. But walking into Paradise is no way to fix things, either." Now that he knew her, he hated the thought of Shandell traipsing around other towns and country roads. Bad things could happen to her, and that path would lead her even farther from home, where she needed to go. And Rachel had quickly come to the same conclusion.

"Not to sound selfish, but I'm disappointed that I'm not going home tonight. You've been so generous, James, and you, too, Rachel. That casserole was delicious, but I just don't belong here. I need to be home, and this is getting ridiculous."

"We want to help you get home, and we have an Englisher friend who would probably help you." Rachel turned to James. "When does Dylan get back?"

"I'm not sure." James knew Dylan would help if he was here. "He said he was going to Chicago for a friend's wedding."

"If I could just get through to my mother, I know she would wire me some money. At least enough to get a car service to Lancaster and take the bus home from there."

"You must keep trying to reach your mother," Rachel said. "I'm sure she's worried sick for you."

"How much is that bus from Lancaster?" James asked. "Maybe we can help."

When Shandell named a sum, he remembered that he had no

cash on hand now. Like most Amish men in their twenties, James had received a small stipend from his parents—most of which he had saved for a house of his own. But after the accident, James had turned all his savings over to his parents to help cover expenses.

"I wish I could help," Rachel said. "But I don't have money just now." James had learned that Rachel had donated her savings, all the money earned from her paintings, to the fund for his medical expenses. What a pair they were! Two hardworking young people, and not a penny to their names.

"I don't want to take your money," Shandell said. "And I don't want to cause you any more trouble. My mom will come through. You'll see."

"Until then, you can stay here," James said. "You've been no trouble, really." He gazed at Rachel through lazy, lowered eyelids. "Except for the surprise you gave this one this morning."

Shandell held her hands up to her face. "That was totally awkward. But I'm glad it was you, Rachel. I would have really freaked out if it had been a bunch of wild Amish guys, like on TV."

Although Shandell sometimes seemed to be speaking a strange language, James appreciated her honesty. "Who are these Amish men on the TV? Plain folk don't abide by having their photos taken, on account of the Bible telling us not to have a graven image."

"You know, those shows. *Wild Rumspringa* and *Amish Run Amok.* I don't watch them, but I've seen the commercials."

"Wild rumspringa?" Rachel's eyebrows arched. "Sounds very spicy."

"And who wants to watch young folk when they're noisy and wild?" James asked, rubbing his chin. "Surely not our parents. They try to look the other way."

For a while, they talked about Englisher television and cell phones and computers. James's father had hoped to purchase a computer for his office, but the bishop wouldn't allow it. Instead, he had hired an Englisher to do bookkeeping, and a few times a week Jimmy went into town to use the computer at this man's office.

Shandell asked about the orchard, suggesting that there might be some work she could do to earn her keep. James thought it was best that she stay out of sight, but then Rachel suggested that it might be smart for the three of them to work together to fertilize the trees near the back of the orchard. Otherwise, James's brothers might wander back here to the sugar shack for a break if they were working nearby.

"Saturday morning, before the treatment," James said. "That would be a good time. I'll send my brothers off to the far end of the orchard, and they'll stay away if they think you're working with me, Rachel."

As the sky began to grow dusky outside, Rachel gathered up the hamper, leaving a good portion of food and snacks behind for Shandell.

"I can't thank you guys enough," Shandell said. "If I can use the shanty, I'll try to call home again tomorrow. My mom will be off, so I might be able to reach her. If I can just get through to her, I'm sure she'll either come for me or wire me the money to get home."

"You can use the phone in the shanty," James said. "Just try to do it when no one is watching." Hearing the words come from his own mouth, James felt a twinge of regret. Sneaking around . . . that part was not right. He should tell his parents now . . . tonight. Surely they wouldn't turn this young Englisher out on the street.

Well, Mamm could find compassion in her heart, but Dat? James wasn't so sure. Whenever talk of Englishers came up, Jimmy quickly went to some dark place, the terrible memory of his childhood friend who had been injured by Englishers. A memory so unsettling that Dat refused to share the story . . . Nay, Dat wouldn't be so quick to accept Shandell.

For now, James had best keep the secret.

PART THREE

Echoes Through Eternity

Withhold not good from them to whom it is due,
When it is in the power of thine hand to do it.
—PROVERBS 3:27

"*That's* a good boy. I'll be back for you in a few hours." With a pat of affection, Rachel left Patches tied up at the hitching post outside the Paradise clinic and headed down the street toward Art at Heart. After yesterday's excitement, she was looking forward to losing herself in her painting for a few hours. Dealing with a runaway English girl brought a person a lot of ruckus and confusion.

She smiled as she pictured Shandell in her Minnie Mouse pajamas and her blue hair. Unusual. That girl would stand out, even among Englishers. Walking quickly past the long stretch of parking lot in front of the Cackleberry Farm Antiques Mall, a shop similar to Elsie's Country Store, but on a grander scale, Rachel wondered what would happen if Shandell was discovered living out in the sugar shack.

Chances were that Rachel's parents would have agreed that this Englisher girl had needed their help. But Jimmy? He would be quick to scold, quick to punish James in whatever way he saw fit.

Even though James was a man himself, nearly twenty-one years old, there was no escaping the authority of an Amish dat.

Thick traffic moved slowly through the center of Paradise, and Rachel took care as she crossed the street in front of a line of vehicles. Here it was the end of April and the tourist season was already picking up. The town of Paradise was similar to Halfway, but bigger, with a huge Christmas store and a working farm on the outskirts that offered daily tours. She passed Leaman Furniture, Zook's Fabric Store, and the Dollar General, where there were many good bargains indeed. Here, the sidewalks were crowded with customers, more Englishers than Amish. Plain folk, who usually greeted each other in passing, joked that if you said hello to every English and Amish person in a town like this, you wouldn't have a moment to catch your breath.

Driving the buggy for James would be a blessing in disguise. Spending most of her days in Paradise would give Rachel the town experience she'd been longing for. Instead of spending her days helping with laundry and sewing, milking and mucking, she would be here on Paradise's Main Street, painting to her heart's content.

A bell jingled when Rachel opened the door to Art at Heart, and as she made her way to the corner of the shop where she'd set up her easel, she was surprised to see a group of customers there, gathered around Pepper, the shop's owner.

"Here she is now," Pepper said, nodding at Rachel. Today Pepper wore a bulky man's sweater over a full print skirt, so long it touched her ankles. Her silvery hair was nearly covered with a bright red kerchief that brought out the rosy color of her cheeks. "This is Rachel King, the artist I mentioned."

The Englishers turned to Rachel, their eyes wide with curiosity.

Rachel nodded, feeling awkward. "Is there something wrong?"

"Not at all. These folks were asking why this easel was set up here, and I told them we were going to have a real Amish artist painting in our store."

"That's what I'm aiming to do," Rachel said. Her face was suddenly warm, and she wondered if her cheeks were glowing pink. When she had asked Pepper about painting in the shop, Rachel hadn't expected that anyone would actually pay attention to her while she was working. Why were these folks staring at her that way?

"We were just saying that we've never met an Amish artist before," said one woman with square black glasses and gold hair cut shorter than most boys'.

"I didn't even know Amish people were allowed to do art," another woman said. "Well, aside from quilting and crafts like that."

"Our bishop allows it, as long as I don't show Amish people in my paintings," Rachel explained as she eased through the circle of customers and stood at her easel, which bore a blank canvas. It was the oddest thing, all these people staring at a pale white canvas.

"What are you going to paint?" asked someone else.

"A farm with a quilt hanging on the line." She had already brought her paints, brushes, and palette from home, and yesterday she had prepped the canvas—without an audience—so that she could begin painting today.

"Have you ever sold a painting?"

As Rachel opened her paint box and found a pencil, she nodded. "I have sold a few." She thought about telling them that a designer had asked for this painting, but she didn't want to sound proud. "I'm very lucky that way."

"She's so modest," Pepper said. "And she's one of my best customers. Rachel purchases all her paints and supplies here. Now let's give her some space so she can do her thing."

Most of the group wandered off to the paint aisle, and Pepper headed over to the register to handle some purchases. Two ladies remained, but they turned toward each other to chat. Rachel was relieved not to have everyone watching her, their scrutiny like hot sunlight beating down on her back.

Pencil in hand, Rachel bit her lower lip and thought about the scene she would paint. There would be a quilt hanging on the line, of course, but for this painting she wanted to capture the burst of life in springtime. She would part the clouds and show streams of sunlight showering the farmhouse. And a fresh purple crocus in the foreground, its hearty flower reaching to the sunlight—that would shout "springtime" to anyone who saw it.

Sitting opposite her easel, she began to sketch on the canvas, blocking out the large crocus first, then the quilt and the farm-house. Next she penciled in the outline of parting clouds and the streaming beams of sunlight. This part would be a mixture of white and gold and yellow and gray. She stood back with a critical eye. Ya, that was enough sketching. She didn't want to overdo the details that would take shape once she had her paintbrush in hand.

As she started mixing purple, white, and two shades of blue for the crocus flower, the events of the last day played out in her head. She had checked on Shandell this morning, dropping off a few slices of homemade bread, along with some sausage links left over from breakfast. The Englisher girl had been ever so grateful, report-ing that she had walked to the shanty last night and tried to call her mother.

"I can't get through to her, and I'm beginning to worry," Shan-dell had reported. "There's probably a reasonable explanation. Maybe Phil isn't telling her that I called. Maybe her cell phone died. But it's really scary not being able to get through to her. I know she would come for me, if she could find me."

"I'm sure she would," Rachel agreed. "But in the meantime,

James and I are glad you didn't go with this Gary fellow. You're better off with a plan to get you home, safe and sound."

With no time to spare, Rachel had promised to come back later, and then walked back to the Lapp home to pick up James for his treatment. During their ride into town, their conversation had focused on Shandell.

"How sad to have a mamm who is too busy to save you," Rachel said. "Some folks have heavy burdens in life. Makes me grateful for my mamm and dat." Betsy and Nate had been strict at times, but there was never any doubt about their love for each other and every child in the family.

"We are blessed to have good families, but Shandell is eighteen. She's a little thing, but not a child. Maybe her mother is teaching her a lesson."

"A girl without a loving family? It breaks my heart."

"That's why we're helping her."

At that moment, Rachel had seen what a kind, strong father James would be. How she loved him!

And she wanted to tell him. Her plans to talk with him about their future had been dashed when she'd come upon Shandell at the sugar shack. Maybe she should have brought it up right then and there, as the horse's hooves clip-clopped along Route 30, but she lost her nerve.

Chickenhearted. Deep inside, she was afraid, scared to hear him turn her away the way he had on Easter Sunday. *You and me, we don't belong together,* he'd said. It still made her sick inside when she remembered it.

With a deep breath, she pushed the worry from her mind and focused on the petals of her first crocus. Six purple petals with yellow at the center. She decided to draw two purple crocuses with a yellow bud behind them.

"Is that a flower?" someone asked. It was the woman with the short blond hair.

"A crocus," Rachel said as she pulled some white onto the side of her brush to do the highlights.

"Very nice. It's mesmerizing, standing here. I could watch all day."

Please don't, Rachel wanted to say. Though she didn't want to be rude to Pepper's customers, she preferred to paint without people looking over her shoulder.

A siren sounded outside on the street. Everyone turned to the shop front, where blue and red lights flashed on the rack atop a passing police car.

"What's going on?" someone asked.

A few customers went to the window for a closer look. Someone mentioned that the police car had pulled up outside the gas station, and there was much speculation about the matter.

Rachel tuned the conversations out and stepped into her quiet world of color and light, shadow and texture. Such a peaceful place to be.

Sometime later, as Rachel was closing up her paints, she overheard a woman telling Pepper that someone had stolen gasoline from the Shell station. "It was a 'pump and run,'" the woman said. "A few witnesses saw him. A young man in a big American car with Maryland plates."

Maryland plates? That got Rachel thinking as she wiped a smudge of violet paint from her hands. Shandell was from Maryland. Was the thief Gary?

☙❧

Rachel waited outside the clinic in the buggy, eager to tell James the news of the thief. For some reason, she felt responsible for bringing this bad man to Lancaster County. Of course, she had not lured him here, but she wished there was a way to stop him.

Once they were on their way, alone out in the open, she shared the story of the police at the gas station. She summed it up, adding: "Maybe we should go to the police and tell them about this man."

James rubbed his chin thoughtfully. "It's not our place to get involved. The Almighty brings justice to those who break the laws of heaven."

Rachel knew that. "But shouldn't a bad man be stopped?"

"We cannot do anything about it. That's the way it is." After a moment, she felt a gentle pressure on her hand. Her mouth dropped open in surprise as he lifted her right hand away from the reins. "What's this?" Tingles of pleasure shot up her arm as his fingertips brushed the smudge of purple paint. "Either you've got a bad bruise or you've been painting again."

She smiled, forcing herself to keep her eyes on the road. "I started on the painting that the designer wants to buy."

Gently he pressed the purple area. "And you're painting with grape juice?"

She laughed aloud. "That's the James I fell for. Always a joke and a spark in your eyes."

"I'm glad you're painting again. How long until you finish and sell it so that Shandell can go home?"

"It's already sold. But it will take me two weeks at least to finish. You can't rush art."

"Most things that matter can't be rushed." He linked his fingers between hers and squeezed her hand. "I'm learning that's true about healing, too."

Her heart sank. "Oh, James, is the treatment not working?"

"Not as quickly as I want it to." He kissed her hand again. "And I want it to work so that we can be together again. I do want to marry you, Rachel. But I stand by what I said before. You deserve a whole man. I won't let you be saddled with anything less."

Tears stung her eyes. "So . . . so you *do* think we belong together? You didn't mean it when you said those things?"

"We belong together," he said. "That's why I pray to Gott that I can be healed so that you can have the husband you deserve."

Rachel swallowed over the knot in her throat. "You are so hard on yourself. And that makes things hard on me, too."

"I'm doing what's best for you."

"Let me be the judge of that, James Lapp."

"Better if we let Gott be the judge of all of us. His will shall be done."

"Amen to that," she said. This short conversation had lifted a cloak of worry from her shoulders. James still loved her. Oh, her heart was glad! As long as they loved each other, they could weather any storm.

"Knock-knock," he said.

This was a game they used to play often before the accident. "Who's there?"

"You are."

"You are, who?" she asked.

"You are the one for me," he said, pulling her hand close to his lips and kissing her knuckles.

Rachel melted against him as joy seeped through her, warm and sweet as drizzled honey. She would have liked to nestle in his arms and kiss him, but she needed to drive, and it wouldn't do for any other travelers to see them kissing in broad daylight.

"I am a lucky girl."

He squeezed her hand, then returned it to the reins. "Like the joke says, you are."

❧ 31 ❧

"What did the little tree say to the big tree?" James asked as Shandell dumped a shovelful of manure onto the soil at the base of a pear tree.

"Um . . ." Shandell swallowed, nearly choking on a breath. "Maybe he said I'm about to wither from the smell of that poop they're dumping over my feet."

Rachel and James laughed.

"It's a strong smell, but you get used to it," Rachel said. She was raking manure, spreading it so that it covered the area under the tree. James had explained that the roots of a tree usually spread out as wide as the farthest branches, so that was a good guide for fertilization.

"I could get used to the work," Shandell said. "But the smell? Not so sure about that."

"Anyway," James said, "the little tree told the big one, leaf me alone."

Shandell laughed out loud. Not that the joke was that funny, but she was giddy, having been up before dawn to shovel manure in the back rows of the orchard. James had worried that she might be seen out and about, but Shandell had been eager to get off her butt and help. Her time alone had been valuable for thought and introspection, but it was beginning to wear on her. She hadn't realized how lonely she'd become until she had dinner with Rachel and James on Thursday, as if they were friends hanging out together. When the opportunity came to help in the orchard, she had jumped at the chance.

Of course, that was before she knew about the smell, which seemed to ooze in through her nose, mouth, and pores. Totally intense. Still, she didn't regret coming out to pitch in. She had been glad to hear Rachel's knock on the door at five-thirty.

Bleary-eyed, Shandell had been impressed to see Rachel standing before her, looking neat as a pin in her dress, apron, and sweater. "Good morning," Shandell said cheerfully. "Do you want to come in?"

"No. I'm going back behind the barn to load fertilizer into the cart."

Shandell raked her hair back out of her eyes. "All alone?"

"James's brothers will help me with it. Peter and Luke can be good workers when there's someone watching. I'll bring the cart over and meet you by the woods there, just at the edge of the orchard."

"Got it."

"And this is for you to use." Rachel handed her an Amish dress in a pretty shade of dark green. "It's mine, so it'll be big on you. I just thought you might want to wear it in the orchard. It's dirty work. Afterward, I can take it home and put it in with the washing."

"That's so sweet. Thank you." Shandell felt a rush of tenderness at the thoughtful gesture. Although Rachel came off as a little distant and methodical at times, inside she had a good heart. Shandell had seen proof of that in many ways. One of the sweetest was when Rachel had tried to warn her once she started to see what a bad dude Gary was.

"This Gary, I think he's hanging around Lancaster County," Rachel had told her yesterday afternoon when she and James had dropped by with food and news. "Someone stole gas from the Shell station today—right in broad daylight. They say there are photos on the security cameras, and the witnesses recall a young man with Maryland license plates on his car." Rachel described how the police car came rushing to the gas station with lights flashing and sirens blaring. Although the gas thief had already fled the scene, they caught the car make and model, and it matched Gary's big boat of a car.

"That has to be him. I have to see those photos from the security camera. I bet they'll be in tomorrow's newspaper."

"Not in *The Budget*," said James. The Amish newspaper did not publish photographs. "But maybe in the *Paradise Ledger*."

"I can't believe he came back here. I told Phil not to send him."

"There are other crimes, too." James had heard about a string of petty burglaries in Halfway, Paradise, and Strasburg. Sheriff Hank was stepping up security in Halfway, adding more personnel on the night shift.

As the details of the crimes became clear, Shandell saw Gary's signature written all over them. She explained that when she'd been traveling with him he had made a game of destroying jars of jam, selling flowers to someone else down the road, and stealing one-of-a-kind items like a baby cradle and a Coke sign.

"I have a very strong feeling that Gary is behind these thefts," Shandell said.

"I don't think you can trust this man," Rachel said. She seemed so motherly, with her head cocked to one side and her blue eyes concerned and penetrating. "Was this Gary your boyfriend?"

"No! Never. He was just a friend. I think he wanted to be more, but after the road trip we took together, that's not going to happen. I will never trust him again. Don't you worry about that."

Rachel let out a breath. "Good." With that, she rose and set out Shandell's dinner—two pork chops, rice, peas, and pickled beets on a paper plate.

"Wow . . . thank you," Shandell said.

"You're welcome." Rachel handed her a fork and knife. "I'll need these utensils back when you're done with them. Don't forget to eat your vegetables."

"You know, sometimes you sound like a mother." Shandell cut into a corner of one chop that had obviously been cooked in a thick gravy. "And you're only a year older than I am."

"Older and wiser. Now eat." Rachel sat with her while James went out to fetch some wood.

Although the bad news about Gary made Shandell sick at heart, it didn't diminish her appetite. As she ate, she was relieved that her Amish friends knew just how bad Gary could be. At least, now they truly understood why she could not accept another ride from him, even if he promised to take her home. But Gary's new crime spree worried Shandell on a deeper level. What was wrong with him? Was he stalking her? Or had he come back here just to take advantage of some more Plain People? Any way you looked at it, the guy was sick.

When James returned, Shandell thought about all the news these two had gathered. "How do you know all this about the thefts? I mean, without cell phones or Internet, how did you find out all this stuff?"

"News travels through an Amish community like seeds in the wind," Rachel said as she'd poured Shandell a cup of milk from a thermos. "James and I heard a lot in town, but my mamm got news from a friend who stopped by for a visit."

"And my father got an earful while he was at the feed store," James added.

"Now we have to go," Rachel had said, "but drink that milk. I don't think you're getting enough to eat. Such a wisp of a thing."

Shandell smiled up at Rachel. "I know I'm petite, but I am eighteen."

"Ya, but you still need milk for strong bones and good teeth. And you're going to need your strength for working in the orchard tomorrow," Rachel had said definitively, pleased to have the last word.

Although she teased her friend, Shandell didn't really mind Rachel's mothering. It was nice to know that someone cared about her safety and health. In some ways, a substitute mother was just what she needed.

Now, as Shandell raked the chicken manure into a wide circle around a tree, she swallowed back the pungent smell. "Strength isn't what you need out here," she muttered to herself. "What you really need is a gas mask."

"Did you say something?" Rachel asked, peering around the horse's head. She had led him up to move the cart forward.

"Um . . . I'm just thinking that taking care of an orchard is no small task." She traded her rake for a shovel and moved to the back of the cart. "I guess I thought you kept the trees trimmed and they just grew."

"Pruning is important. So are fertilizing and insect control." James moved his chair back so that he could pull the rake farther. "But the best part of an orchard is watching the seasons take hold of the trees. In winter, when the world is asleep under a big snow, the dormant trees still reach their branches to the sky. The spring bloom—we're coming up on that—it's nature's celebration. The fat green crowns of summer when trees are thick with fruit. And harvest time . . . that has to be my favorite. As kids, we would stuff our pockets with yellow apples on the way to school."

"You love this orchard," Shandell said.

James balanced the rake on his lap and moved to the next tree. "It's where I belong."

"His grandfather—his doddy, we call it—used to tend the orchard, and he taught James everything he knew about gardening," Rachel said. "James has four brothers, but he's the only one who took to tending trees."

"So far," James said. "We don't know about Matt and Mark yet." He spoke fondly about his grandfather and the importance of keeping the orchard in the family. "There's been talk of hiring someone on to manage. My father thinks it's too much for me, but I know I can do it."

"Well, it must be a huge responsibility." Shandell's shovel scraped the wood bed of the cart. Thank goodness, they had used up most of the chicken poop. James had explained that the animal manure had been composted so that it was no longer raw poop, but from the smell, she had her doubts.

As they made their way down the second row, Shandell asked James questions about running an orchard, and he told her some of the tricks of the trade. She learned that the birdhouses on Amish farms served a dual purpose. The Amish liked to protect nature's creatures, and here in the orchard, birds fed their babies on thousands of larvae that were eager to eat the trees' leaves and fruit. James explained that the trees between the orchard and the sugar shack acted as a windbreak, and they provided more nesting places for the birds.

"That's pretty amazing. You've got the birds working for you, free of charge," she teased.

"Until harvest time, and then we have to wrap some of the trees in netting or hang up scare-eye balloons to ward them off. Especially in the cherry trees. Birds go for the cherries."

"Who doesn't love ripe cherries?" Shandell stood at the back of the cart, shoveling out manure, when a voice called from the path.

"James? Hallo! Is that you?"

Rachel shot up straight, and James's face went white as snow.

"It's my dat!" There was a gasp of desperation in James's voice. "He can't find you here." His powerful arms wheeled the wheelchair away from the cart and down the row, toward his father. "It's me, Dat!" he shouted.

"I thought his father never came out to the orchards," Shandell whispered.

"He doesn't, usually." Rachel moved in front of Shandell, dragging the rake behind her. "He's coming this way. You'd better hide."

"Where?" There was nothing out here but trees, and they were too narrow to conceal her. The tree line was about thirty yards away, but if she made a mad dash for it, Jimmy would spot her right away.

Wheeling around, she saw the cart, its nearly empty wooden bed gaping at her. Oh, please, no! There had to be somewhere else to hide.

"Where can I go?"

"I don't know, but get there quick as a bunny. He's getting closer."

"This is not going to be good." Gritting her teeth, Shandell braced herself against the rear of the cart and hopped up. Manure crumbs smashed under her hands, turning into a slimy clay as she kept her body low and crawled into the cart. As she reached ahead, the borrowed green dress got stuck under one knee, causing her to slip down onto her belly.

Oh, yuck.

"Are you okay?" came Rachel's tense voice.

Lifting her head, Shandell closed her eyes and tried not to breathe. "Happy as a pig in poop."

❦ 32 ❦

In his black pants, jacket, and hat, Jimmy's silhouette was big and bold against the morning sky with its streaks of peach and gold.

"What are you doing way out here?" Jimmy called, closing the distance between them in long strides.

The same question I have for you, James thought, though he was in no position to confront his father. He turned the wheels of his chair as fast as he could, hoping to head his father off and stop him from approaching the wagon. Dat could not run into Shandell; if Dat found out about her, there was no telling what he would do.

"We're spreading fertilizer," James answered. "Rachel and I figured we'd work the rows at the back of the orchard. No need to be tripping over Luke and Peter and the others out there."

Dat slowed as he reached James. "Mmm." His lips pursed as his gaze moved beyond James to the cart.

Did he see Shandell?

Glancing back, James saw Rachel pause in her raking to give a wave. No sign of Shandell. Where had she hidden? The pear trees were young; none of them had trunks wide enough to hide a person, even a small woman like Shandell.

"That's a lot of hard work to put on a young girl," Jimmy said. "Lots of heavy lifting and such. You could bring along one of your brothers to help."

"Rachel's a hard worker. She doesn't mind." James knew his father would pick up on what he wasn't saying: that the two of them wanted time alone—a rare thing for Amish folk.

Dat tipped the brim of his straw hat, revealing his dark eyes, soft and weary. Gone was the usual ramrod-straight poke of his demeanor. And when had those deep creases formed at the outer edges of Jimmy's eyes? The dark half-moons smudging the top of Dat's cheeks were a recent change, too. "I see you've got two rows done."

"Ya. We just started this morning. We'll empty this cart, but then we've got to get on the road to the clinic."

"Two rows is good work for a morning, but it's not good enough." Jimmy squinted against the sun as he scanned the rows of trees behind him, and then pulled the brim of his hat down again. Now his eyes were shadowed and hidden, impossible to read. "The last hour, I've walked the orchard from end to end. I took a quick inventory. There's been a lot of hard work here this week, everyone pulling together. That's a good thing, but May is upon us, and with only half the orchard fertilized, we can't put this off any longer. I'm going to hire the nurseryman old Jacob recommended. The sooner the better."

The news knocked James back like a gust of wind. "Dat . . . no."

"The good care of the orchard cannot be neglected any longer."

"We can handle it, Dat."

"We're too far behind, James. I know you're out here every day, inspecting and telling your brothers what to do, but they slack off when there's no one on them, and you've got your treatment taking you away for most of the day. We need a foreman, now."

"But it's the Lapp orchard. Your father managed it, and his father before him, too. Don't bring in an outsider. I'll talk to Luke about taking on more responsibility."

"I've made my choice. Consider it done. I'm going into town to meet with Orchard Al. He'll get us back on track."

Although James knew it would be disrespectful to argue any more, he could not stop shaking his head. This would not be a good thing for their orchard. Doddy would not want a stranger here, taking shortcuts and throwing down store-bought pesticides to make his job easier.

"You've done a good job here." Dat's voice sounded different; kinder, without the barbs of judgment. "It's time to let it go, James. Time to accept a helping hand." Dat remained for a moment, as if waiting for James to agree.

That will never happen, James thought, digging his fingernails into the rubber armrests of his wheelchair.

With a small grunt, Jimmy turned back toward the path and walked away.

∞ 33 ∞

Such a busy day! Rachel had risen early to work in the Lapp orchard, and then, after a quick breakfast with James's family, off to Paradise they went. Usually, Rachel cherished her time alone with James, but there was no laughing or hand-holding today. Today he tested her patience with his concern over Jimmy's decision to hire on a new ranch foreman.

"He's replacing me," James said quietly. "That's what he's doing."

"There's no replacing you, James Lapp. Get that out of your head right now. And think about the time you'll have to rest. Didn't Doc Finley tell you that sleep was as important to your recovery as exercise?"

"A sleeping man never brought in a harvest," James grumbled.

Let someone else bring in the harvest this year. Rachel wished that James could let go of the way things used to be, but she knew her words wouldn't make it so.

After James was dropped off at the clinic, Rachel navigated

around the crowds of tourists jamming the sidewalks as she walked to the art shop, where there were even more customers than the day before.

"Saturday is our busiest day," Pepper told her when she asked about the people gathered around to watch her paint. It was one thing to turn away from their prying eyes, quite another to have to pull her focus away from her painting every time someone asked a question.

Good thing Gott granted me patience, she thought as she began to block in the quilt on the clothesline. It was slow going, but some progress was made.

As she parted with James in front of his house, she reminded him that she would be visiting in the evening. After all, it was courtship night. James seemed tired, but he didn't disagree. "Are you going to shine a flashlight on my window?" he teased.

"Maybe I will. More likely I'll just come through the front door."

◦◦◦

Once she got home, Mamm asked her to hitch up a buggy and go fetch Bethany and cousin Ruthie from the roadside stand.

"Those girls are so eager to make some sales, they wiped out every jar of jam we had in the pantry," Mamm said as she leaned down to search through a kitchen cabinet. "We're low on Tupperware. I wonder where it all went."

Over to the sugar shack, filled with food for Shandell. Rachel paused in the doorway, tempted to tell her mother everything. Mamm would be disappointed that she hadn't said something earlier, but she would understand that Shandell needed help. With one hand pressed to the wall, she asked: "Mamm? Did you hear about any more stealing in town today?"

"Nay," Betsy answered without looking up from the cabinet. She straightened, placing a square plastic container on the counter. "I'm hoping it's over, just a bad wave passing through."

"Me, too." For a moment she wondered if she was a thief, too, taking her mother's Tupperware. But she was going to return it all, and she lived here. It was different, but Rachel didn't fancy walking on the edge of right and wrong. "I'd best go get the girls," she said, heading out to the stables.

∞

As Pansy trotted down the road, Rachel squinted to make out the colorful fabric waving like flags in the breeze. Were the girls selling Amish dresses?

"They're aprons for cooking," Bethany explained. "Mamm let us use leftover cloth. We've been sewing and sewing."

"They're meant as Mother's Day gifts." Ruthie's amber eyes flashed with joy. "Remy thought Englishers would take a liking to them, and she's right. We sold three today, and a few jars of jam."

"We were hoping to stay open awhile, in case some more customers come by." Bethany slid a few jars to the front of the counter. "Can we stay a little bit longer, sister dear?"

Rachel put her hands on her hips. "Trying to butter me up?" Although she was tired, she couldn't resist the hopeful smiles of these girls. "Just a few minutes. It'll be dark soon, and Mamm wants us home for supper. You're eating with us, Ruthie."

"Denki, Rachel." Ruthie clapped her hands together. "Maybe the next person to come by will want some flowers."

A few cars passed by, but two stopped. Rachel hung back near the buggy, rubbing Pansy. It was good for the two younger girls to handle things on their own.

One customer bought an apron for her mother. The second car contained two women who were on their way to see a show in

Paradise. The blond woman purchased two aprons and some jam. "I'll be back tomorrow for flowers. I would take some geraniums now, but I don't want them to sit in the car overnight."

"We'll be here," Bethany promised. "All day tomorrow."

"They're good flowers. Really hardy," Ruthie said. "Our grand-mother started them in the greenhouse."

Such good little salespeople, Rachel thought with a smile.

As the two ladies were walking to their car, another car pulled off the road, raising dust as it slid to a stop along the gravel at the roadside. The driver, a young man, grimaced as he slammed the car door and passed the other customers.

"You selling any food?" the young man shouted toward the stand.

"We have jam," Ruthie and Bethany answered in unison, then looked at each other and giggled.

"Oh, yeah? What kind of jam is that?" He palmed one of the jars and lifted it to read the label. "Apricot? Nah."

"We got strawberry jam, too," Bethany offered.

"How about bread? You got any bread or rolls?"

"Sorry, mister." Ruthie shrugged. "But that's a good idea."

Bethany shook her head. "Who wants bread for Mother's Day?" she asked her cousin.

The man rolled the jelly jar between his palms. Something about the hungry way his eyes combed the stand made Rachel watch him carefully. There was a tingling sensation at the back of her neck; she sensed danger.

"Have you girls seen a runaway girl around here? She's a shorty. Black hair with blue highlights. Her name's Shandell."

Shandell . . .

This was Gary, looking for Shandell.

Rachel's heart began to hammer in her chest and fear was sour on the back of her tongue. She didn't think this man would hurt her or her family, but facing him was like driving near the edge of a cliff. If one wheel of the buggy slipped, the whole thing could go tumbling down.

She moved away from the buggy and came around the stand behind the girls. Best to let her presence be known.

Ruthie shook her head. "I never heard a name like that before."

Gary's eyes grew round as he noticed Rachel. "How about you? You see a girl pass by, maybe hitchhiking? Not Amish. She's American."

"I just got here," Rachel said, dodging the question. "But these girls work the stand more than I do. They'd know better than me."

"We haven't seen anybody walk by today except Plain folk," Bethany reported.

He stepped away from the counter and grabbed at an apron hanging from a nail. "What's this?"

As the girls went around the counter to take the apron down and talk it up, he backed toward the counter. Eager to move this man on and get the girls home, Rachel went to the buggy to clear away the lap blankets and umbrellas. With a crime spree in the area, it would not do to leave these wares along the roadside overnight.

"Well, thanks anyway, girls." Gary got into his car, and the engine roared.

Rachel caught a glimpse of the license plate from Maryland, and then the car sputtered out with a violent spray of gravel behind the wheels.

"Time to go." Rachel couldn't still the thundering of her heartbeat, and she longed for the safety of home. "We need to load everything into the buggy."

"But we'll be back in the morning," Bethany pointed out.

"We don't want to have things stolen, the way they were last week. And we know there's been a rash of theft in Halfway."

"Then it's good to take care of our merchandise," Ruthie said. "We can bring it back in the morning. It won't take long at all."

"I guess." Reluctantly, Bethany started to gather jars into a sack. "Hold on a second. What happened to the jam that was here on the counter? I just put two out on display and they're gone now."

Ruthie left a crate of geraniums to come over to the counter. "Apricot and strawberry, right? Where'd they go?"

"Oh, honeygirls." Rachel frowned as they did a quick inventory. "They're gone. Someone must have taken them." And she had a strong notion of just whom the thief was.

The stolen jam was all the talk at the dinner table. The table was full, with good, steaming hot food like ham that Dat had grilled outside, along with mashed potatoes, gravy, dressing, buttered corn, and peas. Rachel never could get enough of Mamm's mashed potatoes, creamy but with little bits of solid potato inside.

"Just forget about it," Abe said, sitting tall. "Nothing you can do about it now."

Little Davey was more sympathetic. "Don't be sad. We have more jam, right, Mamm?"

"We do," Betsy agreed.

Still, Ruthie and Bethany felt cheated, feeling the brunt of the second theft from the farm stand in little more than a week.

"Why does this keep happening to us?" Ruthie asked as she added corn to her plate.

"Ours is not to question why." Mamm passed the peas down the table. "Just keep doing what you're doing. It's better to suffer wrong than to commit wrong."

"I think it was that last customer. I'm sure it was him." Bethany's eyes were round as quarters.

"Easy there, half-pint," Ben said. "I've never seen you so mad."

"Someone stole things that belong to me," Bethany said fervently. "More than once!"

"Now, let's pipe down a little bit," Dat said. "It's not our place to judge this man or to punish this thief. It would do us better to look at our own actions. We are made in the image of Gott. We're here to do Gott's work."

Bethany's lower lip jutted out in a pout; she wasn't so quick to accept Dat's advice. "But Dat, someone is stealing from us."

"If that's Gott's will, we must accept it. Turn the other cheek and put your mind to good deeds. A man is starved by cruelty but fed by kindness." Nate held a glass of milk aloft, considering it thoughtfully. "I choose to be nourished."

It was some comfort, hearing her father's words. Better to think about the good she could do than the evil in the world. This reminded her that she was doing the right thing by helping Shandell. What was it Dat had said? Kindness could feed the soul. Rachel never knew her dat was such a wise man. His words stuck with her as she washed dishes, her arms up to the elbows in suds. As they sang some songs and yodeled together, Molly and Ruthie did the drying, while Bethany put everything away. That left Rose free to be out in the stables, tending the horses she loved. Good sister that she was, she would harness Banjo so that Rachel could ride over to visit James.

As the horse's hooves clicked rhythmically on the road, Rachel drew her sweater closer around her and thought what a difference a week had made, in so many ways. Barely a week ago, she had felt her James slipping away, like soil through her fingers. And tonight, the path was lit by a new hope.

She arrived to find James staring at a dying fire.

"So you did wait up for me," she teased. The house was quiet. She knew his teen brothers were most likely out and about, courting their favorite girls. Sister Verena wasn't quite in her rumspringa yet, and his parents had already gone up to bed. "But you didn't keep the fire going."

"I got caught thinking about Dat and this new manager for the orchard."

"It's not a problem you can whittle down tonight, so put it out of your mind." Bending near the stove, she opened the door with a poker and added a log. It would take a hearty fire to chase the cold from her bones. "It's courtship night. I'm here to distract you from this Orchard Al and Shandell and the treatments and exercises you do every day."

"Mmm. By the way, Shandell gave me your dress back for a washing when I brought her food. She was going to eat and go to sleep. I don't think she's used to that kind of work."

Kneeling on the floor, Rachel smiled as she added another log. "Ya, but she really threw herself into it."

"Threw herself right into the pile of manure," James added.

She turned back to catch him grinning. At least his mood had lightened. "Lucky for you, she moved quick and got out of the way so your father didn't see her. That was a close call."

"I was sure Dat saw her. But she picked a clever place to hide. Clever but dirty."

"She's a good girl." Rachel rubbed her arms briskly, trying to warm up. "I have my own bit of news about Shandell. I think I came face-to-face with her Gary, and let me tell you, it was very scary." She stared into the flames as the heat began to blossom around her.

"Rachel . . ." She could hear James wheeling himself closer. A comforting hand pressed her shoulder. "When was this?"

She explained how the young man had come by the farm stand. "He's a good talker with a slick layer of charm, but there's something about him that set my teeth on edge. The way he stared at us. His eyes—there was a hunger there. Like a wolf starving in the snow. And when he left, his car roared and stones went flying from the rear tires. He's an angry one, no denying that."

"I'm glad she decided not to go back with him," he said.

"Ya, and I hope she never has to see him again. Imagine a parent sending that man to pick up a child."

"She's not a child," James said, "though you treat her that way."

"I worry about her."

"I do, too, but we can't whittle that problem away in one night."

Hearing her own words tossed back at her made her snort. Both his hands were on her shoulders now, massaging gently. She dropped her chin to her chest for a moment and basked in the warmth of the fire and James's strong hands.

"Still cold?" he asked.

"I'm getting better." It had helped to share the story about Gary; carrying that block of fear around had chilled her inside.

"I know one way to warm you up."

She tipped her head up and turned to him.

"Kumm." He opened his arms wide. "Sit here on my lap."

She pressed a hand to her mouth. "I don't want to hurt your legs."

"My legs are fine . . . good and solid. It was my spine that was hurt, and that healed months ago. Kumm to me, Rachel. I need to hold you close."

Swallowing over the lump of emotion in her throat, she rose, levered her hands on his shoulders, and eased herself down. The body beneath hers felt sturdy and solid and strong. She swung her legs over one armrest of his chair and leaned into him, wrapping her arms around his neck.

"Is that okay? I'm not hurting you, am I?"

"You can't hurt a strong man like me." His arms were around her, holding her secure, and he tipped his head sideways, toward her face. "You smell good."

"Not like manure?"

He chuckled. "Not at all." His hand moved to the base of her skull, his fingertips massaging the sensitive skin on the nape of her neck. "And you feel good."

Her face was just inches from his, and she could see the shiny dark shadow along his chin, and the long sweep of his dark eyelashes. His eyes were dark and smoky and sometimes, like tonight, shiny as a lake. You could see so much in a person's eyes. Often James's eyes were closed to the world, like windows that had been shut. But tonight, now she could see him, her James, and she could see the love and longing that had been shuttered inside for so long . . . too long.

He tipped his face down and touched her lips in a kiss that sent sweet shivers through her. Oh, dear James! She turned toward him and was lost in his arms. He smelled of lavender and leather—a much better combination than this morning's fare—and she breathed deeply. She couldn't get enough of him!

His hand moved over her shoulder blade, leaving a trail of tiny sparkles of sensation. They knew each other so well, inside and out. There was no doubt in her mind that Gott meant them to be together. It had been her own doubts about baptism last spring that had kept them from marrying in the fall.

Things would be so much simpler when they were man and wife, living together and loving each other in the ways that married couples learned. Those days could not come soon enough. In a few weeks she would begin her classes with the bishop, preparing to be baptized and be a full member of the church. Truly Amish.

In November, they would marry. Oh, James had his worries about that, but she would convince him that she loved him as he was, for better or worse, in sickness and in health.

❧ 34 ❧

Although it was Sunday, James awoke at four, as usual. He sat up in bed and pushed back the quilt, then remembered that it was Sunday, a welcome day of rest. There would be no early morning fertilizing in the orchard, and no trip into Paradise for treatment. Depending on what his mother had arranged, his family would go visiting, or else they'd be hosting family and friends here.

An easy day. Pulling the quilt back over his head, he breathed out a deep sigh and dropped back to sleep. This time, his waking dreams were of walking, or at least trying to walk. He was in the center of the highway, standing on the double yellow line, and a buggy was moving along in front of him.

The driver of the buggy turned back to him, and he recognized Rachel, her blue eyes flashing, her smile dazzling. "Kumm," she called to him, gesturing for him to catch up. "I'll wait for you."

She pulled in the reins and stopped the buggy, and James flexed his arms to jog to the buggy. But as his chest and arms heaved forward, his legs remained in place, as if they'd been nailed down to the street.

He struggled to move his legs, grunting and pushing with all his strength. He had to catch up . . . he needed to go with Rachel . . .

He awoke with a cry, thrashing at the quilt with his arms.

The ceiling overhead, with the small crack that he had memorized over the past months, was the ceiling of his parents' bedroom: the room Jimmy and Edna had vacated so that he could have access to a bedroom on the ground floor.

Because he couldn't walk.

Because he was confined to a wheelchair.

"Dear Gott, am I going to be half a man the rest of my life?"

He ran his hands over the tops of his thighs, thinking about his vow not to marry until he could stand on his own two feet. The thigh muscles were gaining better tone, an improvement either from the electric treatment or from the new physical therapy routine. The pressure of his fingertips was like a comb running down his thigh. He could feel. His legs weren't dead. There was hope.

"Ya. At this rate, I'll be walking when I'm ninety."

He tossed back the quilt and pulled himself up to a seated position. "Don't think I'm not grateful, Father. I'm glad to be alive. But if you could just bring my legs to life, too?"

♒

After breakfast James spent two hours in his room doing his exercises, which couldn't be neglected any day of the week. Then he headed outside into the pale spring sunshine and started wheeling himself toward the barn.

Hannah and Lovina looked up from the lawn, where they were tossing a Frisbee. "Mamm says you're not to go to the orchard, in case you forgot that it's Sunday," Lovina called after him.

"I know my days of the week. And I would never work on a Sunday." Now more than ever, he needed a day of rest. The physical therapy was taxing, and the buggy ride back and forth to Paradise made his days long. He rolled past the Doddy house, where he needed to chase some of the chickens back toward their coops, then on to the barn, where the cool shadows alternated with blocks of sunlight streaming in from above.

"There you go, boy," came Mark's voice from one of the stalls. "All combed down. That's got to feel good. Now . . . your hooves."

"Mark?" James wheeled over to the stall where his younger brother stood behind Rowdy, holding one of the horse's rear hooves between his legs. "I thought I'd find you here." It was hard to separate Mark from the horses, especially the unpopular, unreliable ones like Rowdy, who Mark insisted were misunderstood. "Didn't you brush this horse down yesterday?"

"He likes it," Mark said defensively, "and I do, too. See, it's not all about grooming. With a horse like Rowdy, you need to build trust, or else he'll never learn to pull the plow with the team. And the way to build trust is to spend time with a horse and teach him things. Start with the small lessons and slowly you start to challenge him."

James rubbed his knuckles against his clean-shaven jaw as he listened to the process that sounded similar to the physical therapy the doctors were putting him through. Well, lessons were lessons.

"I came to see if you wanted to come out for a walk with me in the orchard." The Sunday orchard walk was a tradition Doddy Elmo had started with James when he was just a toddler. For various reasons, James's brothers Luke, Peter, and Matt never quite took to it, but Mark had begun to tag along with James and Elmo just as soon as his little legs could carry him.

"I'm not finished with Rowdy, but I guess I can pick out his hooves later."

James knew the horse didn't need much attention on dry days like this. "Rowdy will be here when we get back, but the apricot trees won't wait. They're thick with bud. Some even starting to bloom."

Mark lowered Rowdy's hoof to the ground and went around to pat the horse's withers. "I'll be back, boy."

Reaching up, Mark took his hat from a post in the stable and pulled it on over the dark hair most members of the Lapp family had in common. As they headed down the wide path that bordered the orchard, James recalled coming this way with his grandfather every Sunday, talking about everything and anything that popped into his head. Now the same easy rapport existed between Mark and him as they talked about the family members that would be visiting today, about the end of the school year, which Mark was looking forward to, and about the new manager, Orchard Al, who was due to arrive today before supper.

"Look over there." James pointed his chin toward the apricot orchard. "Amazing, isn't it? You think you'd get sick of it, but every year, come springtime, the new blossoms look better and better."

Mark ran ahead a little and skipped down the row between the pink blossoms. "Why are the apricots always the first?"

James shrugged. "It's the way Gott planned it. We'll see the peaches start to bloom in another week or two. Then the pears, cherries, and apples won't be far behind."

With pale blossoms overhead, he paused in the center of the row to take in the sweet, floral fragrance. The buds had just begun opening, but within a week, these rows would be covered with flowers thick as popcorn balls covering each branch.

"Spring is the best time." Hands on his hips, Mark looked around with a bright smile. "Do you smell that?"

"I do." James was glad his younger brother was growing to love the orchard as he did.

"Remember when Doddy used to slide his feet along in the carpet of petals, stirring all the white dots into the air?"

James grinned. "Walking in heaven, that's what he called it."

"Ya." Mark held his arms wide. "So next week, after all the petals come down, we'll be walking in heaven."

One can only hope, James thought. At this rate, he would settle for walking on earth. Leaning back in his chair, he followed the line of blossoms to the sky, a vibrant blue overhead. He could hear Doddy's voice in his ear. *Nothing like the first blossoms of spring.*

He was lost in the memory of his grandfather's advice, jokes, and riddles when Mark interrupted.

"Who in the world is that with Dat?" Mark asked.

James turned his chair to face the wide path, where Dat was walking with a short, graying man with silver glasses. "I reckon that's Orchard Al," he said under his breath.

Mark's brown eyes opened wide as he took in the new foreman. "He's not as big as I expected, and he looks old."

"He's old Jacob's friend. Sure he's gonna be old."

"James! Mark! Come meet Orchard Al."

Setting his jaw, James wheeled his chair around and started up the lane. From up close, Orchard Al seemed younger than Jacob. Instead of the wrinkles of age, he had round cheeks that were shiny and ruddy like a sun-ripened peach.

Dat introduced the man, who set his hat back and fixed his steely gray eyes on James. "Please, call me Albee. Everyone does. And I understand you're the one I should be going around with. You've been in charge of these orchards for the past year or so. You've done a right good job."

Although pleasure swelled in his chest at the compliment, James kept his expression grim. This was the man who was taking his job away.

Dat had an easy smile for the stranger. "Albee and his wife, Judy, are here for dinner, all the way from Lebanon Valley. They're going to stay with Jacob tonight, then head home and pack up."

Because the Miller orchard was some twenty miles northwest of Halfway, Albee and Judy would live in the Doddy house till the harvest was over. His sons, in their twenties, would manage the Lebanon Valley orchard while he was gone. "You won't even know we're here."

"Ya, good." This Albee was a friendly fellow, but James would not open that door. The sooner Orchard Al was finished here, the better. "We'd best get back for supper."

"We'll go together," Dat said. "Albee has seen enough of the orchard, ya?"

"A fine patch of Gott's earth you got here. Well maintained," Albee said. "Last year's pruning was spot on. Makes the growing season that much easier."

James waited for Dat to agree that his oldest son had managed the orchard well, but the words were not spoken.

⁕

Noon dinner was one of James's favorites—baked chicken coated with cornflakes, along with baked potatoes, buttered peas, corn, salad, peaches, and applesauce. James's aunt Fanny Lapp was visiting with her family, and James was glad for the help that Fanny and cousins Emma and Elsie brought to Mamm in the kitchen. It seemed that Mamm never got a moment's rest these days, but this afternoon, her eyes were bright as she cooed and rocked Fanny's baby, little Tom. And Edna beamed when Judy Miller asked for her recipe for "that wonderful good chicken."

Looking around the dinner table, James still had trouble taking in the changes in their family since that highway accident in January. James's uncle Tom, Fanny's husband, had been killed in the collision that had injured James. Tom was still missed by so many. But just weeks later, little Tom had been born—a boy who would never know his father. There had been such joy and sadness at the same time. Trapped in the hospital, James had listened to reports from his family in a daze of pain and medication.

Fortunately, most of the twelve passengers in the van had survived without injury. Rachel was untouched, as was James's cousin Elsie, who had a special place in his heart for her kindness and constant smile.

During the meal, Elsie talked about Haley Donovan. "Have you noticed the way Haley and Dylan spend so much time together?" Elsie asked. "Don't they always come together, in the same car, when they visit?"

Before James could answer, Jimmy piped up. "They're not coming around here anymore. We had too many Englishers in and out of here. I had to put an end to that."

Elsie's eyes grew wide as she nibbled on a piece of chicken.

The topic would have dropped, but Fanny's son Will seemed interested. "Why don't you like the English?" the five-year-old asked Jimmy.

A good question, James thought, turning toward his father.

Jimmy swallowed as he dropped a bone onto his plate. "I like the English just fine, but the Bible says that Plain folk must live on this earth but not be part of it, the way Englishers are. We need to live in peace with them, but separate. Too many times, Plain folk cross over that line and they lose the old ways."

Although Dat's words made sense, they didn't match what James knew about him. There was no denying that his father disliked Englishers, and that disdain was deep-rooted in a terrible incident from Jimmy's childhood. Unfortunately, James had never heard the whole story. Neither had his brothers or sisters. Every now and then the Lapp children asked Jimmy about that childhood tragedy, and their father shook his head, telling them that it was all long ago and far away.

It may have been long ago, but James sensed that it was never far from his father's mind. Jimmy was carrying the burden of that grief around every day, like a hay bale on his shoulder. James had always known that, though he'd never been brave enough to press his father about it.

After supper, James went out to the yard with the men and children, who decided it was warm enough to play badminton.

"Can I play?" Fanny's three-year-old daughter, Beth, pressed a racket to her face. "Beth a bad mitten!"

That brought a chuckle from the older ones. When Elsie came out a few minutes later, James smiled and nodded at a lawn chair beside Caleb. "Have a seat, Els. Take a load off. It's not often that you get to escape kitchen duty."

"Oh, I don't mind. There's a lot of laughing and yodeling that goes on in a kitchen. And if you have a worry, there's always someone to share your load in the kitchen." She eased back onto a chair and propped herself up with strong arms. Elsie was a little person, born with a medical condition that made her short in stature, with widely spaced teeth. Little people were widely accepted by the Amish because Gott certainly intended to create them as such. Gott did not make mistakes. And whenever James spent time with Elsie, he thanked the Almighty that she was born so special. This was a young person who knew how to let Gott's light shine. "You know, James, maybe you should spend a little more time in the kitchen," she teased. "We need to get you smiling more."

"That is a good plan, Elsie," Caleb agreed.

"It might crack my face," James insisted.

"Well, you probably don't realize it, but you're very lucky to have Judy and Albee moving into the Doddy house. Judy loves to bake, and I hear Albee spent most of his life as a nurseryman."

"Mmm." James turned toward the badminton game.

"Don't growl now. Tell me about your treatment. I heard they plug an electric cord right into your back."

James snorted. "Is that the gossip out there?"

"How does electricity feel?" Caleb asked. "Does it get hot?"

James described the process from start to finish, including the hours of physical therapy.

"Gott's wonders never cease." Elsie clapped her small hands together. "Do the doctors think this will cure you?"

James rubbed his palms against the armrests of his chair. "The doctors think it's going well, but me, I want to be out there climbing trees. It's all too slow. I don't want to wait weeks or months or years to be managing the orchard again."

"James!" Elsie's brown eyes opened wide. "Don't be so impatient. You are improving! Sounds like a miracle to me. Do you think you'll walk again?"

He shrugged. "I've been able to stand."

"That's amazing! Excuse me while I jump for joy."

"This is good news," Caleb agreed.

"But I'm tied to the machine, and I want to be walking already."

"I sure can understand that." Elsie's face was thoughtful as she swung her short legs under the chair. "But some things can't be hurried. Time is a funny thing. We try to measure it in our own way, but Gott's measure is different. He's got eternity on His side."

"It takes a century for Gott to make a sturdy oak tree," Caleb said. "We can't say it's not worth the wait."

"Can't argue with that," James said. He knew Elsie and Caleb were right. Still, it did not ease his impatience with Gott. He wanted to get back to the business of life, and he wanted it now.

Elsie cocked her head to one side as she eyed him skeptically.

"Ah, but you don't feel it in your heart." She tapped her chest with one hand. "I know how that is. Sometimes our hearts and minds are in two different places."

James nodded. His cousin was insightful.

"I guess time is one of Gott's great mysteries," she said.

He tipped his hat back slightly and folded his arms. "What has two hands, one face, always runs, but stays in place?"

"A riddle!" She poked her brother. "Do you know this one?"

When Caleb shrugged, James answered: "A clock."

The chirpy laughter that floated from Elsie's throat made James smile. Maybe time was not on his side, but it was good to know that his family was.

∞ 35 ∞

Crossing off one more day on the calendar Rachel had brought her, Shandell counted the days since her arrival here at the sugar shack. In just a few weeks, she was a changed person! The things that used to matter, getting the coolest jeans and the latest Uggs, none of that was important to her anymore. And the friends she had hung out with—Lucia, Ryan, Kylie, and Gary, well, she could just imagine what they were saying about her now when they hung out in Ryan's garage. Gary would have soured them all on her. Somehow, that didn't hurt her so much. Probably because she had no intention of wasting away time in Ryan's garage when she returned back to Baltimore. Nope, she was going to get back on track for school and get herself a job. If she could just go home, she knew she would set forth on a more positive path for her life.

Getting home was the main problem right now. She hadn't been able to reach her mom. Of course, she had given up on calling the house, since Phil always managed to snatch up the phone. She was beginning to believe that he was keeping her mother away from her. Shandell couldn't even get her mother to take a call on her cell phone, and she had ventured out to the phone shanty a few times, late at night, hoping that Mom would pick up. She was beginning to worry that something bad had happened to Mom. Not that she'd ever seen Phil become violent, but alcohol could bring out the worst in a person. It was so frustrating that there was no way for Mom to call her back. All she could do right now was pray that everything was okay and her mother was safe.

A few times, as she stared into the dark shack at night with the wind howling through the thin clapboards, she felt like the last person on earth. So alone. She wondered if her mom missed her. Was there anyone out there who cared about her?

Thinking back over the past few years, she kept flashing on two girls who were her friends when she had started high school—Patti Santonia and Isabel Chapman. Patti's family had moved to Boston last year, but by that time Shandell had veered off to the kids in Ryan's garage. She wondered what Patti was up to now. And Isabel—the minister's daughter with curly red hair—how was she doing? The last time she had talked to Isabel, they had commiserated about the algebra midterm. "When this test is finished, you should come over," Isabel had told her. "We'll make some brownies and watch a movie." Although she'd agreed, Shandell had known it wouldn't happen. Her new friends would have laughed if they heard she'd spent a Friday night baking, and Isabel's parents would never have let her hang out in some guy's garage with no parents around to supervise. Looking back, she wished she had gone out of her way to keep the friendship with Isabel going. If her cell phone was charged, she would call Isabel right now, but she couldn't call anyone from this one-room shanty.

When loneliness crowded her thoughts, she found some solace

in her Bible storybook. Then one night she remembered what Dad used to say about angels. "You have a guardian angel who watches over you."

Maybe that was true. Since the incident at the Kings' roadside stand two weeks ago, there had been no more signs of Gary . . . no rash of local vandalism or theft. No reports of stolen gas or food at convenience stores. He seemed to have given up on her and left Lancaster County. Good riddance!

That was the good news. The bad news—Shandell had to make numerous trips to the outhouse each day and she felt kind of crummy. It was too embarrassing to explain it to James, but she was going to tell Rachel, next time the two of them were alone.

Although Shandell enjoyed her little morning and night rituals of the one-room cabin, the highlight of each day was spending time with James and Rachel. Every day after James's PT, the Amish couple came back to the sugar shack for a visit—James's exercise journey through the orchard—and the hours spent laughing and eating and talking really flew by.

Shandell loved hearing them talk about their families. Once she had thought it was desirable to be an only child—the star of the show—but from the affectionate and teasing way her Amish friends spoke of their siblings, well, it was sort of like trying to follow a soap opera on TV. James had three sisters and four brothers, and Rachel had eight siblings, and they knew lots of families who had even more kids.

When James and Rachel asked about her family, Shandell told them the truth. "I'll be honest with you. My home life isn't exactly picture-perfect." She admitted that Phil had a drinking problem, and her mom had become a workaholic. "I used to think that she was working hard to stay ahead of all the bills. Now I'm beginning to wonder if part of the reason for her two jobs is to stay away from

Phil. He's surly and mean when he drinks, and the house is dark and depressing. He keeps the shades closed, and he can barely get off his corner of the couch."

Over the course of many afternoons, Shandell's story had slipped out, bit by bit. James and Rachel listened as she told them how Mom met Phil, and how the three of them had lived together happily until Phil lost his job. When Rachel asked about Shandell's father, it was as if she'd unlocked a magic box of memories, and the stories came spilling out, one after another, about how Dad nicknamed her Sunny because of her bright smile, and how he would carry her on his shoulders, and how he would sit with her on the living room floor and let her paint his nails or serve him pretend tea. In winter, he helped her build snow people and in summer he dug in the sand with her at the beach, building sand castles with towers and moats, only to watch them sink and wash away with the tides.

"He was an amazing dad," Shandell told them. "After he died, I spent the first five years thinking he would walk through the front door at the end of each day. And the next five years, I was angry at my mother for letting him die. As if she had any way to stop it." She told them about how her father had been killed in a construction accident. He'd been working on the pipes in a high-rise building when the floor he'd been crawling on gave way. Since she'd been young, she had been spared most of the terrible details. Mostly, she was glad he didn't suffer.

"It's hard to understand why Gott takes some away to heaven so young," Rachel had told her. "So hard when we're left here, hurting and missing our loved ones. But Gott doesn't make mistakes. It's all part of His plan."

"I guess He doesn't," Shandell agreed. "But I've sure made my share of bad choices."

In so many ways, Rachel was a sympathetic, responsible older sister. She was quick to smile or offer a sympathetic nod, and she always made sure Shandell got enough to eat. In the short time Shandell had been here, Rachel seemed to be making up for all the mothering Shandell had missed at home.

And James was like a big brother. When he wasn't cracking jokes or telling riddles, he was a good listener. His comedic bent definitely made a task like hauling water or chopping wood easier, and it seemed the better she got to know him, the more he joked around. He had a million and one facts about trees and birds, and he had taught Shandell how to build a proper fire and skip stones on the stream.

One day, when Shandell was sitting with James, she teased him about marrying Rachel. "What are you two waiting for?" she asked. "You're so perfect together."

"For starters, wedding season is in the fall, and Rachel isn't a member of the church yet. I can't marry her until she's baptized." He explained that Rachel had just begun meeting with the bishop to prepare for baptism in October. Shandell hadn't realized that an Amish person chose to be baptized, but James explained that the rumspringa time, which Englishers made such a big deal about, was often a time when teens sowed their wild oats. "After rumspringa, most Amish decide to join the faith. When you have good family and friends, there's no reason to go anywhere else."

She understood that. "I think most of us want to live the way we're brought up. You have a wonderful orchard here, and you and Rachel have been so generous, but I can't imagine living Plain, as you guys do." She hurled a stone toward the river, and it skipped a few times.

"Good," James said.

"Practice makes perfect," she said. "So . . . don't change the subject. After Rachel gets baptized, you two are getting married?"

He frowned. "This is not something I should be talking about with you."

"Please, humor me. I have no love life or reliable friends or family at the moment. I need a little hope, an emotional lift."

"We want to marry," James admitted, "but when I got injured, I called it off."

"What?"

"Rachel can't be stuck with a husband in a wheelchair. She doesn't deserve that."

"But maybe she wants it. You can't decide for her."

"We'll marry when I can stand on my own two feet. When I'm a whole man again."

"Really. Do you think being a man is about walking?"

"A man shouldn't be wheeled around like a wooden toy."

"I have a cousin in California who was a soldier in the U.S. Army. He lost both legs in Afghanistan, and there's no shame in that. It was rough for him at first, but he's doing just fine now. He's got two kids and he's a computer whiz. A real hero."

"I don't need to be a hero. Just a gardener. A man who can take care of his family's orchard."

"But I've seen you taking care of things from that wheelchair."

He shook his head. "It's not enough."

"Well, I'm sorry about the accident and all, but from my point of view, it's what's inside that makes a real man. Gary—nothing inside. You? Loaded with character."

He didn't comment, but cast a stone into the brook below.

"And, really, don't you respect Rachel's intelligence?"

"I do. I know she's a very smart girl."

"Then let her decide whether or not she wants to deal with you and your issues. Don't boss her around. Think about it."

His dark eyes seemed thoughtful when he turned to her. "And I have a question for you."

"Shoot."

"Where can you get milk shakes?"

She rolled her eyes. "At the Dairy Queen?"

He shook his head. "From nervous cows."

"Do you always crack a joke when the conversation gets too personal for you?"

He tossed another stone. "You're getting to know me well."

෨ 36 ෨

"Oh, honeygirl, I knew something wasn't quite right." Rachel bent over the girl curled up on the bench and stoked her hair. The poor girl was so very sick.

When Shandell let out a tiny moan, Rachel clucked her tongue sympathetically. "I knew you weren't eating right, and now look at you, pale as a sheet." Rachel had arrived at the sugar shack to find Shandell inside the dark cabin, writhing in pain on the hard wooden bench.

"I've been having these terrible cramps," Shandell said, squeezing her eyes shut, "and diarrhea. It's been off and on for a few days now. Sometimes it feels like there's a knife in my belly."

Sympathetic, Rachel rubbed the girl's back and stroked her dark hair gently. "My little sister Molly gets bellyaches a lot," she commiserated. "And one thing Mamm gives her is black pepper. I'm going back to the Lapps and see if I can get a little bit for you. It's a good natural remedy."

Gliding on her scooter, Rachel rolled down the path through the orchard and thought about the sick Englisher girl. Rachel worried about her in so many ways. The more she learned about Shandell's home, the more she cherished her own loving family. Rachel had not been surprised to learn that Shandell's stepfather had a problem with alcohol. Although the Amish community did not condone drinking, everyone knew someone who had had too much to drink. Some Amish youth on rumspringa binged on beers—especially the boys. Rachel had never tried alcohol, but then she was one of those Plain girls who was content with her lot.

As she approached the main house, she bit her lips together. It would be a challenge, borrowing from an Amish kitchen. Fortunately, James's sister Verena was the only one in sight when she got there.

"James is still out checking the orchard with Albee, but I'm wondering if you have something for a stomachache." Rachel didn't say whose stomach ached, and Verena didn't ask.

"There's black pepper in the pantry," Verena said. "That's what Mamm starts with when we're sick. And honey helps, too. A little bit before eating. We don't have any lemon, but pepper and honey will do you for now."

"Denki." Rachel went into the pantry and helped herself to two paper cups, one for each home remedy.

"Are you staying for supper tonight?" Verena asked as she checked on a bin of rising dough.

Sometimes Rachel stayed to supper with the Lapps after she and James returned from his treatment. It was easier to catch a ride home from one of James's brothers after supper. "Not today. I have plenty of time to ride my scooter home during daylight." The days were getting longer—praise Gott!—and the orchard was beginning to fill with fluffy blossoms. What a pleasure spring was!

Rachel smiled as she rode her scooter back to the sugar shack, going out of her way so that she could pass the peach orchard, now in bloom. The fat blossoms filled the air with their sweet perfume, and the way they lined up so neatly reminded her of the frosting flowers on the edge of a wedding cake. She didn't see James and Albee, but she knew they were out there, talking and looking for signs of pests and disease.

Just the thought of James brought a smile to her lips. He was doing so well, looking healthy as a plow horse. The extra sleep did him good, and the new therapy was building up the muscles in his arms and legs. And the treatment! Well, the time spent at the Paradise clinic had taken a lot out of James, but it was all worth it. The treatment was working!

She had just learned the exciting news a few days ago when she arrived early to pick James up. The receptionist at the clinic told her that James was still in the physical therapy center. She went into the big room and, lo and behold, he'd been standing there! Standing on his own, with just a walker nearby to help him balance.

It was a miracle—had to be!

"Praise be to Gott!" she'd gasped, catching his attention. The doctors and medical technicians all looked over at her, too.

"Amazing, isn't it?" Doc Finley asked. When she nodded, he explained that James was doing better than anyone anticipated. He had exceeded the progress of earlier patients in this study, but then his case was a bit different, with less damage to a different area of the spinal cord.

The medical explanation blurred in Rachel's mind. She saw her James standing up, and seeing was believing!

"You're staring like an Englisher tourist," James said.

"I know and I don't care. You're standing on your own two feet, James."

"I am. But it's because of the treatment. Every day, I need the electric treatment to make it onto my feet."

"It's a start, James. A wonderful good beginning." Unable to contain her grin, she moved closer to him and crossed her arms over her sweater. "And now we can start planning the wedding," she whispered. She wouldn't have said this in front of Plain folk, but she knew that the others weren't close enough to hear. "You said you couldn't marry me until you stood on your own two feet. Well, thanks to the Almighty and these doctors, you're standing now."

Wavering ever so slightly on his legs, James turned back to Rachel, his dark eyes sparkling with mirth. "I guess you've got me now."

"I do." Her smile couldn't contain the joy shining in her heart. James was getting better. Gott had answered their prayers.

With a heart full of excitement, Rachel couldn't wait to tell everyone, but as they rode home in the buggy, James had cautioned her to wait.

"I'm not walking yet," he said. "If Dat hears that I'm standing, it would be just like him to cut off the rest of the treatment. We can't let that happen."

"Would your dat really do something like that?" She had always thought of Jimmy as a good, kind father.

"We can't take that chance."

She had agreed with James. It had been hard not to say something to Shandell when the three of them were together, but Rachel had kept her word.

Now, ironically, Shandell's health was getting pokey as James was getting better.

When Rachel arrived back at the sugar shack, she was glad to see Shandell sitting outside on a chair facing the stream.

"Look at you! Out of bed. Are you feeling better?"

Shandell gave a little smile. "I think the fresh air helped." Her face was still pale, but her skin had lost the sheen of sweat and fever.

"How are the cramps?" Rachel asked.

"Gone for now. But they've been coming and going over the past few days."

"Well, I've got some home remedies that should help you feel better." Rachel went inside to mix up some honey and pepper with warm water.

"Thanks, Rachel. Did anyone ever say that you'd make a good nurse?" Shandell called after her. "Oh, that's right. You Amish finish school after eighth grade. Wow, that's an educational plan that would have worked well for me. Except I'm not so good with the farm work. Fertilizer is not my friend."

With an amused grin, Rachel handed over the cup. "You're getting about as funny as James. Now drink this up, and I'll check on you tomorrow."

"Thanks. I don't know what I'd do without you. I mean it."

Rachel shrugged off the compliment, but as Shandell's dark eyes held hers, there was no denying it: She was getting mighty attached to this dear girl.

❦ 37 ❦

The pear trees were thick with fat white buds on the verge of blooming as James wheeled himself over a mound of grass to get closer to the trees. On the lookout for leaf rollers, a type of caterpillar that liked to eat leaves and flowers, James reached up to grab a leafy branch. "I don't see any caterpillars, but if we're going to spray for them, we need to do it soon."

"That's what I was thinking," Albee said from across the grass divider. Hand atop his hat, he tipped his head back to examine the higher branches. "Got to make a decision, and I just wanted your advice."

They did not spray pesticides when they weren't needed, but then Albee knew that. James sensed that this was the new foreman's attempt to gain his trust.

"No need to spray."

"That's what I thought." Albee nodded. "Just wanted to be sure."

True to his word, Albee and his wife had been quiet tenants in the Doddy house, keeping to themselves and taking their meals on their own unless invited to the Lapp home. A few times Judy had come over to help Mamm with quilting, and they talked about canning and making jam later in the season. And it had been something of a relief not to be responsible for the orchard while his treatment took so much of his time. Still, James did not want to open up to this man. Albee was living proof that James's injury was taking him away from the orchard he loved.

"Any day now, these buds are going to open up." Albee's voice held wonder and anticipation. "This is a very good time of year to work in an orchard."

"My grandfather used to say that spring hadn't sprung until the trees were in bloom." Even as James answered, he saw the resemblance between his grandfather and Albee Miller. Was that why Dat had hired this man? Maybe he missed his father more than he let on. Jimmy and Elmo had not worked side by side the way Elmo and James had, but there had been a strong respect and affection between father and son.

As the two men continued inspecting the row of pear trees, James squinted into the light and imagined Albee to be his grandfather. Both men had that same spry step, that habit of tipping the head back and staring up at the tree branches and sky, as if the real hub of the wheel of life was somewhere up above. *Looking up to heaven?* James wondered. *Maybe they know something the rest of us still have to figure out.*

"Who is out there in the sugar shack?" Albee asked suddenly, taking James off guard. "I see you coming and going there every day, but there's smoke coming from the chimney long after you're gone, and I know a responsible young person like you wouldn't leave a fire untended."

James could not lie to this man. "It's an Englisher who fell on some hard times. Rachel and I are helping her. But no one else knows she's out there, and I didn't want to bother Jimmy with the details. Having Englishers around . . . it's a sore spot with my father."

"That's your way of telling me to keep it to myself." Albee stroked his gray beard, his soft eyes thoughtful. "When I took this job, I told your father I wouldn't meddle in the family business, and I'm a man of my word." He let out a breath. "For what it's worth, I've never seen anyone loitering about there. Just as long as that fire is under control."

"It's under control," James assured him.

"Then I guess we're finished here, except for one more thing. I've been talking to your father about the upkeep of the orchard. It's clear that he knows the business end well, but the trees? Not so much. He doesn't understand how much work is done out here. He's lucky to have you, James, with your knowledge and experience. You've done a good job holding this place together."

The old man's praise stirred up a maelstrom of emotion that rose in James's throat and lodged there, a thick, salty knot. Such kind, welcome words. Words James had longed to hear from his father, not from this stranger.

James was glad that his eyes were shielded from Albee's view by the wide brim of his hat.

Although the healing continued and James was now able to take a few steps on his own, he kept the news to himself. Rachel had found out his secret when she came into the clinic that day, and he figured she deserved to know. But spreading the word at home meant he would have to share with his father, and right now he could not face his father's cutting comments and disapproval. If James showed how he could stand, Dat would be disappointed that he couldn't walk. Show the man two steps, and Dat would wonder why he couldn't climb a tree yet. James told himself that Dat's dis-approval had more to do with the Englisher doctors than with James. He wanted to believe that. But in the light of day, it was clear that Dat was disappointed with his oldest son.

So James did his walking at the clinic and kept to the chair at home and in public. Knowing he could stand on his own, he was losing that feeling of being trapped. Now that he wasn't stuck in the chair all the time, he didn't mind it so much.

One day after church, when he'd been left off near a group of men his father's age, he noticed how they seemed to forget he was there. Was it because he was quiet among them, or because they thought his brain had stopped working along with his legs?

Most of the people James's age were eating at tables or going through the line for a sandwich or to spoon out some coleslaw, beets, or potato salad. Children were scattered here and there, some of them corralled by their mamms to come and eat. Having fin-ished their church supper, the older men talked about the weather and the growing season. Now they were on the topic of Englisher doctors.

"We're glad for Doc Trueherz making the house calls and staying on top of things," said old Jacob, who was out of his wheelchair and walking with a cane. "When I had the breathing problems and coughing attacks, I thought it was from the accident. Turned out that was wrong. Ha! What do I know? Doc Trueherz found that I have a heart problem. Ay-fib, they call it. Got me on a heart medi-cation now and I'm feeling fit as a fiddle again."

"Glad to hear it!" Bishop Samuel grinned. "Sometimes these Englisher doctors can bring us back to health, Gott willing."

"And sometimes the Englishers are the ones causing the prob-lems," Dat said, singing his usual refrain. "Did you hear about that buggy accident in Berks County?"

"A tragedy, and it could have been prevented," said the bishop. "The car that hit the buggy was driven by a drunk driver."

Holding a bird's head that he had whittled, Mark came over to show James, but James held up one finger, a signal to keep quiet for a moment.

"Our cousin knew the woman killed in the buggy. Ida Fisher was her name." Jacob's forehead wrinkled. "She had twelve children and a hundred and fourteen grandchildren."

"The English are so careless on the roads," Jimmy said.

Samuel shrugged. "Sometimes. Folks make mistakes, Englisher and Amish."

"But the Englishers, with their buses and trucks and fast cars." Dat folded his arms across his chest. "They make the road dangerous for Plain folk."

"This is true, but these accidents, they are not mistakes. Gott doesn't make mistakes."

"I'd be happy if I never had to see an Englisher again." Dat scowled. "Nothing but problems."

"We must live in peace with all of Gott's creation." The bishop narrowed his eyes. "What is this bad feeling toward Englishers, Jimmy?"

"It's about that bus driver, isn't it, Dat?" James moved into the conversation.

"Nay. I simply choose to live separate, as the Bible says."

"What happened with the bus driver?" Samuel asked.

"When Dat was a boy, a bus hit one of his friends," James offered, glad that the bishop was probing a bit.

"This I don't know about." Samuel pushed his spectacles up on his nose. "Was there an accident when you were a child?"

Although Jimmy had never wanted to share the details, he was compelled to answer when the bishop asked the question.

"It was long ago. I don't talk about it."

"Your friend was hurt," James said, leading the way. "Mamm said he recovered over time. How did it happen, Dat? You never told any of us the story."

"This is something to hear." Samuel's gray eyes were thoughtful. "Tell us, Jimmy."

"It was a terrible day. Even thinking back on it now, all these years later, it gives me indigestion."

"That will ease with time if you get the bad memory out," the bishop said. "How old were you?"

"Just a boy. My friend Paul and I were around the same age . . . eight or nine years old. Paul Beiler. We were inseparable. We played together all the time, and he helped out here at the orchard when he wasn't needed at his parents' chicken farm. We each had a scooter. A scooter was very important to us boys, because it was our only way around. It makes a five-mile trip to your friend's farm go a lot faster. Well, one summer day it was very hot, and Paul and I, we decided to ride our scooters into town to get ice cream."

"Was the ice-cream shop around back then?" Mark asked. "The same one?"

"It was." Jimmy nodded. "Only we didn't make it there that day. We were riding along the highway, the two of us side by side, talking. I was on the right side, near a cornfield. It was August, and the corn was yay-high, far over my head. Paul was scootering along beside me, and we were talking about something and then . . ." His brows creased as he stared off in the distance. "It just happened."

James knew the chilling feeling that came with remembering, although his memory of the highway collision that had injured his spine was blessedly hazy.

"A tourist bus came up behind us. Suddenly. It must have been coasting because we didn't hear the engine or the brakes. It was just there. And one minute Paul was riding along beside me, and the next minute, he and his scooter were flying, right in front of me. They landed in the cornfield. And the bus, it just kept on going.

"A hit-and-run." Jimmy let his chin drop to one hand. "When I found Paul in the cornfield, facedown, I thought the life was gone out of him. Thank the Almighty, I was wrong."

"And you being a boy." Jacob shook his head. "You must have been all shook up."

"I was," Dat admitted quietly.

Mark's shiny eyes were on their father. James felt the same keen interest. It wasn't every day that Dat opened up.

"Later on, when the police found the driver and asked him what happened, he told them that he never even noticed hitting anything. He didn't see or hear anything. It was like Paul wasn't even there."

"Did you go and talk to the driver?" Albee asked. "Did the bishop and your dat take you there to offer forgiveness?"

Jimmy shook his head. "We were told to stay away." He waved his hand. "Some legalities. The bus company was worried about the driver getting blamed in a lawsuit."

"Were you mad at the driver?" Mark asked.

Dat turned to him and frowned. "I was very angry. My father told me that Gott wanted me to forgive that driver. He said I had to let it go."

And had Dat forgiven the man? Although James couldn't know the answer to that, he now understood why his father struggled with the summer invasion of Englishers in local towns.

"What happened to Paul?" Mark asked.

"He was in the hospital for months, but when he got out, he was able to walk and talk again, same old Paul. His family moved north, up to another district, so that they could afford to buy some land to farm. But I still see him when he visits. Ten children, and already a grandchild."

"Gott is merciful," Samuel said.

As the conversation moved on and James talked to Mark about his whittling, he was glad to have learned this about his father. Sometimes, to understand a man, it helped to know something about the boy.

∞ 38 ∞

The rubber soles of Shandell's boots trod quietly on the path as she walked by the light of the bright sliver in the sky. Moonlight cast a blue sheen over the grass and leaves, a silver glow over the stone and dirt paths. Trekking through the night was surreal; she felt as if she were an actor in a movie.

I'm like a pioneer, or an undercover agent, stealthily cutting through woods and fields. She had made it past the Lapp farmhouse, a white two-story home that was now dark and quiet. These country folks really did rise at dawn and go to sleep at sundown, and now that she had lived without electricity for a few weeks, she understood how that worked.

She'd made so many trips to this phone shanty, she'd stopped counting. But tonight she was propelled by worry for her mom and concern for her own health. The stabbing cramps had been coming on more and more frequently, and when they were at their height, she worried that she was going to die all alone in that sugar shack.

By the time she reached the phone shanty, the song of the crickets had died down, but the chorus of frogs was on, full force. Usually she couldn't see them, but one rainy night, they'd come out along the path to the outhouse. Now, that was creepy.

Closing the little door of the hut behind her, the tiny space seemed warmer, then suddenly too warm—airless and blazing hot! Groaning, she pressed her hand to her forehead, as if that could tell anything. Was she getting a fever?

She called Mom's cell phone number and closed her eyes as it began to ring.

"Hello?"

Shandell was so startled to hear her mother answer after all this time, she couldn't find words at first. "Mom? Is that you?"

"Shandell! Honey, I've been so worried about you."

Her knees sagged in relief. Her mom missed her.

"Where are you?"

"Still in Lancaster County, in that small town. Halfway. I've been calling a lot, but Phil always answers at the house, and whenever I call your cell there's no answer."

"I'm sorry. Things have been crazy here. Phil hid my cell phone from me, and . . . It's hard to talk about, especially on the phone."

"That's okay. We can talk about it when I get home. Some people are helping me here, and as soon as they've saved the money, I'm coming home."

"I will send you the money right now, but I have to warn you, there's no going back to the house."

Shandell wondered if the fever was making her hallucinate. When she pushed her hair out of her eyes, her forehead was on fire. "I—I can't come home?"

"There is no home, nowhere to go, not anymore. I had to, to . . ." Her mother's voice cracked.

What the heck? Mom was crying.

"I've moved out of the house," Chelsea told her. "I'm staying with my friend Teresa, sleeping on her couch, actually. Teresa's been great, but I . . ."

"Mom, what happened?"

"Everything is falling apart." Chelsea let out a breath. "I should have seen this coming, but I was so buried in work. Head in the sand. I'm sorry, honey, but I just couldn't do it anymore. I couldn't put up with Phil's drinking. You were right about that. I didn't realize how bad things had gotten until I went to take the recycling out one night and there were six shopping bags full of beer cans. Six shopping bags!"

Shandell's lips curled as tears filled her eyes. Phil had really lost it.

"I told him he had to stop drinking or get out of the house. I tried to reason with him, but it was a waste of time. He refused to leave, and the police can't kick him out from his place of residence. So we're stuck for the moment."

"Stuck how?"

"He gets to stay in the house, and I'll have to look for another place for you and me. But first I have to get my name off the lease. What a mess. I'm so sorry, Shanny. I know I've let you down."

The words were lost on Shandell as she pictured her bedroom. Gone. She would never get to sleep there again.

She had nowhere to go.

"I'm sorry, honey. I know I've been hard to reach, but things will get better from this point on. I've got a lead on a place for us. You can help me check it out when you get back."

Listening to Mom talk about moving furniture and finding a new place, Shandell fought to hold back the tears. These past few weeks, she had longed for the comforts of home and now it was gone? She ached for her mother and for herself. That house was her home. All her things were there. Her bed. Her clothes and jewelry and posters. Her stuffed animals and a fat box of notes she had collected over the years from her friends.

"Mom? What about my stuff?"

"We'll retrieve it from the house. Don't worry about that right now. Tell me how you've been? Still in Halfway? Where should I send the money? Western Union?"

"I'm fine," Shandell lied, pressing a hand to her hot forehead as she tried to sort through Mom's questions. She pressed her face to the tiny window of the shanty and wondered why her thoughts were so jumbled. Swirling like the stars overhead.

"Shandell? Do you want me to come and get you right now? Tell me where you are."

"I'm staying at an orchard outside Halfway, but you won't be able to find me in the dark, and I can't . . . I can't walk into town right now."

"I wouldn't want you walking after dark. Give me an address and I'll use my GPS."

"I don't know the address." She rubbed the sweat from the back of her neck. Why was it so hot in here?

"Then I'm going to wire you money. I'm sure there's a place in Halfway. Tomorrow go into town and ask around. There'll be a hundred dollars waiting for you."

"Okay." Shandell's voice sounded hollow, echoing the feeling inside her. The emptiness. Exhausted, she sank down to the rough floor of the shanty. Her head was a ball of fire and she was hundreds of miles from where she wanted to be. Hundreds of miles from home. No . . . there was no home. She would never return to the home she had focused on these past few weeks.

As Mom talked about apartment hunting, Shandell leaned against the whitewashed boards of the shanty and found herself drifting . . . adrift. The little shack floated off, gently rising over fields and rolling hills, lifting into the sky like a hot air balloon.

When she opened her eyes, she was slumped down in the tiny shack and her mother was saying good-bye. Somehow, the rest of the conversation had slipped through her fingers like water from the creek. "Come home as soon as you can, honey. I've been so worried about you. Call me tomorrow if you want a ride."

"Okay, Mom," Shandell said on a sigh.

She hung up the phone, put her hood up, and braced herself to step into the night air. It wasn't that cold, but she shivered as soon as she stepped out the door.

What a wreck I am.

Sorrow weighed down her feet as she tried to walk. She plodded on, her mind racing away from her then circling back like a boomerang. Oh, what was wrong with her?

The crushing cramps came just as she passed the Doddy house, and she had to stop and hunch over as the pincers dug into her belly and held on for what seemed like an eternity. And then, the pain lifted and she was able to straighten and continue on. The sugar shack was a dark hulk against the blue night. She was glad to see it, but it wasn't home. That made her want to cry, but no tears came. She was all dried out.

The next thing she knew, she was back in the sugar shack, frantically slipping her boots on for an emergency visit to the outhouse. She was really falling apart! As she hugged her jacket closed and traipsed down the dark path, she tried to bring logic to her warped brain. Her cramps were getting worse, and now she felt weak and feverish, wracked by chills and sweating. She needed to see a doctor. Sick at mind and heart, she put up her hood, folded her arms, and pushed into the darkness, one step at a time, one foot in front of the other.

39

"What else can we do?" Rachel asked James as they waited for Mark to hitch up a buggy for their ride into the clinic. "I found her passed out in the dirt. She's taken a turn for the worse, and I've tried every remedy under the sun."

"So she must go to the clinic with us." James shrugged as he pulled himself out of the chair and held on to the hitching post. He had kept the news of his progress a secret for the most part, but he had revealed a bit to Mark as he couldn't bear to have the boy lifting him in and out of a buggy. "What did you tell Mark?"

"That she's my friend, and she's sick, and we're taking her to see Doc Trueherz."

"Well." James's dark eyes met hers, and the understanding that glimmered there melted her heart. "You told him the truth. That's good."

"She's already in the back of the buggy, lying down, with a blanket." Concerned about Shandell, Rachel had brought her some medicine made from the boiled-down leaves of blueberry shrubs, but found her collapsed on the ground when she arrived at the sugar shack.

"Shandell, what happened?"

"The path to the outhouse, it's too long," Shandell had murmured as her head lolled back toward a lacy green thatch of weeds.

"Did you have a rough night, honeygirl?" Rachel asked gently.

"I can't go home." Shandell's eyes shone with a strange light. "There's no home, no house. It floated away. Floated over a cornfield."

"Maybe in your dreams. Did you have a nightmare?" Rachel pressed her hand to Shandell's hot forehead. "You're burning up with fever. Can you sit up?"

Shandell propped herself up on her elbows for a moment, then lay down. "My head's too heavy."

Worry was a thorn in Rachel's throat as she rode her scooter back to the Lapp barn. The Englisher girl needed a doctor, and since they were headed to the clinic, there was no reason not to bring her along.

Quickly, she hitched up a cart and brought it back to the sugar shack. Since there was no way Shandell could walk the path through the orchard, this would have to do. Although Shandell wasn't particularly fond of riding in a cart after her manure experience, it wasn't difficult to get the girl to lie down in the wooden cargo area. Rachel felt a bit guilty, involving Mark in helping the Englisher girl, but he seemed unfazed as Rachel helped Shandell ease out of the cart and settle into the backseat of the buggy.

As they rode into town, the rocking motion of the buggy and the steady clip-clop of the horse's hooves seemed to soothe Shandell a bit, but every now and then she would stir and murmur feverish things that Rachel could not make sense of, calling for her mommy and whimpering that she couldn't go home.

"Poor wounded dove," Rachel said, wishing that she could offer Shandell some relief.

James rubbed his chin thoughtfully. "Why is she so sick?"

"I can't say. But I think Doctor Trueherz will know."

"And how will we pay for the doctor?"

Rachel winced. "From the money we were going to use to send her home?" She was almost finished with the second painting, having learned to work in a bubble and pretend that the Englishers watching her at Pepper's shop weren't there.

"It probably won't be enough. Medical bills are expensive."

"I know. Maybe she has medical insurance. We'll have to find a way."

⚭

Fortunately, Doc Trueherz's wife, Celeste, sensed the urgency of Shandell's condition. She pointed the way for Rachel to help Shandell into an exam room without delay. James followed, his face taut with concern.

"I'll have him look at her as soon as he gets off the phone." Celeste eased Shandell down onto the table and strapped the Velcro blood pressure cuff around her upper arm. "Just relax now. We're going to take care of you, get you comfortable. Shandell? Can you hear me?"

"Mmm. Where's my mommy?"

"Your mother isn't here, but you're going to be okay," Rachel soothed her.

Celeste Trueherz pumped the cuff up, asking Rachel, "How long has she been disoriented like this?"

"That started this morning, but she's been sick for a week or so." Rachel described Shandell's symptoms as Celeste took notes on a clipboard.

"At the very least, she seems to be dehydrated." Celeste rubbed Shandell's upper arm. "We can give her some IV fluids here, but the doc might want her in the hospital."

The hospital! That would cost a small fortune. Rachel shot an anxious look at James, but he seemed surprisingly calm as he reached over and took her hand.

"We'll do whatever it takes," James said, for her benefit and for Celeste's. "And we'll pay her bill."

Celeste looked up from the clipboard, squinting at them. "Why would you do that? Besides, she may have health insurance. But we're not going to worry about that right now. Doc treats everyone, insurance or not. Either way, she's going to be here awhile." Celeste turned to James. "You had better get over to Dr. Finley's office. We know where to find you if we need you."

☾☽

Soon after James left, Henry Trueherz strolled into the exam room with Celeste on his heels. "Morning, Rachel. I see you've brought me a friend." He picked up the chart. "Sick for a week or more. Okay. We'll have a look at her and we might want to run some tests. Have a seat out in the waiting room and we'll come get you as soon as we're done with the exam."

Rachel nodded, then went over to take Shandell's hand. "I'll be right outside."

As Rachel backed away, Shandell reached for her. "No! Mommy, don't go."

Moved, Rachel touched her cheek. No one had ever called her Mommy before, and although she knew it was the fever talking, it pleased her to imagine the children who might need their feverish brow soothed one day. She hoped and prayed that she and James would marry in the fall and start their own family soon.

Thirty minutes later, Rachel was summoned to another room in the clinic—this one with three hospital beds. Fast asleep, Shandell seemed tiny, tucked into the white sheets of one of the beds. A few tubes ran down her body, one taped to her arm and another clipped onto one fingertip. Rachel had seen these gadgets used on James when he had been in the hospital.

"Is it very bad?" she asked Doc Trueherz, who was writing some notes on a clipboard.

"She's definitely dehydrated, but I think she'll be fine once we get some fluids in her," the doctor said. "It sounds like you used some sound home remedies, trying to treat her. Some of those things probably helped."

"But she wasn't getting better," Rachel said.

He nodded. "We're thinking it's a bacterial infection. Could come from unpasteurized milk, but I know the Lapps don't have a cow. You mentioned that she's been using water from a stream. My best guess is that that water is the source of the bacteria. She's got to stay away from that creek. In the meantime, antibiotics aren't called for here. We've just got to flush this thing out."

This was something Rachel hadn't thought of. "Does she need bottled water?"

"At the very least. We're going to keep her here for the day. I know that James finishes his treatment around two or three. We'll get Shandell hydrated and see how she's feeling this afternoon. You're free to stay with her or come back later."

Rachel thanked the doctor and headed out. As she walked to Art at Heart, a new burden was heavy on her shoulders. Where would Shandell live now? Weeks ago, Rachel might have been able to convince her parents to take the girl in for a bit. But now? After she and James had kept things a secret for so long?

They had really gotten themselves into a pickle. Whatever happened from here, there was one thing she knew for sure. They were going to need that money to help Shandell, and the sooner the better. Good thing she was almost finished with the second of the three pieces for Kiki Grant.

Pepper was helping a customer when Rachel entered the shop. In Rachel's work space, the painting seemed to smile at her. The crocuses in the foreground were bold and bright and hopeful in front of the peaceful scene of a Sunshine and Shadow quilt draped over a clothesline. She removed her black sweater and set to work on the finishing touches in the sky, the sunbeams and the small flowerbed near the house.

As she worked, Rachel tuned out the conversation behind her until one voice broke through the glaze.

"The rumors were true. Rachel King, painting before our eyes!"

Rachel turned to see the designer, Kiki Grant, with her hands clasped under her chin.

"Is that the piece you're doing for me?" Kiki's eyes grew round with wonder.

"It is." Rachel stood back, her paintbrush tipped in the air. "What do you think?"

"I love it! I am thrilled to death. And the client will be so pleased, too." Kiki stepped forward and did a quick check with a paper tape measure from her pocket. "The dimensions are perfect. It's all good, and nearly complete, right?"

Rachel nodded. "Finished today, I think."

"Fabulous. I had to stop in when I heard that you were painting here. What a great idea. Everyone around here is talking about you."

The idea of her name being bandied about made Rachel want to take her paints home to the safety of her old room. "I needed a place to paint in Paradise while waiting on a friend. He's getting medical treatment at the clinic, and he needs to be here every day."

"Aren't you a saint." Kiki pressed a hand to her breast. "You know, we have a lot of wonderful local artists in the area, but none of the painters are Amish, and that's what people want. Authenticity, the real deal."

"Well, I am real." Rachel smiled, knowing that she could not properly explain why she didn't want all this attention.

When Kiki took a photo of the painting to show her client, Rachel thought of the time it would take to complete the next painting and her immediate needs. She asked if it would still be possible to work on commission.

"How about this? I'll come back tomorrow for the finished painting, and I'll give you a check for the first two."

"That would be helpful," Rachel said, "but you can pay Elsie Lapp when you pick up the painting at the Country Store. And I'll have the third painting to you in a few weeks."

"Oh, I know your word is good," Kiki said. "That's one of the benefits of working with Amish people like you."

Rachel knew that there were good and bad folks in all walks of life, but she was glad the Amish were known for their honesty. She thanked the designer and got back to work so that she could finish the painting.

Tomorrow, they would have more than enough money for Shandell to travel home, though she probably wouldn't be well enough. Wasn't it peculiar? They would have the money at last, but now Shandell was sick. You never knew what the Almighty had in store for you. As Mamm always said, nothing lasts forever, not even your troubles.

∞ 40 ∞

Shandell rolled over on her side and snuggled into the crisp white sheet. To be nestled in a bed—even this stiff cot in Dr. True-herz's office—was heavenly. She reached for the covered cup on the end table and took a few sips of Gatorade through the straw.

"You're awake," came a voice from the door.

Shandell rolled over to face Celeste, the doctor's wife, who seemed to be in charge of the office. They'd had such a nice talk earlier when Shandell had awakened on the cot in the doctor's in-firmary. Celeste reminded Shandell of her own mother, whom Ce-leste had promised to reach for her.

"And you're drinking. That's good. Remember, small sips for now."

"How long have I been asleep?" Shandell asked, her voice creak-ing.

"A few hours. How are you feeling?"

"Better. I can think straight, at least. My body isn't so weak, though I'm still wiped out."

"That's understandable. I finally got a call through while you were sleeping. Your mother is anxious to talk to you."

"My mom?" Hope sparked in Shandell's chest. "Is she here?"

"She'll be heading this way as soon as she finishes work this afternoon. When she heard you were sick, she was ready to lam right out of there, but I told her she was better off waiting. You'll probably be napping most of the day, and the doc wants to keep you on IV fluids through the afternoon."

"Okay." Shandell was happy to stay right here in this soft bed and wait for her mother. "My mom is coming. You don't know what a relief that is."

Celeste patted her shoulder. "Oh, I know. A mother's love is the best medicine."

"I really miss her."

"She can't wait to see you. Said she was sick with worry. I told her I'd take good care of you until she got here." Celeste pumped up the cuff until it squeezed Shandell's arm.

"I can't believe it. This is the end of a really long journey."

"So I heard. Your mom said you've been away for weeks, and Rachel told me you've been living in a sugaring shack."

"I don't know what I would have done without James and Rachel's help." As Shandell pictured her mother's broad smile, she remembered the conversation they'd had the night before when Mom had told her that she'd left Phil. At the time, it had seemed devastating to lose their home that way, but now, with the perspective of a clearer mind, Shandell realized it was a positive development. It would be good to be free of Phil and his illness, and wherever Chelsea and Shandell went, they would make a home together. Living in the sugar shack, Shandell had learned that a home was not the four walls around you, but the people you shared your days with.

"Your blood pressure looks good," Celeste said, "and your fever is gone. You young people bounce back fast."

Shandell smoothed her palm over the white sheet. "This is such a tidy place. Like a little hospital."

"We aren't equipped like that, but the doc had the idea to put some beds into this room, and I have to say, they've gotten plenty of use. The bulk of our patients are Amish folk, who usually do not want to be checked in to a hospital. If their condition isn't too serious, Henry will let them stay here during the day and monitor their progress. It saves them a trip to Lancaster, as well as a good deal of money."

"Well, thanks for saving me, too," Shandell said, her heart full of gratitude.

Celeste smiled as she made a note on her clipboard. "You are very welcome, but it's what we do."

As Shandell sipped more of her drink, she felt a swell of appreciation for this place, Lancaster County, where people put themselves out to lend a hand to strangers. She was glad Mom was coming, but she felt a twinge of regret at the thought of leaving Halfway behind.

🏵 41 🏵

When James found Shandell in Dr. Trueherz's office at the end of the day, she was sitting up, eating a Popsicle, and her face was pink and healthy. He was glad to see her back to her old self again.

"I have good news." Shandell smiled, her lips purple from the grape Popsicle. She was still hooked up to an IV line; James recognized the tubing running into her arm and the bag of clear fluids hanging from a metal hook beside her. "My mom is coming to get me! Celeste talked to her on the phone, and she insisted. She's driving up when she gets out of work."

"And the doctor says you should be good to go by then," Celeste told Shandell, "though you'll need to take it easy."

"Do you know what made Shandell sick?" James asked.

"Doc thinks it was something environmental, possibly unpasteurized milk, or bacteria in the water. Shandell explained how she was drawing water from the creek. Let me tell you, E. coli is not your friend."

"Well, we only have pasteurized milk at my house," James said. "So it must have been the water."

"Which I always heated up," Shandell said. "I saw in one of those survival shows that you should heat water from a stream before you drink it, just in case."

"A very good idea." Celeste nodded as she tossed away the disposable thermometer stick. "But did you bring it to a boil? Did you boil the water you washed your hands in? The water you used to brush your teeth and wash?"

"Not exactly," Shandell admitted.

"That stream contains many strains of bacteria, and it's very likely that bacteria is causing the diarrhea and subsequent dehydration. We won't have the test results back for another day or two, but we're going to treat this as if it's E. coli from the stream. Which means, no more exposure to this water source."

"That won't be a problem, since I'm going back to Maryland," Shandell said.

"Everything looks good." Celeste smiled as she wrote on the chart. "I'm taking out the IV; that will give you more mobility."

James nodded slowly. "So . . . at last, you get to go home."

"Back to Maryland, but we can't go home. Mom is splitting up with my stepfather, so I guess we'll be in a motel for the time being. Mom told me all about it last night when I called her from the phone shanty. I think I was too sick to totally comprehend it."

"This makes sense of some of the puzzling things you said on our way here this morning," James said, wondering how she could be smiling when things had gone so very wrong.

"Really? What did I say?" When he told her a few of the things, she moaned. "Aw. I really was a mess."

"A high fever like that can bring on a sort of delirium," Celeste said.

James nodded. "You were in a bad way. I'm glad you're feeling better."

"I am. Especially now that Mom is coming for me." Shandell's dark eyes shone in the light. "But I'm going to miss you guys. It'll be nice to have a bed and running water and all, but I will definitely miss our chats."

James squeezed the armrests of his chair as he looked up at the Englisher girl who had seemed so mysterious when he'd first stumbled upon her in the back of the orchard. Now he could see that she was not that different, not in the ways that mattered. "It's been good knowing you, Shandell."

⚭

When Rachel arrived a few minutes later and learned the news, there was much hugging and back-patting and sighing between the two women. James held back a grin as he watched them say their good-byes with promises to write letters—snail mail, as Shandell called it. The two of them were like peas in a pod.

While Rachel went around to the hitching post behind the clinic, Shandell walked James out to the vehicle parking lot.

"How come you never let anyone push you?" Shandell asked as they stepped into the spring day, a breezy day with short stretches of bright sun peeking out between fast-moving clouds.

"I used to think that was the sign of a weak man," James said. "Now, not so much. The more I can move on my own, the more I see that walking is not what makes a man strong. If there's a strong, sturdy oak inside, no one notices the chipped bark on the outside."

Her nose wrinkled as she squinted. "Is that a riddle?"

He chuckled. "Sort of." The riddle of life.

She asked him to take good care of her possessions, which he and Rachel would hold on to until she knew her mailing address in Maryland.

"I don't mean to be a baby, but please, please, be careful with my *Bible Stories* book," Shandell said. "My dad used to read it with me, and it's one of the last keepsakes that remind me of him."

"We will be very careful with your book," James promised.

Both James and Shandell were watching the parking lot entrance, waiting for Rachel to pull off the quiet side street with the buggy, when a dark green car cruised by, its motor roaring louder than most.

Shandell jerked upright. "Is that . . ." Her face reflected her horror. "It is! It's Gary."

The hairs on the back of James's head rose, his skin prickling in alarm. This was the man who had lied to Shandell and left her a hundred miles from home.

Shandell was already looking around for a place to hide, but they were in a wide-open spot on the center of the pavement. She lunged over to the right and dove behind the closest parked car.

"Did he see me?" she called to James. "Did he stop?"

"I don't think so," James said under his breath as he watched the slow-moving car glide off down the street, the red taillights disappearing behind the bank on the corner. "He's gone."

"Oh, that was close." Shandell rose, dusting her hands off on the seat of her jeans. "What is he doing here?"

Was Gary still looking for Shandell, or had he come back for another reason? There was no telling, but it would be best for Shandell to stay out of his way. "You'd best be careful."

"I will. I'd better get back in."

She was interrupted by the roar of an engine and a squeal of brakes. Dust rose as the big green car slid into the parking lot and skidded to a stop.

Gary was back.

In an instant the car door popped open and a tall, rangy man emerged, his arms spread wide. "Shandell! It's you, baby. I've been looking all over for you."

Jarred, Shandell stepped back, ducking to a spot where James could no longer see her. "Go away, Gary. I mean it."

"Aw. Don't be that way. We need to talk. Come on in the car, where we can have some privacy." Edging forward, Gary never took his eyes off Shandell as he spoke.

This one has the eyes of a hunter, James thought. Cold, calculating, determined.

The door behind Gary remained open and the heavy beat of music thrummed from the car. Fear clamped around James's gut like a vise. To his right, Shandell was trying to get to the clinic's door, but Gary was tracking her, nearly on her.

"You'd best go, friend," James said firmly. "She doesn't want to go with you."

"What are you going to do, *friend*? Leave a tire track on top of my boot?" Gary's smile was smug. "An Amish guy in a wheelchair—two strikes against you. I know, you Amish don't fight. Don't even defend yourselves. You'd be a waste of my time, but this one—" He made a grab for Shandell, clamped on to her arm, and jerked her toward him.

"Ow! That hurts. Cut it out."

"Just get in the car and we'll talk about it." He tugged on her arm, but she resisted, sitting down in the gravel.

"Why do you make things so hard?" he growled. When she kept trying to free her arm, he braced himself and started pulling, dragging her across the gravel to his car.

James sorely wished he had the full power of his legs so that he could stop this man. But what if he did? He wasn't going to hurt him. He would not fight him. That was not the Amish way.

But he had to stop him from hurting Shandell. And if Gary managed to push Shandell into his car, there was no telling her fate.

As Shandell protested and Gary tried to pick her up, James turned to the car. He had never driven, but he knew how an automobile worked. Most Amish teenaged boys had some experience with cars. James knew that a key was necessary to make the engine run.

The key.

Moving quickly, he wheeled over to the open car door and leaned inside. He couldn't reach around the steering wheel from his chair—not far enough to get the key. But there was a bar over the door. Gripping the bar with one hand, he rose from his chair and levered himself into the driver's seat. From there, he grasped the key, pushed it in, and twisted toward him.

The engine stopped.

"Hey! Get out of there!" Gary shouted as he grappled with Shandell.

With the key tucked in the pouch of his chair, James maneuvered himself out of the driver's seat and wheeled the chair free of the car. Snatching the keys, he wound up as if he was pitching a baseball and threw with all his might. All the workouts with weights had paid off; the keys sailed over the hedges at the border of the parking lot and landed near the savings bank.

Gary looked up, giving Shandell the chance to slip free of his grip and scramble to her feet. "What are you doing?" Gary barked at James, lunging toward him.

After that, everything seemed to happen at once. Rachel steered the buggy around to the front of the clinic, calling for Ranger to whoa when a police vehicle shrieked around her, its lights flashing. Dr. Trueherz and Celeste came storming out of the clinic, their white jackets sailing behind them in the breeze. Two other police vehicles squealed to a stop at the parking lot entrance, and James recognized Sheriff Hank as one of the men who emerged from the Jeep.

Gary put his hands up when the two cops confronted him. "I

didn't do anything wrong, Officers. I'm just trying to talk to my friend here."

A female cop nodded at the green car. "Is that your vehicle?" she asked.

"Yes, ma'am, and I'd be happy to get in it and get out of your hair, but that guy over there took my keys."

James expected all eyes to turn to him, but Sheriff Hank interrupted, pointing a finger at Gary. "Gary Anderson, right? I know your plate, make, and model. You're a film star around here, young man. We've got you on camera stealing from a few different merchants in Lancaster County."

Gary's jaw dropped. "Now hold on, Officer—"

"Save it for your attorney," Hank said. "Cuff him and get him in one of the cars."

James watched the cops walk Gary over to their car. It was over. Although the Amish put no stock in the laws of the Englishers, James felt relief to see this man taken away.

James did a quick check on Shandell, who stood a few yards away, talking with Celeste and the female officer. He could see that her hands were trembling, but otherwise, she seemed okay.

Doc Trueherz pointed toward the bank. "Did you throw his keys over into the next parking lot?"

"I threw them as far away as I could."

"That was clever thinking. You don't want to take on a guy like that."

James didn't want to take on any man. Raising a hand against a fellow man was strictly forbidden in the Amish faith. "I couldn't protect Shandell from him, but I stopped him from taking her away."

"That you did."

42

After the police handcuffed Gary and tucked him into the back-seat of a patrol car, Shandell felt a sweeping sense of relief. Sweet, safe relief. The police were arresting Gary . . . taking him away. Removing one enormous burden from her life.

In that moment, she felt as if she could breathe again.

And then everything came rushing at her, fast and furious. They wanted her name and address. Her school or employer. What was her relationship with Gary? What was she doing here in Lancaster County? "If you've been staying here for the past few weeks, where have you been living?" one tall cop asked.

Shandell opened her mouth, but the words stuck in her throat. She didn't want to drag her Amish friends into this situation involving the police.

"On our farm," James answered for her. "She's been staying in the sugar shack at the back of the orchard."

Shandell hoped that was enough information to satisfy the police, but then the head guy stepped in and started asking questions.
Sheriff Hank was tall, and the navy cop uniform with the bright
gold star on the chest made him seem intimidating as he towered
over Shandell. How long had she known Gary Anderson? Had he
hurt her just now?

"I'm a little sore," she admitted, "but mostly scared." She rubbed
the side of her hip that had been dragged over the gravel. "He
wanted me to go with him, and he's very pushy that way. Controlling."

Something sparked in Sheriff Hank's eyes. Sympathy? With
snow-white hair and crinkles at the edge of his eyes, he seemed like
a man who could see through to the truth. A wise man. "I have a
feeling you can help us out, young lady."

"I'd like to help." She hadn't done anything wrong; why was
she so scared? Suddenly, her vision was blurred by tears and her
throat felt thick and her legs were wobbly beneath her. "I gotta sit
down."

To her surprise, Celeste was right there with a wheelchair for
her. "Sit, honey. You take it easy."

"Hank, this young lady is a patient of mine," Dr. Trueherz said.
"If you want to talk, you're going to have to step inside the clinic
and take it in measured doses."

"My pleasure." The sheriff cast a look at the police car, where
they had Gary in the back. "You know me. I'm always glad to step
away from the drama. You guys head inside, and I'll finish up with
James and Rachel."

As Celeste wheeled her inside, Shandell overheard one of the
cops ask the sheriff if they should send a unit out to the Lapp orchard to investigate.

Investigate what? Was she a suspect now?

Shandell turned back to look at her Amish friends. Rachel stood beside James's chair, the two of them facing the sheriff with respect and a little fear. They didn't deserve this. Now her friends were in trouble because of her, and there was nothing she could do to stop it. A little sob escaped her throat as they approached the door. This time when she cried, tears streaked down her cheeks.

43

James frowned when Rachel turned the buggy down the lane that ran to the Lapp orchard. This was not going to be a good afternoon. The thought of facing his father squeezed his chest with dread, and each trot of the horse made it wind tighter, as if in a vise. He knew that the news of his involvement with the young Englisher girl had beaten him here. Most of Halfway would be talking about the thief who had finally been arrested, and the young woman who had been hiding out at the Lapp orchard. Shandell had asked how word could travel so fast without a telephone or Internet in the house, but James knew how folks reacted to a bit of news. They made a stop on the way home, hitched up a buggy, or wrapped up some cookies to take to their neighbor. As Doddy used to say, big news had strong wings.

"It's a juicy story," Rachel had admitted as they talked it over on the way home. "I imagine tongues are wagging now."

The gossip did not concern James nearly as much as his father's reaction did. He had been foolish to think that he could keep such a thing hidden. He should have told his parents in the beginning, when it all seemed so simple. A young woman had needed help, and the Lapp orchard could give her shelter.

"Look at that," James said as they passed the orchard. Down the row of the plum trees, he could see his younger brothers working with Albee, most likely spraying for black knot. In the pen outside the barn, Mark was working with one of the horses, probably his beloved Rowdy. "It looks just like every other day. You'd never know that all hell was about to break loose."

"We gave food and shelter to a girl who needed it," Rachel said evenly. "It was an act of charity, not a sin, even in this strange situation."

"Mmm." James loved the purity of her heart, but Rachel's explanation would not wash with Jimmy. For Rachel's sake, he prayed that her parents would recognize her goodwill. "Do you think your parents will understand?"

"Ya. They don't like secrets, but they will see past that chip in the cup."

James was glad to see that his parents did not wait on the porch or come running out after him. At least they did not see the situation as an emergency.

As Ranger trotted up the lane, Mark climbed out of the pen and came to greet them. "Do you need a ride home, Rachel?" he offered. "I've been practicing driving the buggy, and Mamm says I've got it down."

"No, denki. I've got my scooter here." Rachel climbed out of the buggy and stood watching as James swung his legs around and eased his body to the edge of the open carriage. Getting out was much easier than climbing in.

"Here you go." Mark handed him his two canes, which he kept stashed in the back of the buggy.

As James moved to the compact wheelchair, he noticed his brother staring.

"Dat says I'm to send you to his office, soon as you get home." Mark pushed his hat back and scratched his head. "Does it have something to do with the Englisher girl who was sick?"

James nodded. "I'll tell you about her sometime—the true story."

"I'll be heading home," Rachel said, touching James's shoulder, "but I'll be back tomorrow."

I hope so, James thought as he watched Rachel walk away, the skirt of her dress billowing in the breeze. Such a fine, kind woman.

Years ago, Jimmy had set up his office in a small outbuilding behind the barn. As James rolled closer, he could see his father's silhouette inside the window. He would be sitting at his desk, steaming like a tea kettle. Bracing himself, James pushed open the door and worked the chair over the lip at the threshold.

"James?" Jimmy wore reading glasses low on his nose, though he didn't seem to be engaged in any of the five or six piles of papers on his desk. "Kumm."

Maneuvering around a file cabinet, James parked himself right in front of the desk. Face-to-face with his father, he saw the changes that usually went unnoticed: new creases in his forehead, puffy eyes, gray sprinkled through his hair. Ya, Dat was getting older, but he had also lost a brother and a father in less than two years. Jimmy rarely talked about those two men, but James knew his father had loved them.

"So." Jimmy removed the glasses that made him resemble his father. "You hide an Englisher woman in our orchard without telling anyone."

"It was a simple act of charity," James said, recalling Rachel's words.

"You invited an Englisher to live on our farm after I told you it was forbidden. You understood that there would be no outsiders here in our home." The low husk of his father's voice was penetrating. "Haven't I warned you of something like this? Do you know what folks will say when they hear of this?"

"There will be gossip, I know, but maybe some folks will understand the goodwill of helping a person in need."

"There will always be someone in need. We do our best to help other families in our community. The Amish community. We don't get involved with Englishers who wander down the road. Where is your common sense, James?" He tapped his head. "Sometimes I wonder what's going on in that noggin of yours."

"The Plain People help each other. I know that, Dat. But it would be cruel not to help an Englisher who is right in front of your eyes."

"The Englishers have their own systems for helping people. Welfares and charities and whatnot. It's not our concern." Jimmy leaned forward, his dark eyes shiny with anger. "This girl is not one of us. She is not our concern. She will not be yours, either. And that is that!"

She is already my concern, James thought as his father turned to his file cabinet. James knew that his father would act as James had if he had gotten to know Shandell as a person. Instead, she was lumped in with all rude, fancy Englishers.

Outside the window, James saw a short, spry man walking down the lane with a large spray can in one hand.

Doddy . . .

What would he say to this problem?

"What we do in life echoes in eternity."

The voice was clear as a bell, though James knew it was simply a part of his memory. Elmo Lapp had been a man who chose his actions carefully. Good deeds and kindness had the power to echo through the rolling hills, far and wide. In that moment, James appreciated the irony that his good deed was echoing through Halfway in the form of gossip. Doddy would get a good chuckle out of that.

James missed him every day, and he imagined that Jimmy was still sore from the loss of his father. And then Uncle Tom, Dat's brother, killed in a car accident just months ago. Dat must be reeling from the pain.

And then, there was the young Jimmy Lapp—the boy who had seen his young friend knocked off the road by an Englisher bus. It was the pain of that experience that made Jimmy hate Englishers. James understood that now. But hatred was a dangerous thing. Like an infestation of Oriental fruit moths or aphids, hatred could take hold of a tree and, bit by bit, destroy the entire orchard.

His gaze dropped to the desk, where his father had printed pages of photos and text spread out. James caught some of the words: *Our pears are always sweet and delicious!* and *Try our eat-over-the-sink peaches!*

It was copy for a website for Lapp orchards, something Dat was putting together with the help of a Mennonite man who had a knack for computers. Jimmy believed that their orchard needed a website to stay competitive, and James suspected he was right.

"Dat . . . you work with Englishers every day. Clive, who manages the delivery trucks. And you spend a lot of time with Ira Doscher, getting all this together for the website."

His father frowned. "Ya, so?"

"If one of these men had a problem, you would try to help them, wouldn't you?"

"Sure."

"Because you know them. You don't lump them in with other Englishers."

"What are you saying?"

"It would help if you met Shandell, just once. She would like to thank you, and if you see that she's a real person who needed our help, I think you would understand. Remember the Golden Rule—"

"You have broken the rules of your parents and your bishop," Jimmy interrupted. "You have shown disrespect to your father. You have stepped over the line of what's right and proper. And you've taken things from our home for this Englisher to use. That makes you no better than a common thief."

Borrowing a few cups and forks—James didn't see it as stealing, but he would not argue the details with his father right now. It would only seem to prove Dat's point about disrespect.

"I want this trespasser off our land," Dat said.

"It's done. She's staying with Doc Trueherz."

"And I have half a mind to end your treatment in Paradise until you get it through your thick skull that you are a member of an Amish church and you have promised to live Plain, not all entangled with Englishers. Ya, I think you've been spending too much time in town with the Englishers."

This was exactly what James had feared. This would crush all hope. "Dat, please." He kept his voice low and contrite. "Please take some time to think before you make that choice."

"And why is that? Because you think the heat of the moment will cool and I'll let you do what you like?"

"Not that. It's because the treatment is helping me, Dat. I don't fancy spending my days there, with all the exercising and repetition, and you haven't made it easy for me to get in and out of Paradise. But the treatment is working, slowly but surely. I can stand for more than an hour now, and I've taken a few steps with the help of a cane. And I've learned how to get myself in and out of a buggy."

Jimmy sat back in his chair, his head cocked to one side. "And you've kept this a secret, too?"

"I held on to it because I was afraid it wasn't enough, Dat. No matter what I do, it isn't enough for you. I get half the orchard fertilized and you are disappointed about the other half. I learn to walk a step, and you want a mile." James rubbed his brow. This was hard to put into words, and he didn't want to be tripped by emotion. "I was saving it all up, thinking you might be pleased when I could walk again like a normal man."

Jimmy's lips were pursed in a frown. "What are you saying? That I favor the others because you can't walk anymore?"

James shook his head. "You have always been hardest on me. Maybe because I was firstborn. I'm not complaining, Dat. You've pushed me hard, and I'm probably a better man because of it. I'm not asking for you to look the other way. I'm just asking you to give me a chance to continue the treatment. It's helping. It's giving me hope. I don't want to lose that."

"I'll think on it." Dat's dark eyes squinted shut as he stared off in the distance. "But I don't see why you should be allowed any favors after all you've done. Bringing in an Englisher and lying to hide it all from your family. It was wrong, James, and I can't abide it. The cornerstone of faith is truth, not tolerance."

"But Dat, it was you yourself who taught me the Golden Rule: Love your neighbor as yourself."

"We are finished here." Jimmy leafed through the papers on his desk as if James were no longer there. "I have nothing else to say."

Swallowing over the knot in his throat, James stared out the window again. That man in the orchard wasn't Doddy, but Albee Miller. And James's father could not control everything. He could tell James what to do, and James would likely go through the motions to appease him. But he could not make James turn away from Shandell. James would not give his father that power. James would not give it to any man. James would follow his Father in heaven, who taught man to love his neighbor.

❦ 44 ❦

Six weeks later, Rachel leaned against the counter at the Country Store and marveled over the power of Gott to heal. Dear Shandell, who had returned to Halfway after a month in Maryland, now guided her new boss through the shop with confidence and good humor. The hollows in Shandell's cheeks had filled out, the blue tint was gone from her hair, and her shiny black mane reminded Rachel of a feisty horse. A colt that needed to be trained, but not broken. Nay, you would never want to break such a strong, determined spirit.

Shandell had recovered, and she had returned to Halfway to stay, with a job at the new bed-and-breakfast. Her mother, Chelsea, was also moving to the area to be near her daughter and get a fresh start. Gott was great!

"A FRIEND IN NEED IS A FRIEND, INDEED." Shandell put her hands on her hips as she admired the plaque. "That's perfect for us, right, Rachel? I would love to have this for my room."

Rachel smiled as Elsie removed the plaque from the wall and handed it to Shandell. "It was handcrafted by Adam King, Rachel's cousin," Elsie said.

Shandell ran her fingers over the grooves in the wood. "It's beautiful, but it's the sentiment that really appeals to me. It will help me remember the time when my life hit rock bottom and Rachel and James pulled me up."

A smile warmed Rachel's face at the sweet sentiment, and she beamed with pleasure and intrigue as she watched Shandell guide her boss through the shop.

"Add it to our pile," Zoey said with a wave of her hand.

Shandell was here to help Zoey Jordan choose merchandise to decorate Halfway's newest inn. Zoey and her husband, Tate, were the owners of the Halfway to Heaven Bed and Breakfast, scheduled to open in a former Amish farm right next door to Elsie's home. The inn was being advertised as an authentic Amish experience. "Overnight stays in a historic Amish home!" And though Zoey seemed to have very good intentions, she didn't seem to know much about Plain living.

"How about these plaques with the sayings painted on them?" Zoey asked, holding up a framed piece made by one of the local Amish women and reading it aloud. "KISSING WEARS OUT, COOKING DOESN'T. Oh, that would be great in the kitchen! Would it be authentic?"

"Many Amish homes have one or two hangings like that on the walls. We don't have a lot of decoration, otherwise."

"That's what I told Zoey," Shandell said. "I know I'm not Amish, but since I came out of hiding I've been inside enough houses to know that flowered wallpaper and chandeliers are not the way to go if you're trying to create an Amish experience."

"Oh, I know, I'm learning that lesson. That was my attempt at Victorian decorating." Zoey rolled her eyes. The woman, who was in her early thirties, had a round face, a bright smile, and a gift for gab. Today she wore a cute little straw hat that framed her fluffy blond hair nicely. "Shandell has a knack for marketing and a love for simplicity—two things that I lack, I'm afraid." She turned to Shandell, dimples appearing as she smiled. "You vetoed my choices for the names of the rooms."

"I did, with good reason. Zoey and Tate wanted to give the rooms names instead of numbers, but I had real issues with the Making Whoopie Pies room. And it seemed wrong to call the lobby restroom the Outhouse."

Everyone chuckled at that. Elsie's high-pitched laughter blended well with Ruben's low, hearty laughter. Such a good couple they made!

And the way Shandell's face shone when she laughed . . . it brought Rachel such joy. "Oh, and some paintings!" Zoey rubbed her hands together as she came upon the wall displaying Rachel's artwork. "We have to have some work by Miss Rachel King, one of our local heroes."

Although Rachel smiled, part of her wanted to run to the back room of the shop and hide. Such praise made her face grow hot with embarrassment. Funny, how the very thing that had been frowned upon by the Amish community was considered an act of heroism by the Englishers. As she watched Shandell and Zoey choose various paintings, Rachel still felt a maternal tug toward the Englisher girl. Helping her had been a joy, a true blessing, not some fantastic feat. Although Shandell didn't need her loving care anymore, Rachel knew that they would always be friends. She hoped that the experience of taking care of someone in need had been Gott's way of preparing her to be a mother.

That was part of her new dream—to marry James and raise a houseful of children in a home close to the orchard so that he could work the land he loved. The notion of having a house in town, here

among Englishers, now seemed laughable. Her experience of painting in the art shop had shown her that she was not a city girl, after
all. She didn't know how far he would progress with his new therapy, but that was in Gott's hands. One thing she did know was that
she loved him with all her heart, and a heart full of love was a happy
heart, indeed.

∞

Although James's dat had threatened to forbid further medical
treatment, so far he had let James continue going to the clinic six
days a week. That was a very good thing, as the treatment was re-
newing James's strength and giving him control of his legs, slowly
but surely. Still, James worried that his father would change his
mind and forbid James from further treatment. James didn't want to
talk about it, so Rachel could only guess at the strain and conflict
that had been caused between father and son when James decided
to take in the runaway girl.

Rachel was happy to drive him every day. Their special time in
the buggy gave them a chance to talk—a very private time that
most couples weren't privy to, except for the weekend courtship
nights.

Art at Heart was still the place where she spent most of her days,
but after she finished the third painting for Kiki Grant, she began
to break up her day with other errands. Being on display, like a tiger
in the Philadelphia Zoo, was not something she enjoyed. She now
had a hefty sum saved, and she kept the money in a little sachet, tied
up with a bow. Their house fund—or so she hoped.

One Saturday night, Rachel was up in the attic room, dabbing
paint onto a canvas, creating a crazy quilt of color, when a light appeared at the windows. The beam bounced around the window-
panes like a giant firefly.

Stepping into the cool breeze at the open window, she looked down and saw James standing in the yard with a flashlight.

Standing there, as if it was the most natural thing in the world!

"Praise be to Gott!" It was a sight she thought she would never see again.

Rachel hurried downstairs to greet him. "What are you doing here, standing in my front yard?" she teased.

"I came to court my girl." He smiled, nodding toward the buggy. "How about a little ride? I've got enough control to sit right and steer the horses."

"Is that so?" She folded her arms across her chest, fighting the tears of joy that stung her eyes. "Oh, James, you've come so far! I know you've worked for it. You've worked hard every day. But it's such a blessing. I think it's a miracle."

"Gott is great. Kumm. Let's get away before we wake the whole King family."

Sitting close to James, Rachel was grateful for his warmth as they rode in silence. The silvery moon, the scattered stars, the midnight sky and quiet, rolling hills wove a beautiful, peaceful picture all around them. She had never attempted a night painting, and now she wondered if she could ever capture this lovely serenity on a canvas.

"So, how long have you been driving?" she asked.

"Just a few days. Mark's been taking me out to practice."

"And you kept it a secret from me? I thought there were no secrets between us."

"No secrets, just a surprise." He turned the buggy into a farm lane and pulled the reins to stop. When he turned toward her, he seemed hearty and strong, his shoulders so broad and his legs secure on the running board. "At first I didn't want to say anything because I didn't want to get your hopes up."

"Oh, but hope is a very good thing." She flattened her hands against his chest, loving the warmth there. "I never stopped hoping for you, James . . . and for the two of us."

He wrapped the reins on the stump and slipped his arms around her waist. "You never did. I was lost in the dark for a while, but you? You were like the brightest star in the sky, always shining, lighting the way. You showed me the path . . ." He walked his fingers along her shoulder, tickling her slightly as his fingertips trailed up along her jaw. He pressed a fingertip to her lips. "You showed me the way back to you."

Rachel thought her heart would burst with love and joy as he gently cupped her jaw and pressed his lips to hers. His kiss was a wild explosion of stars and sunlight and blossoming flowers. Oh, the power of his kiss!

She pressed her body closer, entering the warm cocoon of his arms. He smelled of wood smoke and lavender, and his body was the perfect fit for hers as she pressed against him. This was where she belonged, tucked into James's arms, loving him, needing him. Her senses tingled and her pulse raced as they tumbled from one kiss to another, lost in each other under the starry sky. Time slipped away as they nestled together.

Her lips were swollen from kissing when he slid his mouth across her cheek to her ear. "I love you," he whispered, his breath hot and moist against her bare neck.

"And I love you." Her voice was husky from passion.

"I'm glad you're taking classes to get baptized. I know it's only the beginning of June, but autumn will be here before you know it. First baptism, and then wedding season. I can't wait to marry you, Rachel, if you'll still have me."

"I want to marry you, for better or worse," she said. "Though I may want a proper proposal, Mr. Lapp."

"We've been through that. I gave you a proper proposal years ago. Don't tell me you gave away our clock?"

"How could I do that? I've kept it close. Sometimes right under my pillow at night. Sometimes the ticking sound is soothing."

"Well, I'm glad it's still working." He grinned. "Did I ever tell you the riddle about the clock?"

"Two hands, one face, always runs, but stays in place."

His brows shot up. "You really do know me well."

They chuckled together, and then he captured her hand and pressed it inside his jacket. Amid the welcome warmth, she could feel the steady thump of his heart. "Feel that? It beats for you, Rachel. One day that clock may burst its springs, but as long as this heart beats, it beats for you."

In the back of her mind, she had always known that, but it was oh-so-sweet to hear him say the words.

∞ 45 ∞

The screen door slapped closed behind her as Shandell went out on the back porch. "Sorry," she called, knowing that the noise could be annoying.

"No worries," Zoey answered from the kitchen window. "That door spring is on Tate's fix-it list, which seems to be getting longer every day. Good thing he likes to tinker."

"Good thing," Shandell called as she headed out to the clothes-line to check the two quilts drying in the sun.

The fan quilt, with its turquoise border and colorful fans repeated in small blocks, was dry and smelling springtime fresh. She eased it from the line, folding it first in half, then quarters, careful not to let it touch the ground. The lovely old quilt had been in Zoey's family's attic for years, which explained the need for a good washing to get out the musty smell. But now that it was clean, Shandell understood how this beautiful handmade quilt had inspired Zoey to open the Halfway to Heaven Bed and Breakfast.

With her arms full, she headed toward the porch, her flip-flops slapping on the wood.

Since she'd come out of hiding, summer had unfurled in Halfway, with bold blue skies, scorching heat, and fields of green. Even now as she gazed out from the porch, the sky and fields opened up around her, broad and bright with possibility.

New possibilities, every day. She had not imagined the blessings God had in store for her when she'd been holed up in the sugar shack. But once Doctor Trueherz and his wife took Mom and her under their wing, so many other things had fallen into place. Celeste had won over Mom, and Dr. Trueherz had introduced them to Dylan Monroe, a therapist and social worker who had helped Shandell in so many ways. Dylan had hooked her up with a free group therapy session over in Paradise, and he had been awesome in getting her this job at the Jordans' inn, a position that included room and board.

The icing on the cake had been her mother's decision to move up here. Dylan had helped Mom in her job search, and Celeste Trueherz had found a small house for her to rent—an adorable little cottage with a rose trellis and a wishing well. Mom deserved a fresh start, and Shandell was glad Chelsea had found a friend in Celeste. Whenever Shandell stopped by, those two were either on their way to the movies or sitting on the patio, sharing stories and iced tea. Yup, the town of Halfway now seemed like a much kinder place than it had when she'd first gotten stuck here.

Even the sheriff, Hank Hallinan, was now one of her go-to guys. He had scared the stuffing out of her when he'd first started interviewing her at the clinic. She had thought back to those days she'd been riding around aimlessly with Gary, and wondered if maybe she was guilty of some crime.

"If someone steals gas but you don't know it and you're riding in their car, does that make you an accessory to the crime?" she had asked him.

He had mulled that over. "You didn't know?"

"I didn't. Well, I knew about some things he stole. Some fried chicken and snacks. But that was after he took the stuff. And then, when he started stealing in front of me, I tried to talk him out of it. I told him to pay. I also told him to take me home. I begged him to take me home. He didn't listen."

"As far as I can tell, you had no intention of breaking the law," Sheriff Hank had told her. "If anything, you were a victim yourself. With a little more of a chronology and some corroboration, we might be able to charge him with attempted kidnapping."

"Oh." Shandell didn't want to hurt Gary; she just wanted him out of her life, forever. "I'll tell you everything that I remember, but honestly, I don't know why he got so obsessed with me riding around with him. I was never his girlfriend."

"For whatever reason, he targeted you. That happens some-times." He sat back, his sheriff's badge winking in the light. "We're lucky things turned out this way. It was wise of you to hide out for a while."

Looking back on the past two months, Shandell couldn't believe the drama in her life. A road trip. A runaway. Attempted kidnapping. Living Amish. Homeless. A medical miracle. Her life sounded like a supermarket tabloid!

Now, as she centered the quilt on the double bed in the room called Rural Retreat, she took in the space with its wall plaque, plain white curtains, and walls painted a pale shade of peach. There was a watering can in the corner that Zoey had painted turquoise and filled with silk flowers, and the old dresser was polished to a shine, though its edges bore some cuts and nicks, signs of true wear and tear. Maybe the room held a bit more decoration than most Amish homes, but it was more authentic than the chandeliers and wallpaper that Zoey had initially chosen.

On the wall adjacent to the bed was one of Rachel's paintings—

one of Shandell's favorites because it showed the sugar shack with its roof coated with a layer of sparkling snow. Shandell had a fondness for that old cabin because her life changed there. But of course, the place was just an old shack. People like Rachel and James were the ones who had saved her when she had nowhere else to turn. People like Dylan Monroe and the Trueherzes were the catalysts of change. And her new bosses, Zoey and Tate, had the courage to take a chance on her, and trust her with their home and their van.

Fluffing up the flowers in the watering can, she surveyed the room with a surge of pride. Rural Retreat was ready for guests, as were two other rooms on this floor. If they stayed on track, the inn would be ready to open next week when their first group of guests was booked. Apparently, lots of people wanted to experience how the Amish lived.

So far, Shandell was committed to working for the Jordans through the summer. After that, she wasn't sure, but she was glad to have options. Zoey kept saying that she hoped Shandell would stay on, and Dylan had steered her toward a community college in Lancaster County that would let her make up her missed high school classes in the fall. Shandell liked the Jordans, but she didn't want to make them surrogate parents; if she stayed on, it would be as an employee, earning her keep. "You're at a crossroads in your life, with many choices to make," Dylan had told her. "And just because you choose one direction doesn't mean you can't change your mind. Go forth. Make mistakes and learn from them. The path is yours. Just keep moving ahead."

❦

The van was easy to drive, although the logo "Halfway to Heaven Inn" painted on the door was a little embarrassing. It was nearly lunchtime, and Shandell was thinking about stopping at the diner for fries on her way through Halfway.

She sang along with a song on the radio, glad to be in an air-conditioned car on this hot, sunny day. Tate had sent her to the hardware store in Paradise for a special plumbing wrench that would fix the leak in the third-floor bathroom.

As the van sailed down a hill toward a farm stand, she pressed the brake to slow down and wave. It was the farm stand that she had stopped in with Gary, all those weeks ago; the one where he had stolen a flat of flowers and a couple of jars of pie filling. That had been the dawning moment, the moment when she had realized that he was a thief and that he had no intention of taking her home.

The two girls working the stand waved back, the white strings of their prayer kapps blowing in the breeze. She recognized Bethany and Ruthie King, Rachel's sister and cousin. She had met them last week when she'd come to the stand with money from her first week's pay at the inn. That had been weird. So embarrassing to explain that she'd been with that loser Gary when he stole their stuff.

But the girls had been so nice about it. They'd heard that Gary had been caught. And they knew who Shandell was. "My sister talks about you all the time," Bethany had said. "She's Rachel King."

Well, that had really blown Shandell away. Small world.

Heat waves shimmered over the black asphalt as the van rose up another hill. It was a hot one out there!

She had just cracked open a bottle of Gatorade in the cup holder when she came upon the horse and cart listing on the side of the road. Something was wrong with one of the wheels, and the cart tilted toward the cornfield. That didn't look good.

Hitting the brake, she slowed the van and pulled over. "Hey, there. Need some help?"

That was when she noticed the Amish man. He was wearing a

black suit and straw hat, and he bent over, gripping the edge of the cart, as if he'd been vomiting.

"Are you okay?" As she approached along the shoulder, she could see that the wheel had broken off its axle. "Wow, look at your wheel. This cart isn't going anywhere. Are you all right, sir?"

"Just resting," he said without looking up. His distress was obvious, and she knew that the open road with the noonday sun beating down was no place to be resting.

"Is there someone you want me to call? It's really hot out here." When he looked up, his face was pale and damp. "There's nothing can be done that will be done," he muttered, closing his eyes.

Well, that didn't make much sense. "What was that?"

"It's the . . . no matter. It's all under *Gott und Himmel*."

She frowned. Was he having a stroke or something? "I'm no doctor, but you look overheated." She knew the symptoms of dehydration; she was a self-made expert on the topic. "Why don't you come with me?" She reached out a hand, hoping to take his arm, hoping that he would come along. She couldn't leave him here, and she didn't want him to be mad at her for calling an ambulance. Already, she had a bit of a rep as a drama queen.

Much to her relief, he took her hand and straightened. "Let's get you into the van, where it's cool. You can sit awhile and drink some Gatorade."

He didn't answer, but he didn't resist at all. When she opened the door, he climbed right into the passenger seat. She handed him the open bottle. "Small sips," she said, and he obliged.

Taking a seat behind the wheel, she looked over at the older man, who sat with his eyes closed. Occasionally he would rouse and take another sip, and a deep breath. That was good. He seemed to be coming out of it, his skin pink and dry now.

"It is really hot out there," she said sympathetically. "I'm going to give you a ride into Halfway, okay? That seemed to be the direction you were going. Or do you want me to take you to the clinic in Paradise?"

"No, no clinic. I must get the berries to Halfway."

"The berries?"

As he became more cognizant, he explained that his cart was loaded with strawberries—dozens of flats of dark red berries that were going to spoil in the sun if he didn't get them to the market now. Zook's market, in Halfway.

Shandell sighed. "Your cart isn't going anywhere, but I've got an empty van here." Would the Tates be mad at her for moving berries when she was supposed to be working for them? What if the berries stained the inside of the new van?

One more glance at the Amish man, stubborn and determined as he mopped his brow with a handkerchief, was enough to get her going. "Let's do it," she said, pushing open her door.

The berries, ripe and shining in the sun, were contained in cardboard flats. Well, at least that would save the van. The man began handing her stacks of three flats, and she transferred them into the van, using the side and rear doors to maximize space. The whole thing only took about twenty minutes, but in the scorching heat of the sun, it seemed like a day in the desert.

As she drove, she called Zoey to let her know what was going on. "So I'm driving this Amish man to Zook's market, with a van full of strawberries." When she explained about the heat and the broken wheel, Zoey approved of her decision to help. It occurred to Shandell that Zoey and Tate should meet them at the market and help unload. This could be the perfect chance for the newcomers to connect with the Old Order Amish community.

Fortunately, Zoey understood that this was a rare opportunity. She and Tate were waiting at Zook's market when their van pulled up. Some of the Amish people seemed surprised to see the man pull up in a van. Two older Amish men asked him questions in Deutsch, but he waved them off.

"Work first, talk later," he said. He showed Shandell and the Jordans the table where the strawberries were to be set up for sale, and a young boy of eleven or twelve waiting there promptly jumped up and began to pitch in.

They needed to wend their way around shoppers and other vendors, but with the Jordans pitching in they unloaded the strawberries in record time.

When it was done, the Amish man mopped his brow in the shade of the barn. "Thank you," he told Shandell, then turned to the Jordans. "Thank you all."

Tate, with his charming manner, jumped in and introduced himself and his wife. "And this is Shandell Darby, the assistant manager of our inn. We didn't get your name, sir." The Amish man's eyes opened wider as he turned back to Shandell. "I'm Jimmy. Jimmy Lapp from the Lapp orchard."

Shandell's mouth dropped open. Of course! Those dark eyes, those broad shoulders. This was James's father. She felt a little sick inside. This was the man who really hated her.

"Mr. Lapp . . . I didn't realize you were . . ." She rolled her eyes. "Do you know who I am? I guess this is God giving me a chance to apologize."

He nodded. "At first, I didn't recognize you without this blue hair I've heard so much about. But now? I recognize you. I see that the Good Samaritan now has a name. It's Shandell."

ꙩꙩ 46 ꙩꙩ

"That's a new personal best, James." The physical therapist pumped a fist in the air, and James grinned, recognizing the celebration sign that Englishers loved to give. "You can now stand on your own for an hour and a half."

"It's progress," James said. "Should we try awhile longer?"

"If you think you can do it, let's go for it," JJ said, making a note on his clipboard.

Keeping his breath steady, James looked away from the clock and noticed an Amish man standing just inside the doorway. He blinked, startled to recognize his father.

"Dat?" He was the last person James had expected to see here.

"Don't let me interrupt." Jimmy removed his straw hat and held it to his chest. "I know you've got exercises and therapy and whatnot, but I've come to see all this hard work I've been hearing about."

James didn't know what to say. He had long hoped for his father's approval of his treatment, but he had never expected Jimmy to appear here at the clinic.

JJ looked up. "Is this your father?"

James introduced the two men, and JJ gave Jimmy a quick rundown of the treatment and James's improvements.

"Around here, your son is like Superman," JJ said. "There's no challenge too big for James, and he's a hard worker."

Jimmy nodded. "We like to have a good work ethic in our family," he said, "but James got the best of it, I think. His brothers, not so much."

Is that my dat talking? James wondered, pleased to be recognized. Dat had never noticed James's hard work at the orchard.

After a short chat, JJ backed away and Dat stepped up to James.

"I met your Englisher friend today. Shandell."

The news set James slightly off-balance. He touched the bar, steadying himself. "Really? Did she come by the house?"

"Nay. She rescued me." Turning his hat in his hands, Jimmy told the story of the Good Samaritan who had come along and saved him and his strawberries.

The hand of Gott moves gently, James thought, knowing it was the will of the Almighty to bring Shandell and Jimmy together.

"I talked to Bishop Samuel about . . . well, many things. I see that you getting help and medical treatment from Englishers doesn't take away from your Plain living. Samuel pointed out that Plain folk use cars for things like doctors' appointments and whatnot. I just benefited from a vehicle to get me out of the sun and bring my produce to market. If it helps you get to treatment, we can hire a car to take you back and forth."

"Denki, Dat. You know, a few weeks ago, I would have gladly taken a car. But going in the buggy every day with Rachel, it's been a good time for us." He faced his father, daring to meet those penetrating, dark eyes. "You made the right choice on that, Dat."

Jimmy looked down. His eyes were on the hat that he turned in his hands. "Sometimes a father is hard on his sons. Especially the oldest."

"Because a father must be a teacher. Remember Doddy's favorite expression about the grindstone of life? 'Life is a grindstone,' he used to say. 'Whether it grinds you down or polishes you up depends on what you are made of.'"

Dat gave a short laugh. "He said that all the time when I was a boy. He'd be hard on me for goofing around, and when I complained, he'd say that he was trying to polish me into something smooth and shiny."

When Dat looked up at James, his eyes twinkled with tears. "A father does what he thinks is best for all, but in the end a man is just a man and Gott is the Almighty. You'll see what I mean in a few years, when you have children of your own."

A smile tugged at James's lips. Ya, he would. God willing, he and Rachel would have a dozen children of their own.

He clapped James on the shoulder. "I'd best get going. I just stopped in to say . . . good job, son. You're proof of Gott's great love."

෯෯

From the doorway of the physical therapy room, Rachel watched the father and son. Tears stung her eyes at the reconciliation that was long overdue. It was an answered prayer.

As tears blurred her vision, she saw the two men as a scene in dabs of color. The cool ocean blue of mats beneath them. The stark black and white of Jimmy's clothes, opposite the softer gray of the shorts and T-shirt the doctors had James wear here. The warm chocolate brown of Jimmy's eyes. The blush of pleasure on James's cheeks.

She swiped at her tears and smiled. Such beautiful colors! But what color would she put on the halo of sunlight around them—the swirl of healing and relief and love? Oh, those were wonders that only the Almighty Father would capture in color. His perfect masterpiece.

ACKNOWLEDGMENTS

I am grateful to loyal readers who share my enjoyment of escaping to a simpler lifestyle. In this age of gold cell phones and global messaging, I cherish the opportunity to write about a society with traditional family values. Instead of looking to institutions outside the home for education, religion, and entertainment, the Amish—like James's father, Jimmy Lapp—strive to keep these functions in the home.

No one can surpass Dr. Violet Dutcher's eye for story detail, cultural detail, and the nuances of Amish living. Many thanks to Dr. Vi for the inspiration and encouragement she provides.

A huge shout to Junessa Viloria, the one and only editor who seems to love these characters as much as I do. Working with you is always a joy.

And to the excellent staff at Ballantine Books, denki!

ABOUT THE AUTHOR

ROSALIND LAUER grew up in a large family in Maryland and began visiting Lancaster County's Amish community as a child. She attended Wagner College in New York City and worked as an editor for Simon & Schuster and Harlequin Books. She currently lives with her family in Oregon, where she writes in the shade of some towering two-hundred-year-old Douglas fir trees.

*For updates, bonus content, and
sneak peeks at upcoming titles:*

FIND THE AUTHOR ON FACEBOOK
FACEBOOK.COM/ROSALIND-LAUER

Read on for an exciting preview of

A Simple Charity

THE NEXT
LANCASTER CROSSROADS NOVEL

BY ROSALIND LAUER

*T*he purple of dusk still cloaked the sky as Fanny Lapp lifted her five-month-old son from the buggy and cooed to soothe him. "I know, I know. It's too early to be awake. You can sleep when we get inside." Shifting the little one onto her shoulder, she walked the small path bordered by red and yellow pansies and knocked on the door.

Today promised to be a warm one, with the wonderful good blessing of a new baby for Lizzy and Joe. Seeing a child into the world was the sweetest delight a person could know—though it came with its inconveniences. When she had agreed to help out Anna Beiler for a spell while the midwife went to visit her family in Florida, Fanny had not imagined herself traipsing through the night with her own baby in tow. How quickly she'd forgotten that babes came into the world on their own schedule, whether it be stretched over three long summer days or as quick as a teapot comes to the boil.

First-time mothers could be a trial, not knowing what was to come, but Lizzy King was different. Maybe because Lizzy knew about the dark patch of sorrow and grief Fanny was working through. Or maybe because it had taken this couple longer than most to be blessed in this way. Lizzy was old by Amish standards, but that wouldn't make her any less of a mother once her baby was born.

The door was opened by Market Joe, a young Amish man with a broad, friendly face and thick black-framed glasses. "It's Fanny," he called to his wife, opening the door wide. "Come." With the excitement and nervousness of a first-time father, Joe scampered over to Lizzy, who stood leaning over a chair, breathing through a contraction.

Stepping inside, Fanny smiled at the young man and his wife. Ah, how dear they were to her heart! Although Joe King and his wife, Lizzy, were not family, Fanny felt a special attachment to the couple, who had shared her family's fears and grief after the tragic accident six months ago. Joe and Lizzy had been in the van with Fanny's husband, dear Tom, who had been taken by Gott.

The house smelled sweet, like cinnamon and sugar. "Someone's been baking," Fanny said.

"Lizzy made cookies, in the middle of everything," Joe said. "And you brought little Tommy this time. Come. We've got a place for him." He scrambled back behind Fanny to close the door.

"Lizzy." Fanny rocked Tommy back and forth as she made a quick assessment of Lizzy, who wore exhaustion on her pale face. A midwife had to learn much from the first look at a mother, especially since a husband, who was the one to call in a fit of jitters, rarely passed along details of his wife's condition. Instincts told Fanny that the baby was still a good two hours away. "Looks like you're coming along fine."

"You were right about staying on my feet." Lizzy gripped the top of the ladder-back chair so firmly her knuckles were white. "I baked a batch of snickerdoodles. That got things moving along."

When Fanny had come out last night around ten o'clock, Lizzy had been resting in bed, still in the very early stages of labor. Since her pains had been nothing more than occasional cramps, Fanny knew she need not stick around. She had left the couple with instructions that Lizzy do some walking, and a promise that she would return before dawn.

Fanny felt her son's head stirring on her shoulder as she spotted a pile of quilts set up on the living room floor.

"We made a *Budda Nesht* for Tommy," Joe said.

"Looks cozy." Fanny squatted down beside the nest of blankets and placed her son in the center of the thick bedding. His lips formed a pout, then opened slightly as a look of peace softened his face. Covering him with a soft blanket, she bent down to kiss his forehead. "Sleep well, *Liebe.*"

"It's good you've returned." Joe stood at Lizzy's side, rubbing her back. "She's been walking and standing most of the night, just like you told us, Fanny."

"I knew you would follow advice. You're a good patient, Lizzy."

"Maybe not so much. I'm sorry for getting you out here last night, what with the baby not really coming yet. When everything started, I got a little scared."

"It was no problem at all," Fanny said, comforting the younger woman. "The first baby usually takes its time, but this is all new for you. I liken it to a road you've never traveled before. You need good directions and a companion at your side. Joe has taken good care of you. Now it's my turn."

With her little one tucked away, Fanny took charge of the situation. The house was tidy, but Lizzy looked tired, and she needed to be strong for the pushing part of labor. "You go into the bedroom and change your clothes. You've done a good job walking around, but now you need some rest."

As Lizzy waddled into the bedroom, Fanny turned to Joe and asked if Doc Trueherz was on his way. Fanny was happy to help Amish mothers bring their babies into the world, but the doctor was always in charge.

"I called, and Celeste said Dr. Minetta was coming."

"Not Doc Trueherz?" Lizzy paused in the hall, strain showing in her face. Most everyone liked Henry Trueherz, the country doctor who had served the Amish for years.

Joe readjusted the black-framed glasses on the bridge of his nose. "The regular doc's gone to the city. This Minetta fella is filling in."

"He's a good doctor, too," Fanny said, holding back her concerns. Both times she had encountered Dr. Minetta, she had been assisting Anna, and both times he had been late. Most doctors were not familiar with the farm roads and unmarked lanes of Lancaster County, which Doc Trueherz knew well from twenty years of house calls. Dr. Minetta had arrived so late to one of the births, the baby had been diapered and wrapped. Fanny hoped he would be prompt today.

Fanny sent Joe out to the buggy to fetch her things—two heavy cases of supplies and medical gadgets that Anna had loaned her. As she washed her hands at the kitchen sink, Fanny was startled by her reflection in the window with the dense night still behind it. Her dark hair was neatly pulled back under her white prayer *Kapp*, but her cheeks seemed hollow, her eyes wide and dark like a wise old owl. My, oh my, but she could use a good night's sleep. She was beginning to understand why Anna was always yawning at quilting bees. Ah, but to hear a baby's first cry, to bundle an infant in flannel and hand it over to the mother—those sweet moments were worth a little lost sleep.

In the bedroom, Lizzy had changed into a robe that stretched

over her wide belly and had slipped fluffy socks on her feet. Her
kapp hung from a peg on the wall, and her golden-blond hair was
unpinned, still twined in a braid that ran down her back. The bed
was already covered with a mattress pad and clean sheets.

"Look at that. The bed's all ready to go. Now we just need your
baby to come," Fanny said as she motioned Lizzy to sit on the bed.

"We've been waiting so long," Lizzy said as she scrambled back
on the mattress, then quickly looked away. Amish women didn't
usually talk about such things—pregnancy and the like—but certain things had to be told to a midwife or doctor, and Fanny knew
about how Lizzy and Joe had waited. Most Amish women had their
first babies within a year of marriage, but Gott had given Lizzy and
Market Joe a different path. Lizzy was in her mid-twenties and having her first child.

Fanny propped up some pillows and had Lizzy lean back. Smoothing a hand over the young woman's forehead for a quick check of
her temperature, Fanny was relieved to see Lizzy relaxing between
contractions, drawing in a smooth breath and sinking back against
the pillows.

"No sign of fever, and it's good for you to close your eyes. You're
going to need strength for what's ahead."

"Where do you want these bags?" Joe asked from the doorway.
He hung back sheepishly, knowing a man's place was not in this
bedroom right now.

"Here." Fanny pulled one of the heavy bags close to the bed,
thanked Joe, and sent him back out to the kitchen. "Why don't you
go put some water on to boil?" she told him. The tradition of boil-
ing water was steadfast during Amish home births, though the most
practical use for it was making tea.

Guiding her hands over Lizzy's taut belly, she felt the baby's head
pointed down and securely engaged. "All good. Let me just count
the baby's heartbeats." The listening piece of the stethoscope was

cold, so Fanny rubbed it with her palm. "Don't want to send you and the baby jumping," she teased.

"I'm not going anywhere," Lizzy murmured.

With the cup of the stethoscope pressed to Lizzy's belly, Fanny found the rapid thud of the infant's heart. Using a stopwatch from Anna's black bag, she counted the beats. "A hundred and forty," she said aloud. "A good, strong heartbeat."

Lizzy smiled, though her lips thinned as a contraction took over. "Ah, Fanny, I need this baby to be born," she said, wincing. "Please! Give me my baby now!"

Fanny helped Lizzy move to her knees so that she could rock her way through the wave. Tears glimmered in Lizzy's blue eyes as she searched the room for relief.

"Look at that calendar over there. What a lovely picture. Looks like Niagara Falls. That's it."

"I didn't think it would . . ." Lizzy moaned. "I didn't think it would hurt so."

"No one knows until it happens," Fanny said gently, but she doubted that Lizzy could hear her. Although Lizzy had been told what to expect from her dutiful visits to the clinic in Paradise, Fanny had always found that all the well-told stories and directions flew out the window when a woman was in the throes of labor. A midwife's simple words and calm explanations could wash over a laboring woman like a warm balm. Fanny stayed close until the pain subsided and Lizzy closed her eyes again.

"The contractions are getting closer. I'm going to send Joe to watch for the doctor. You rest."

"Got to go." Lizzy pushed herself up on her elbows and edged off the bed. "I need the bathroom." She took two steps, leaned forward, and gave a cry of pain. She gathered her robe up and peered down at the linoleum floor. "My water."

"It's clear. That's a good sign, and it also means that your baby will be here soon."

"Oh, Fanny, it's taking so long and I'm about spent." Lizzy dropped down to a squat, her head resting against the bed. "This little one will never come."

"Your baby will come." Fanny smoothed a strand of blond hair away from Lizzy's forehead. "They always do." She helped Lizzy to her feet. "Off you go. After that, you come back in here. This room is your little cocoon, ya? We'll spin a warm, soft nest of love around your baby as it comes into the world."

Lizzy gave a wan smile, then headed down the hall as Fanny quickly fetched a rag to wipe the floor. Attending any birth was an act of charity for Fanny, but she didn't want to overstep her bounds. Where was that doctor?

Keeping a calm way about her, Fanny cleaned up the floor and started two cups of tea brewing. Joe asked how it was going, and she told him there was time to go down the road to get someone in the family to cover for him at the King Family Cheese stand in the city. Joe wanted to be here when his baby was born, but he was a bit squeamish about hanging around now. "Go," Fanny told him, "and keep a look out for the doctor when you're on your way back."

Inside the bedroom, Lizzy was curled on her side. Fanny helped her up to a sitting position and handed her a cup of honeyed tea with a dose of blue cohosh, an herb that stimulated labor.

"*Denki.*" Lizzy sipped gratefully. "The doctor . . . he should be here soon, ya?"

"He's probably trying to find his way on the back roads." Fanny perched in the chair beside the bed. "I do wish we had a birth center here. That's how things are done back in Ohio. All the doctors and Amish know where to go when the time comes. Makes for fewer mixups, and it can be a lot of fun, women together with their newborns for a few days."

"That sounds like a very good thing, Fanny." Lizzy's face was puffy from strain, but she didn't complain. Her amber eyes focused on the picture of the waterfall.

Fanny recognized that look: the turning point when a woman realized she must give herself over to the pain, trust it, ride it out.

Sitting nearby and cradling a mug of tea, Fanny remained quiet as Lizzy's pains ebbed and flowed. This was the bulk of Fanny's duties: watching and waiting, serving and cleaning up.

Not so long ago, Fanny herself had been attended by Doc Trueherz and Anna when Tommy had been born. At the time, Fanny's heart had been heavy with sadness over Tom's death. But the minute she held the baby in her arms and kissed his wrinkled brow, she had recognized the blessing of family that Gott had granted her.

Every day she thanked Gott for the older ones, who helped keep the household running smoothly. Twenty-one-year-old Caleb was a man now, a good Amish man with the same patience and strength his father had possessed. Emma, head teacher in the one-room schoolhouse, had won over the hearts of the children of Halfway with her steady, serious manner. Elsie knew how to make chores into fun for her younger siblings, who couldn't resist her bubbly laughter and big heart.

And then there were the little ones, the children Gott had blessed Tom and her with. Five-year-old Will was a typical boy, rambunctious and full of questions about everything under the sun. Beth was Fanny's little helper around the house, rolling cookie dough into balls and sweeping up a dust storm with her tiny broom. And the baby—a strong little thing with a sweet smile for his siblings, who loved to hold him and tell him stories. How Fanny loved being mother hen to her brood of chicks!

Lizzy let out a little cry, then scraped in a deep breath and moaned quietly as the pain took her. Willing the young woman to blossom with the pain, Fanny slipped out of the room to check on Tommy. He was up on his little fists, rocking and crooning.

"Time to eat, little one." She took him into her arms and sat down in a rocking chair. His eyes soaked up her face as she smiled down at him and got him nursing. "Such a good boy, plucked from your crib in the middle of the night without a fuss," she cooed. Of course, babies didn't seem to care much where they were, as long as Mamm was near.

She ran a thumb over the crease in his little forehead. "What have you to worry about?" she teased as he nuzzled into her.

The sound of the creaking bed inside reminded her of dear Lizzy, and Fanny flashed back to her first time, when she gave birth to Will. At the time, her husband Thomas had been the knowing one, having had three children with his departed wife.

For the most part, Amish women went through the paces quietly when they had their children. And that was a good thing, with so many women having ten and twelve children. Fanny had seen her grandmother Martha handle them with a steady gaze, a minimum of words, and a firm hand in the years when Fanny had assisted her mother and grandmother, who were midwives in Ohio.

Rocking gently in the chair, Fanny warmed over thoughts of the large family she had left behind. As a girl, she had been content to help out at the birth center in Sugar Valley. She had been happy as a lark with her family and friends there, until she had fallen for David Fisher, who had been visiting from Pennsylvania. Hard to believe that was more than ten years ago.

When David had asked her about Sugar Valley, she'd told him that it was a good stretch of Gott's acres. "Everything I love is here in Sugar Creek," she said.

"Not everything," he'd responded. "I'll be heading back home next week, and I don't want to go without you."

Verhuddelt though it seemed, it had felt right as rain to follow him back here to Lancaster County and get married soon as wedding season allowed.

The Fisher clan had welcomed her here in Halfway. Many of them were bakers, with a successful shop in Halfway, but her David had wanted to work the land. He had been handy with machinery and good with animals—apt skills for a farmer. They had been living in a small outbuilding on the Fisher farm, saving up for their own house, when David died in a farming accident. She had been hanging wash outside on the line when she got the word. And suddenly, in the blink of an eye, she became an Amish widow living in a settlement hundreds of miles from home.

Although the community had supported her, she had not been comfortable living on their charity, and with her marriage so new, she had never felt completely accepted by David's family. Although the words were never said, she sensed that they were disappointed David didn't choose a wife from here in Lancaster County. The family was never cruel to her, but she didn't have a friend among them.

Fanny had been making plans to return to Sugar Valley when the bishop had asked her to help out a family in need. Thomas Lapp needed a woman to come in and do some cooking and cleaning and minding his young ones, seven-year-old Elsie, ten-year-old Emma, and Caleb just coming into his teen years. Fanny had accepted because it was the charitable thing to do, and she'd stayed because the children had won her heart, along with their kind, thoughtful father.

A gray cloud of grief had hung over her, but Fanny had learned how to occupy her hands to ease her mind. As months went by, her heart began to mend, and Tom and the children kept her on her toes. One year after David's death, to the day, Tom came into the quiet kitchen while she was cutting vegetables and the children were off doing chores. His muscular arms were brown against the blue of his shirt, and instead of taking his usual seat at the table, he had stood behind her, his hat in his hand.

"It's time that we talk, Fanny." She turned to find his eyes glimmering, his fingers pinching the brim of his hat nervously. "I haven't said anything until now, out of respect to David, may he rest in peace. But I want you to know that I believe Gott sent you to us, Fanny. You're like a part of the family now. And I'm asking if, well, if you ever see fit to court again, I'd like to be on the top of your list."

Fanny told Tom that she hadn't planned to court again—and she held true to that plan for a few weeks. But as time passed, she had realized that, in large and small ways, Tom Lapp had become a good friend to her. A dear friend. And though she tried to push him away, after a year of working in his household, he had already found a place in her heart. He didn't push her, but he was always there by her side, kind and good.

"How is it that the carrots have all this space, and yet they grow right against each other?" she had asked Tom one day as they'd worked together in the garden. "See this?" She held up two fat carrots that had twined so close, they were nearly one.

Tom stepped over the broccoli and came to kneel by her side as he examined the tangled carrots. "Maybe carrots are like people," he said, pushing back the brim of his hat so that she could see the glimmer in his eyes. "No one should be alone. People could spread out over the land, and yet, we live together. A community, a family. A couple."

With a broad smile, she put the two carrots in her pail. "I was only talking about vegetables, Tom."

"I know. But I've been looking for a way to talk about this, and carrots are as good as any." He took her hands in his, capturing her eyes. "Marry me, Fanny. You know I love you, and you're already a mother to my children. *Kumm,* now. Can't you find room in your heart for an old widower like me and three children who need you?"

It wasn't the first time he had asked her . . . but somehow, that day, she did find the room in her heart and the courage to say yes. Thankfully, the children were at school, so no one was there to see the two of them kissing in the garden, promising love and faith in the narrow rows between fat bunches of broccoli.

Dear Tom! Somehow he had found the twisted, narrow path to her heart.

Placing the baby on her shoulder to pat out the gas, Fanny rose and swayed back and forth. "Your father was a good man," she told her son. "How he would have loved you, little Tommy. But it was not part of Gott's plan."

She and Tom had enjoyed eight good years of marriage before he passed, and Gott had blessed them with three children, as well as Tom's three, whom Fanny was still raising as her own. Getting old, those three, but she smiled as she thought of their little family. It was up to her to manage the household now—a big job, but Gott never gave a person more than she could handle. Fanny's heart was still heavy, and there was no getting over the emptiness Tom had left behind. But Gott had blessed her with wonderful children.

Setting Tommy back in the budda nesht, Fanny made herself a cup of tea and brought it into the bedroom, where Lizzy lay on her side, her eyes focused on the picture of the waterfall. All was good.

Just then Lizzy was jolted from her resting place with a fitful cry. She rolled to her knees on the bed, lost in a strong wave.

That was when Fanny noticed the dark stain on the plastic sheet. The once clear waters had turned brown, the color of dried leaves on October. That meant the baby was in some trouble. Without wasting words, she tended to Lizzy, then went to find Joe.

Fanny tried to calm her racing heart with measured steps to the kitchen. A panicked midwife was no help to anyone.

She was relieved to see Joe was back, pacing. "Is the baby coming?"

"Soon, but there could be a problem. We need the doctor, Joe. A doctor or nurse, and there's no time to waste. Go now, and find Doc Minetta."

He pressed his straw hat onto his head. "Is Lizzy all right?" he asked, his eyes growing round with alarm.

"I'm more worried about the baby. If you can't find Dr. Minetta, call Doc Trueherz's office again. Tell Celeste we need help and—" She stopped short of telling him to call an ambulance. There wasn't an emergency. Not yet.

"I'll call the doc's office. And I'll get folks out on the road to watch for him and send him our way." As Joe hustled out the door, Fanny pressed her hands together at her chin and said a silent prayer that Gott would bring this baby to them in good health.

Then, with a deep, steadying breath, she turned and went back inside to tend to Lizzy.